Devine Justice: Matriarch of Crime

A fictional biography inspired by Tilly Devine Palmer's life.

Charis Constantine

The author respectfully acknowledges the past and present traditional owners of the land of the Indigenous people, the traditional custodians of this land, and respect their culture and identity which has been bound up with the land and sea for generations.

Publisher: Inspiring Publishers,
P.O. Box 159, Calwell, ACT Australia 2905
Email: publishaspg@gmail.com
http://www.inspiringpublishers.com

A catalogue record for this book is available from the National Library of Australia

National Library of Australia The Prepublication Data Service

Author: Charis Constantine
Title: Devine Justice: Matriarch of Crime
Genre: Fiction
ISBN: 978-0-6450780-5-3

Acknowledgements

No project in a writer's life is completed without support and contribution, so....to my exceptionally talented youngest daughter Chaianne, a huge thank you for the magnificent cover design for Devine Justice. To my friend and Beta Reader, Trish Burton for her numerous rereads of this epic adventure without complaint. To my dear friend Michael Semchison for his advice, assistance, and for writing the foreword. And to Tilly Devine herself, for dropping hints "from beyond" for me to write this book. And to all those friends and fiends of Tilly's—thank you for the inspiration.

Sources

The Dictionary of Sydney

State Archives and Records, New South Wales Government for information and photos for the book cover.

State Library of New South Wales

Australian Dictionary of Biography

Public Record Office, London

Australian War Memorial

Drug Traffic by Alfred McCoy

Razor by Larry Writer

The Shark Arm Murders by Alex Castles

'Alleged Theft of Tiepin', The Sydney Morning Herald (Monday, 13 July 1931)

Trove

Truth Newspaper

The Bulletin

'Maroubra Affray', The Canberra Times (Wednesday, 16 September 1931)

Daily Mirror, UK

The Daily Telegraph

Public Record Office, Victoria

L. Straw, Leigh S.. Angel of Death (p. 290). ABC Books. Kindle Edition.

Sydney Morning Herald

Outback Family History blog

State Archive

Toby Creswell, Notorious Australians

James Morton and Susanna Lobez, Gangland Australia

NSW Registry of Births, Deaths and Marriages, Guido Caletti, Death Reg No: 13849/1939 District of Sydney.

'Shooting in House. Death of Guido Calletti – Witnesses Story', Sydney Morning Herald, (22 September 1939)

NSW Police Gazette

NSW Government, Registry of Births, Deaths and Marriages

Registry of Births, Deaths and Marriages, Victoria

7

All reasonable efforts were taken to obtain permission to use copyright material reproduced in this book, but in some cases, copyright could not be traced. The author welcomes information in this regard.

*This book is dedicated to women who know we are not
measured by our hardships, our faults, and our tragedies.
To women who refuse to allow her past to dictate who she is and
who she will become. To women who are on their journey of
self-discovery. We are woman and we are strong!*

The born female criminal is, so to speak, doubly exceptional, first as a woman and then as a criminal ... criminals are exceptions among civilised people, and women are exceptions among criminals ... As a double exception, then, the criminal woman is a true monster.

—Cesare Lombroso

Foreword

1900, the Victorian era of England was coming to an end and a new century had just begun. For most of its citizens, it was a time of chaos, poverty, social injustice, illness and for thousands, an early ignominious death. Huge numbers of the populace had moved into major cities where they tried to survive in the reeking morass of overcrowded slum accommodation, contaminated water, poor nutrition and when they could find them, jobs in harsh working conditions for pittance wages. Violence, disease, and many forms of death were common.

It was also the year that Matilda Mary Twiss was born. She grew up in squalor and hardship and at age fourteen, she saw her world get even worse with the outbreak of The Great War. Europe was in chaos. Conditions deteriorated even more and rather than toil in the drudge houses for subsistence wages, Tilly began what she saw as an opportunity not only to survive but engage in a more lucrative trade— that of prostitution where she could make far more money to support herself and her small family. Ambitious, determined, and with a plan to remove herself from the ubiquitous life she had been born into, Tilly set upon a path that was to not only do just that, but take her to the other end of the world where she would make a name for herself as one of the most infamous organised crime bosses in Sydney Australia.

At the age of fifteen, Tilly met Australian Serviceman, James Edward Devine, a ne'er-do-well, hard drinking shearer from Melbourne with grandiose ideas, who was always looking for an easy score. Believing his tales of a good life, lies regarding his family's monetary comfort, and charming her with hollow promises, the teenager agreed to marry him and later to follow him to Australia when the war ended. She did and thus began the journey on the road to Devine Justice.

Her marriage to Jim Devine was mostly one of abuse and deceit on his part. He was a consummate liar and user, always looking to make a quid at anyone's expense but his own. He set himself up as Tilly's pimp. With her quickly learned expertise of 'street smarts' and acumen for business, Tilly established her first brothel. Knowing the trade well and the pitfalls for young women who came into it, she looked after her girls and paid them fairly. She also found out that many of the Police establishment could be bribed and used that to her advantage.

Matilda Devine became Sydney's most infamous resident, and her wealth was legendary, all amassed from criminal activities in prostitution, stolen gold and diamonds, and drug trafficking. She was also known to be volatile and violent, and not adverse to using strong arm methods against criminal competitors like her arch vice rival Kate Leigh. She owned much real estate in Sydney, luxury cars, high fashion clothing, and always travelled first class. However, over time, much of her wealth went to pay fines and court costs for her numerous charges including the use of firearms, attempted murder, and other convictions over a span of five decades. Tilly also had a reputation for flamboyant acts of generosity and compassion. She became a legend in her own time.

Matilda Mary Twiss aka Tilly Devine aka Matilda Mary Parsons passed away from cancer in 1970. After decades as the "Crime Queen" of Sydney, she died almost ignominiously, few came to her funeral and the Press, once avid to report her misdeeds, virtually ignored her. The only public eulogy given her came from then current Police Commissioner, Norman Allan, who simply stated, "She was a villain, but who am I to judge her."

Perhaps the course of Justice was Devine after all.

"I have known Charis Constantine for several years, mostly through our mutual passion for and the breeding and showing of quality horses, but also for our shared interest in literature and a good story. Some of which arose from my carrying the responsibilities of a Storyteller in my culture and sharing them in the Public and International forums. After retiring from my teaching obligations in Tertiary Education, Charis approached me to help her edit her first novel The Pink Rose, which I did. This led to further forays into the creative mind and diverse imagination of this talented writer as one of her regular assistants and editors. The amount of research she does in establishing the premise, history, and attention to detail of relevant events occurring in the time frames in which her stories are set is amazing. This tale is an epic fictional biography based upon the actual events of a real person whose infamous life and reputation is part of Australia's history during the 20th century. Pop Culture now has seen and defined Tilly Devine as being one of Sydney's most colorful personages."

I am honored to have been asked to write this foreword for Devine Justice.

Michael R. Semchison
M.Ed.St., Gr.Cert.Ed.[HE]
Published writer, Lecturer, Researcher,
Cultural Advisor, Storyteller, Artist,
Equine Entrepreneur

Side notes: Information source Wikipedia.

Peter Kenna wrote a play called The Slaughter of St. Teresa's Day (1973 Currency Press), based on Devine's life.

The song *Miss Divine* from the 1990 Icehouse album Code Blue is about Devine.

A popular cafe-nightclub in Canberra ACT is called Tilley's Devine Café Gallery.

A wine bar in Darlinghurst, Sydney opened in 2011, named Love Tilly Devine in honour of Devine.

In August 2011, Australia's Channel Nine commenced screening *Underbelly: Razor a True Crime* television drama series that deals with the Leigh/Devine Sydney gangland wars in the 1930s. The series was based the 2002 Ned Kelly Award-winning book by Larry Writer.

Chapter One

In the Beginning

In the late 18th century wealthy businessmen, physicians, and professionals were attracted to Camberwell for its fresh air and clean water supply. Grand mansions, large houses, and landed estates were built, establishing a well to do neighbourhood.

No more than a few minutes away would find you in one of the filthiest, soul-destroying slum areas in London. The lives of residents in this area of Camberwell were ravaged by high violence, high crime, and abject poverty. The putrid labyrinth-like streets denied any growth of grass or flowering gardens often seen in more affluent areas. The grimy, sooty brick tenements were barely blessed by the sun, which was normally blocked by clouds of smoke and soot from the local industrial factories.

Most of the neighbourhood dwellings were ramshackle two to three-storey houses, which often sheltered up to twenty-five adults and children. Cow farms and piggeries operating close to these dwellings making the smell in the area almost unbearable. Absence of basic sanitation facilities in their homes was so bad that most people preferred to defecate in the street, over the road gratings or in out-of-sight corners rather than use the putrid crowded privies. Its people were too poor to afford pride. The resulting effluent often leaked into the water that the families in Hollington Street shared from a common standpipe at the end of the street.

This was the demoralising world Matilda Mary Twiss was born into on the 8th of September 1900. She was raised in a four-room rented dwelling at 57 Hollington Street Camberwell, with her bricklayer father, Edward Twiss, and her mother Alice, along with seven siblings.

The Twiss family's home backed onto another house. Their small yard, as well as those around them, were filled to the gills with fetid refuse. There were holes in the rotted wooden flooring, the stairs were broken with several of the steps missing, and the ceiling plaster in the rooms often fell on their heads. Hot summers and freezing winters regularly brought sickness to the children due to the lack of ventilation and heat in their home.

The family led a hand-to-mouth existence, enduring deplorable poverty on the subsistence labouring wages earned by Edward. The Twiss children, like most children who lived in the poverty-stricken area, went without shoes, and mostly dressed in rags whether it was summer or winter. Families who lived in 'The Well' which the area was commonly known as, in reference to a well once located off Camberwell Grove, generally survived on scraps of food often scavenged from rubbish in the surrounding wealthier villages.

Tilly's mother never used a tablecloth, instead she would spread sheets of disused newspapers on the table. Most nights the family were served a slice of bread and dripping, wet down dog biscuits or a stew made from a penny's worth of dog meat bought from the local market stall on Saturday mornings.

Alcohol abuse, domestic violence, crime, and high mortality was the norm in Camberwell. Nevertheless, through the darkness that life filtered upon the residents, they were still a close-knit community. They would fight each other one day and help one another the next, be it by sharing a few vegetables for a meal, darning already often darned socks, or nursing a sick mother and caring for her children until she was well again.

To bring more money into their home, Alice cleaned the houses of the neighbouring wealthy whenever the opportunity arose. This helped her buy extra food and much-needed medicine for when her children were sick.

At times, Tilly would consider running away from Camberwell. The houses with broken windows, dirt-smeared walls and abused women screaming for help, was often too much for her to take. But most of all, she wanted to flee the destitution she and her family endured.

Due to her family's dire financial circumstances, Tilly was forced to leave school at twelve years of age. She found employment at Watkins & Co. Bookbinders, one of the pernicious sweatshop factories in Camberwell at the time. At this workhouse, Tilly and her fellow co-workers toiled twelve hours a day for six days a week binding over a million bibles a year. The paltry one-pound weekly earnings offered little assistance to her family, but it was enough to help buy bread, milk, and cheap cuts of meat.

Most afternoons after work, Tilly visited the nearby respectable areas of London. She spent time at art galleries, checking out shop windows or sneaking into theatres to watch a silent movie. It confused her that just a few streets away from the slum of Hollington Street there was a whole new world filled with a treasure chest of wealth and happiness. It didn't take Tilly long to realise that with money she could live a different life, one that held many promises compared to the poverty-stricken life her family and neighbours suffered.

One afternoon whilst walking home with Amy, a fellow factory worker, she revealed that she was considering quitting her job to work as a prostitute. She told Tilly that her twenty-year-old cousin worked the Strand on weeknights and made between six and ten shillings from each 'punter' because the men preferred the younger girls.

"That's more than we make in a fuckin' week slaving over those heavy binding machines!" Tilly exclaimed. Her mind was already calculating how much money she could make each week to help her leave the hell hole of Camberwell.

Prostitution was not an uncommon profession among women from the destitute areas of London. Every night men would find women soliciting their bodies and sexual favours along the main road and alleys of Soho, Piccadilly Circus, and the Strand, hoping to earn enough money to put food on the table for their families.

Never being slow to make a decision, Tilly knew she had finally found a way to realise her dream of living a life of luxury by selling the only asset she possessed—her body. Thus, began Matilda Twiss' foray into the world of crime and prostitution.

Several months shy of her fourteenth birthday, Tilly quit her job without telling her parents and made her way to Soho. Once there she strolled along the streets, studying what the women were wearing and how they attracted their clients. As she dared to venture through one of the litter strewn alleys, Tilly stopped upon hearing footsteps behind her. She turned around and saw a slim, tall, well-clothed man approaching her.

"You can't trust these dark alleys day or night milady. Only drunks, thieves and tarts walk these lanes. I don't think you're any orf those. Or are you? What's your price little sweet'art?"

Tilly froze on the spot for a few seconds before stuttering that she was lost. However, the man was a savvy local and could smell a nervous newcomer who was fresh to the game.

"I'm Raymond. I know the girls who work these parts. A few of 'em work for me. You're new 'round 'ere I see. A young and pretty thing like you could make herself a few pounds a week if she wanted. If you work for me sweet'art, I can protect you from the punters and the other strumpets."

Tilly took a step back, startled that the stranger being could read her so well. The thought of being attacked had never crossed her mind. Nor had she considered that she would be considered competition by the other street workers. But the most important thing the young teenager had not contemplated was how to have sex with a man. She was still a virgin.

"I've not done anything with a man before. But I need money. My family needs money. A friend told me that 'er cousin makes a few pounds a day. If I can make that much, it'll 'elp my parents."

"What's your name, pretty?" the pimp asked.

"Tilly... Tilly Smith," she replied with more bravery than she felt.

"Pleasure to meet you, Tilly...ah...Smith." He grinned derisively. "I'll teach you 'ow to please men. I'll show you every trick there is to get 'em to finish quick so you can do more clients every day. You're young an' pretty. The ol' men will finish before they get their cock out orf their drawers. Don't give 'em their money back. You've already done your job. Come with me. I've got a room at the boarding 'ouse down the street."

When they entered the rented room, Tilly remained at the door and took in the shabbily and sparsely furnished room. She had always thought that she would be married before having sex. In her imagination her and her groom would be spending their wedding night in the Bridal Suite at the London Savoy before leaving for Paris for their romantic honeymoon. Instead, she was standing in a disgusting boarding house room furnished with a table that held a jug and wash basin, an old wooden chair, and an old bed with a lumpy mattress and soiled bedding.

Raymond stripped off his clothes and sat on the bed, watching Tilly expectantly. The teenager's heart was beating hard and fast. She had never been naked in front of anyone before, except for her family at bath time when they all bathed from the same bucket of warm water. She hesitantly removed her clothing as Raymond watched her every move.

"C'morn girl, git your kit orf! I 'aven't got all fuckin' day!"

Tilly's face flushed with embarrassment as she placed her left arm timidly across her breasts while pulling her bloomers down with her right hand, slowly slipping her feet out of them. She remained where she stood as still as a statue, not knowing what to do next.

"What are you waitin' for, a written fuckin' invitation! Git on the bed!"

Reluctantly, the trembling teenager took four slow steps toward the bed and laid down beside the man she had just moments ago met. The pimp didn't give her any time to prepare. As soon as her head hit the pillow, he raised himself above her and forced her legs wide apart. Tilly turned her head away in shame and trepidation as she felt his weight upon her: "Open your fuckin' eyes and look at me! You'll 'ave to look at the punters while you're fuckin' 'em!"

Tilly closed her eyes tighter. She couldn't look at the pimp. She wanted to get off her, but her voice seemed to be trapped inside her throat. A sudden burning pain between her legs elicited a pained scream from Tilly as he forcefully pushed himself inside her. "Please don't. It hurts!" Her cry of distress had barely escaped her lips before the whoremonger slapped his hand hard over her mouth. "Shut up 'ore! Before this night's over, you won't feel any pain and you'll love it when a cock's inside you."

Tilly choked back her sobs as Raymond told her how good she felt and that she would make a lot of money. "Men love a blonde tart, 'specially one that's new and's got a tight 'oneypot!" he said after he had finished.

"Go over and wash yourself. You've got more to learn, me pretty. Me and me mates will 'ave you ready to please the punters by the end orf the night."

With the bedsheet gathered around her, Tilly made her way to the basin, becoming alarmed when she saw blood on the towel. "I'm bleeding!"

"I broke your maidenhead. You'll be fuckin' right. Get yourself washed so you're ready for when the other blokes arrive. Tomorrow you'll be workin'."

By the time Tilly's "lessons" had finished during the early hours of the morning, she could barely walk. Her legs and body ached from all the men her pimp had forced her to lay with. He had told her that she was only going to see three of his mates, but by the end of the night, she had serviced five men. As the last one was leaving, she saw him pass Raymond a pound note.

"You fuckin' made money from what those bastards did to me! I want my fuckin' share or I'm goin' 'ome and you'll not make another fuckin' penny from me!"

Raymond threw a pound note onto the bed and told Tilly to meet him outside the tobacco store on Compton Street at ten o'clock the next morning.

"You made ten fuckin' pounds or more. I want 'alf or you can lay on your back and make your own fuckin' money!"

"You've got fire in your spirit. Don't push me too far." The pimp warned as he threw another four pounds on the bed.

Trembling from the sudden loss of adrenaline, Tilly slowly made her way home. She stopped when she reached their street's communal standpipe and cleansed herself of the blood and semen that had run down her legs.

Creeping through to the bedroom so as not to wake her sleeping siblings, Tilly rifled through the clothes on the floor in the corner of the room until she found a clean dress and underwear and changed. She then crept through to the kitchen and threw her semen-stained skirt under the rubbish in the bin.

When Tilly arrived at the tobacco store the following day, it wasn't Raymond waiting for her, but one of the girls that worked for him.

"I'm Jean. Raymond told me to get you started this morning. You'll walk the strip with me, and I'll show you 'ow to work the men. Next week, you're on your own, so make sure you fuckin' learn fast. While I'm nannying you, I'm missing out on me own work and I 'ave kids to feed. Raymond must like you. The rest of us were thrown straight to the streets to work and 'ad no bastard to 'elp us."

Tilly's first couple of clients refused to use the rented room, preferring to be serviced in the alley at the back of the tobacco shop. She was a little clumsy with them at first, but the Johns didn't seem to mind. They were older gentlemen who would pay a pretty penny to feel the soft and supple skin of a young woman again.

The first week seemed to pass slowly for Tilly, but by the end of the second week, she had become more confident. The clients were so pleased with her service that she had even picked up a few extra shillings as tips, which she secreted behind a loose brick near the Chinese laundry.

The men found Tilly delightful, even though she was out of her depth the first few days, she was a quick study and learned how to play the game. Raymond, pleased with the feedback, gave his new worker her own stretch of Soho to work. Her minder, Jean, was pleased when the babysitting job was over. She hadn't made half the money her charge had and was forced to work the weekend to recoup her loss.

After almost two months of streetwalking, Tilly had mastered the art of prostitution and had not encountered any violence or robberies her co-workers had experienced.

However, Tilly's run of good luck ended during her tenth week when a punter jumped from the bed and grabbed her by the throat while she was undressing. "Give me your fuckin' money or I'll break your fuckin' neck."

There was no way Tilly was going to surrender the money she had worked so hard to earn. Using her street smarts, she offered him faux fear before agreeing to give him the money. Letting down his guard, the would-be robber released her so she could retrieve her stash from under the filthy mattress. Then, pretending to reach under the bed, Tilly quickly spun around, flicked open her straight razor and slashed the man across his face. Blood splashed across the wall as the punter took a step toward her screaming: "I'll kill you, you fuckin' bitch!"

Tilly didn't back down. She lunged forward, slashing at his arm twice as he protected his face. "Get the fuck out orf 'ere before I cut your fuckin' balls orf!"

The would-be robber turned and fled, yelling that he was going to put her into the police as he rushed down the stairs.

Within three months, the foul-mouthed, hot-tempered blonde teenager had acquired regular clientele who booked her several times a week. Colin, a man she visited several times a week, worked for the local council. He had a fancy flat in Soho and paid for Tilly's cab fare there and back. He had one stipulation—she must always dress respectably whenever she came to his home so his neighbours would think she was there on council business.

Sex with Colin was quick or sometimes non-existent. He was more interested in feminine company more so than intercourse. They would talk about his family, his sick wife who was hospitalised, and the travels he had experienced. Tilly grew fond of Colin and soon trusted him enough to confide in him about her ambitions of rising from the slums of Camberwell and becoming a wealthy woman living in middle-class London.

Colin gave her advice on how to save her money and explained that investing in real estate would see her set for life. He had a soft spot for Tilly and always gave her a pound tip whether they had sex or not. He told her that the extra money was for her to put toward her first property purchase and not to share it with her pimp.

Six months later, when she felt confident enough in her trade, Tilly decided to work for herself. She had learned a lot from Raymond and had become adept at using her knee and straight razor whenever the need arose. But she was tired of moving from room to room and dodging rents that were in arrears because Raymond had not held up his end of paying the landlords. Working for herself, Tilly knew that she could pay her own way and no longer be required to service Raymond and his friends or have sex with traders in lieu of one of his debts. Another advantage of working for herself was that she would earn more than ten to fifteen pounds a day—a far cry from the average take-home pay of four to five pounds.

Being a responsible daughter and sister, Tilly shared her weekly earnings with her family. But her parents began asking questions about the amount of money she was bringing home. Unable to tell them the truth about her sudden extra income, she told them she had found a second job in another factory. Sensing something was amiss, her father told her that he would walk to work with her the following morning. Just before dawn the next morning, Tilly snuck out of the house and by Midday, she had rented herself a three-roomed furnished flat in Soho.

7

Tilly had been working the streets for almost a year when World War I began. It was a good time for a young, vivacious, and streetwise teenager to make money selling her sexual favours. Soldiers on their way to or from active service passed through London in their hundreds of thousands. Many trawled the streets of Soho, Piccadilly Circus, and the Strand seeking a street walker's company. More naïve soldiers than not found out the hard way that Soho, the Strand,

and various other prostitution haunts of London, were not for the fainthearted after falling victim to violent pimps, grifting prostitutes, and pickpockets.

However, as is the risk of any illegal activity, in February 1915 Tilly was arrested for prostitution and appeared before a magistrate in Bow Street Court. No-one asked how old she was, the magistrate didn't even look up from the paperwork on his bench as he fined her three shillings for her first prostitution offence. Tilly was released after paying the fine and immediately caught a cab to her strip in Soho. After all, she had to catch up with the money lost from her fine and make up for the wasted hours waiting to appear before the magistrate.

The following Friday night, Tilly answered a knock at the door at her flat to find two American soldiers standing on her step. Assuming the only way the men could have known her address was through one of her regular punters, she invited them in. The soldiers introduced themselves as Larry and Bob from Illinois. Tilly explained that she wasn't working, but given they were American GIs, she would see them one at a time. The younger and nicer looking of the two, Larry, was invited into her bedroom first. Bob, whom she asked to wait, suddenly lunged forward, and grabbed a handful of her hair, tightly twisting it as he forced her to the floor.

"You look good on your knees. Now get down on all fours, whore. You can take us both at once!"

Enraged, Tilly grabbed hold of Bob's right leg, and latched onto his calf, biting him hard enough to draw blood. Larry leapt to his buddy's defence as Bob pulled hard on Tilly's ponytail attempting to free his leg from her mouth. When Bob was finally free, Larry dragged Tilly across the rough wooden floor to her bedroom. Then, after a Larry punched her to the side of her head, Tilly fell unconscious to the floor.

When she came to, Tilly found herself being held down and bent over the bed by Larry who was anally raping her. As she furtively looked around her bedroom, she noticed the furniture had been upended and Bob was emptying drawers in a frenzied search for money.

Feigning unconsciousness, Tilly waited for Larry to finish before reaching under her pillow for her concealed straight razor. Then spinning around, she slashed the rapist across his abdomen before escaping half naked out into the street.

Just minutes later, she returned home with two men from the Dog and Duck pub to protect her in case her attackers had remained in her flat. She was relieved to see they were gone, but her flat had been completely ransacked and her mattress and settee, shredded.

Tilly rushed into her bedroom to find the loose floorboard under which she had hidden the previous day's earnings pulled up and the cash missing. She thanked the men who had escorted her home and gave them a few shillings from her purse to buy themselves a beer before seeing them out.

Once alone, she went to her bathroom and lifted the linoleum in the corner, removing her hidden stash. She then bathed and dressed before making her way to the Coach and Horses pub. There she met with Dick the Dealer, who was able to obtain almost anything provided you had the means to compensate. Tilly wanted a pistol, and as luck would have it, Dick just happened to have a Webley Navy issue .44 with ammunition. She paid him his asking price of two pounds for the revolver and twenty bullets, and promptly left.

Armed and feeling somewhat safer, Tilly returned to her old haunt at the Strand to start making up for the stolen money. For the first time in her short prostitution career, she worked almost forty-eight hours straight, earning a cash windfall of seventeen pounds, almost double the amount the GIs had stolen.

The rape and robbery changed Tilly. She became even more obsessed with making money. She had decided that men had stolen her hard-earned pounds, so from then on, she would steal from those who used her services. Most of the time she got away with her pilfering, at other times the men discovered the missing cash and demanded it's return or threatened to report her to the police. On one occasion, however, one of her punters was so incensed that she had stolen five pounds from his drawer, he reported her to the police.

The following morning, Tilly was arrested for prostitution and theft. The magistrate came down hard on her. Tired of having prostitutes appearing before him and sentenced her to three months imprisonment. She was also ordered to make reparation to her victim of the full amount she had stolen.

7

By 1916, the once innocent and naïve teenager, had become a tenacious and street savvy streetwalker. In just three years, she had been arrested and charged for prostitution, theft, and assault eight times. Each time

Tilly appeared before court she paid the penalties imposed instead of accepting a gaol sentence. She didn't mind paying the fines, they were a pittance compared to the fortune she was making. Tilly was on the way up. She was living in a nice flat with modern furniture, wore the latest in fashion and had helped her parents purchase the home she was born in.

After managing to save over five hundred pounds, Tilly saw her dream of living a life of luxury become a reality. She inquired about purchasing a terrace house in Dulwich, an area in the East End of London that she had always favoured. However, upon speaking to the realtor and hearing that the property was priced at two thousand pounds, Tilly was crestfallen.

Determined to make up the additional funds, Tilly took to working longer hours each day and weekends as well. It was important to her that she could fit into 'polite society', and to ensure that she would, she attended a dance school every Tuesday night. On Friday afternoons, she received deportment lessons from a woman who was once a lady-in-waiting to Queen Victoria.

Tilly spent a lot more time with Colin after his wife died. She had experienced the better side of life with the kind gentleman. They often went on outings to museums, art galleries, stage plays, and dined at well-to-do restaurants. Tilly decided that she would drop her shortened name and become 'Matilda' when she finally saved enough money to leave the life of Tilly the prostitute behind. She then hoped to attract a well-situated gentleman and become his wife.

One night whilst she was working the Strand, Tilly was approached by a tall, handsome and rugged-looking Australian soldier. She had heard some of the local lads calling the Aussie boys 'Diggers' and gave him a cursory once-over. Not spotting any suspicious bulges that could have been a pistol or truncheon, she smiled toward him.

"How much sweet'art?" The soldier inquired.

"Ten shillins' for a good-lookin' bloke like yourself, lovey," Tilly replied in her Cockney accent. Smiling, she appraised the Digger, before raising her skirt a little further up her leg.

"Where's your pimp?" He enquired as he suspiciously looked around.

"I work alone. I don't need no bastard takin' me dosh."

"Fuckin' bullshit! No sheila works without one. He better not come at me while I'm fuckin' you!"

Although finding the Digger lacking charm and his behaviour just as crude as most of her English punters, Tilly didn't feel that he was the least bit intimidating. She led him to her regular dark nook between two shop fronts and they got down to business.

"Do you wanna join me at the pub for a beer?" he asked after they had finished the deed.

"That'll be another ten shillins' 'andsome."

"You're a sly fox aren't you, but I'm good for it." He laughed before he and Tilly made their way to a nearby pub.

After spending most of the night drinking, they rented a room at a local boarding house, where the soldier presented Tilly as his wife.

"What's ya name, lovey?" the boarding house owner asked.

"James Devine, but my mates call me Jim," the soldier replied.

James and Tilly spent the entire night together. The larrikin Digger enthralled the unworldly teenager with tales of the Australian Outback, claiming he owned a kangaroo farm and came from a well-to-do family. He also bragged that he was a 'gun' sheep shearer in the local country town where he lived. The captivated teenager sat beside James on the bed in wide-eyed wonderment while he blew his own trumpet, filling her head with stories about Australian sunsets, starry skies and a mansion filled with servants. She listened with naïve interest as he told her about shearers coming to his farm from all around Australia, challenging him to a competition of who could shear more than two hundred sheep in one day…

Tilly may have had minimal schooling, but she was intelligent, shrewd, and driven to succeed in life. After hearing Devine's stories about his life in Australia, she planned on hooking the Aussie Digger and making him her husband. She found the steely blue-eyed, tall, and good-looking man an attractive prospect to escape her wretched life in England and start anew.

Chapter Two

The Aussie Kangaroo Farmer

James Edward Devine was born in Colac, Victoria on the 22nd of August 1892 to James Henry Devine and his wife, Theresa Alice. He was the fourth of six children.

After meeting and marrying Theresa in Glen Innes, New South Wales in 1883, James and his bride returned to his hometown of Fitzroy, Victoria. After many months of living hand-to-mouth in a boarding house, the newlywed husband finally found employment as a barman at the Cavan Hotel in Brunswick Street.

Unfortunately, the owner of the hotel was facing bankruptcy due to the economic depression and drought and was forced to lay off staff. Being the last to be hired, James was the first to be fired. From then on, the Devines moved around a lot with their parents as they sought employment opportunities.

It is not surprising that Jim, having lived such a vagabond existence as a child, was endowed with the spirit of adventure and devil may care attitude. Living in such poverty, he also learned to protect himself when the better off kids from the towns where his father found odd jobs, teased him about his dirty and tatted clothing. Those days taught him the art of taking the knocks, the black eyes—the fat lips and how to fight as though his life depended on him winning.

Due to jobs being scarce in Victoria and having a family to support, James moved his family to Quairading in Western Australia where he found work as a lead station hand on Blackmore Downs cattle station. Theresa took a position as head cook in the main house where she was in charge of the scullery maids. The children were educated with the other cattlemen's children on the station. When not in class, the Devine children joined the other station employees' children with chores around the property.

James Junior, who preferred to be called Jim, enjoyed life on the station and the roustabout experience it offered when he was older. While living at the Station, Jim learned numerous trades—felling trees, fencing, repairing saddlery, castrating bulls, repairing windmills, as well as cattle and sheep mustering, but most of all he had become adept at shearing sheep. Each year, he looked forward to shearing the ewes before the summer lambing began. Jim didn't mind working in the corrugated tin shed carrying out the back-breaking work during the hottest days of summer. He craved the feeling of the metal shears in his hands and the sheep between his knees as he clipped away its fleece. But most of all, he relished the competition between him and the other shearers as they tried to beat the ringer's record.

During shearing season, he eagerly waited for the shed boss to ring the bell as the sheep bleated in the pens while he and his fellow shearers honed their blades. Then at the shrill sound of the bell, they dashed to grab a sheep, quickly dragging them to their cubicle and the race was on as they competed against the shed's ringer to be the one who sheared that one sheep more than his record.

Jim was good but he never quite beat the ringer, whose record was three hundred and seventeen sheep in eight hours and twenty-two minutes. Jim's record was three hundred and four sheep in the same amount of time.

In late 1907, Jim became entangled with some blow-ins from the city. They were on the run after carrying out robberies and break and enters throughout New South Wales, South Australia, and Victoria. Jim was a young and very impressionable sixteen-year-old teenager, standing six feet in height and was quite well-built. He enjoyed spending his free time with the miscreant mob, picking up bad habits of smoking and drinking along the way.

In September the following year, two of the men were apprehended while stealing rum from the station master's cellar. They were gaoled in the Wayfarer Downs' cells awaiting the arrival of the police from Perth. Later that night while sitting around the campfire, Jim listened as the other gang members discussed breaking their mates out and heading to Perth.

"I can come with you!" Jim offered. "I want to get away from here and look for a job in the city."

"Sure, mate. Meet us at the north gate at midnight," Bluey, the redheaded gang leader replied. "It won't be fuckin' easy. We'll be sleepin' rough and stealin' what we can to make money until we find work."

"I'm up for it for sure!" Jim excitedly countered.

Although he found life with the brigand gang exciting, Jim felt they treated him more like a lackey than the man he believed he was. Most of the robberies they had committed yielded only small sums of money, of which he received the lesser amount from the bounty due to both his age and being the last member to join the gang.

After nine months of travelling the Top End with the brigands, Jim left the gang and went out on his own. Over the following years, he found odd jobs as a handyman, shearer, and roustabout, he also made a bit of money prize fighting. Life on his own had hardened him. He had become a strong fighter, and shearing sheep as well as farm labouring had made him physically fit. In January 1913, after winning another competitive boxing match, Jim decided it was time for him to return to the city and try to carve out a life for himself.

It was whilst he was at the Court Hotel in Perth, Devine first learned the news of the threat of a world war. The hotel owner, Con O'Brien, was sitting along the bar drinking a beer with its patrons.

The conversation at the bar had turned to talking about the risk of a war. The men discussed how the Germans were building up strength in their armies. The growing concern in Britain was that they would have the numbers to dominate Europe. The men at the bar were in accord. They were all prepared to fight for the King if he declared war upon Germany.

Jim was fortunate to obtain part-time employment at the Court Hotel and the local general store. He also picked up a shearing contract for a local grazier, Robert Murphy, who had witnessed Devine's impressive speed at shearing when filling in at a neighbouring station.

Perth became home for Jim. He had employment, rented a room at the pub, and had no end of feminine companionship. Life seemed like it was on the up-and-up.

Jim started attending the local horse races and won a bit of money. Thinking he was on a lucky streak, he told Tommy the Bookie to place a twenty pounds bet on Radnor, the favourite in the inaugural Cox Plate that was running at Ascot. However, the bookie told him he'd heard that the favourite had suffered with a little colic overnight and talk on the track was that Artesian was now the horse to beat.

Radnor won the race and Jim lost twenty pounds. Disheartened to have lost such a large sum, he continued betting to recoup his losses. Unfortunately, he continued to lose more than he was winning, and more than he was earning.

Several weeks later whilst drinking at the bar, he learned that the bookmakers at Ascot Racecourse were nobbling certain horses to win, drugging them with caffeine and cocaine. Angry and bitterly disillusioned, Devine left the pub and waited outside the track for Tommy. When the bookmaker opened the door to his Waverley car, Jim jumped out from behind a tree and grabbed him by the throat.

"You'll give me fifty fuckin' pounds now or I'll slit your fuckin' throat you thieving cunt!"

"I…I don't have that much money on me." The bookmaker stuttered.

"Either give it to me or I'll rip the bag from your fuckin' hands and look meself!"

The bookie warily opened his satchel and pulled out a wad of notes and passed them to Jim. Not satisfied that he was giving him all the money he had, Devine snatched the satchel and emptied several more wads of cash and coin onto the ground.

"You fuckin' swindling bastard!" Jim roared as he backhanded the bookie.

"I gave you my share of the takings. That money belongs to other punters!"

"I'll give you half back if you agree to pay me twenty fuckin' pounds a week, otherwise I'll let the police and the punters know your game and there'll be a lot fuckin' more of this!" Devine threatened before punching the bookie in the stomach with such force he doubled over, winded. Still not appeased, he grabbed the bookie's head and brought his knee up to his face, breaking his nose. "Next time I won't be so fuckin' polite!"

Every Saturday night from then on, Jim met the bookie at the local pub to collect his newfound revenue. However, he became greedy and demanded more than the twenty pounds he was collecting from Tommy.

Expanding his extortion racket, Devine started attending race meets at Belmont Park and the trots at either Fremantle racecourse or in East Perth at the cricket grounds. Whilst attending the race venues, he would watch the bookies, jockeys, and owners carefully until he ascertained those who were nobbling their horses, and then blackmailed them too.

Devine made a steady income from his racetrack standover business and before long had given up his hard-labour work and was enjoying a lifestyle like that of the landed gentry. He wore expensive suits and shoes and bought himself a 1910 Renault.

Jim's standover life came tumbling down when he turned up to receive his regular payment from Tommy. Met by three thugs instead, Jim was punched and kicked into unconsciousness by Tommy's new protectors. They left him lying on the ground after throwing a few pennies over him. News of his beating spread through the racing community like wildfire. The other bookies Devine was shaking down soon followed suit and hired their own bodyguards, ensuring their safety from further intimidation.

Forced to return to labouring work, Devine contacted Robert Murphy, the grazier he had a contract with previously. However, he was turned away for not having fulfilled his contractual obligations.

When Great Britain declared war on Germany on the 4th of August, Jim considered enlisting, but was told there were already enough men signing up in the bigger cities. The publican told him and the other young men wanting to join in the fight, that Joseph Cook, the prime minister, would announce a call to arms when needed.

With most of his station hands enrolling in the armed services, Robert Murphy sought Jim's help. Although reluctant at first, Devine demanded thirty pounds for every hundred sheep he shore and ten pounds more if he was the only shearer. Murphy's back was against the wall. There was only himself and his fifteen-year-old son left to work the station. He was forced to agree to Jim's demands.

With most of the stations and farms left shorthanded, the Murphys allowed Devine to work at other properties for a week at a time to help his neighbours out. The hours were long and tiring for him, but at times Jim had relief when itinerants seeking work arrived. As with most travelling labourers, they often only remained the month, and as soon as they had received their wages, they were off to the next town.

While working for Larry Williamson, a neighbouring station owner, Devine met Betty, his seventeen-year-old daughter. She was quite a free-spirited and forward young girl. When Jim was repairing her father's broken windmill, she openly flirted with him, often bending over far enough to reveal her cleavage. Over the following months, when working on the Williamson's property, Betty became more overt in her sexual advances and innuendo. Jim tried to ignore her, but one cold winter's night when he was spending a week at the station branding and dehorning cattle, Betty crept into his room. Fearful that her father would find her in his quarters, Jim told her to leave.

"He's dead drunk and snoring in his chair. He won't wake up till sunrise." Betty said as she stripped off her clothing.

Knowing he was on a good thing bedding Betty every night—Jim began making excuses to visit the Williamson's property. Betty assisted by removing parts from the windmill and other station equipment. However, almost a year later, Betty told Jim she was pregnant and demanded they get married.

Devine didn't wait around for the visit from her father, he left straight for his quarters at the Murphys, packed his gear before heading to the Court Hotel. He later told Con he was hitching a lift with one of the seasonal labourers to Sydney where he planned to enlist as a soldier. Low on cash, Jim asked the hotelier if he'd be interested in buying his car. Con paid him fifty pounds for the car and wished him luck.

For the first few days in Sydney, Devine enjoyed drinking his days away in pubs and spending his nights in local brothels. Feeling the itch for some adventure, on the 16th of February 1916, he made his way to the enlistment booth outside the Sydney General Post Office. After reading the associated information leaflets, he signed the *Attestation Paper of Persons Enlisted for Service Abroad* and the Oath to 'well and truly serve'. He was commissioned to the 11th Depot Battalion until he was transferred to the No.4 Company, Tunnelling Corps, on the 1st of April 1916.

Several weeks after his transfer, Jim was promoted to Acting Corporal. However, he was reverted to Sapper rank on the 9th of May due to insubordination toward a sergeant. He was then officially appointed to the 1st Reinforcements, 4th Tunnelling Company of the Australian Imperial Force at Rosebery Park, New South Wales. On the 22nd of May, Sapper James Devine boarded the *HMAT Warilda* to set sail for Plymouth, England.

During the voyage, Devine was struck by the indomitable courage of the men aged from sixteen upwards, all of whom were in happy spirits. Unlike him, the thoughts of the death, torture and suffering they could be sailing to, seemed far from their minds. But those thoughts haunted his mind every moment of the day and intruded his sleep of a night.

While the *Warilda* was docked in Cape Town, South Africa for a brief stopover, Devine and several other men went Absent Without Leave. The recalcitrant soldiers were disciplined for their non-consensual leave during the voyage.

When they sailed into port on the 18th of July 1916, Jim's Company, along with the Four, Five, and Six Companies, disembarked and made their way to Amesbury and Tidworth to train for action at the front.

While at Tidworth Military Camp, Devine played poker with several of the other soldiers at the barracks and before long ran up a huge gambling debt. Out of money and chances of further IOUs, he once again went AWOL and was on the hunt for easy targets to rob.

Whilst in Soho, Devine came across a lone prostitute who was easy prey for the ignoble soldier. He asked her for her price and followed her down a nearby alley. When they were out of the sight of any passers-by, he grabbed her by the hair and held his pocketknife to her throat, demanding all her money. Terrified, she pleaded with him not to hurt her as she emptied the coins out of her blue velvet purse.

"You've got more than this. Eight fuckin' shillings? Give me every penny you fuckin' have or you won't be walking the streets for a month!"

"I ain't got nothin' more. I gave you all I 'ave!"

Devine didn't utter another word. He closed his pocketknife and ran out of the lane, disappearing into the night. Over the following week, the aberrant soldier robbed several prostitutes of their money, once almost being shot by a pimp. If it weren't for a passing milk cart offering him cover, he would not have survived that day.

During the fifth day of AWOL, and broke again, Devine sought out another prostitute to plunder. As he watched from his vantage point at a nearby inn, he spotted a young buxom blonde walking along the Strand. However, after asking the girl for her price, Jim saw the spark of fire in her eyes and decided not to rob her but take advantage of her services. He saw that there was something different about this girl—she had a boldness and strength which he respected. But what most impressed him was her sexual prowess. In her he sensed a kindred spirit.

Her name was Tilly.

During their time together, Devine continued to fill Tilly's head with fanciful stories about the kangaroo station he and his mother owned in Central Australia. He told her about the country dances they hosted at their property, the station hands he oversaw since the death of his father and the wealthy life he led. And being a virile Aussie man, he made himself out to be quite the Lothario—back home.

Devine thought that he had cannily eluded the military police whom he assumed were searching for him. But his luck ran out one evening as he and Tilly walked arm-in-arm out of Daly's Theatre in Leicester Square. Hearing a man calling out his name, Jim turned to see who it was and saw two MPs running towards him. The chase was on.

"Go back to the boarding house!" He called out to Tilly before making his escape down Charing Cross Road. When he looked behind, he noticed that one of the officers had disappeared, but the second cop was still in close pursuit.

Instead of continuing down the street, Devine decided to veer off to the left into St. Martins Place where he secreted himself under a parked car. He watched as the ensuing MP ran past him and waited a few moments before crawling out and taking off in the opposite direction. About two hundred yards up the street the second MP suddenly stuck his arm out from behind a black Overland touring car. Jim was knocked flat on his back by the cop's outstretched arm.

Dazed, Jim remained where he fell. The breathless officer that had passed him earlier, approached Devine and growled, "You led me on a fuckin' wild goose chase, you fuckin' bastard!" before pulling Jim to his feet and duly returning him to Tidworth

Confined to barracks for nine days as punishment for desertion, thoughts of the young blonde prostitute consumed Devine's mind. Again, not learning his lesson from his previous jaunts, Jim escaped the barracks as soon as he was released from detention.

Heading straight to Tidworth train station, Jim secreted himself in nearby bushes until boarding a train to Charing Cross station. Upon his arrival, he hired a cab and directed the driver to take him to the tobacco shop on the Strand. Devine was disappointed when he saw that Tilly wasn't in her usual spot. He walked to the boarding house several yards up the street and paid upfront to rent a room for a week before heading to the local pub. Four nights later he came across Tilly leaning against the brick wall front of the tobacco shop.

"I've been here waiting four days for you!" He called out as he crossed the street.

"I took some time orf. What can I do for you today, my 'andsome Digger?" she flirted.

Jim took Tilly back to his room and they fell into the same comfortable chatter as before. He told her he wanted to leave the army and live with her in England. His motives were in no way altruistic—to him Tilly was a meal ticket for an easy life of money and leisure in London and then later, Australia.

Not wanting to be embroiled in trouble with the armed forces, Tilly used her feminine wiles to encourage Devine to return to his barracks, promising she would help him remain in England after the war ended. She had no intentions of remaining in Britain. Since hearing Jim's stories about the kangaroo farm and life in the Australian outback, she had thought about nothing much else.

"Jimmy," she whispered as she gently caressed his face, "the King and our country expect you to fight the Germans. I've 'eard the army shoot deserters. I couldn't bear it if anything 'appened to you. My father says the Germans are outmanned and the war will be over soon. Stay with them and collect your wages. Be brave and get yourself a medal and maybe a commission."

"Or I could end up a fuckin' fly-covered rotting corpse on the battlefield. This isn't my war, Till. Us Diggers are just a pawn in a game of military fuckin' chess!"

His words stabbed at her heart. Tilly wished he didn't have to return to war and the threat of death, but if he didn't, she knew he would surely face the firing squad. She had no other words to make him see sense after what he had just said. Tilly knew it would be better for both she and her Aussie soldier to have a future together if he remained alive.

"Jimmy, I don't want you to die. Neither of us 'ave been in a war before and we 'ave no idea what's going to 'appen. But I know if you don't return to Tidworth, you'll be 'unted down and court-martialled when you're caught, and you could face a firing squad. Ask the commander if you can do clerk work or kitchen duty. Anything to keep you out orf the fighting..."

"I've got to go. There's a card game on at the publican's house. I'll see you when I get back," Devine said as he looked at his watch.

"Well, I need to work. I've got a family to 'elp and rent to pay. I'll see you tomorrow morning before I start," Tilly replied as she climbed out of bed. "Think about what I said."

When Jim handed her ten shillings as payment for her services, Tilly refused to accept the money. She had plans to change the Digger's mind and what better way than stroking his ego. She told him she enjoyed his lovemaking and companionship much more than she did his money.

The following morning, Devine spent half the day in bed listening to stories Tilly shared from some of her soldier punters about their jobs at the AIF Headquarters in London. "If you 'andle all the business papers and the 'iring and organising staff at your kangaroo farm, you should be able to get a position in the records department."

"Mum keeps the books. I do the hard yakka on the station."

"'ard yakka?"

"Its Australian pidgin learned from the blackies," Jim said.

"Blackies?"

"Yeah, the black fellas. Aborigines. The outback is full of 'em."

"I've never 'eard of them."

"They are the natives of Australia. They work for practically nothing and most are good workers. Those that don't go walkabout."

Tilly was more interested in convincing Jim to return to the barracks than learning about Aboriginals walk-abouting in Australia. "Jimmy, I 'ave to go to work. I'm over an 'our late for one of the blokes as it is. I'll see you back 'ere tonight." She smiled as she stretched across and kissed him on the cheek.

"I think I'll go back to Tidworth. After my confinement for ack willy is done, I'll speak to the commander about transferring to headquarters."

"Oh, Jim, thank you! I'm so 'appy! If you get a job there, we can see more of each other without worrying about MPs breaking down the door!"

When Devine returned to the camp, he was immediately arrested and due to handing himself in voluntarily, received one week's detention and a forfeiture of nine days' pay by the Commanding officer.

On the 29th of August 1916, Jim was sent to the Australian Divisional Base Depot in France. The following day he was enlisted in the 1st Australian Tunnelling Company and was told that they would soon be leaving for Messines Ridge to dig tunnels and line them with explosives.

7

Whilst attending training at the No. 2 Command Depot, Jim reported sick and was admitted to the 2nd Canadian Casualty Clearing Station. The staff nurse was not surprised to find he was suffering from a venereal disease. On the 7th of December, he was transferred by Ambulance Train to the 8th Stationary Hospital where he underwent treatment for syphilis. Upon discharge from hospital, he spent a day at the Rest Camp in Boulogne before being transferred to the Australian General Base Depot at Étaples in Northern France.

On the 13th of February 1917, Devine was transferred to the No. 2 Command Depot in Weymouth, England, for permanent base duty. Four days later he became ill again and was admitted to the Isolation Hospital. His syphilis had not been properly treated so he remained in isolation for the required fortnight and was then transferred to the Verne Isolation Hospital at Portland until he was discharged back to Weymouth on the 24th of February.

Devine remained at the Command Depot for some months but found the arduous training too much and absconded on the 7th of June. Once again, he made his way to the Strand in search of the blonde, nubile Tilly. Being unable to find her, the insubordinate soldier booked himself into the boarding house.

"What, no missus tonight, sir?" the housekeeper asked.

"She'll be here in a few days."

Two days later, Devine came across Tilly outside the tobacco shop. "I've been searching all over the place for you," he exclaimed. "You're a bugger to find, love!"

"I 'aven't been working. I missed you and didn't want another man touching me," Tilly lied. "But I need to buy food, so I came out to find a punter or two tonight."

"Take the night off, sweet'art. I'll take you out to dinner then it's afters at your place."

After the German daylight raid on London on 13th of June 1917, causing the death of over one hundred and fifty people and injuring more than double, Devine acted as Tilly's pimp and protector. When Tilly felt she had made enough money, she and Jim would take time off to see a movie at the local theatre and dine out at restaurants.

London was unsafe with the Germans targeting the city. Whenever she heard the sound of an engine in the sky, Tilly would hold her breath in fear and look skyward to check to see if there were more Zeppelins or Gotha bombers. She was always relieved whenever she saw that they were English warplanes.

Two weeks later when they were returned home from the Strand, Devine was surprised when apprehended by two MPs who had jumped out from the side of the flat. He was taken back to Weymouth, where he was confined to barracks for fourteen days and forfeited two weeks' pay for his AWOL stint.

Whilst confined, Tilly and her money-making abilities never left the young soldier's mind. He had witnessed for himself the amount of money she made and knew that with his help, she could double the amount, if not treble it. Devine paced the barracks, frustrated at not being able to put his plan immediately into action.

After serving his detention, Jim instantly sought leave from the barracks, which was denied. Unperturbed by again risking the forfeiture of his military pay and further confinement, Devine went AWOL on the 9th of July.

After catching a train to Soho, Devine robbed two prostitutes of their earnings before making his way to Tilly. Within ten minutes of his arrival, Tilly told Jim that she was pregnant. "Is it my kid?" the shocked soldier asked.

"Orf course it is. You know I use rubbers with my punters. You complained about it enough times when I first fucked you!" She spat in defiance and hurt at his inference.

"Well, fuck knows how many men you took a shine to like you did me," Devine spitefully retorted. "Yeah, and those condom bastards break."

"Not with me they don't! Now fuck orf. Get out orf my flat and don't fuckin' come back!"

After a fiery discussion, Jim decided to continue their relationship. As far as he was concerned, he could send Tilly out to work once the baby was a few weeks old.

The following day, Tilly took Jim home to meet her family. To say her parents were unimpressed with their daughter's choice of husband would be an understatement. After the introductions were over, Tilly helped her mother serve tea and scones while Devine vilified the King and the British government for forcing Australian men to join the war.

Seeing her father holding on tight to his temper, Tilly lightly touched Jim's arm and whispered: "Stop talking about the war."

The Twisses had already lost family members and they resented being forced to entertain a soldier who, instead of fighting against destructive enemy forces, preferred to go AWOL and live the life of a fancy man.

On the 12th of August 1917, Jim married sixteen-year-old Matilda Mary Twiss at the Sacred Heart of Jesus church. The teenage bride and her parents lied to Canon Murnane, stating that she was twenty-one-years old. The only attendees were Tilly's immediate family and two of her friends. Edward Twiss gave his daughter away to Devine as her mother sobbed and patted her eyes with a handkerchief sitting in the first pew. Alice Wesley stood beside Tilly as her Matron of Honour. An army mate of James's, Richard Hirsch, standing as Best Man.

The newlyweds had not left the church grounds before Devine turned to his bride and told her that he expected her to remain working as long as she was able.

"Why Jim? You 'ave money. You told me you are rich!"

"Fuck, my mother warned me to watch out for bitches like you who'd be after my money! I can't touch any of it until I return to Australia. So, you've got a long wait. That's if I keep you that long."

"Why is that? It's your fuckin' money. Why should I fuck 'alf orf London when you've got money!"

"It's fuckin' *family* money. I have to wait until the old girl falls off her perch before I can get a fuckin' penny! That's the end of it. If you don't like it, you can fuck off!"

With her hopes broken, Tilly farewelled her parents and siblings before returning to her Soho dwelling where she and Devine consummated their marriage. Later, while standing naked in the kitchen and pouring himself a beer, Jim noticed four MPs walking through the front gate before dividing to surround the flat. Not wanting to be caught stark naked, he raced through to the bedroom to get dressed, only to be confronted by an MP climbing through the bedroom window. Woken by Jim's shouting, Tilly asked him what was wrong.

"I'm about to be fuckin' arrested again!"

Jim was sentenced to six days confinement to barracks and forfeited three weeks of his military wages.

Between the 1st and 3rd of September, no more than two weeks after his release from confinement, the wayward sapper was again AWOL. During this reprobate's sojourn, Devine shook down several prostitutes for their money, so violently assaulting one that she was rushed to hospital. The women didn't report the robberies and assaults. Prostitutes knew the risk of rape, robbery and bashings were part and parcel of their profession. But Jim also knew the women working the streets to feed and clothe their children were too afraid to report and run the risk of being imprisoned and having their children taken by the authorities.

This time Jim didn't make it to the flat. He was receiving oral pleasure from a streetwalker in Piccadilly Circus when he was seen and captured by passing MPs. He was confined to barracks for three weeks. A fortnight into his detention, Devine was admitted to the 1st Australian Dermatological Hospital at Bulford suffering another bout of venereal disease.

When Tilly arrived at the barracks to visit Jim, she learned that he had been admitted to the infirmary. Concerned that he was seriously ill, the worried young wife rushed to the military hospital and asked to see her husband. The clerk told her that he was in isolation and when she asked what was wrong with him, he refused to reveal the illness. He did tell Tilly that if she waited, she could speak to her husband on the telephone. Tilly anxiously waited at the clerk's desk until he handed her the candlestick phone.

"Hello, Jimmy. What's wrong? Why are you in the 'ospital?" Tilly asked, her concern evident in her voice.

"Nothing for you to worry about, love. I've been having dizzy spells. They think it might be food poisoning but stuck me in isolation in case it's the flu." He lied.

During the telephone conversation, Jim was only interested in talking about the amount of money Tilly was making and asked her for eleven pounds to cover a gambling debt. Tilly became a little short with him and complained that she was tired of working such long hours because he kept going AWOL and forfeiting his army wages. She told him that with her being pregnant, she had to compete harder to attract punters.

"Don't you fuckin' dare speak to me like that. Give me the money, or you can fuckin' stay here and I'll go to Australia without ya, baby or no fuckin' baby! Now shut your big fuckin' mouth or I'll have it shut for you!"

Tilly replaced the earpiece back into the cradle, stood up and left without uttering a word.

On the 21st of October, Tilly was shocked to learn that a Zeppelin had dropped a six-hundred-pound bomb on Camberwell the previous night. The radio broadcast stated that some areas had been destroyed and at least a dozen people were killed. Terrified that her parents and siblings may have been hurt, she tried to catch a cab, but in the mayhem that followed the bombing she was unable to hail one. She rushed back to her flat, and after hiding her earnings, Tilly raced next door to Ronald and Betty's.

As Ronald approached Camberwell, the catastrophic damage caused by the explosion was devastating for them to see. Tilly was stunned to see the damage of several shops on Calmington Road. Tears stung her eyes as Ronald slowly drove along the road and she saw that most of the redbrick Victorian terrace houses that had once lined the street, were now rubble. People were standing around looking grief-stricken. Tilly wiped away her tears with her handkerchief. She had never thought that Camberwell would be target by the Germans.

"I 'ope the families got to the shelters before those bastard Germans dropped the bomb…"

When they arrived in Hollington Street, Tilly was relieved to see her family home was still standing. "My family is safe, thank God," she rasped. "Mum still 'as the black curtains up at the windows. They're probably too scared to leave the 'ouse.

"It's a terrible mess, Till. I hope they killed the commie bastards!" Ronald angrily replied.

"All the windows are shattered!" Tilly gasped.

Tilly and Ronald spent the afternoon with her family. The conversation centred around the bombing. Her father related how he and her mother had sat huddled with her siblings as they listened to the bomb blast, terrified that they were about to die.

"Oh, Mum, I wish I were 'ere with you all. I 'eard the bombing at Piccadilly Circus, but the last place I thought would ever be bombed, was 'ome! I can't wait for this bleedin' war to be over and 'opefully they'll kill the Nazi bastards!" Tilly fumed.

"Darling, there are just as many innocent people in Germany as there is in Britain. We can't wish ill on an entire country for the evil done by a few," Her mother gently replied.

As Tilly was about to suggest to Ronald that it was time for them to leave, a knock sounded at the front door. When her brother William answered the door, their cousin Henry came rushing in. His eyes were red and swollen, his cheeks tear stained. He sobbed as he tried to explain why he was there.

"D…D…Dad was killed in the bombing! Mum wanted me to come and tell you!" He wailed.

Tilly's dad fell back in his chair. He and his brother were close. His wife sat on the arm of the chair, holding him close to console him.

"I'm sorry Henry. Your Dad was a good father and uncle. Tell your Mum that I'll come around and see you all next week when things are a little more settled." Tilly said as she hugged her cousin.

Tilly handed her brother, Richard, thirty pounds and told him to give the money to their father when he was feeling better. She hugged her parents and sibling's goodbye before she and Ronald left.

"It's going to take years to fix Camberwell. I still can't believe this 'appened. This will be the undoing of fuckin' Germany!" Tilly seethed.

7

On the 2nd of January 1918, Devine was transferred to the Anzac Provost Corps in Tidworth. He hadn't seen Tilly since their argument, nor had she answered any of his daily letters. The only correspondence he received during his sentence was from his brother, Thomas who had written to say he was being shipped back to Australia after injuring his left hand while fighting the Germans in Pozières. Thomas wrote how he had been carried from the field by overtired Australian stretcher-bearers who did not give up trying to save him even though bullets flew above them and dirt from exploding bombs showered them as they carried him to safety. Jim felt a lump in his throat as he thought of his younger brother bravely facing battle while he spent most of the war escaping it. He bowed his head in shame.

7

Heavily pregnant, Tilly found having sex with any more than four or five clients a day too tiring. The freezing cold weather was also affecting her. She often wished that she were already in Australia, sitting in the warmth of the sun instead of selling herself on the street in the falling snow. The long hours she worked to cover the losses due to Devine's army wages which were again being used to pay his AWOL fines, she found unfair.

After working from eleven o'clock in the morning, she would leave around eight o'clock at night. On her way home, she would buy a sandwich or a pork pie and be in bed and sound asleep within an hour of arriving at the flat.

On the 11th of January, after she had not long finished servicing a client, Tilly's waters broke. Until then, she had not experienced any symptoms of labour, not even a twinge. Concerned that the baby was coming so early, she hailed a taxi.

By the time she arrived at the hospital, her labour pains were four minutes apart and she complained that she felt like her lower back was breaking. "My baby is early. It can't be born yet!"

"Calm down and we'll take you to the ward. What's your name sweet'art?"

"Mrs. Devine. I feel like pushing! This 'urts so much!"

"Don't push until we get you undressed and ready."

"I can't 'elp it. I can feel something between my legs! I think the baby's 'ead is coming!" Tilly shrieked. "I need to push! Please!"

"When was the baby due?"

"End of next month! I need to push!"

The nurse quickly removed Tilly's bloomers and helped her onto the bed. "Now lay back and spread your legs so I can check you, sweetie… Oh, sweet Jesus! Yes, push my dear, push as hard as you can."

After only a few pushes, the baby was born. Tilly, still surprised that she had given birth so quickly, looked at the nurse's distressed face. "What's wrong? Can I see my baby, please? What is it, a boy or a girl?" she asked, her voice strangled with fear.

"It…it's, it's a girl." the nurse replied as she quickly wrapped the baby up in a towel.

"Alice, 'er name is Alice Theresa Devine." Tilly smiled as she held her arms out for her daughter. "She's named after my mum and my 'usband's mother."

"I'm sorry, Mrs. Devine but I must take the baby to see the doctor first," Nurse Richards almost whispered as she rushed from the room.

Anxiously waiting for the nurse to return with her Alice, Tilly broke down in tears fearing that there was something terribly wrong to cause the nurse to leave the room so quickly.

Ten minutes passed before Nurse Richards returned, carrying Alice wrapped in a hospital blanket. All the new mother could see was a shock of brown hair. As Tilly asked to see her daughter, a doctor entered the room and stood at the end of her bed.

"Mrs. Devine, before the nurse hands you your baby, there's something I need to tell you. Your daughter has been born prematurely and deformed because you're infected with syphilis," he coldly explained.

"What? I can't be!" Tilly exclaimed in horror. "There's no possible way. I'm a married woman. My 'usband is a soldier!"

"I'm sorry to tell you that you are indeed infected. Your daughter is jaundiced and is quite small and… Mrs. Devine, your daughter exhibits deformities consistent with congenital syphilis. Soldiers are known to be the worst offenders of spreading the disease."

Tilly turned her head away as guilt washed over her. She didn't want to tell the doctor she was a prostitute. She had taken precautions against becoming infected. *How could this happen*? She took a few deep breaths, wiped away her tears and sat up in the bed with her arms outstretched. "Please, I need to see my baby."

The doctor nodded toward the nurse who then laid the tiny baby girl in her mother's arms. Tilly removed the blanket covering her daughter's face and gasped in shock. Her tiny face had cratered necrotic holes where a nose, eyes, and mouth should have been. Her skin was yellow, and she made horrid gurgling sounds instead of a cry.

"What will happen to 'er? Will she live?" Tilly asked as tears welled.

"Her deformities have corrupted her nervous system. I'm afraid your daughter will die within a matter of days, perhaps even hours."

"There must be *something* you can do for 'er. Is she in any pain? Please 'elp Alice if she is," Tilly pleaded as her tears overflowed.

"The nurse will take her now. Your daughter needs to be placed in the special nursery." The doctor replied in a matter-of-fact voice. "I need to treat you with salvarsan for the syphilis infection. Your husband will also need to be notified and see a doctor for an immediate check-up. I advise you to refrain from your marital duties until your doctor deems you cured. If you become pregnant again whilst infected, the child will also be afflicted with syphilis. But if you must indulge, please encourage your husband to use a prophylactic."

Tilly shuddered a sob as she kissed her Alice's little hand before passing her to Nurse Richards, who immediately covered the baby's face with the blanket and hastily made her way out of the room.

The heartbroken mother sobbed into her hands, blaming herself for her daughter's illness and wondered how she could ever face Jim again.

Almost a half an hour later, the doctor re-entered the room and asked Tilly to turn over for her an injection to treat the syphilis. "This is the first of several injections over the next week or so. You will then need to come into the hospital clinic to continue your treatment until you are cured. The nurse will move you to a private room. You need to be isolated from the other mothers and babies." The doctor jabbed her with the hypodermic and then left the room.

Late that night, Tilly went for a walk around the hospital. She was unable to sleep worrying about how she had become infected with syphilis and grieving that she was the cause of her daughter's impending death.

She had asked one of the nurses earlier in the evening if she could visit Alice but was told they were too busy. The nurse promised to ask the sister to bring her in when it had quietened down. Tilly wasn't willing to wait any longer. She had already waited for over eight hours.

As she walked along a corridor, Tilly heard a doctor talking nearby and ducked into an auxiliary room that was next to the nursery, not wanting to be caught. Waiting for the footsteps to pass by, she looked around at the medical equipment and linens. Not hearing anyone outside, Tilly turned to leave but stopped when she heard a strange noise. Walking toward the sound, she was horrified to see her baby laying on a bench in front of an open window. It was a freezing cold night and snow was falling. She rushed across to Alice, wrapped a nearby sheet around her and hugged her close. She sobbed upon realising they had left her baby out in the cold to die, discarded like a diseased piece of rubbish.

After checking that no-one was in the corridor, Tilly rushed back to her room and snuggled under the blankets as she held her little girl close. To make sure the nurses couldn't see she had little Alice, she curled her body around her. About a half an hour later, a nurse came in and placed a cup of tea and a biscuit as well as a glass contraption with a black ball on one end, on the bedstand.

"Precious, I need to show you how to express your milk to make you feel a little more comfortable. If you don't, you could get sick with mastitis. I also need to show you how to wrap your breasts, so they don't move around too much."

The young mother refused to acknowledge her presence.

"I'll come back to see you early tomorrow afternoon. It's been an upsetting day for you, love. Try and get some sleep." The nurse gently touched Tilly's shoulder and quietly left the room.

The pain in Tilly's breasts woke her at two o'clock in the morning. She looked down to check on Alice and found her cold and blue. Knowing her baby had died, she let out a heartbreaking wail which brought two nurses rushing into the room. They were quite perturbed when they saw her sitting up with her daughter in her arms. When one of the nurses attempted to take Alice from Tilly's arms, she swung her out of her reach.

"You fuckin' killed 'er! You left my baby out in the cold, and you all fuckin' killed 'er!" Tilly screamed. "You're supposed to protect the sick and dying! Why, why would you do this to an innocent baby!"

The sister in charge walked straight over to Tilly and asked for the baby. When she refused, she wrested Alice from her arms. "Be quiet and calm yourself. There are other mothers and babies in this hospital who need their sleep. We only did what was right for your child. Something you should have thought of before you riddled yourself with syphilis!" The sister barked.

"Go fuck yourself, you fat fuckin' cow!" Tilly spat back. "You fuckin' murdering 'ore! I don't fuckin' care who 'ears me! *You killed my daughter!*"

The younger nurse tried to calm Tilly down after the sister took the baby away. "I'm sorry for your loss Mrs. Devine. Let's calm you down now before the sister returns with a sedative. What she did with your baby is what we do here for the little ones we know are going to die. You must thank God that he led you to your little girl, so she was able to die in her mother's loving arms."

"Fuck God and fuck the sister!" Tilly seethed before turning over and facing the wall.

"I'll make you a nice cup of tea and that will help calm you down," the nurse said as she walked out of the room.

The sister returned a few minutes later with a doctor. She didn't give Tilly a chance to utter a word, she held her down while the doctor quickly administered a sedative. Moments later, the heartbroken teenager fell asleep.

As soon as she woke up the following morning, Tilly got dressed, left the hospital, and hailed a taxi to take her home. She asked her neighbour, Ronald, if he would drive her to Tidworth to see Jim. Noticing that she was no longer pregnant and the redness of her eyes, Ronald knew something terrible had happened. He told her to wait in the car and said that he would be out as soon as he grabbed his coat.

Devine was as heartbroken and consumed with overwhelming guilt when Tilly told him their daughter had died from syphilis and that she was being treated for the disease. He knew he couldn't blame her, as he was currently being treated for the infection himself. He also knew he was the cause of his daughter's death.

"I don't know 'ow I caught it," Tilly sobbed. "I'm so careful with the punters and check their cock before I 'ave sex with them. You know what I'm like. But some'ow I got it and it killed our little girl."

"It wasn't you. It… it was me. I'm sorry, Tilly. I'm being treated for it here. That's why I'm in the infirmary. I caught it from one of the whores in a brothel I visited when I was drunk."

Tilly didn't say a word. There were no words. The man she married had killed their child. She stared at her husband long and hard, then throwing him a look of repugnance and disgust, stood, and walked away. She ignored Jim as he called for her to come back. She ignored his pleas for her forgiveness.

She could scarcely hold back the tears as she returned to Ronald's car. The ride home was silent. When he pulled up outside Tilly's flat, she remained in the car. Ronald sat in silence beside her, knowing she would speak when she was ready.

"I can't go in there. Can you take me to my mum's 'ouse, please?" She pleaded. The last place Tilly wanted to be was at home where a crib and baby's clothing awaited the arrival of her much-wanted newborn.

"Sure thing. If there's anything we can do Tilly, you know Betty are here for you." Ronald softly whispered as he gently patted her hand.

"Thank you, Ronny, but you can't bring my baby back from the dead," Tilly whispered.

"No, unfortunately we can't. I'm deeply sorry for your loss, Tilly."

Two days later, Jim knocked on the Twiss' door. His father-in-law reluctantly admitted him. The distressed husband offered Tilly flowers and silk stockings and begged for her to forgive him and return home.

"You're fuckin' AWOL again aren't you! 'onestly Jim, you just can't stay out of fuckin' trouble and I'm left to make the money because the army takes your pay in fuckin' fines!"

"I've got special dispensation for leave on compassionate grounds. Our baby died and you need me. Till, please, come back home with me. Betty and Ronald have moved all the baby belongings from the flat, so you won't be upset seeing it all again."

Tilly had spent most of the time grieving in the bedroom of her childhood home. Her siblings slept in the living room, giving their sister privacy. She was unable to tell her parents how her daughter had died. Preferring to shield them from the tragic truth, she told them she was stillborn.

Her mother said that even though she and her father didn't like Jim, he was the father of the baby and it would be better for them both to grieve together. Tilly had already decided that she would cope better with her daughter's death if she was to return to what she knew best, working the streets. She had also determined that, for better or for worse, she was married to Jim and she wouldn't give up her chance to leave Britain. Australia held such promise for her future, and as Jim's bride, it was almost as good as an immigration certificate.

"I'm fuckin' warning you, if you ever 'it me or fuck another woman again, I'm gone for good!" Tilly threatened before turning around to collect her belongings and say goodbye to her family.

CHAPTER THREE

Ack Willy Jim

Devine had lied to Tilly about the army granting him compassionate leave. He *was* AWOL. Tilly discovered the falsehood when the military police turned up on her doorstep a week later. Once again, she was forced to lie and told the officers she had not seen Jim since the week after their daughter's death. As he reached the threshold of the flat, one of the MPs turned around and told Tilly that if they discover she was hiding her husband, they will turn her flat into wrack and ruin when they next turned up to look for him.

"You fuckin' lying bastard!" Tilly spat when Devine stumbled into the living room rotten drunk later that night. "The MPs were 'ere and 'ave threatened to come back! You're fuckin' AWOL again! When will you stop bringing fuckin' trouble to our door!"

"Fuck it woman! I'm just fuckin' ack willy. I haven't shot the fuckin' king! Would you prefer that I was in Beersheba so you can get a fuckin' war pension?" Jim roared as he slapped Tilly hard across her face.

"Listen 'ere, you drunken bastard, get out orf my fuckin' flat! I told you the next time you 'it me it would be the last! Now get the fuck out!" Tilly screamed as she picked up a vase from a small table beside the settee and threw it at him.

In a rage, Devine threw furniture and whatever else was nearby around the room, smashing a chair through the front window. Fearing another beating, Tilly fled to the safety of the bedroom. Closing the door behind her, she pushed an Edwardian chest of drawers across it, moments before Jim tried to open the door. Cursing and swearing, he threatened Tilly that he would run her through if she didn't let him in.

A loud banging at the door quickly silenced the irate husband. When he looked out the window, he saw two MPs standing on the bottom step. Not wanting to be arrested, he raced to the bathroom and secreted himself in the wall space he had constructed behind the bath.

Tilly was relieved by the arrival of the cavalry. She let them in without saying a word and nodded toward the bathroom. The officers went straight through and noticed it was empty, but a small gap in the wall caught an officer's attention. He leaned over the bath and pulled on a piece of loose Masonite and was surprised to see the wall open to reveal their AWOL soldier crouched behind it. Jim was immediately arrested and returned to the barracks.

"Please, let me stay just one more day. I give you my word that I'll give myself up to you at midday tomorrow. My daughter died. I'm a drunken bastard right now, but I need to make amends with my wife. I'm sure you understand…"

He hadn't shown it to Tilly, but Jim was in mourning for his daughter. He hadn't spoken to her about the heartbreaking guilt and shame he felt for being responsible for her death. He was supposed to be at war to kill the enemy, not his own flesh and blood. That night he had turned to snorting cocaine to blur away his anger and numb the sadness, pain, and guilt.

"You've been given enough chances!" One of the MPs growled as he roughly pulled Jim out of the crouch space. "If it were up to me, I would have shot you for desertion, you fuckin' coward!"

Again, Devine was found guilty of being absent without leave. He forfeited one week's pay and returned to the Training Depot at Parkhouse. There, he resumed gambling and the Aussie card-sharp realised he was playing against professional swindlers and had been out sharped. Two days later when he was unable to pay his debts, Jim wrote to Tilly requesting thirty pounds so he could pay a gambling debt. Tilly was sick and tired of sending her husband money to pay his gambling debts and threw his letter into the fire.

Several weeks later, angered by his wife's ignorance, Devine seized upon the first opportunity to escape. He had accrued a major gambling debt of fifty-five pounds and needed money to pay the burly Englishman he was indebted to. The corporal had threatened to slash his face so badly that he his own mother wouldn't recognise him. Devine knew the threat would be carried out—he had witnessed the violence he had carried out on previous debtors.

Devine headed straight to the Strand.

Tilly saw Jim coming and immediately took off to the alley, hiding herself behind a lorry. But he had seen her first. A small scuffle ensued, and Tilly threatened to scream if he didn't let her go. Devine placed his hands in the air in a show of defeat and apologised, stating that he was at his wits end trying to get the money together to pay the debt before he was maimed or even killed. Tilly told him that she would only give him the money if he returned to Parkhouse before he was reported missing. Devine begrudgingly agreed.

As luck would have it, four hours later Jim crept into the barracks and resumed his normal duties without being called up to the commander's office.

Two weeks later, Devine and his squad were marched out to the Training Depot at Parkhouse. 'Training' is an inaccurate description of the activities enjoyed by the soldiers at the depot. Their days were devoted to playing games of cricket, football, weight training, and inter-squadron fencing and boxing tournaments.

After hearing the rumours around camp that the end of war was imminent, Jim sent Tilly a letter advising her of the gossip. He wrote that if the talk were true, he would be sent back to Australia as soon as a ship was available. He also told her to save as much money as she could so they could enjoy time in Sydney before he took her home to meet his mother.

Excited at the prospect of living in a mansion, Tilly worked long hours so she could buy the clothing and shoes befitting a lady of leisure when she arrived in Australia. She was a little nervous at the prospect of leaving England but was looking forward to saying farewell to prostitution forever.

However, knowing that he would soon be Australia bound, Jim's flights to freedom from the barracks continued. He was absent from the Parkhouse muster parade on the 6th of May after receiving a letter from Lucy, a woman he had met in a Soho bar several months before. He and the buxom redhead had struck up a romance and spent a few nights together during a previous jaunt. He made his way to her flat and spent the night and voluntarily returned to the barracks the following day. For his brief time of ack willy, Devine was sentenced to three days field punishment enduring eighteen hours of hard labour.

Tilly was unaware of Jim's latest AWOL junket. She was too busy working her butt off for their arrival in Australia. Jim however, had no morals or guilt about his affair. As far as he was concerned, Tilly had sex with men every day, so he felt he was owed a few women on the side.

On the 9th of May, as soon as he had finished his field punishment, Devine again left the barracks without permission. He spent the first three days with his red-headed mistress, before making his way to the flat. Back in Soho, 'Big Jim' as the locals had started calling him, began pimping his wife out again almost every day and night. The long hours were exhausting for Tilly and she asked Jim for a day or two off. Not wanting to lose the chance of making any money, Devine introduced her to cocaine, so she was able work the hours he expected.

On the 2nd of August, the Military Police showed up at the flat looking for the ack willy soldier. They had not long missed him. Devine had left only ten minutes before to buy more cocaine. The MPs searched the house, including the hideout in the bathroom. Not finding him, they warned Tilly that it would go easier on her husband if he turned himself in as soon as possible.

When Jim returned home, he was already in a foul mood and Tilly's news about the visit from the Military Police tipped him over the edge. Infuriated, he picked up one of the wooden chairs in the kitchen and slammed it across Tilly's back, calling her a fat useless bitch for letting them enter their home. She fell to the floor screaming in agony as he started kicking her, roaring at her to 'shut her fuckin' mouth or he'll do her in' as he continued the assault. Hearing her distressed screams, Ronald and Betty helped Tilly escape to their house before driving her to the hospital. Devine didn't try to stop them. He sat down on the settee and finished off a bottle of beer in almost one gulp.

The following morning, after receiving information from Ronald, an MP climbed through the bedroom window of the Devines' flat. Once inside, he unsheathed his pistol and abruptly woke the rogue soldier before arresting him.

"Mate, can you let me get dressed first?" Jim asked as reached for his trousers hanging over the bed end.

"After what you did to your wife you deserve to be dragged in half naked, you fuckin' bastard!"

7

On the night of the 5th of August 1918, Tilly was abruptly woken by the shrill sound of whistles. Knowing that whistles were used to warn of an impending air raid, the bruised and battered teenager left her hospital bed and limped to the hallway. The sisters and nurses were rushing around wheeling patients and sick children to the operating theatres which they considered to be the safest rooms of the hospital. Tilly returned to her shared hospital room and helped the woman in the bed next to her into the corridor and followed the nurses down to the theatres.

When all the patients and hospital staff were in the operating rooms, the lights were dimmed, as they anxiously waited for the German bombs to detonate around them. They wiled away the time with songs and stories to keep the frightened patients minds off the terrible fear that at any moment, they could feel the blast of a bomb, or worse…

Just after midnight, a doctor rushed through the door. The room fell silent as he excitedly revealed: "One of the Zeppelins was intercepted and shot down in a huge ball of flames! The others dropped their bombs at sea! They didn't even make it to land! We're safe! God save the King!"

7

Life with Jim Devine was far from what Tilly had expected. Even though her parents were poor and didn't own much, they loved and respected one another. Her father had never raised a hand to any one of them. She longed for the love and respect her parents shared and not be treated as little more than a pimp's prostitute.

The tender moments she and Jim had shared early in their relationship were gone. Her marriage, even though it was in its infancy, was marred by verbal and physical violence which, more than once, had seen Tilly being treated at the hospital. No longer wanting to live her life as a doormat and money-maker, as soon as she had recovered from the beating, Tilly packed her suitcase and headed to the West End of London. She had heard the other streetwalkers talk about a brothel that was run by a woman and felt she would be much safer working there until Jim had left for Australia.

Upon her arrival at the brothel, Tilly was surprised to count at least fifteen women working in the four-bedroom house. Mavis, the brothel Madam, told her that she could have a room in her tenement for free, but she was to be paid fifty percent of her earnings as rent and protection dues. Tilly had no problem with the house percentage. She would be somewhere safe where Jim wouldn't find her. She also knew that being the new girl in the house, she would attract most of the clients.

Mavis showed Tilly through the sparsely-furnished rooms of the brothel—just a bed and a table along a wall that was topped with towels and a china basin and jug for bathing.

"I run a clean house 'ere. Check the punter's cocks before fuckin' 'em. Make sure they're clean, take the money upfront and then wash up good when 'e's done. Fuck as many as you can, lovey. The soldiers will love you, especially those Aussies. Those boys prefer blondes. You'll make a lot of money 'ere," the Madam claimed. "You can start tonight. You and Caroline will share this room. There'll be about ten other girls on as well, so dress to be noticed, sweet'art."

As she went to the back room the girls used to prepare for work, Tilly met four prostitutes that were working the day shift. One of the girls, a brunette named Ruthy, struck up a conversation.

"You're going to have to get rid of those bruises, sweet'art. 'ere, let me do your makeup. I'll have you looking shiny and new in no time… Did a punter do this to you?"

Tilly lied and said that she had been bashed and robbed by an American soldier in Soho. Ruthy was very sympathetic and gentle as she applied the makeup. When Tilly asked what it was like to work in the brothel, Ruthy told her that at times you had to offer services 'out of the ordinary' to get the men in. She said that sometimes there were up to twenty girls working a shift and the ones that had specialties, were always busy.

"Do you make much money 'ere?" Tilly asked.

"I'm pretty straight, so I don't make as much as some. But I also work at a few other brothels. I'm here tonight because I have some regulars to see. You need to grab a punter as soon as they come in, otherwise you could be waiting all night for a room. There you go, shiny and new like I said."

Tilly thanked Ruthy, grabbed her suitcase and headed out to speak to the Madam. She told her that she had made a mistake and rushed out through the door before catching a taxi home. After repacking her clothes into the chest of drawers, Tilly returned to the Strand, knowing that migrating to Australia was her only salvation from prostitution and poverty.

At his court-martial hearing on the 20th of August, Devine pleaded guilty to being AWOL. He was sentenced to twenty days of detention and forfeiture of twenty-four days' pay. This time the Australian Army showed him no leniency and sentenced him to the Lewes Detention Barracks, known as 'hell on earth'.

On the 2nd of October while working her strip at Soho, Tilly noticed the police walking toward her. She quickly entered the tobacco shop and handed the tobacconist a shilling and three pence for a tin of Pall Mall cigarettes and walked out the door as if she was an innocent customer. As her feet hit the footpath, she was grabbed by one of the constables and arrested for soliciting.

She appeared before Magistrate 'Hanging Henry' Hollingsworth. Tilly was warned by the other women in the cells that he detested prostitutes and was quite nasty with his condemnation of those who plied the trade.

Instead of her usual defiance, Tilly stood silent and listened to the degrading names the magistrate called her as he berated her for her choice of profession. She was ordered to pay a hefty fine of forty shillings or spend twenty-one days in the Bow Street cells in lieu of payment. Tilly thanked the magistrate for his leniency and told him that she would prefer to pay the fine. As soon as she finished signing the paperwork at the courthouse, she returned to the street to make up for the forty shillings she had lost.

While visiting Jim at Lewes, Tilly sat through his tirade of abuse and insults after she told him how much money she was earning. She explained that without the regular influx of ANZAC soldiers due to the upcoming Armistice, her income had suffered. She was relieved that there were bars between them. They probably protected her from another flogging.

Heartless and greedy to the core, Devine demanded that she work longer hours for the money they needed for Australia. "You'll fuckin' stay here until you've made enough money. I'll be on one of the first ships out and without my signature on the papers, you don't fuckin' get into Australia!"

Tilly tried to work longer hours, but with less soldiers, the rationing of food and war widows taking to the streets to feed and clothe their children, the punters had a wider selection of women to choose from. Having no choice, she began offering more repulsive services to attract the kerb-crawling men.

To ensure she had enough personal funds for Australia, Tilly always added a few pounds each week to her hidden stash in the kitchen.

She was going to make sure she had enough fancy clothes, shoes, and jewellery to impress her mother-in-law, thereby ensuring she would accept her as Jim's wife.

Her life was peaceful without Jim turning up on the run from the army every other week. She missed him when he was the gentle Jim but was pleased to be safe from his violence when drunk or high. Betty and Ronald also took good care of her; watching out for her to return home, they would often invite her over for a meal.

Jim, on the other hand, was extremely unhappy at Lewes. He was upset and often paced the cold stone cell, fuming about Tilly's lack of visits. She had also stopped sending him money, which made life even more difficult with the army still taking his pay for his AWOL stints.

On the 11th of October, eight days after his release from detention, desperate for cash, he left Tidworth without leave once more. As soon as he arrived at their flat, Devine found Tilly asleep and abruptly woke her and ordered her to get dressed.

"What the fuck are you doing 'ere? Are you fuckin' ack willy again?"

"I wouldn't be if you'd sent me fuckin' money! Now, get the fuck out of bed. You're going to Soho!"

Over the following weeks, Devine pimped his wife out in Camberwell pubs, Soho, and the Strand. He also took advantage of his escape by gathering a group of criminal associates he had met at East London pubs. Through his nefarious league of villains, Jim was able to amass more money by using Tilly and the men's girlfriends as decoys to lure men into dark corners with the promise of sex and then robbing them.

One night, Tilly felt unwell and refused to work. Intoxicated and enraged by her dissent, Devine punched her in the mouth before grabbing a handful of her hair and throwing her across the room. Tilly's head hit the corner of the kitchen table, causing a gash above her right cheek.

"Get the fuck out and work, you lazy sow! You're sick because you're getting' fat and lazy. Eat less and work more, or I'll throw the food into the fuckin' street!"

Dazed and bleeding, Tilly escaped her husband's violent rage by running into the street and hiding behind the hedge fence of a nearby corner shop. She remained there almost all night as she watched Jim from behind the hedge, stomping up and down the street looking for her.

That night, as she had often over the past months, Tilly thought about running away and starting a new life elsewhere in England. She had several clients who had taken a shine to her and offered to take her away from the sex trade. Whenever Jim became violent toward her, Tilly often thought about taking one of them up on their offer.

When she returned home the following morning, Tilly found Jim sober and in a more favourable mood. He apologised to her for hurting her, faithfully promising never to hit her again. He told her he just wanted to return home with money to show his mother that she had her own wealth. Jim explained that if she arrived penniless, his mother would think she had married him for his money and demand a divorce.

Tilly understood how protective mothers were of their sons and bathed before leaving with Jim to work in Soho.

When he wasn't pimping Tilly out, Jim remained at the house drinking beer or sleeping while she worked the Strand. Whenever he wasn't with her, Tilly would secretly drop money off to her mother because Jim had forbidden her from sharing their money with her family.

That afternoon after he had discovered that she had given her family five pounds, Jim smashed a beer bottle across Tilly's head, causing a gash above her left eye and knocking her unconscious. When she came to, she lay still for a moment, confused at first about where she was and what had happened. Through blurred vision, Tilly saw Jim leaning over her and she noticed that there was blood all over his shirt. Her head was throbbing, and when she touched her forehead, her hand abruptly recoiled at the touch of wet blood.

"What the fuck 'appened? What did you do to me?" Tilly screeched.

"You made me fuckin' do it. If you fuckin' did what you were told and didn't give your parents money all the fuckin' time, it wouldn't have happened!"

"It's *my* fuckin' money. All *your* fuckin' money goes to the fuckin' army! You can't keep your fuckin' cock in your trousers or be the soldier you fuckin' signed up to be! I'm sorry I ever met you!"

Enraged by her insolence, Jim grabbed Tilly by her throat and pulled her toward him. For a brief moment, the teenage girl thought she was about to die. She refused to look away and defiantly looked Jim in his eyes and told him that if he hurt her, she wouldn't be able to work, and they'd have no money to show off to his mother. Her rebelliousness worked. Devine turned to walk out the door.

"Such a fuckin' tough man! You'd rather beat the shit out of a woman than fight the enemy! You fuckin' coward!"

Her personal insults were the final straw. Devine slapped Tilly so hard to the side of her head that she fell to the floor. He then kicked her in the stomach twice before yelling at her again: "You're nothing but a dirty whore! I don't know why I even fuckin' bother with you! There's plenty of other women in London who'd jump at the chance to emigrate to Australia. I might go find one!" He roared before stomping out the front door, slamming it behind him.

7

Holding fast to her dream of a new life in Australia, Tilly once again took Jim back when he arrived home sober four days later. Through Tilly's prostitution and his league of criminals, Devine was making a substantial amount of money, however, it was never enough for him.

Whilst Tilly was out working, Devine and his gang would break into wealthy addresses and businesses, selling the bounty of stolen jewellery, food cigarettes, and other items through the black-market. Their loot made each of the men a lot of money which they shared amongst themselves. Jim never accounted to Tilly about the money. He had made it and saw no need to share his 'spare change', as he called it. Devine used the money for gambling, after telling Tilly he had given up betting for good. She had no cause to doubt him, as he no longer asked her for money to pay his debts.

At 6:30 am on the 30th of October, the Devines were abruptly woken by banging at their front door. Knowing the hammering of the Military Police, Jim secreted himself behind a fake wall he had built in the kitchen after his bathroom hideout had been discovered. Tilly waited for him to be safely out of sight before moving the table against the kitchen wall and answering the door, inviting the police inside. The officers told Tilly to sit down while they asked her questions about Devine's whereabouts. She answered their questions diligently and told the officers that she and Jim had parted ways whilst he was in Lewes. She admitted to seeing him several times over the past months but said he hadn't told her where he was staying.

Satisfied with her answers, the men left. However, Jim wasn't so sure about them not coming back. He knew that Armistice negotiations were taking place between United States and Germany, and it would be better for him to hand himself in than be charged in Australia as a deserter.

Devine surrendered to the Military Police at ten o'clock that night. He didn't want to miss out on his chance to return to Australia and set up a flat for himself and Tilly. He had big plans for his wife to start working the East Sydney streets, knowing the Aussie men would fall for the rosy-cheeked blonde and he would make a mint.

Whilst on detention, Devine learned that the German soldiers were suffering heavy losses. One officer told them that the Allied forces were keeping them from advancing. The men cheered and started placing bets on when the war would end.

On the 2nd of November, a District Court Martial was convened at Sutton Veny where Jim entered a plea of guilty. After receiving a severe dressing down for his dishonourable conduct and for missing his ship to Australia, Devine was sentenced to two weeks detention at Lewes.

The sound of cannon fire, the constant artillery bombardments, and watching his fellow soldiers fall in battle, was never experienced by Devine. He had never stepped foot on a battlefield. He had spent most of the war in an infirmary suffering with syphilis, being ack willy or serving detention for being Absent Without Leave. He knew he would not return to a hero's welcome in Australia but would be seen for what he was, a disgraced soldier.

A week after arriving at Lewes, Devine and the other incarcerated soldiers learned that Germany's leader, Kaiser Wilhelm, had abdicated as the German Emperor and King of Russia. They were told by one of the guards that the cowardly leader had escaped to Amerongen in the Netherlands, and Chancellor Max von Baden refused to surrender, but had requested an armistice.

The men cheered knowing that they would soon be returning home.

CHAPTER FOUR

Australia Bound

Almost every person in the world who owned a radio were on tenterhooks waiting for the announcement that the war was over. The world rejoiced when they heard that Turkey had succumbed to Austria and surrendered. They now awaited the news that their loved ones would be coming home. People worldwide listened keenly as the radio announcer broadcasted that Germany had sent representatives to General Foch to discuss the suspension of hostilities. They knew that an announcement of peace would soon follow.

Australians celebrated the armistice early on the 9th of November after hearing whispers from family, friends, and neighbours that the war would soon end. There were outpourings of emotion, jubilation and grief in every town, village and city, as elated Aussies rejoiced the end of the war to end all wars and mourned the death of loved ones who would never return home.

On the 12th of November, the headlines of Australian newspapers read: *Official: Armistice Signed, The War Is Over!* and *Armistice Signed by Germany.*

The Guardian reported the signing of the armistice, with the following editorial:

'The war is over, and in a million households, fathers and mothers, wives and sisters will breathe freely, relieved at length of all dread of that curt message which has shattered the hope and joy of so many. The war is over. The drama is played out.

The old order in Europe has perished. The new is hardly born, and no one knows what its lineaments will be. Tomorrow we shall be brought up against the harsh immediate problems of re-establishment.'

7

Meanwhile, on the overcast and misty morning of the 11th November 1918, crowds gathered outside the gates of Buckingham Palace awaiting the King to officially proclaim the end of the war. The morning newspapers were sold out almost as soon as they hit the stands, causing newspaper publishers to print several editions.

Tilly and her sister, Caroline blended into the crowds along the Strand waving their flags alongside thousands of Londoners. The sisters, like countless others having suffered the loss of family during the needless war.

"Feel that breeze, Caroline…it's the winds of change. Many changes…" Tilly wistfully uttered.

At precisely 11:00 am, a typewritten notice announcing the cessation of hostilities was hung on the railings outside the palace gates. Cheers immediately rose from the crowd as they called out and pleaded for the King to appear and make a speech. "We want King George!" They cried. The air was filled with electric fervour. Sincerity, warmth, and laughter had replaced fear, anger, and sadness.

At 11:15 am King George dressed in his Admiral uniform and looking happier than he had in some time, appeared on the palace balcony. The Queen, hatless and wearing a fur coat, stood alongside him. Queen Mary stood to the right if her son, waving a British flag in celebration of the end of the war. Princess Mary and the Duke of Connaught smiled and waved at the crowd.

"With you I rejoice and thank God for the victories which the Allied arms have won, bringing hostilities to an end and peace within sight." The King cheerfully stated.

The joy that the war had ended was clearly evident on the Royal's faces. The soldiers presented arms and the Irish Guards' band played the national anthem as the spectators joined in with the slow refrain. After the short speech, the band immediately began playing *God Save the King*, the crowd cheered the King as they proudly waved their British flags high in the air. King George removed his cap and nodded his head toward the crowd as the Queen waved a Union Jack, bringing even more cheers before the royals waved and walked back into the palace while the band played *Rule Britannia*. Tilly had been clicking away on her recently purchased Kodak Medalist camera, catching memories that would last her a lifetime.

Tilly, Caroline, and thousands more, cast their steely reserve to the winds as they celebrated with spontaneous bouts of cheers and screams. Men and women cried with joy, children ran around waving the British flag, excited that they would soon see their fathers again. Hundreds and thousands of people assembled at Trafalgar Square and Buckingham Palace, throwing coloured paper in the air to celebrate that peace would soon embrace the world.

As she and her sister searched for a taxi along the Strand, Tilly stopped and watched the King leading the royal motorcade through the pouring rain. Beside him sat the Queen smiling and waving out the window.

As the cab made its way along the streets swarming with jubilant people, Tilly thought about how easy it was for most to forget for just a day, an hour, a minute, that the war had been a cataclysmic event. Empires had fallen, millions had died, and hundreds of thousands more were maimed or crippled. Those that didn't forget sat with their heads in their hands-on footpaths and porches of their homes, knowing that their loved ones would never be returning.

She sighed to herself, *"No more soldiers will be killed or injured in the mud and horror of the trenches. Nurses and doctors who served in war camps will no longer awake to another dawn of hopelessness. Soldiers will no longer dodge bullets, shellfire, and mines. But there will be more tears for family and mates of those who died. At least the senseless war is over."*

7

Tilly was surprised to receive a letter from Jim six weeks after the Armistice. He wrote that he was free, and again stationed at the training barracks. He told her he was waiting to hear when he would be returning to Australia. Her heart skipped a few beats as she read '*I want us to look as smart and modern as possible when I present you to my mother. Work that beautiful arse of yours off and make as much money as you can so we can buy clothes and a car that will make us look like royalty'.*

Tilly sighed. She wondered if Jim's mother was more fair-minded and polite than he was. She couldn't bear to live in a home with so much angst and demanding behaviour. She closed her eyes and tried to imagine living on the kangaroo station in the hot Australian outback, shuddering when she realised just how isolated she would be living in the middle of a desert. Comparing living in isolation to the crushing poverty that forced her to sell herself on the streets, Tilly decided that the station life had to be a far better alternative.

That night when she returned from working in Soho, Tilly sat down to a meal of pork pie and chips and replied to her husband's letter. She told him that she had saved a little money and explained that with the men returning to their countries and the ANZACs being confined to barracks, she wasn't making as much money as she had during the war. She tried to placate the anger she knew Jim would be feeling by telling him that she had saved just over one hundred pounds. She still kept her stash a secret from Jim. Tilly wanted to keep that money to use for a train fare to Sydney if she found living on the kangaroo station too difficult.

Two weeks later, Tilly received a reply. Jim said he would be shipping out to Australia in mid-March and asked her to visit him and bring whatever money she had. Her reply was crisp and to the point. Tilly told him that she thought it would be best if she kept the money until she arrived in Australia.

Jim almost choked on his anger when he read the letter. He made an appointment with his Commanding Officer to request leave to see his wife before embarking to Australia. His request was denied. Not impressed by the rebuttal, he responded as he always did whenever he didn't get his own way, Devine absconded from the Longbridge army training barracks. After walking for almost two hours, he managed to pick up a lift to London, and finally, after hailing a taxi, he was on his way to Soho.

Devine stopped by a local garage and asked the man if he knew where he could hire a car. The mechanic sent him to a car yard in the next street. There, Jim hired a 1913 Prince Henry Vauxhall and headed straight to the flat.

Tilly returned home, surprised to find her husband asleep on the settee. Seven empty beer bottles were scattered on the floor and an unfinished meal of fish and chips was on the table. She silently crept into the bedroom in fear of waking him and being interrogated about money. Tilly also didn't even bother washing, she just lay on top of the bed, almost afraid to fall asleep lest Jim came into the room.

Later that morning, Tilly was abruptly woken when Devine thundered into the bedroom and demanded she get ready.

"When was the last fuckin' time you worked Whitechapel?"

"Jim, for god's sake, it's six in the fuckin' morning. I didn't get in until after midnight. Let me get some fuckin' sleep and I'll work tonight." '*Wait…what did he say? Whitechapel?…*' She thought to herself. "Work Jack the fuckin' Ripper streets? I've never fuckin' worked there! I'm not risking getting' sliced up for you or Australia!"

"You'll do as your fuckin' told. I'm not missing the boat home for you to be a lazy cunt and stay in bed all fuckin' day. No wonder you're not sending me any money! You're sleeping instead of fuckin' working!" He roared as he pulled Tilly from the bed. "Clean yourself fuckin' up and get in the car! And what the fuck are you on about Jack the Ripper streets? The blokes at the barracks said nothin' about any killer. They said Whitechapel needs new girls because the whores there are old and ugly. You're fuckin' goin' there or I'll take one of the other girls from Soho and they can make the fuckin' money for me!"

Tilly had always steered clear of Whitechapel because of the Ripper stories she'd heard throughout her childhood. She knew they had occurred thirty years previously, but the horrifying deaths of the prostitutes and darkness of the town terrified her. She knew well of the poverty and disease that was rampant in the area and ensured that she had plenty of condoms to keep herself free from venereal disease. Tilly had also heard that women from 'the Chapel' sold themselves for four pence or less, a stale loaf of bread or at times, a pork pie. When she climbed into the car beside her impatient husband, she told him she wouldn't drop her price to less than five shillings.

"You will if you're not making any money and if you fuckin' know what's good for you! I'm not sitting in the car all day and night for nothin'!"

"All fuckin' night? Any bastard tries anything with me, I'll slash his cock orf!"

"Just you worry more about making money than this ripper bullshit!"

Tilly was surprised that Jim knew which streets for her to work. He first dropped her off outside a tobacco shop along Berner Street and parked the car a little way down the street so he could keep an eye on her. She was fortunate and attracted three punters during the first half-hour. Only one of the men complained about her price, but he quickly paid up when he realised Tilly wasn't going to barter her body for any less.

By late afternoon, she had earned over four pounds, but it wasn't enough money for Jim Devine. He told her as soon as she finished dinner, she would be working along Commercial Street until she made at least another five pounds.

The dimmed gas lamp-lit street and the foggy dark alleys where Tilly was forced to take her punters was terrifying. If Jim weren't nearby, she would have serviced the men where she stood. By two o'clock in the morning, she had surprisingly made almost double what she made on the Strand and her Soho haunts. She was loathed to admit to herself that Jim was right. But she hoped to never work the malodorous Whitechapel streets again.

Devine was pleased when Tilly told him that she had made just over eleven pounds—the other three pounds were savings for her private kitty.

"We'll go home, grab some kip and come back tomorrow. It's best to strike while the iron's fuckin' hot!"

7

Several weeks later, Tilly felt unwell. She was constantly tired, and nauseous around food, her sense of smell was in overdrive and her breasts felt a little tender. Thinking back to when she'd had her last period, Tilly realised it had been at least two months. She started to cry. A baby was the last thing she needed, especially before leaving for Australia.

Tilly didn't want to meet Jim's mother pregnant. However, when she told him, he was cautiously overjoyed. They both attended the doctors and were tested for syphilis and were clear of the disease. It was a relief for them to know their child would be born safe and well.

Jim promised Tilly that while she was pregnant, he wouldn't have sex with any prostitutes or sleep around. As much as she wanted to, she didn't believe him. She knew her husband too well. Tilly made him use a condom to make sure she wouldn't be infected again if he broke his promise as he usually did.

Tilly hoped that being pregnant again would jolt Jim into returning to the training barracks or at least seek proper employment. Once again, she expected too much. He warned her that he would be imprisoned in Australia for five years if he were to hand himself in and he would be of no use to her and the baby in gaol. Devine also had an answer for not finding work… he would never be able to find a job that paid as much money as she was able to earn.

Working to pay the bills, put food on the table and purchasing baby needs, Tilly continued plying her trade. From midday until the early hours of the morning, she worked the pubs or streets competing against desperate war widows who dropped their prices to two shillings just to be able to buy food for their children.

Jim became concerned about less money coming in and knowing that Tilly would soon discover that he had gambled away most of their savings, he suggested she open her own brothel and make money that way.

Tilly gave his suggestion some thought but was worried that running a bawdy house from her rental premises would not only upset her neighbours, but she'd also run the risk of being evicted. She didn't want to be on the streets pregnant.

"You're as big as a fuckin' whale already and you're not even six months along! The men will refuse you soon and you'll be stuck with drunk and pox-ridden bums! Do it, or I will find someone else!"

"You'd be fuckin' them more than makin' money orf them! I won't do it, Jim! I won't lose my home, and I won't upset Betty and Ronny!"

Tilly knew that standing up to her husband could entice another beating, but she trusted that he wouldn't touch her and risk causing a miscarriage. Her intuition was spot on. Jim threw a chair across the room in anger before storming out of the front door without saying a word.

As she neared her seventh month, Tilly became fed up with working the hours Jim forced upon her. No matter how much money she made, he still wanted more. "I want my pockets loaded with money when we arrive at the station. I want my mother to think that I did well for myself in Britain…"

Not being able to cater to her husband's demands anymore, Tilly asked Ronald to report Jim's whereabouts to the Military Police.

Two nights later, the Devines' sleep was interrupted by a loud banging at the front door. Jim was well aware that knock meant that his jig was up. He headed straight for the bathroom to jump out of the window.

Tilly opened the door and admitted two MPs before sitting on the settee while the men searched for the renegade soldier. Jim's voice suddenly broke the silence when he roared out a string of curse words after one of the officers caught hold of his shirt as he attempted to jump the back fence. The MPs, accustomed to Jim's escape attempts, were well prepared and had stationed five officers around the flat.

At his court-martial hearing, the subversive Sapper was sent to the half-century-old Lewes barracks on four months detention and also forfeited sixteen weeks pay. In the military prison that overlooked the south-east coast of England, Devine laboured in the prison's workshop alongside Sinn Fein members arrested during the Bloody Easter uprising of 1916. He didn't mind working with the Irish rebels. His father had often told him tales about his uncles who were members of the Society of United Irishmen and fought against the British.

7

Life went on the same for Tilly. She continued giving her father money and worked the hours she could around her never-ending morning sickness. Several times she passed out and when she regained consciousness often found herself on the ground or on a bench surrounded by concerned streetwalkers.

The pregnant teenager knew she should give up working. The pregnancy was taking more of a toll on her than her previous one had. But, with Jim taking one hundred and fifteen pounds from the money she had made to pay his gambling debts, she needed to recoup as much of that money as possible. She still had cash in a private kitty that Jim had never found. But that was her emergency fund, and she didn't want to use it unless she was desperate.

Daydreaming about life in a large country mansion surrounded by nothing but sheep and kangaroos, and being the fine lady of the house, kept the naïve teenager going. She often imagined herself sitting at a table under a shady Jacaranda tree, sipping tea with her mother-in-law as her children played with joeys and lambs while Jim was out overseeing the station. Those dreams alone made her life working as a prostitute worth it.

Devine was discharged early from Lewes on the 7th of September and returned to Longbridge Deverill training barracks. There he was ordered to pack and prepare for demobilisation aboard the *Raranga* the following day.

Stunned to be leaving so soon, he asked his sergeant if he could see his wife before he left—telling him how it was imperative he talk to her about emigrating to Australia. The sergeant told him that there was no time, and with his appalling AWOL record, he didn't trust that he would return. Devine pleaded again to see his wife, advising his superior that Tilly was pregnant and would be upset at not saying goodbye… The sergeant ordered him to return to barracks and write a letter and assured him that she would receive it even if he hand-delivered the letter himself.

Defeated, Jim returned to his quarters and wrote a letter to Tilly to bid her farewell and advised her on what to do, where to go, and who to see with regard to migrating to Australia. He wished her luck giving birth to their child and said he would see her again and meet their son or daughter in Sydney.

Two weeks later, the heavily pregnant Tilly waited in the crowded hall at Horseferry Rd, Westminster, alongside other war brides with and without children. A young soldier approached, offering her a chair, advising her that due to her condition, she would be seen to as soon as possible.

After answering an army clerk's questions and handing him the certificate proving her marital status, Tilly was told that the department would contact her by mail with further details about her voyage to Australia.

Tilly was both excited and nervous. Although pleased with the ease in which it took for her to migrate to Australia, now she had to wait and hope the ship sailed before the birth. She wanted her child to be born an Australian.

7

Jim and his fellow soldiers sailed into Sydney on the 29th of October 1919.

Unlike many of the other soldiers, there was no-one waiting for Devine when he disembarked. He walked by soldiers openly embracing and kissing their wives, girlfriends, and fiancées. With his head down and hands in his pockets, the thought of Tilly making her way to Australia gave him the uplift he needed. With a new spring in his step, Jim made his way to the closest pub to inquire about the local prostitution haunts.

Having minimal funds, Devine sought lodgings in a boarding house until what was left of his army pay was forwarded to him. Unimpressed by the disgusting food and slovenly state of the accommodation, he roamed the Sydney streets picking up ladies and spending the night with them. The women were so enamoured by the dapper 'returned war hero', that they treated him like a king.

7

At 3:17 am on the 2nd of November, Tilly delivered Frederick Ralph Devine, a healthy baby boy. She remained at her parents' home with her newborn son for several weeks but knowing Jim would be expecting a large bundle of cash when she arrived in Australia, she returned to walking the streets when her son was just two weeks old.

For one so young, Tilly was burdened with a lot of responsibility. She was taking care of her family as well as her son. Her dreams of giving birth in Australia were now shattered. She had only received one letter from Jim, and that was hand delivered by a sergeant from Longbridge shortly after he had left. In the short note, Jim said that he will be waiting for her at Circular Quay whenever her ship arrives. He added that he would rent a flat, so they had somewhere comfortable to stay to use as a base while they shopped up big before making the long trip to his farm.

Baby Freddy was cared for by Tilly's mother while she worked. The young wife and mother was determined to make as much money as possible before sailing to Australia. She wanted nothing more than to make Jimmy and his mother proud.

7

With money in hand after receiving his army wages in late November, about the time he was discharged from the AIF, Jim went searching for a furnished flat. Not having much money after squandering most of his military pay in AWOL fines, Devine settled upon a dowdy and unkempt flat in the overcrowded, squalid area of Glenmore Road, Paddington.

7

On the 23rd of November, Tilly received official mail from the AIF. She eagerly opened the letter and was excited to have finally received the documents to travel to Sydney aboard the steamship *SS Waimana*. But she gasped when she saw the departure date—the 25th of November. In a sudden panic, Tilly rushed to the living room and told her parents that she was leaving to Australia in two days. Her father dropped the newspaper he was reading, her mother immediately began sobbing. "Oh, my darling, so soon! This is such a shock!"

"Yes Mum, a big shock!"

Shaking her head free of her upset, knowing she had only two days to pack and prepare herself and Frederick for the voyage, Tilly asked her father collect Caroline to help her pack up her flat.

A couple of hours later, with the help of her sister and brother, Tilly had packed her clothes and personal belongings. She left the furniture and everything else for her parents to sell.

On the eve of her voyage, Tilly's father nervously asked her to sit down telling her that he and her mother needed to talk to her.

Tilly's mother sat opposite her with tears welling in her eyes. As a mother, she understood how difficult the task ahead was going to be, so she patted down her skirts, inhaled deeply and took Tilly's hands in hers. "Your father and I have discussed keeping Freddy here with us. Being on a ship for so long at his tender age could make him terribly ill and could kill him. You're young and have much to do before you're ready to cope with a baby in a new country. After you and Jim have settled in properly, you can come and take him to live with you. I know it'll be hard leaving your baby boy behind, love, but his health is more important, and it will be unsettling for him with the upheaval and turmoil of having to travel so far..."

"But Jimmy 'asn't seen 'is son yet. It'll break 'is 'eart. And I'll miss our sweet Freddy. Leaving 'im here while I'm workin' is one thing but leavin' my baby 'ere for months on end...'e won't know who I am when we come back for 'im." Tilly sobbed as her eyes brimmed with tears.

"Is it worth the risk of losing another baby, Matilda? The ship's journey is going to be hard enough for you. It will be even harder for a three-week-old baby. Think of him. You know he'll be well looked after here." Her mother pleaded.

After a little while, Tilly nodded. Her heart was breaking, but she'd heard the ships had minimal facilities for women, let alone children. She also heard how war brides and their children would be sharing the voyage with returning soldiers, which meant they would take precedence over the women and children for essentials and medical care. Tilly was also aware of how cold the first leg of the crossing would be for her baby. Her mother was right. The troopship was no place for her infant son.

In the predawn darkness on the morning of her departure, Tilly cradled her son in her arms. In the chilly solitude, she wept as she whispered that she loved him, and she would come back for him as soon as she and his daddy were settled in their new home. She told him that he would soon be living on a kangaroo and sheep station and would grow up to be big and strong, just like his daddy. She held her son close as tears burned her cheeks as she stood and took the torturous and heartbreaking steps to the living room.

With a heavy heart, she took in a deep breath and handed Freddy to his grandmother, who promised to care for him and love him until her return. Her siblings hugged and kissed their sister, each heartbroken to see her leave.

Her father held her close. Tilly had never seen him cry before. "You make sure he looks after you, my love. If things don't work out, you'll always have a home here." He said before letting her go and tearfully walking into the kitchen.

"Remember that we love you, Mattie. It's hard to let you go, but we know you love your man. Hurry back, love. Your beautiful little boy will be waiting for you." Her mother whispered, her voice trembling with emotion.

Tilly couldn't speak. She picked up her trunk and struggled to carry it to the waiting cab through the teeming rain. Before climbing into the back, she turned and waved to her family who were standing at the living room window. She blinked away the tears as she saw her son snuggled in her mother's arms. Quickly closing the cab door, she told the driver to take her to the Tilbury Docks and forced herself to continue looking forward, defying the tears that blinded her vision.

Upon her arrival at the docks, Tilly was surprised to see so many women, some pregnant and others with children holding onto their skirts as they stood in line amongst the soldiers. She anxiously waited to board the *Waimana*, wondering what life in Australia would be like.

When she thought about meeting Jim in Sydney, Tilly began trembling, fearing his reaction to her arriving without Freddy. Tears filled her eyes when she wondered what her mother-in-law's expectations of her would be, and how upset and heartbroken she would be about not meeting her first grandchild. *"Will she accept me without her grandson, Jim's heir?"* she whispered to herself.

Tilly shuffled along behind the other passengers as each person boarded the ship. She stared at the *Waimana*, knowing it would be her 'home' for up to eight weeks surrounded by hundreds of strangers as they sailed across thousands of miles of ocean together. When she finally reached the gangway, Tilly stopped and closed her eyes. *Am I doing the right thing? Should I stay 'ere with my son and family and forget about Jimmy and our plans?*

"C'mon love, move on up. I've got a wife waiting for me in Sydney!" A man shouted from the rear of the line. "The longer you take, the longer it will be before the ship leaves."

Tilly apologised and took one hesitant step after another as she boarded the troopship that would take her to a new and unknown life on the other side of the world.

The *SS Waimana* was one of thirteen 'Bride Ships' as they were disparagingly known. They were hastily prepared to convey the British wives and children of ANZAC Diggers to Sydney and New Zealand. Inside most of the ships, the dodgy bathrooms, toilets, and living areas were almost death traps due to the perfunctory manner in which they were constructed. The women were told the *Waimana* had been renovated to the standard of a second-class passenger liner and were surprised to find a filthy and cockroach-infested ship instead.

At least the men and women were berthed separately. The men's quarters were a lot more comfortable than women's, but the ladies were pleased that there was a women's only hospital, bathrooms, and lavatories which offered them a small amount of comfort and privacy.

To assist the mothers whose children misbehaved due to boredom, several of the soldiers kept the kids amused with songs, plays, and hide and seek games. Not having seen their own children in many years, the returning soldiers enjoyed entertaining them.

Tilly suffered terribly with seasickness the first few days of the voyage and spent most of her time with her head over a bucket. It didn't help that her section of the ship was overrun with rats, forcing her and the other women to set traps and throw whatever vermin they caught overboard.

The women hadn't minded the hardship at first. They were on their way to their new future with their husbands or boyfriends. But when a terrified scream of a baby broke the silence one night and the mother found a rat biting her son's finger, all hell broke loose.

The captain of the ship ordered the soldiers to hunt down the remaining rodents and throw them overboard. The nursing staff gave the mothers large bottles of Lysol to clean the floors and walls of their quarters and bathrooms. Over five days, women and soldiers who had offered their assistance, were on their hands and knees scrubbing every floor and wall in the living quarters, kitchen, pantries, hospitals, and bathrooms. Every effort was made to disinfect the *Waimana* from stem to stern in an attempt to cleanse the ship of any disease the rats had carried aboard.

Despite their efforts, several infants were still being treated for rat bites to their fingers and toes. Two weeks later, there was an outbreak of measles, infecting numerous children onboard. The rough seas also often threw the little ones around. Several times it was so rough that two boys suffered broken legs, and a two-year-old girl had broken her arm. Tilly herself was thrown against a metal pole, badly bruising her shoulder. Each day, she and all those aboard hoped the voyage would soon end, and they would be off the 'rat ship' and back on solid ground.

Once she had recovered from her seasickness, Tilly helped the mothers with their sick children and took the healthier ones to the crèche to give their overwrought mothers some respite. When the children were resting or otherwise entertained, the mothers enjoyed time chatting over a cup of tea and biscuits or scones. Some days soldiers would join the women and dance to the tunes their fellow brothers in arms played on their harmonicas to help keep up moral.

While resting on her bunk with a cup of tea one morning, her mother's cautionary words echoed through Tilly's mind. As much as she missed her little Freddy, she was grateful for her mother's foresight. The *Waimana* was not fit for any child of any age, let alone a young baby.

CHAPTER FIVE

The Darkness Down Under

On Tuesday the 13th of January, Tilly was thrilled to be finally sailing in Australian waters. The trials and tribulations she had endured during the voyage, had not made her feel as anxious as she was about seeing Jim again. As she stood at the deck railing, the teenage wife excitedly searched the faces in the waiting crowd as the ship steamed into Circular Quay. Her breathing was rapid and shallow. Her pulse pounded in her temples as she worried about the long journey to Western Australia and meeting her mother-in-law for the first time. She placed her right hand on her churning stomach as she slowed down her breathing in an attempt to quell the overwhelming panic that consumed her soul.

The ship's crew started assembling the travel weary passengers for disembarking while soldiers stacked trunks and other items on the deck. The sergeant in charge allowed six people at a time to collect their luggage before directing them to the growing line at the gang plank. Once Tilly had secured her trunk, she joined the queue of women and soldiers who were eagerly waiting to be reunited with their husbands and wives.

Over the previous weeks, Tilly had watched as women debarked at Freemantle and Melbourne, now it was her turn. She would see her husband again after four long months apart. She took in a deep breath of the stifling hot, humid Sydney air, slowly releasing it in hope that it would give her some relief from the acrobatic butterflies in the pit of her stomach. Somewhere in the distance, a military band played a song she'd never heard before, only to overhear the soldier behind her tell his wife that the song was *Waltzing Matilda*, a song he said she would hear almost every day in Australia.

As Tilly fanned her face with her documents, she wondered how Australians survived such sweltering heat. She was dressed in a brown loose-fitting dress, stockings, black pumps, and a green feathered Tam O'Shanter floppy hat and was sweating from places she never knew possible. The backs of her knees were wet, she could feel sweat trickling down her spine and between her breasts, and she suddenly wished she were back home in the cool of London.

The time came for Tilly to leave the ship. She took in a deep breath, picked up her trunk and carefully walked down the gangway and onto the wharf. A man dressed in a black suit diverted her to another line outside offices along the quay. A sign written on white paper read: 'Passport and Marriage Lines'. She joined the line and stood behind a mother with two fidgety, excited little girls who kept asking their overwrought mum when they would see their daddy.

Tilly winced. The girls' pleas shot through her heart like a lightning bolt. She missed her son desperately and had kept herself busy on the ship in a failing attempt to keep him off her mind. Tilly's anxiety returned and her hands trembled as she thought of what Jim would say when he saw her without their son.

Tilly turned away from the little girls and watched as women ran into their loved ones' arms. The longed-for embraces had finally become a reality. She felt a stab to her heart when she witnessed the tears, laughter, and the release of pent-up emotions when long separated couples were finally reunited.

Tilly wondered if Jim would greet her with such passion and elation. Their relationship had not been an affectionate one for quite some time, but she hoped after being separated for so long, he would have missed her and at least offer a loving homecoming.

Tilly finally reached a desk where a man in his late fifties smiled as he stood and indicated for her to take the seat opposite him. "I hear the voyage over was quite a rough and worrisome one," the immigration officer remarked. "Can I have your papers please?"

"It wasn't too pleasant," Tilly nervously replied as she handed her documents to the officer.

"Stamped AIF letter, marriage certificate, birth certificate, health certificate and you. Everything is in order. Welcome to Australia, Mrs. Devine."

"Thank you. Where do I go now?" Tilly asked.

"Out through that door and into the arms of your waiting husband, I expect." The officer smiled as he pointed to a door.

As Tilly made her way through the emotional and elated people on the dock, she scanned the men's faces. Not sighting Jim amongst the throng of people, the nervous teenager made her way towards the road and finally caught sight of her husband standing beside a cab.

When he spotted Tilly, Devine took several steps forward and told her to hurry as the cab was costing him money. There was no affection or welcome kiss. There was no questions about the voyage. Jim remained as thoughtless and inattentive as he had been before leaving England.

"Where's the baby? What is it? And, you better have brought the fuckin' money if you know what's good for you!"

"We 'ave a son, Jimmy! I left little Freddy at 'ome until we're settled. Then we can go back and fetch 'im. And yes, I have the fuckin' money. But now I think both me *and* my money should 'ave stayed in London!"

Open and closing his fist in anger, Jim climbed into the cab, leaving the driver to secure Tilly's trunk to the baggage compartment and help her into the cab. "The little bugger is better off with your parents than here. It's gonna take some time to get set up,"

The hustle and bustle of the trams and motor cars surprised Tilly. She'd heard that Australia was a backward colony, yet she could see for herself that it wasn't true. She found that the city might not be as populated as London but could see there were certainly plenty of people and buildings in the area.

"What do you mean by get set up? What about going 'ome to your mother?"

"Never mind about her. Just be ready to start working tomorrow."

"What about the kangaroo farm and your mansion?" Tilly anxiously asked. "Why do I need to return to work if you're rich?"

"Kangaroo farm! That's one of the funniest things I've ever 'eard from a fellow Pommy!" The Cockney cab driver interjected.

"Yeah, these limey sheilas aren't too bright," Jim flippantly retorted.

"Good-oh mate. I get 'em all in my cab. They think they're comin' to paradise and end up in the middle of the desert."

Tilly closed her eyes for a moment. She tried to swallow the lump rising in her throat as she struggled to hold back her tears. Not only was she a stranger in a new land, but she was with a man who had lied to her about his life and she was now trapped a million miles from home.

"What do you mean work, Jim?"

"What you did in London! We'll talk about it more when we get home."

When they arrived at the flat, Tilly was appalled by its decrepit state. She looked around the shoddily furnished kitchen and living area in disappointment. When she saw a large cockroach climbing the wall, she screamed and bolted for the door.

"Don't worry about the fuckin' cockies, you'll get used to them."

Absolutely bereft, Tilly ran into the filthy bathroom and locked herself inside. She sat on the side of the bath and sobbed into her hands hysterically. A few minutes later, she looked out the window and became even more depressed when she saw the squalor that surrounded her. *"I can't fuckin' believe it. I'm stuck in 'ell with a lying cheating 'usband. I just want to go back 'ome."*

"Get outta there. I need to piss!" Jim roared as he slammed his fist on the bathroom door.

Tilly wiped her eyes and opened the door. She looked at her husband but couldn't find the words she wanted to say. He smirked and walked into the bathroom, closing the door behind him. When he returned to the living room, he found Tilly standing at the open front door. "There's no mansion, is there? You brought me 'ere to spread my legs and make money for your fuckin' beer and gambling."

"Shut the fuckin' door and your big fat mouth! If it was good enough for you to sell yourself in fuckin' London, then it's fuckin' good enough for you to do it here."

"Everything you told me was a fuckin' lie! What kind of fuckin' man are you pretending to be lord orf the fuckin' manor to get a woman to marry you! You desperate cunt!"

Jim's face was almost crimson with fury as he clouted Tilly across her right ear with his opened hand, knocking her clear across the room. Knowing what was coming, Tilly tried to run past him to the front door to escape, but he caught hold of her dress and pinned her against the wall. "You're here now whether you like it or fuckin' not. I'm not asking you to do anything you haven't done before. We worked well together in

London and we'll do it again here. Just until we make enough money to buy a farm, and then we're through with it all."

Defeated, Tilly sat on the settee with her head in her hands wondering what kind of hell awaited her on the streets of Sydney.

Exhausted, heartbroken, feeling a little seedy after the long voyage and learning the disturbing truths that awaited her upon arrival, Tilly sighed and made her way to the bedroom. She looked at the bed where Jim expected her to her to sleep. It was as disgusting as she expected. A dirty lemon coloured blanket, two uncovered pillows and a mattress covered by a filthy sheet, and an old chest of drawers greeted her. Tilly thought she had left the slovenly rooms and poverty-stricken surroundings behind. She swallowed hard when the slamming of her trunk on the floor alerted her to her husband's presence. "I'll start work in the morning Jim. No-one should live like this. I 'ope I make enough money to buy new bedding."

Their discussion was interrupted by a knock on the door. Jim seemed excited when he returned inside about twenty minutes later.

"Don't worry about starting work tomorrow, love. You just travelled from a world away, wait until Friday. You need a few days rest and I have some business to sort out in the meantime."

7

Tilly hit the Sydney streets on the 16th January after Jim had the taxi drop her off along the dirty half mile on William Street in the heart of sin city, in Woolloomooloo. With her blue eyes, rosy cheeks, cream complexion and sexual expertise, men came in droves to part with ten shillings to spend just a few minutes with the English Rose. In the first five days, Tilly earned in excess of forty pounds and purchased not only new bedding, but a new silky oak double bed and mattress as well.

Jim was ecstatic about the money that had crossed his palm and pushed his wife to work longer hours. For the following months she worked seven days a week to take advantage of her being the new girl on the scene.

Tilly marketed her sexual prowess at the local prostitution haunts along Riley, Forbes, Palmer and Bourke Streets in Darlinghurst, and along Crown and Cathedral Streets in Woolloomooloo. Within six months she had garnered a large regular clientele base. The well-known prostitutes, who had long ago staked their claim to the streets, quickly learned that the petite blonde girl from the streets of London was no pushover. One streetwalker learned the hard way when she was so savagely beaten by Tilly that she was hospitalised for weeks, and another prostitute ended up with a broken nose.

Thence began Matilda Devine's reign over the streets of Sydney.

7

Mindful of the amount of money she was making, Tilly didn't want Jim to squander any of it. So, she decided to find a safe place to hide a few pounds each day to add to her emergency funds. Whilst working in Glebe, she had often admired the stained-glass window in St James' Church that commemorated the men who had died during the Boer War. One afternoon, she decided to go for a walk around the church grounds and spotted a loose brick in the rear wall. Looking around to make sure no-one was watching, Tilly quickly removed the brick and placed two pounds in the hole before replacing the brick and leaving.

Within the first six months of living in Australia, Tilly had earned a massive six hundred pounds. One night, she told Jim she needed a break for a few days as she was too sore and exhausted to work. He told her she could take the week off—he had just spun a deal with a supplier in Darlinghurst to sell opium and cocaine.

The time off gave Tilly the opportunity to spend some of her hidden pounds on herself. Her first stop was a hair salon to have her hair dyed and curled. She shopped at exclusive city boutiques, buying furs and diamonds, looking more like a lady from the upper-class than a girl born in a slum. During her week of freedom, she often stopped at cafés for coffee and scones and enjoyed watching the colourful variety of people pass by.

Finally, she was able to breathe and enjoy life in Australia while Jim was setting up his new business hooks.

Jim was also happier. He was making more money selling cocaine and opium than he made pimping his wife. At times, he wasn't as heartless as he appeared. He knew Tilly was missing their son. He often heard her crying of a night and whispering Freddy's name. He hoped the time off would help her heart mend and for her to realise that it was in the best interest of their son to continue living with her parents... and where he should stay.

In his own peculiar way, Jim loved Tilly. When he was a good husband, he was loving, gentle and kind. He often bought her gifts of jewellery and shoes. Mind you, it was out of the money she was earning, but to Jim, it was his money too. The flip side of the coin was when Jim was bad, he was malignant. It was when he was like this, Tilly often remained away from the flat due to his violent moods.

Devine also liked to waste his money in one of the various illegal gambling dens in Woolloomooloo. He wasn't much of a winner, but he sure was a prolific loser. One night he was on a roll whilst playing poker and won just over one hundred pounds with a royal flush. Not wanting to push his luck, he left and decided to visit a tattoo parlour down the street before returning home.

When he arrived at the flat, he woke Tilly, who was soundly sleeping, and proudly showed off his tattoo of a horse head inside a horseshoe, with the words 'Good Luck' written across a red ribbon, on his right forearm.

"You woke me up to show me that?" Tilly grumbled. "Jim, I worked until late tonight and 'ad to catch a cab 'ome because you forgot to pick me up."

"You've got legs, use them!" Jim angrily replied before dropping on the bed fully clothed, his back to his wife.

"Yeah, I fuckin' work my arse orf to pay my soliciting fines and your fuckin' gambling debts. Just like it was in merry old London town. I wish I were back there now with my son!"

7

Twelve months after her arrival, Tilly was tired of being arrested and fined for soliciting, so she convinced Jim to purchase a Cadillac. From that day on, she found it a lot easier to solicit and service clients using the car as a travelling boudoir. The seats also made a warmer and more comfortable bed than being pushed up against a hard brick wall or laying on the dewy grass when servicing the punters. An added bonus was having Jim nearby, armed with a baton and an army-issue Webley Mk IV revolver. She knew she was safe if rival gangs and pimps showed up. The car also made escaping from the police much easier.

One night when Jim drove Tilly to the home of one of her regular clients, he didn't wait outside. Instead, he drove off to attend a rat fight.

The fighting den at the scabrous slum-house at Riley Street in Surry Hills was a regular haunt of his.

The area was known as Frog Hollow, which was aptly named due to it being the home of countless frogs. It was also the dwelling place and headquarters of notoriously dangerous Sydney crime figures and where police maintained a high presence.

Riley Street was the filthiest and vilest slum area in all of Sydney, a place no respectable citizen dared enter. The haphazard overcrowded tenements were built on and around a sheer cliff that plunged from the western side of Riley Street, and residents were only able access their homes by dimly lit, steep stairways. The houses were dark and poorly ventilated with defective drainage and sewers. Poverty, the plague, venereal disease, and illness were rife, as were frogs, rats, and cockroaches.

Devine made his way down the rotting staircase into a makeshift cellar and entered the smoke-filled room smelling of blood, rats, dogs, body odour and stale beer. Kerosene lamps hung from wire above the ring, illuminating the twelve-feet square fighting pit as the referee called for the dog to be brought into the blood-soaked arena. When the timekeeper nodded at two men, one poured rats out of a hessian bag, while the other, the owner of a fox terrier, dropped his dog into the pit. Two men then quickly covered the arena with wire mesh to prevent the rats from escaping.

Jim made his way to the bookie and placed a bet before finding somewhere to stand around the arena. The men cheered as more than forty large rats quickly dragged the fox terrier to the ground and they began tearing the dog apart. After its grisly death, the dog's body was removed, and a bucket of bleach and water was then thrown across the pit before the next dog was brought into the ring.

The men cheered loudly as a dog named Gunner, the champion Jack Russell Terrier, trotted into the arena. Money quickly changed hands from punter to bookie until the odds were too high for the gamblers to make a halfpenny back from a pound bet. Jim wagered fifty pounds at seven to one on Gunner to win.

The men stood back and watched as the rat handler poured fifty rats from his sack into the pit. After his handler released the rope lead from around his neck, Gunner leapt into the arena. Two minutes and forty-three seconds later, covered in blood and gore, Gunner stood at the far side of the pit, the victor in the bloodied arena laden with shredded vermin.

The dog's owner picked him up and gave him a drink of water and a piece of meat before washing him down. Once clean, his loyal applauding fans pressed forward to pat him and congratulate the owner on a job well done.

The rat handler collected the rats and laid them out in a circle on the table for the referee, who struck the animals three times on the tail with a cane. Not one rat moved. It was a clean kill. Gunner's prize for a record kill was a blue ribbon and a leather collar.

When Tilly had finished, she arrived outside her client's residence to find her Jim missing. Thinking he'd gone to buy cigarettes, she stood against the fence to wait. After waiting for twenty minutes, she determined that he was probably at the Tradesmen's Arms pub or one of the gambling dens and refused to wait any longer. She walked down the street with her finger on the trigger of her pistol until she hailed a cab to take her to the pub. On her arrival she told the cabbie to wait and headed straight to the back room where the barmen illegally served alcohol after six o'clock closing. When she saw that Jim wasn't there, she returned to the cab and told the driver to take her home.

It was almost midnight when the final fight was about to begin. Jim and the remaining men placed their bets. The owners of the four dogs stood by the pit as the rat handler descended the stairs with a sack filled with rats. This was the main fight of the night that most men came to see. The gambling area was standing room only as the men pushed and shoved each other to get a better view of the pit.

Two hundred rats were emptied into the pit before Charlie, the fox terrier was released from his rope. In one giant leap, the terrier was in the pit and immediately started ripping into the rats. After two minutes, the protective wire mesh was lifted, and Charlie was immediately pulled out as the rat handler sorted through the dead rats and placed them into a bucket. The next dog to jump into the pit was a Jack Russell terrier named Rusty and again after two minutes, he was retrieved from the arena and the dead rats collected. In turn, two more dogs, a stocky Staffordshire bull terrier named Jimmy and an Airedale terrier named Buttons were thrown into the pit.

They were immediately swarmed by the rats. Buttons was pulled out of the arena by his owner after just sixty seconds of fighting. He had lost his left eye during the ferocious battle. His early retirement earned Buttons an immediate disqualification.

The winner of the night was Jimmy the Staffordshire bull terrier. He had killed seventy-four rats within two minutes. The men cheered, as the owner collected his winnings before leaving for home with his champion, and to care for Buttons, who he also owned.

Jim pushed his way through the crowd to receive his winnings which was a grand total of fourteen hundred pounds. He placed the notes in the inside pockets of his jacket before driving home. Most of the other men made their way to the Sunbeam Hotel, a seedy and unkempt pub, to celebrate their winnings or to commiserate their losses.

When Devine arrived home, he found Tilly sitting on the settee. "You fuckin' left me at the punter's 'ouse. Anything could've 'appened to me in the street. I 'ad to catch a cab," she snarled.

"What the fuck was that old man going to do to you? You see him every week for hours on end. You're safe, so stop your fuckin' whining!"

"You probably lost all my fuckin' money down at that fuckin' rat 'ole. You still stink orf the fuckin' place!"

"Don't fuckin' yell at me," Jim sneered as he threw the roll of cash at Tilly. "Count the fuckin' money and shut the fuck up!"

Tilly's eyes lit up as she counted each note, throwing her head back and laughing when she reached the final pound note. "You were on a lucky streak tonight, weren't ya!"

"Yeah, seven hundred fuckin' pounds worth sweet'art!"

"I 'appen to know a girl that's worth every…single…penny." Tilly smiled as she walked towards the bedroom stripping off her clothing along the way.

The next morning, Tilly was back at work. Jim drove the streets of East Sydney while Tilly serviced clients in the back of the Cadillac. Business was quite brisk that day. Punters were rolling in at a steady pace until Jim stopped the car outside the Hopetoun Hotel and solicited an off-duty police constable who was new to the area. He immediately arrested both Jim and Tilly.

The following morning, Tilly stood before the magistrate and was sentenced to three days in gaol for whoring and a further forty-eight hours for obscene language when she told the magistrate to go fuck himself. Jim stood quietly by her side and was released after paying his fine of two pounds.

Five days later when he met Tilly outside Long Bay women's gaol, Jim greeted her with an unusual display of affection. Once she was in the car, he rolled the shirt sleeve up to his elbow and showed her his left forearm.

"Jim! You did that for me?" Tilly almost squealed in delight when she saw the new tattoo bearing her name.

"You don't need to make a big thing of it. It's just ink."

"You must 'ave really missed my money!"

"Shut the fuck up and get your fuckin' bloomers off woman, I need a fuck!" He rasped knowing that the tattoo would get him whatever he wanted for a few days.

When they were only yards away from the gaol gates, Jim stopped the car and told Tilly to jump in the back. Almost naked and with legs everywhere, the Devines made love as if they didn't have a care in the world. Their open-air show gave the inmates and prison guards in a passing tramcar a bit of a treat as well.

Over the following months, Jim became more heavily involved in drug dealing. He was selling marijuana, opium, heroin, and morphine through pubs and to street workers around the city. But cocaine was the drug that made him the most money. He had learned that mixing boracic acid into the cocaine, he made a lot more money.

Jim purchased his cocaine from Thomas Burgess, a chemist in Surry Hills. He paid the pharmacist twenty-two shillings for the cocaine, then cut it with the boracic acid, before selling two-hundred-and-fifty bags for five shillings each. He was proud of his business skills and profit margin, but most of all, he was happy that Tilly didn't know how much money he was making.

One afternoon, Tilly was arrested when she was caught shoplifting with a fellow streetwalker. She and Eleanor Kaye were stealing clothing from a department store and were apprehended by a store detective. They were charged and held in the police cells overnight. The following morning, the women attended court and were fined three pounds each before being released on a three months' good behaviour bond.

"Why the fuck were you shoplifting?" Jim raged when Tilly told him what had happened.

"It was a joke, Jimmy. I didn't think we'd get caught! Elsie broke the fuckin' elastic on her silk knickers when she was shoving a dress down them. Then 'er knickers fell around 'er feet. It was fuckin' funny! Our laughing caught the store detective's attention…"

7

Jim's drug empire came crashing down when local prostitutes began turning up on the street looking like cadavers. Their skin was as dry as paper, their eyes were sunken deep into their sockets, and the bridge of their noses had all but disappeared, leaving the nostrils widely dilated. Jim knew it must have had something to do with the cocaine he was selling, as many of the women were his clients. He stopped selling the cocaine in fear of being arrested.

It was a fortunate decision. Two months later, Sergeant O'Brien from Surry Hills police station, made it his mission to rid Darlinghurst of drug dealers. He had learned from an informant that a man by the name of Charles Passmore was selling bad cocaine at eleven o'clock every Wednesday night on the corner of Woolcott and Craigend Streets, Darlinghurst.

At ten o'clock the following Wednesday night, O'Brien set up surveillance at a house down the street from the corner. Just before eleven o'clock, a tall well-dressed man with grey hair arrived at the corner and the sergeant watched as he was given money before each person that approached was handed a small paper bag. O'Brien left the house through the back gate and cautiously made his way to the corner and caught the drug dealer unawares. He immediately arrested him while police officers, who were hiding in areas near the corner, nabbed the buyers.

Passmore was formally charged and spent the night in a cell. The cadaverous cocaine addicts were offered immunity if they testified against Passmore, which they agreed to do.

The following morning when he appeared before the court, O'Brien told the magistrate that Passmore had a long criminal record and gave him detailed information about his crimes. Before finishing, the sergeant stated, "Passmore is lord and master of a dope combine and has waxed fat and flourished through the agency of his hopeless clients. Every Wednesday night at about eleven o'clock, he would be standing at the corner of Woolcott and Craigend Streets, Darlinghurst, handing out the deadly packages of cocaine to scores of addicts."

The magistrate fined Passmore fifty pounds, the harshest penalty at the time under the *New South Wales Poisons Act*. Passmore paid the fine immediately, left the court and continued his cocaine trade.

CHAPTER SIX

The Best and the Worst of Them

The early 1920s were quite profitable for the Devines. Jim, however, wasted most of his money on alcohol, cocaine, and gambling. In fact, he would lay a bet on almost anything as long as the odds were good. Tilly's life hadn't changed. She still sold herself on the streets, and she was still married to a man who treated her more like a cash cow than a wife. And Freddy was still in Camberwell.

Unfortunately, most of the money Tilly had made, Jim gambled away at poker games, dog pit fights and horse racing. Fortunately, she had squirrelled away a great deal of her earnings in several hiding places in their rented Surry Hills home, but Jim found two of her caches. From then on Tilly decided to hide all her money behind the loose bricks in the walls at St. James' Church…

After finishing work early one night, Tilly and Jim drove to the refreshment room at Tom Ugly's Point for a snack. Tilly ordered corned beef sandwiches and a bag of her favourite chocolates. After she paid, the manager accused her of stealing a glass from the counter and hiding it under her coat.

"Where the fuck is the fuckin' glass?" Tilly yelled as she opened her coat wide enough for the kiosk owner to check.

"I saw you holding the glass in your hand and now it's gone!" she yelled.

"I put the fuckin' thing back on the shelf!"

"There were four there, now there's only three. Give it back or I'll report you to the police!"

"Go get them. I don't have your fuckin' glass!"

Tilly left the kiosk and when she told Jim what had happened, he told her to ignore the stupid fuckin' bitch. However, after one bite of his sandwich, his charitable mood quickly changed. "She can shove this fuckin' sandwich up her fat arse!" Jim thundered as he tossed the sandwich back into the paper bag before storming into the kiosk with Tilly close behind.

"You call this fuckin' food? The corned beef is off! I wouldn't feed it to a fuckin' dog!"

An argument ensued between Jim and the kiosk owner. Fearful of being attacked, the shopkeeper threw a jar of jam at Jim, demanding that he and his wife leave her shop, or she'd call for the police. Both Tilly and Jim pitched items back at her and left when a car pulled up outside.

The following morning, two police officers knocked on the Devine's door and demanded they accompany them back to the Darlinghurst police station. After Westbrook, the kiosk owner, identified Jim and Tilly as the people who had stolen from her and assaulted her. They were charged with maliciously damaging her property. Westbrook also demanded reconstitution of a cash register, four jars of jam, and other goods to the value of £17/12. The Devine's denied the accusations and were bailed to appear in court.

On the 23rd of September 1924, the Devines appeared at the Central Police court to fight the charges. They made compelling witnesses and they fought hard to prove their innocence and won.

Later that night after styling her hair in her favourite kiss curls and ringlets, Tilly left to work along her section of William Street. She'd fought tooth and nail to secure the strip as her own. Her face and body bore the battle wounds of countless fights with other streetwalkers and pimps to win the prime location. Tilly carried a scar above her right eye from an altercation with a streetwalker named Sonya. Tilly was the victor. However, when Sonya's pimp heard that his girl had lost the valuable strip she had worked for over five years, he attacked Tilly with his straight razor slashing her forehead and left hand. But Tilly was no slouch when it came to street fighting—she grabbed her pistol and shot the pimp in his left thigh.

After making twenty pounds, Tilly set off to catch a cab home. She had taken no more than a dozen steps when she was approached by a man who asked her the price for her time. He was a well-spoken gentleman, so Tilly assumed he wasn't a threat and told him it would cost him ten shillings. He agreed to the price and followed her to the niche she used behind a nearby shop. After the sexual deed was completed, the punter refused to pay.

"Pay me the fuckin' money or else I'll cut ya fuckin' balls orf, ya thievin' bastard."

The man shoved Tilly before taking flight down an alley near a butchery. He pushed her so hard that she fell to the ground, but recovering quickly, an enraged Tilly soon caught up with the fee-evading felon. After catching hold of his coat tails, she swung him around, and knocked him to the ground. Putting the boot hard into his stomach, Tilly gave the man a good going over, landing a final blow to his crotch with her right foot. The punter's screams were heard by a passing policeman who promptly came to his rescue. Tilly was arrested and later charged with malicious wounding, incurring a two pounds fine.

Early in 1925, Jim was so busy resurrecting his drug business and gambling that he rarely had the time to drive Tilly to her regular appointments and to her strip along William Street. With Jim taking the car, Tilly was forced to catch a cab, and often at times, a tram.

Whilst riding a tram one morning, Tilly happened across some government papers that had been left on the seat by the gentleman that had been sitting beside her. She picked them up and flipped through the pages, hoping to find information on where to hand them in. As she perused the documents, the word 'prostitute' caught her eye. She started reading a passage on page twenty-three which was a parliamentary discussion about a decree stating that under the *New South Wales Police Offences Act of 1908*, it was an offence for a man to operate a brothel, act as a pimp, or profit from the earnings of prostitution. But what really caught her attention, was there were no laws against *women* owning or operating a brothel. Tilly's heart skipped a few beats in excitement.

The twenty-four-year-old prostitute may not have had much education, but she had business savvy and was extremely shrewd. She knew she could make around seventy pounds a week working as a prostitute, but she also calculated that she could make at least six times that amount if six women worked for her in a brothel.

Finding those documents by chance was fortuitous for Tilly—she had clued herself up on the *Prostitution Act* and instead of working that day, she looked for a decent property to establish as a brothel.

On the 21st March, while she was browsing real estate offices for a suitable house, she happened to look through the window of a barbershop. Her breath caught in her throat and she flew into a rage. Sitting in the barber's chair was the man who had called her a whore while she was drinking at the Paragon Hotel at Circular Quay several months before.

"You fuckin' bastard!" Tilly screamed as she pushed open the barber shop door and rushed toward the terrified man. She swung her right arm and slashed him across the face with her razor. As he raised his arm to protect himself, Tilly slashed him across his right hand and then across his forearm. Blood gushed from the gaping wounds as he collapsed to the floor screaming for help. Tilly wasn't finished. She kicked him in the stomach and laughed; "Not so fuckin'smart-mouthed now are you, you fuckin' cunt!"

When she had finished, Tilly looked around the room at the astonished onlookers and threatened that she would hunt them down and give them the same if they spoke to the police.

Tilly made her way home and threw the blood-stained razor in the gutter outside her Crown Street house. Once inside, she washed herself clean of the blood before changing into another frock and stockings. She was wiping blood off her shoes when Jim burst through the door.

"What the fuck have you done woman?"

"I slashed that fuckin' bastard who called me a 'ore when we were at the Paragon!"

"Fuckin' Jesus! Where?"

"At the barber's in Surry 'ills" Tilly replied as she calmly checked herself in the mirror.

"How many fuckin' witnesses were there? This is all we fuckin' need. You stupid fuckin' bitch!" Jim spat before storming out of the house.

At seven-thirty the following morning, Tilly was rudely awoken by a loud knocking at the door. She turned to ask Jim to answer it, but he wasn't there. When she peeked out the bedroom window, three policemen stood on the steps. Mumbling, she donned her dressing gown and made her way to the door.

"Mrs. Devine, I'm Constable Roache. I'm here to ask you questions about the slashing of Mr. Sidney Corke yesterday at the Surry Hills barber shop."

"I was 'ome all day yesterday, constable. What a 'orrible thing to 'appen! I 'ope the man isn't too 'urt."

"Mrs. Devine, my fellow constable and I found a bloodied razor in the gutter not more than thirty yards away. You also fit the description of the attacker in the statements made by the victim and witnesses. We're entering your premises to conduct a search." The constable solemnly stated as he and two other policemen pushed their way past her.

When one of the police officers emerged from the bathroom with her bloodstained frock and stockings, Tilly knew her goose was cooked. She asked if she could get dressed and grab her handbag before they took her to the police station.

At the Central Police Court on the 23rd of March, Tilly was bailed on a charge of maliciously wounding Sidney Corke. The victim had been standing at the back of the court watching the proceedings. The wound on his face was covered with gauze and plaster tape, his right hand and forearm were also bandaged. As Tilly left the courtroom, she cast a malicious smile toward Corke that would have terrified the devil himself.

Knowing she would more than likely be sent to gaol, Tilly continued with her plans to buy a brothel. She knew that she would need more money than she'd saved, not only to secure a property but also to pay for luxuries and bribes whilst she was in prison.

On the 25th of May, two days before her return to court, Tilly happened across an advert for a house at 191 Palmer Street, Darlinghurst. The house wasn't much to look at, but it was cheap. She planned to make a few renovations and knew that after adding new furnishings, décor, alcohol and sparsely clad prostitutes, the house would look better in no time. By four o'clock that afternoon, she had signed the deeds to the property and was handed the keys of the first house she had ever owned.

Arriving at court on the 27th of May, Tilly was stylishly dressed in a lacy black dress, wide-brimmed black hat, a red fox fur, and a pearl necklace. She stood before Magistrate Scholes and offered him her most demure smile. The stipendiary magistrate listened to the prosecutor as he read the police report about what had taken place at the barber shop. He also read the doctor's report about the injuries Corke had sustained. Every now and then, the magistrate glanced from the witnesses across to Tilly with either a raised brow or a look of disgust on his face.

When called to the stand, Corke stated that he was a confectioner from Sydney. He told the court about the twelve stitches to his forearm and the nineteen stitches on the wound to his hand and how he would never regain the full use of it. He said that the razor wound across his face required seventeen stitches and he would always have a scar. He stated he was stunned by the vicious attack and denied ever seeing the defendant before…

After Corke had finished his testimony and returned to his seat, the magistrate asked the prosecutor's next witness to take the stand. After Constable Roche's evidence was heard, the magistrate dismissed him before perusing a few sheets of paper handed to him by the prosecutor. The magistrate took some time reading the sheets of paper, then placed them in front of him before asking Tilly to stand.

"Mrs. Devine, I have just finished reading your charge sheets and find your behaviour to be devoid of morals and common decency. To attack a complete stranger with a razor while he was going about his daily business is absolutely reprehensible! I see that you have more than seventy convictions recorded against you. It is incumbent upon me to teach recidivist offenders like you a lesson. For the crime with which you are charged, you are liable to imprisonment for five years. I feel…"

A shrill scream interrupted the judge and he looked aghast when Tilly fainted. After she was brought back around by smelling salts, she wept when the magistrate sentenced her to two years light labour at Long Bay Women's gaol.

As the prison tramcar approached the entrance of the gaol, Tilly craned her neck to see which guard was on gate duty. She was delighted when she saw Tommy at the gate. He was one of her favourite warders. While they were stopped at the gates, Tilly dropped a few pounds to the ground for him to buy her chocolate and food, as well as a generous tip on the side. The guard tipped his hat in acquiescence and watched after the tram as it continued its way to the main building.

Tommy, as Tilly affectionately called him, was quiet by nature but had a restrained intensity about him that she found charming. His wife had died leaving him with three young children. The amiable warder also had a soft spot for Tilly. He was one of the few people who were able to break through her tough exterior and reach her soft side. Before leaving gaol at the end of every sentence, Tilly always slipped him ten pounds to buy something special for his children.

Whilst in prison, Tilly used her time wisely. She kept her head down and completed her work promptly so she could return to her cell to study the *New South Wales Police Offences Act*. One afternoon while she was reading the papers, she came across a section titled, *Prisoners' Detention Act*. Upon reading it she learned that under a health regulation within the *Act*, even though she couldn't be arrested for operating a brothel, she and her working girls could be arrested and detained for suspicion of having a venereal disease. She also discovered another problem under the *Vagrancy Act*—police had the power to arrest and imprison prostitutes who walked the streets.

Determined to beat the government, Tilly decided the only way around the Act was if she and her girls had monthly certified health checks. She felt that being in receipt of proof that they were clean of any diseases, they would circumvent the *Acts* and not be arrested. She wrote down a business plan for her brothel and decided she would dominate the sex industry in the East Sydney area.

One morning, Tilly was sitting on a bench in the exercise yard watching the sun as it rose over the high stone wall. She closed her eyes and inhaled the aroma of porridge wafting from the kitchen. When she opened her eyes, the gaol's pet magpie rested on the branch of a nearby tree. Tilly smiled as the bird shook out its feathers after preening itself, emanating a light cloud of dust while vigilantly keeping its kind russet eye on her all the while.

The tranquillity of the morning was abruptly shattered by the loud crack of a pistol shot, and Tilly watched in horror as the bird fell dead on the grass just a couple of feet away. She looked toward the guardroom and saw Roger Browne, one of the cruellest warders at the gaol, standing outside the dormitory with a smirk on his face. Enraged by his cruelty, she assaulted Browne so violently that he was rushed to the Sydney infirmary for treatment.

Tilly was placed in isolation for one month and the gaol's superintendent cancelled her release. Tommy advocated on Tilly's behalf, advising the administrator that she had been overcome by emotion after witnessing the shooting of the women's pet bird. He also reminded the superintendent of the multiple accusations of violence and sexual assaults perpetuated by Browne by numerous women prisoners. The administrator considered Tommy's petition, and the fact that Tilly had been a model prisoner and released her from isolation.

When she arrived back in her cell, Tilly was surprised to find two biscuits and a slice of fruit cake wrapped in brown paper on her bed, and a newspaper on the wooden chair. She smiled to herself as she read the newspaper, pleased that it hadn't had sections cut out like the normal prison-issued newspapers, and made a mental note to give Tommy a larger bonus before she left.

Tilly didn't find her stints in prison too difficult. In fact, she enjoyed the peace and solitude, and considered them a break from prostitution and her husband's foul temper. She rarely had any problems with her fellow inmates. Most were intuitive enough to know not to take her on. Those that didn't learned the hard way that Tilly's firecracker temper was quick to ignite. She often scoffed at other prisoners when they called the prison guards 'miss'—*I need the toilet, miss, I'd like to go to the chapel,* and *How long are we outside for today miss?* Tilly never spoke in such a servile way nor displayed a whit of subterfuge or duplicity. She didn't have to. She was well-liked and looked after by most of the prison guards due to the monetary gifts she bestowed upon them.

7

Whilst his wife was incarcerated, Jim's new haunt became the Fifty-Fifty Club, which was owned by the up-and-coming crime king, Phil 'The Jew' Jeffs. The club was Sydney's best-known secret illegal casino, cocaine palace, and sly-grog joint. Jeffs also used the club as a high-class brothel. The upstairs apartments were where his important clients were 'looked after'.

To keep his business operating, Jeffs paid a fortune in bribes to crooked police and council aldermen. Due to the restrictions imposed on the sale of alcohol after six o'clock, keeping the nightclub and upstairs brothel safe from police activity was important. A number of prominent politicians and gentry who occasioned the establishment ensured the bribes served their purpose, knowing that if they were ever caught on the premises, it would cause a major scandal.

The club was a dark place and was made even more tenebrous by the thick cigarette smoke permeating the room. Conversation was almost impossible due to the noise made by the spirited patrons and the loud music played by the band. Every night, a local four-piece jazz band played long sets with a variety of raucous songs. Jeffs paid the band a little more than their fee so they'd take shorter breaks because the more the patrons danced, the thirstier they became and the more money he made at the bar.

One night during a poker game at the club, Devine accused one of the players of drawing a card from the bottom of the deck. Threats and counter-threats were spat between the two men before the table was violently overturned. Beer and whiskey splashed the other players as cards, ashtrays, cigarettes, and cash were strewn across the floor.

Jim's opponent pulled out a knife, so he unsheathed his trusty Pistole Parabellum that he'd purchased on the black market during the war. Pandemonium ensued as people fled the dancefloor and headed for the exit.

The two men glared at one another, neither uttered a word, each daring the other to make the first move.

The card sharp threw his knife at Jim, missing him by less than an inch. A shot rang out during the melee and the card cheat fell to the floor. Moments later he was dead.

Jeffs ran down the stairs wearing nothing but a shotgun. As soon as he saw the body on the floor, he told his staff to clear the club. Jim remained behind and paid one of the bouncers ten pounds to get rid of the dead man.

The man knew the perfect place to dump a body. He took a trip with a couple of cement blocks and rope down to the asbestos works along the Parramatta River, an area that was frequented by great white sharks…

7

After spending less than fourteen weeks in Long Bay, Tilly was released on a good behaviour bond. The judge warned her that if she broke the law, she would be sent straight back to gaol to finish her sentence as well as the added time for whatever crime she had committed.

Tilly had no intentions of going back to prison. She had a plan to put into action and she wasn't going to let any bastard stand in her way.

CHAPTER SEVEN

The Spirit of Enterprise

The mind of a woman can be a devious one,
but she gets the job done

Upon her release, Tilly decided she would no longer live under the misogyny and servile role that women had endured for centuries. She was resolute. Matilda Devine was going to live by her own rules, on her own terms, and live the life of luxury and leisure she had always dreamed about.

She forged ahead with her plan. With the money she had set aside, Tilly began refurbishing the dingy old cottage. Due to the global financial crisis, there were very few jobs in Sydney, so finding willing workers was easy. Prostitutes too.

Within a week of putting the word out, she had employed eleven women between the ages of fifteen and forty-five. They came from diverse backgrounds—from the disadvantaged illiterate to the private school educated, and inner-city homeless teenage girls. Poverty didn't distinguish between classes.

Several of the women were seasoned streetwalkers Tilly had worked with in the past. Others were lonely, single women who hoped to find a rich farm cocky who would carry them away from the poverty and violence of city life. But mostly she hired desperate housewives who wanted to keep their children together and not be forced to relinquish them to the orphan school because they were unable to feed them.

Tilly was determined to be a good brothel Madam. She had done the hard yards and knew the business from the bottom up. Now she planned to reach the very top. She taught the girls personal hygiene and also explained how douching with Lysol would kill sperm and prevent an unwanted pregnancy.

Within three months of opening her Palmer Street brothel, Tilly strutted around the 'Loo sporting her newly-coloured platinum blonde hair and an expensive one-hundred-and fifty-pounds silver fox fur. To show off her extravagant fur coat and new diamond rings, Tilly would often sit at a table outside the Greek-owned Canberra Café on Oxford Street, Darlinghurst, sipping coffee and enjoying traditional Greek sweet pastries.

Jim was also more dapper in appearance. He was swimming in the money from receiving a percentage of Tilly's brothel income as well as his own money from selling cocaine and marijuana. Now wealthy enough to procure suits and coats from Zink & Sons Tailors, he could be found every three months indulging in the Oxford Street clothiers' premises being measured and fitted for a new three-piece suit made from newly imported plaid fabric.

For the Devines, life was all about power and making money, spending it, enjoying it, and partying—but what was most important of all to Tilly was to become the queenpin of East Sydney!

Tilly enjoyed a drink, but unlike her husband, she didn't touch drugs. She learned her lesson when Jim had started her on cocaine in London. Jim didn't care about the threat of prison. As far as he was concerned, he was born under a lucky star and had gotten away with crime most of his life, so he continued to wear his devil-may-care attitude.

Unfortunately for Tilly, Jim's abuse continued. With the popularity of cocaine and marijuana rising, more and more drug dealers cropped up. This meant less money for Jim, forcing him to rely more on Tilly for money.

One evening, desperate for money to pay yet another gambling debt, Jim demanded money from Tilly. She had already given him his weekly cut of ten percent and told him he wasn't getting any more, no matter what he did to her.

"I know you're fuckin' hoarding the money somewhere around here! You can either give it to me now or I'll rip the fuckin' place apart!"

"Go right ahead and I'll throw your cocaine into the fuckin' loo!"

"Yeah, you think you'll do that, you fuckin' bitch?" Jim roared as he took hold of Tilly's right arm and wrenched it up her back. The sound of a bone snapping and Tilly's agonised scream shocked Jim so much so that he quickly released his grip. Tilly swung around and grabbed a vase on a nearby table and threw at her husband, gashing his left cheek.

"Take me to the fuckin 'ospital before I run you though!" She threatened.

For the weeks that followed their violent altercation, Jim dutifully drove Tilly to the brothel every day and picked her up at eight o'clock sharp every night. Tilly made sure he never forgot for a moment during that time that he had broken her arm.

7

While Tilly and Jim were sitting outside the Cowper pub at Woolloomooloo one morning, Tilly noticed a young blonde girl sitting on a brick fence across the street. She looked visibly upset. Tilly walked across and gently placed her hand on the young girl's shoulder.

"Oh 'ere, 'ere lovey, what's the matter with a pretty girl like you? Are you alright, sweet'eart?"

"I've had a fright. My friend was attacked by a woman with a razor at our refuge this morning and I don't know where else to go."

"There, there, now sweet'art. There's always somewhere to go around 'ere, so don't you worry about that," Tilly said as she sat beside the girl.

"I don't know anyone, and I can't go home..."

"Well, you know me now, lovey. I'm Tilly Devine. I'm well known around these parts. Maybe I can 'elp you." Tilly tapped the frightened teenager's pert nose to reassure her. "What's your name, sweet'art?"

"Dulcie Markham."

"Well Dulcie, I'm pleased to meet you. Let me take you 'ome and freshen you up a bit. A nice bath and a full stomach will 'ave you feelin' better in no time."

Within the week, Dulcie was sporting a new wardrobe of clothes, had her hair styled and makeup applied and was making a fortune at the Palmer Street brothel.

7

Tilly's foray into crime quickly brought about the wrath of Kate Leigh who considered herself the Crime Queen of Surry Hills and surrounds. She told Wally Tomlinson, her lover at the time, that as far as she was concerned, the 'Loo, Surry Hills, and Darlinghurst wasn't big enough for two madams, and she would see Tilly gone… one way or another. A bitter feud of one-up-womanship ensued that would almost bring East Sydney to its knees.

One afternoon, Tilly and Kate literally almost bumped into one another in Oxford Street, Darlinghurst. Sparks flew from each woman's eyes.

"It's you, ya fuckin' bitch," Kate seethed. "Who the fuck do you think you are setting up houses in *my* areas?"

"There are enough men in Sydney for a 'undred fuckin' brothels, you gapped tooth bitch! Now fuck orf!" Tilly spat.

Both women stood their ground, each waiting for the other to make a move or be the first to walk away. Tilly glowered at Leigh, and Kate glared at Tilly. Until that moment, Tilly had never really given Leigh much thought. As far as she was concerned, East Sydney was big enough for the both of them, but if it came to who would come out on top, Tilly was damn sure it would be her.

The blowing of a horn broke the women's stand-off. Kate walked toward a car that had stopped at the side of the road. She opened the car door and snarled: "If I see you near any of my fuckin' girls, I'll rip your fuckin' face off, ya cunt!"

"Too late, ya fuckin' ugly dog! My business is good…my girls are the best in East Sydney. The punters are comin' to *my* place in droves!"

Tilly's derisive taunt was too much. Kate threw her handbag onto the car seat and in a seething rage, charged toward Tilly while her back was turned. Tilly kicked off her shoes and threw her handbag over to a nearby fence just as Kate's right fist came swinging toward her. Tilly blocked the punch and ducked an oncoming left swing, returning with a hard hitting right and punched Kate brutally across the side of her head before bringing up her left fist in a quick uppercut. "You fuckin' coward! Attack someone from behind!"

Tilly grabbed a handful of hair on each side of Kate's head, yanking it down before kneeing her in the face, fracturing Leigh's nose. Kate staggered back clutching at her face, her head spinning as blood streamed from her nose.

Tilly laughed before turning to retrieve her handbag. "Is that all ya made orf? Ya fuckin' soft as a pillow!"

Eyes afire with rage, Kate lunged at Tilly, grabbing a handful of her hair, jerking her head backward. Kate maintained her grip and punched the side of Tilly's head, casting her face first to the ground before laying the boot into her stomach and ribs. "I'll fuckin' show you who's a fuckin' pillow, you scar-faced trollop!"

Tilly tried to get up before Leigh swept a kick to her back, knocking her back into the dirt. Then in a monumental show of strength, Tilly raised herself up from the ground in time to avoid another kick. Kate leaned toward Tilly again, spitting as she abused her. Tilly took advantage of her enemy's closeness and brought up her left fist in an uppercut that knocked Leigh off her feet. Tilly swiftly recovered, got to her feet, swung around, and smashed her heel into Kate's face. Dazed, Leigh's head snapped back, her mouth fell open and she fell flat out onto the road.

But Tilly wasn't finished. She'd learned the hard way on the streets of London that to rule your territory you must conquer your enemy. Darlinghurst, Woolloomooloo, and Surry Hills were hers and she refused to cede them to Kate Leigh. Tilly was younger, faster, and tougher than Kate and she was determined to teach her who the top hen was. So, she grabbed hold of Kate's collar and rammed her right knee straight up under her chin before dropping her elbow twice into her chest and face. Then taking hold of Leigh's hair, Tilly dragged her to the ground, grabbed hold of Kate's arm and stretched it out across the gutter and brought her foot down hard, breaking her elbow.

Kate could scarcely breathe. She knew she couldn't fight anymore. Weakened and in excruciating pain, Leigh pleaded for Tilly to stop. "You've… fuckin'…won… this… round…" she gasped.

Tilly walked over to her handbag and removed her Webley revolver before approaching Kate's driver. "Get her to the fuckin' 'ospital. And if any orf you fuckin' bastards try anythin' else, I'll fuckin' put a bullet in every single one orf you!"

7

Tilly's brothel business acumen was almost genius. Through her earnings, she purchased 193 Palmer Street, the house that was attached to her brothel. She also bought another house in Chapel Street, a small cottage in Woods Lane, and yet another house in Berwick Place, which she had tastefully renovated and furnished. She was proud of the impressive property portfolio she had accumulated in such a short time. To celebrate her new acquisitions, she bought herself a 1925 Morris Bullnose car.

Due to the economy, there was an influx of travelling prostitutes looking for a prime location to make their fortune. Most had heard that the only madam to work for in Sydney, was the brassy Tilly Devine. Those women who received Tilly's seal of approval, were charged board and lodgings to live in 193 Palmer Street, whilst they worked for her. And to keep Jim off her back, she allowed him to sell her girls 'snow', the prostitute's drug of choice during the 1920s.

In each of her brothels, Tilly had a printed menu of services and prices offered by her girls, whether it be to a gentleman in one of her elegantly decorated bedrooms, or a cheap quickie in the back alley for the lower-class punters. She also had strict rules that her girls always wore makeup, had the latest hair style, and insisted that they paraded around her brothels wearing the best French silk lingerie and stockings.

A proficient gingerer from way back, Tilly educated her girls in the miscreant art. She told them that the house received fifty percent of any money they stole from clients, but any tips they received, were their own. Tilly was an expert at wrapping her merchandise to make them irresistible to men. She wanted the clients to be more attracted to her girls than their wives. The more punters through her brothels, the more money Tilly had to spend on furs and jewellery.

7

"Jim, we're rolling in the money now. I have a few trusted women I can leave in charge of the brothels, and I was thinking that I should take a trip 'ome and bring Freddy back." Tilly was guardedly optimistic that Jim would be happy to have the son he had never met home with them.

"Are you fuckin' mad woman! Why fuckin' bring him here now? He's almost seven years old and wouldn't know us if he fuckin' met us in the street! He's better off staying with your folks. At least he fuckin' knows them. Surely, you're not so fuckin' selfish that you'd rip him out of a loving home!" Jim fumed.

"Selfish? I'm the fuckin' selfish one James fuckin' Devine! If you weren't my fuckin' 'usband, I'd fuckin' run you through and dump your body at Tempe Wetlands! 'e is *OUR* son and should be 'ome with us! You've never laid eyes on 'im. 'e's looks just like *YOU*! Freddy is your flesh and blood! 'ow can you deny 'is right to be with us. 'ow can you keep me from being a mother to my own son!" Tilly seethed.

"You want your son? Go get him, but don't expect me or your fuckin' precious brothels to be here waiting for you. No child of mine will be hanging around no whore house! It's him or me and your brothels!"

Broken-hearted, Tilly turned and walked away. She picked up her purse and gloves from the hallstand and made her way to her car without uttering a word. Jim had proven to her that money was more valuable to him than his own son. She felt like a coward and an uncaring mother for not wanting to give up her brothels. But Tilly knew that she could give Freddy a much better life as a brothel madam, than living on government pay outs or working in a shop or factory. She resolved herself to continue sending money to her parents so *her* son could continue to live a better life thousands of miles away.

7

In November 1926, thirty-two-year-old Norman Bruhn, a violent standover man and hopeful crime boss from Melbourne, arrived in Darlinghurst. He had become embroiled in a bitter argument with his former associate, Squizzy Taylor. He and his gang robbed Dottie Patrick's sly grog shop and had forced her prostitutes to strip off their clothing then searched them for hidden cash, stealing whatever money they found as well as their jewellery. Bruhn also ransacked Dottie's private office, stealing a further one thousand pounds. Unbeknownst to Bruhn, Taylor was a part owner in the brothel.

Squizzy Taylor, who Bruhn once loyally served as his lieutenant, was incensed by the flagrant robberies perpetrated by Bruhn and his gang. He called a meeting with his former co-conspirator to discuss Dottie's brothel raid, and the police interest he was attracting to Fitzroy due to his brass-necked illegal activities. Concerned that the meeting was his death knell and knew Taylor had the numbers. Preferring to keep breathing, Bruhn, his prostitute wife, Irene and their young sons, Noel and Keith, shot through to Sydney on a train.

Upon their arrival, the family stayed in a nondescript hotel in Surry Hills until Bruhn could raise the funds to rent a house. After settling his family into the room, his first call was to the Limerick Castle Hotel. There he learned during a conversation with some men at the bar, the address of a local brothel and sly grog shop. The directions he was given led him straight to 104 Riley Street, Surry Hills—Kate Leigh's sly groggery and brothel.

Using the same strategy as he had in Melbourne, Bruhn secreted himself behind a tree and laid in wait to ambush a punter leaving the Riley Street address. He didn't have to wait long. No more than fifteen minutes later, a well-dressed man furtively left the infamous house of ill repute. Bruhn listened to the hastening footfall of his unsuspecting prey closing the gap between them. When the mark was just a few steps away, Bruhn pounced on him, king hitting the midnight brothel creeper. Felling the man to the ground, Bruhn robbed him of his wallet and watch. Then making sure no-one was around, he took off, leaving the man lying unconscious on the footpath.

Having his sights set on taking over Sydney's underworld, Bruhn began frequenting pubs to get a feel for the city and its felonious goings-on. It didn't take long for like to attract like and he developed connections with local thugs and gang members. One bloke he met, an easy-going pickpocket named Anthony, procured him a job at the docks where he worked under the alias, Norman Noble.

Within months, Bruhn had initiated some of the most brutal and heinous underworld figures into his newly formed gang. They included homosexual albino, Frank 'Razor Jack' Hayes, George 'Midnight Raper' Wallace, Lancelot McGregor 'Sailor the Slasher' Saidler, and John 'Snowy' Cutmore. All came with a swag of charges, gaol sentences and criminal talents to ensure that the Bruhn gang was one to be feared.

Bruhn's aim was for him and his gang to barrage Tilly and Leigh's illicit businesses with robberies and assaults, in hope the women would go scampering in fear and Bruhn would take over their businesses.

"A woman's place is in the kitchen or in bed with their fuckin' legs spread. If these bitches think they can run the fuckin' underworld, they're about to learn a big fuckin' lesson!" Bruhn vowed.

Just moments into raiding Tilly's brothel, the men turned heel and ran when she burst into the room brandishing a pistol in each hand. "You fuckin' cunts get out of 'ere before I empty these fuckin' pistols into your fuckin' arses!" She roared before letting off several shots. To make sure the men knew she was a force to contend with, Tilly chased after them, shooting at their car as they clambered inside. Another shot rang out, followed by the primal scream of a man, and the screeching of car tyres as the 1922 Summit sped off down the street.

Their venture into Leigh's grog shop the following week gained them more than a bullet wound to the wrist that their partner in crime had received from Tilly. The gang robbed the ill prepared Kate of her day's earnings as well as a crate of whiskey. Wallace, who never missed an opportunity to enact his deviant behaviour, gave Kate's breasts a bit of a feel up, and copped a punch in the mouth.

"You fuckin' slut! Punch me in the fuckin' mouth!" Wallace bellowed. Then, being the gentleman that he wasn't, the 'Midnight Raper 'grabbed a handful of Kate's hair and dragged her over to the settee. Leigh fought with all her might, but the brawny brute of a man was far too strong. He forced Kate over the back of the settee, held her down by the nape of the neck and ripped off her imported French silk knickers.

"We've got no fuckin' time for this!" Snowy shouted. "Bruhn will be well fuckin' pissed off if we get caught because you can't keep your fuckin' cock in your drawers!"

"Get the fuck out and keep watch! Shoot any bastard that tries to come in!" Wallace growled as he viciously raped Kate from behind.

Kate didn't make a sound. She knew she was outmanned. She was no slouch in the revenge department and had plans for Wallace. She would make sure he would pay dearly for every violent thrust of his cock and bruise on her body.

7

The *New South Wales Pistol Licensing Act 1927* imposed a mandatory six-month prison term for anyone found carrying an unlicensed weapon. These laws forced criminals to find a new weapon and brought about the 'bloody razor' era. The normally innocuous, everyday shaving device became the weapon du jour for Sydney crime figures. Razors were inexpensive and easily purchased at any pharmacy. Most criminals, gang members and a certain brothel madam, brandished the cutthroat razors as their tool to threaten, intimidate, disfigure... or kill. Within days of the new firearm law, the newspaper headlines blared about the unparalleled barbarity of razor assaults throughout the city.

Tilly was ahead of the other criminals. She had used a straight razor for protection whilst working the streets of London, and it sailed with her to Australia. After losing her original straight razor to the police as evidence after the Sidney Cooke incident, Tilly had purchased herself a newer version.

Realising that Bruhn was out to seize control of both hers and Leigh's territories, Tilly kept razors close to hand at home and in her brothels.

She also made sure that her revolver was loaded and nearby in case she was ever ambushed.

Bruhn and his accomplices were making a villainous name for themselves around East Sydney. The docks gave him legitimacy and legal earnings, but the nights brought him the adventure, adrenalin, and violence that he craved. Dissatisfied with the money he was making robbing prostitutes and sly groggeries, he ventured into cocaine trafficking, turning him a handsome profit.

In late November 1927, Tilly was warned that Bruhn was planning another raid on her brothel but didn't know which one of the premises was the target. To ensure the safety of her girls and her money, she hired local thugs to protect her brothels in readiness.

Unbeknownst to Tilly, she had hired several of Bruhn's gang members to protect her Woods Lane brothel. At ten thirty during a busy Saturday night, Bruhn, Hayes, Wallace, and Saidler burst their way through the front and back doors of the Woods Lane house.

Bruhn grabbed hold of one of the young workers arms as she raced out of her room to see what the commotion was about. He pulled her against him, held a cut-throat razor against the terrified girl's throat and threatened to slash it if anyone made a sound or attempted to escape. Her partially clad client rushed into the hallway and was immediately elbowed in the face by Saidler, knocking him to the floor.

"I'll deal with him," Hayes grinned as he grabbed the client by the collar of his shirt and dragged the horror-struck man back into the bedroom, closing the door behind him.

"You!" Wallace roared from the doorway. "You, the one with the big fuckin' lady bumps! Get your arse over here!" Wallace demanded of a woman standing in the opposite corner of the room. Eloise gingerly approached him, attempting to cover herself with a shawl as she walked across the room. "You're comin' with me!" He sneered as he grabbed the girl by her hair and pushed open the door to the first bedroom. When he saw one of the working girls and her client cowering under the bed, he told them to get out before he slit their throats.

"I'll do anything you ask. Please don't hurt me," Eloise whimpered after Wallace threw her across the bed.

"Do you think you have a fuckin' choice! Get on your fuckin' hands and knees and spread those arse cheeks, you mangey bitch!" Wallace snarled as he pulled Eloise closer to the edge of the bed.

A sudden loud scream from the room Hayes had taken the client, pierced through the fracas in the waiting room. "Sounds like he's scored a bullseye!" Snowy snickered. "The fuckin' queer bastard."

That night, Bruhn and his mob of miscreants robbed Tilly's girls of over five hundred pounds and their jewellery. They also stole countless pounds and watches from the clients. It was a great haul for Bruhn and one that he hoped to repeat the following night at one of Leigh's groggeries.

7

The violence occurring in East Sydney earned the suburban area the reputation of being the 'Chicago of the South'. The extreme savagery became the concern of local newspapers, including the *Truth*.

On the 15th of January 1928, The *Truth* newspaper printed an editorial that would affect New South Wales criminals in a way that previous laws had failed to do. The *Truth*, generally known for sensationalising and proliferating scaremongering, actually did something right for New South Wales:

'This is the hour of glistening blades and crimes of violence, particularly razor slicings are part of the daily increasing carnival of bloodletting. It is no longer possible for decent citizens to walk the streets without fear of sudden and terrible attack. The harvest of hackings and slicings and stabbings is being garnered in all parts of the metropolis. The razor has found its place in the pockets not only of the original razor gang, but in the hands and thoughts of hundreds of nondescripts who have found that a well-honed blade is a weapon that strikes fear in the hearts of innocent victims.'

7

One night in mid-March, Tilly was in the Palmer Street brothel kitchen enjoying a glass of whiskey. Her rooms were full, a further half dozen clients waited in the living room, kept company by their chosen girl until a room was available. She was about to turn on the radio when a young blonde-haired, blue-eyed woman knocked on the kitchen door.

"Hello, are you Tilly?" The well-spoken girl asked.

"Yes, I am lovey. What can I do for you?"

"I'm looking for work. Are you looking for any girls?"

"Pull up a chair, love and 'ave a drink with me," Tilly said as she stood and walked over to a cupboard returning with a glass.

"You're a pretty little thing aren't you. What brings you 'ere? You're too pretty and upper-class for 'ouses like this."

"I need money. I've been with enough men to know what it's about and I can start straight away."

"What's your name?"

"Nellie Cameron."

"Well, Nellie, you're a bit ripe on the nose, sweet'art. Why don't you follow me to the bathroom and once you've had a bit orf a wash, you can start. Make sure you douche yourself with the Lysol, mind. You'll find it on the stand. We don't want any unwanted pregnancies, now do we."

"No. I don't ever want any babies."

"One day you'll change your mind. Now, you're a fine-lookin' sort, so you'll be chargin' the blokes six shillings each. I get 'arf. Cheat me, and you'll wish you were never born."

"I wish I was never born most days." Nellie mewled.

"Well, love, you let Tilly 'ere look after you."

That night, fifteen-year-old Nellie serviced eleven men. At six shillings per client, Tilly made more money from Nellie than any girl had ever made in one night in her brothels.

Over the following weeks, Tilly learned a lot about Nellie's life and what she'd suffered. She also was aware of how much she had given up by leaving a life of wealth and respectability and traversing to the shady side of Sydney. Tilly also recognised the façade of a tough, independent woman with an unbreakable heart that Nellie projected to hide the heartbreak and humiliation of her past. She was living that same pretence in regard to her marriage.

Tilly set Nellie up in her new house at Berwick Place. "Now, you make sure you bathe after every punter. I don't want you stinkin' like some fisherman's wife. Use plenty of rose water and remember douche yourself with Lysol. The better you smell, the better they pay!"

Berwick Place was the brothel where the higher-class girls worked, and where Tilly made the most money. The clientele included prominent businessmen, politicians, high ranking police, overseas dignitaries, and businessmen of great importance. Those men often sent overseas guests, when in Australia on business, to Berwick House to grease the wheels a little.

Nellie was finally able to settle into the brothel after she had placated the other five girls who worked in the house. The women were initially jealous of the blonde-haired beauty, but when she sent men their way after she'd already serviced a few, Nellie earned their respect. From then on, the women worked together as a team, and began offering threesome deals to their clients, bringing extra money into their house, and pleasing their Madam no end.

7

On the afternoon of the 22nd of June, Tilly sent a barrow boy to deliver a note to Jim. She had learned that Bruhn was collecting standover money from one of the heroin dealers in East Sydney. She had paid her informant ten pounds for the Darlinghurst address, before passing it on to Jim.

In heavy fog the following night, Jim secreted himself within the bushes in a garden of a Charlotte Lane house while Bruhn was handling a business matter at Mack's seedy cocaine and sly grog den. Unbeknownst to Devine, Bruhn's business wasn't reciprocal with the man he was visiting. He had actually held up Mack, robbing him of his daily takings.

Jim watched from his hiding spot as Bruhn rushed from Mack's house and when he was several feet away, he leapt out and yelled; "You fuckin' cunt! Stealing from my fuckin' wife and raping her girls!"

Before Bruhn could utter a word or grab for his pistol, Devine fired his Webley revolver five times. Each bullet found its target as the repetitive crack of gunfire resonated through the lane, shattering the quiet of the night. Jim didn't wait to make sure Bruhn was dead. He fled over the back fence and raced to where he had parked his car. The shrill blast of a police whistle sounded as the voices of several men and the piercing scream of a woman sounded in his wake.

Gas lights lit up the houses along the lane as concerned residents, dressed in their night attire, others in suits and fur coats returning home from an evening on the town, came out into the street. All were shocked to find a man shot and bleeding within yards of their homes. Two men tried to help Bruhn but could only offer him solace when they discovered the magnitude of his injuries.

Constable Blench was the duty officer walking the beat that night. He ran towards the lane from a block away and approached the group of silhouetted figures. When he reached the crowd, he saw Bruhn lying on the cobbled road clutching his bloody chest and moaning in agony.

The ambulance arrived and Bruhn was rushed to the hospital. The constable, who'd had previous dealings with Bruhn, went directly to his home and told his wife about the shooting. Visibly shaken by the news, Irene left her boys with her neighbour and Constable Blench drove her to the hospital.

"I suppose it was that Kelly again. The bloke that did the other fellow in." Irene remarked.

"Who's Kelly?" Blench asked.

Irene ignored the question as she watched the doctors cleaning up the blood from her husband's wounds.

Detective-Sergeant Miller arrived at the hospital before Bruhn was wheeled into surgery. "Do you know who shot you, Mr. Bruhn?"

"I won't be a copper. I won't shelf anybody. Go away, I'm too sick. I don't want the police to interfere in this."

A magistrate arrived at the hospital in the hope of obtaining a dying deposition. But Bruhn stuck to the criminal's code replying to the magistrate's questions with: "I don't know who shot me," rasping the same answer when asked again.

During surgery, the doctors removed a bullet that was lodged near Bruhn's left kidney, he had also suffered two bullet wounds to the left side of his chest, a fourth bullet was lodged in his left cheek, and a fifth went through his upper leg. During surgery, Bruhn's heartbeat had slowed to a critical level, forcing the surgeons to perform an emergency thoracotomy. Upon opening his chest and spreading his ribs apart, they discovered a catastrophic wound in the blood vessels that fed his lungs. Bruhn died moments later.

No-one was ever arrested for Bruhn's murder. There were no suspects, or a description of the killer. The police said it was almost as if the shooter had disappeared into thin air.

New South Wales Police Commissioner James Mitchell stated during an interview with the *Truth* newspaper that Bruhn was killed due to his cocaine business: 'The shooting is clearly interwoven with drug trafficking'.

Bruhn's razor gang disintegrated soon after his demise.

Chapter Eight

Nellie Kelly, Cameron Bourke

We Loved, We Lost Touch, We Moved on

Ellen Katherine Cameron was born to wealthy parents at Waterloo on Sydney's North Shore on the 1st of October 1910. She was the youngest child of Colin and Lillian Kelly.

The beautiful home Nellie was raised in was built in 1868 on a forty-acre allotment her mother had inherited. The mansion had fifteen rooms, which included three bathrooms and two internal toilets. The family was attended by a cook, four maids, three gardeners, a coachman, and a groom.

Lillian, like most women of means of the time, spent several hours a day tending to her display of African violets, ferns, and aspidistras or in her hothouse. The locals considered her gardens the best in the area.

Nellie, the name Ellen preferred, attended the exclusive St. Vincent's Catholic girls' private school at Potts Point, excelling in all subjects. However, home life wasn't as happy as it once was after her father returned from the war. Colin's legs were severely damaged when a shrapnel shell exploded forcing him to use crutches. Not only was Nellie's father physically injured, but he also returned addicted to morphia and suffering deep psychological scars. Nellie often woke in the middle of the night because of her father's terrifying screams.

Colin was no longer a happy loving father. Gone were the fairy tales at bedtime. His stories were about the war—the blood, the mangled bodies, and the agonised screams from his fellow soldiers.

One afternoon, Colin left on one of his walks and never returned.

Lillian became more and more melancholy, too depressed to face the world, she left young Ellen in the care of the housekeepers and remained in bed.

School and dance lessons were the saving grace for Nellie over the months that followed her father's abandonment. She also felt neglected by her mother. She understood that she was missing her husband and was hurt that he had left without a word, but she too was hurting. Her dad had also left her without saying goodbye.

If not for Martha, a close family friend, Nellie would have lost her mother, too.

Martha arrived one mid-morning with a crate of fresh off the boat hydrangeas and lilies. She helped Lillian out of bed and into the bathroom and prepared her clothes while she bathed. No-one could ever say no to Martha. After a morning tea of tea and scones, they headed to the hothouse.

The fresh air, conversation, and Martha's cheery smiles, laughter, and her ready ear, brought Lillian back to life. That afternoon when Nellie returned home from school, her mother rushed down the veranda stairs to greet her with a beaming smile like she had before her father left. It was a welcoming sight. At bedtime, Lillian like she had in the past, lay beside her precious daughter and played 'count the freckles' as she softly touched the spots on Nellie's face.

Colin Kelly's contact with Nellie was sporadic to say the least. She received the occasional Christmas and birthday card, but he never supported his daughter financially or emotionally. Her mother never asked him for financial assistance as she was wealthy in her own right. However, despite many personal and legal attempts requesting Kelly to visit his daughter, he remained aloof and distant.

In 1920, Lillian met Robert George Cameron, a culturally refined and well-educated gentleman during a brunch at a friend's home. Robert, a naturally shy and reserved fellow, finally summoned the courage to invite Lillian to a picnic in the park. Nellie was also welcome.

In 1921 Lillian discovered that Colin was living with a woman in Mascot and had fathered a son and a daughter to her. When Nellie was eleven years old, her mother was granted a divorce.

It wasn't love at first sight for Lillian and Robert, but there was an intense friendship between the two, and five months later, Robert proposed marriage. They set the wedding date for three months later. Initially, Nellie was ambivalent about having a stepfather. She had developed an inherent distrust of men. To her, father's broke promises and forgot their old children. Her father's new children were the ones listening to his songs and being read nice stories now, feeling safe and loved...

In January1922, Lillian and Robert were married in a beautiful ceremony with Nellie attending as a flower girl. The wedding was on the social calendar of Sydney's elite, with friends and family travelling from interstate and Great Britain to attend.

Not wanting to upset Nellie's life and uproot her from her family home, Robert decided to sell his house and move in with Lillian and Nellie.

Nellie and Robert developed a father and daughter relationship. He always playfully teased her about her gapped teeth, and like her father, complimented her on her ginger golden curls. Robert often read to her in the garden and at bedtime, attended her dance recitals and school performances and treated her like a princess.

Robert was the man both Nellie and Lillian needed in their lives. He was gentle and all about love, family, and protection. He was kind and led by example, a confident and steadfast role model, husband, and father figure.

Nellie and Lillian finally lived a full, harmonious life and thought nothing would ever ruin their happiness. Nellie loved her stepfather so much that she took on the Cameron surname.

Lillian's newfound happiness inspired her to start a small nursery business. Robert placed an advert in the local paper for labourers to help with the heavy lifting and delivery of orders. The men were given orders to remain away from the main house and not to approach the madam, her daughter, or their maids.

One afternoon in September 1925, Nellie's blissful life of security and happiness was shattered. She was walking through her mother's hothouse admiring the jonquils and freesias when she was suddenly grabbed by the throat and thrown to the ground. When she looked up, she saw the bloodshot eyes of Henry Baker, one of the labourers, staring down at her.

Nellie tried to escape his grip, but she was half the size of her attacker who easily pinned her down into the dirt. Baker clamped his dirty hand over her mouth threatening that if she screamed or struggled, he would kill her and then her parents.

Baker gripped Nellie's wrists together above her head with one hand as he removed her bloomers with the other. She had no idea what the man was doing and squeezed her eyes shut with embarrassment. Nellie struggled again to dislodge him and felt the hot sting of a slap across her face, before he clasped his hand around her throat, choking her. He waited until she was gasping for breath and removed his hands. "Next time I'll let you die!"

The frightened teenager closed her eyes as her molester fondled her breasts, squeezing them until they hurt. She trembled in fear as she felt the hardness of his groin rubbing against her leg. Nellie held her breath as the flesh on her knuckles tore as she pressed them into the stone covered earth. Then with one painful thrust, he forced himself inside her.

Nellie screamed out in pain as he pushed himself inside her again and again…When Baker was finished, Nellie couldn't look at him, she felt so dirty and ashamed. Every part of her body hurt, especially between her legs. Baker stood and tied up his pants before growling at her to get up.

"Here's a halfpenny," he said as he threw the coin at her. "That's all that fuck was worth! Next time you'd better be nicer to me or else! Tell your parents about this and I'll burn your house down with you and your parents inside."

Too terrified to say a word, Nellie watched as the labourer left and slowly raised herself to her feet. She felt a wetness running down her legs and when she looked down, she saw that she was bleeding. Horrified, she ran into the house and took refuge in her bedroom. Afraid her mother would find out about what had happened, Nellie removed her clothes and threw them into the fireplace. She stood in a daze in front of the fire, watching as her clothes burned as hot as the pain of the rape still throbbed within her loins.

The chiming of the grandfather clock striking four times in the hallway brought her to her senses. Robert would be home within the next half hour. She needed to make herself presentable and join him in their customary cup of tea before dinner.

Nellie headed for her bathroom and splashed water between her legs and gently washed her intimate parts before cleansing the blood and semen stains from her legs. Silent tears rolled down her cheeks as memories of her rape played through her mind. She closed her eyes as she tried to stave off the memories of the labourer's glaring eyes and sour whiskey breath as she dressed in freshly laundered and pressed clothing. After calling for her maid, Honour, Nellie sat on the chair at her dresser and waited for her hair to be braided. She tried so hard to pretend all was well. When she was presentable, Nellie went downstairs.

Her mother was reading a newspaper in the parlour. She gave her a kiss on the cheek and gently caught hold of her hand. "Where have you been?" She asked.

Nellie took a deep breath. "I was in the garden reading a book."

"Which book my darling?"

"*My Brilliant Career*. Mavis gave it to me at school. It's remarkably interesting Mama." Nellie said as she sat carefully on the chair, trying not to wince.

"I've not heard of that book. What's it about? Is it suitable for a young lady to be reading?"

Nellie told her that she enjoyed reading about Sybylla Melvyn, the heroine of the story. She explained how she felt sorry for her because she was a misunderstood girl, forced to live a life that wasn't her own. "I feel like Sybylla sometimes. I wish I were born a boy and jump into creeks and ride into bushland on a horse…"

"Why ever would you like to be a boy? You'll never find a fine young man to marry acting like such a ruffian." Her mother smiled as she picked up a plate of jam biscuits and offered one to her daughter. "I'm afraid it's a boring afternoon tea with me today. Your father is working late."

"I don't mind, Mama. I don't feel like a cup of tea. Would you excuse me so I can go to my room and read my book please?"

Long hours passed that night. Nellie couldn't sleep. She tossed and turned as she replayed what had occurred in the hothouse. She wanted to tell her mother but feared the threat Baker had made that they would all be killed.

Nellie got on with her life as best she could and maintained her silence about her rape. It was a shameful secret lodged in her heart and throat that was ready to choke her every time she contemplated revealing the awful occurrence. She stayed away from the hothouse and when her mother asked her for flowers for the nursery, she would ask one of the housemaids to accompany her. She was fearful of being alone.

At night, Nellie huddled under her bedclothes and wished she could die. She learned to sob soundlessly into her pillow as the painful memories of the labourer's savage face haunted her every moment. Through the day she coped as well as she could, taking herself into a parallel place in her head where the rape hadn't taken place.

She thought once the bruises on her thighs and arms faded, she would be healed, and the memories would vanish. But they didn't, and over time she began to lose her sense of self. Her trust in adults after the rape was shattered, and keeping her secret became almost as destructive as the assault itself.

Lillian noticed her daughter's strange behaviour and her loss of appetite and sudden lack of personal hygiene. One evening she asked her if she was all right. Nellie wanted to tell her what had happened, but whenever she attempted to talk about it, she remembered Baker's terrifying eyes and threats, so she smiled and told her mother that she was fine.

However, Nellie's parents and teachers could see that she was no longer a happy-go-lucky girl. At school, the sisters became concerned about her. She was easily distracted in class and her schoolwork was less than exemplary. One afternoon her teacher noticed that Nellie had not returned to class after lunch, so she sent two students to check the toilets and search the grounds. When the girls approached the main quadrangle, they saw her lying on the cobbled stones at the centre of the recreation area in the pouring rain.

The girls told their teacher who immediately rushed to the courtyard and ordered her back to the classroom before she caught pneumonia.

"Have you ever laid in the rain and counted the raindrops?" Nellie asked, almost as if in a daze.

"Certainly not, child. One of sound mind would never consider such a ludicrous task," Sister Bridget scolded. "Get up this instance. If I catch a cold from this, it will be the stick for you!"

That afternoon, Sister Bridget accompanied Nellie home in the family carriage. Her mother was taken aback when her daughter entered the parlour with the nun.

"I'm afraid this isn't a social call, Mrs. Cameron. I'm here in regard to the concerns myself and her teacher, Sister Monica, have about Ellen and her odd behaviour."

"Katie, bring in tea and scones please," Lillian directed her maid. "I'm sorry, Sister Bridget, I don't understand. What's happened, Ellen?" Lillian asked, directing her attention toward her daughter.

"I find school boring, Mama. I'd rather be outside or stay at home than sitting in a classroom all day listening to boring mathematics and Bible studies."

Lillian and Sister Bridget almost choked on their scones at her reply. "Ellen! You must apologise immediately to Sister Bridget! I'm dismayed by your impudence and rudeness!"

"Why Mama? Doesn't John 1:4 state that 'I have no greater joy than to hear that my children are walking in the truth' and Psalm 34:13 also tells us to keep our tongue from evil and our lips from telling lies? I'm telling the truth and now I must apologise for it?"

"Dear child, in Matthew 12:34 it preaches that it is as easy to put the tongue to a good purpose as to an evil one. Misuse of the tongue is a sign that one's heart is not in the right place. As our Lord Jesus warned us, 'out of the abundance of the heart the mouth speaks'. Which means you must speak with love and respect at all times."

"Respectfully, Sister Bridget, I would much rather speak the truth than falsehoods. I don't enjoy school anymore and I would prefer to remain at home with my mother."

Embarrassed, Lillian looked at her daughter as if she didn't know who she was. She had never spoken to anyone with such disrespect and had never blasphemed before.

"Ellen, you will stop this disrespect immediately. I don't understand what's got into you. Your behaviour will not be borne by Sister Bridget or me. Go to your bedroom!"

"But Mama, I haven't done anything wrong, save be truthful."

"Ellen, you were found by Sister Pamela lying in the middle of the courtyard in the rain, uttering nonsense about counting the raindrops. Your schoolwork is not up to the standard of your past work, and you are easily distracted in class. This is not the behaviour we expect from you or any of our girls at St. Vincent's Catholic school. You were one of our best students, and now you're heading toward being one of the most ill-mannered and disappointing pupils in the school's history!" Sister Bridget reprimanded.

Ellen ran from the house.

Her mother stood to go after her, but Sister Bridget asked her to sit down so they could speak about Ellen's future at school.

Nellie bolted through the main gates and kept running until she was in the midst of bushland. When she finally stopped, she sat atop a sawn-off tree trunk, crying as she wondered what she could do. Her mother had never been so cross with her before. She knew Sister Bridget would more than likely suspend or expel her. She was so confused. She loved school, but she could no longer concentrate on the lessons.

She walked aimlessly through the mud, wanting to return home but not wanting to become embroiled in another argument with her mother and Sister Bridget. The sound of crackling branches stopped her in her tracks. Nellie turned and looked in the direction the noise was coming from, waiting for her mother or father to make their way through the trees. However, it wasn't the faces of her concerned parents that she saw, but of Henry and he was with two other men.

Terrified, Nellie lifted her skirts and ran in an attempt to escape. A few hundred yards down the track she found a spot to hide and lay in the bushes hoping the men would stop looking for her and leave. The frightened girl lay as still as she could, too afraid to breathe lest they heard her as they walked past.

There was a sudden, deathly quiet. Nellie strained to listen for footfalls, and after several minutes of stillness, she left her refuge and started running towards home.

And just as home came into sight, a hand grasped her shoulder. For a moment, Nellie was paralysed. Her heart leapt into her throat as she helplessly watched as Baker and the other man approached.

Baker slapped her across the face with such force that it knocked her hard against the man who had caught her. Tears welled in her eyes and her cheek burned as blood filled her mouth. He then placed his hand underneath her skirt, before grabbing hold of her legs and dragged her down into the mud on the ground. She started screaming, hoping someone, anyone, would hear.

But no one came.

Nellie twisted her body around in another attempt to escape, but a sudden blow across the side of her head caused her to let out a heart-wrenching cry. Baker growled at her to shut up, and Nellie was hit by another blow which almost knocked her unconscious. Her limp body fell to the ground as Baker began to pull down his trousers while the other man held her down to the ground. She screamed for help and scratched as she fought to protect herself as Baker attempted to remove her pantaloons. The third man knelt beside her and ripped open the buttons of her blouse, revealing her cotton and lace camisole. Henry forced himself inside her as the other two men held her down. Nellie screamed as his weight and movement rubbed her body against the rocks and twigs in the mud, turning her skin bloody and raw. His invasion of her once again tore at her insides as she screamed and struggled against the men.

"Shut the bitch up O'Reilly!" Henry yelled.

O'Reilly, a recently released convict, punched Nellie to the side of her face. She shook her head to try and stop the dizziness before attempting to kick Baker in the groin. She watched in fear as he pulled his arm back before delivering another crushing punch across her face, knocking her unconscious.

When Nellie regained consciousness, she was disoriented. Her mind was in such a fog she barely remembered how she came to be in the bush. Seconds later, memories flooded back. Her body hurt as she tried to sit up and when she did, she saw that her clothes were covered in blood and her breasts were bare and covered in bite marks.

A noise caught her attention and she squinted through the darkness until she saw the three bastards that raped her.

"We're finished with you for now so don't worry your pretty little head. We'll visit you again soon and bring more friends to be pleasured by our little princess. Pity you slept through the fun. I'll make sure you are wide awake next time," Baker smirked. "Newham, give her the money."

A bald fat man laughed as he threw three shillings in the mud beside her. Baker threw another two shillings. "You breathe a word of this, and I will come to you in the black of night and cut your parents' throats while you watch." He laughed.

Too afraid to move, Nellie remained in the mud and cold for a few minutes before painfully dragging herself to her feet. She didn't know what time it was, but she knew it was late. Clouds covered the stars and the wind bit against her bare skin as she stumbled in the direction of her home. When the mansion came into view, there were no lights on, but a lamp was burning in the front parlour and she saw the silhouette of her father standing at the window. She crept through the side gate and climbed the ivy-covered trellis up to her bedroom window.

Once in her bedroom, Nellie gingerly cleaned herself with the jug of water and once again threw her filthy clothes into the fireplace. Quietly, she rummaged through her drawers and wardrobe filling her carpet bag and school satchel with as many clothes as possible.

Tears pooled in her eyes knowing that she had to go somewhere—anywhere. She could never return home. Nellie couldn't endure another rape and knew if she remained in Waterloo, she would never be safe. Nor would her parents, not after Baker's threats.

She wiped her tearstained cheeks as she quietly crept across the hall and entered Robert's private den. Walking close to the wall, bypassing the creaking floorboards in the centre of the room until she reached his large oak desk. Slowly, she opened the right-hand drawer and reached toward the back, retrieving a tin box. She opened the lid and removed several pound notes before closing it and returning it to its hiding place.

When she passed her parents' bedroom, she almost burst out crying, knowing her mother would be heartbroken when she realised that her daughter was gone forever. She then left by the servants' door hoping that her stepfather would not hear the closing of the door.

And thus, passed Nellie's childhood. Her heart went into hiding. The rapists had severed fifteen years of innocence. Nellie was oblivious to where she was going and what lay ahead, but when the first train arrived at Waterloo station, she paid the conductor and left the carriage when the train stopped at Surry Hills station.

Nellie spent the day walking the streets or sitting in cafés drinking coffee and eating sandwiches. She had no idea what she was going to do. She asked several waitresses if there was work available but was told with the depression, jobs were difficult to find.

That night, she went in search of a boarding house. She walked down narrow lanes as she splashed through puddles, passed dumpsters and piles of rubbish. This was a world she had never seen before. It seemed for a moment that the unlit streets might completely consume her, but she soon passed through the periphery of darkness and was walking through a main street brightened by lamplight.

She finally came across a boarding house along Windsor Crescent where she booked a room for a week and paid for it in advance. The landlady showed her to her room and lit the lamp. When she left, Nellie retrieved a nightie from her satchel. Undressed, she was able to see the injuries she had sustained during the rape. She gently ran her fingers across the finger mark bruises on her thighs. Her body still ached all over. Her breasts were bruised, and her buttocks and the back of her legs were covered in bruises and scratches from the rocks and twigs.

Laying back on the bed, she sighed with relief. She was safe from Baker. Never again would he or his friends attack her. She would look for a job in the city and make a new life for herself and never return to Waterloo, or to school.

Nellie checked the money she had taken from her stepfather's tin. She had just over thirty pounds. It was enough money for her to survive on for a few months. But in her desire to gain her independence, Nellie's bourgeois upbringing was her undoing. She splurged on her newfound freedom, spending almost a quarter of her money on restaurant food and on clothing and shoes.

With her money depleting, Nellie knew she'd need to find work soon to keep a roof over her head. She heard that the Sargent's Pie Factory in Darlinghurst was recruiting staff and applied for a position. However, when she walked around the corner into Oxford Street, she saw a sign for Professor Bolot's Dance Academy. Excited to have come across the studio, Nellie rushed inside and spoke with the owner, Crimean migrant John Bolotinski.

John was impressed with Nellie's dancing technique and poise, and after joining her for several dances on the dance floor, he hired her to start teaching classes the very next day. The teenager was so overjoyed with finding employment that she danced almost all the way back to the boarding house.

Over the following weeks Nellie enjoyed working at the studio with her flamboyant, eccentric boss. Of an evening when the last class finished, they would sit in his office and drink cocktails. However, the work was only part-time, and Nellie needed to make more money to keep up with her spending. On her days off from the academy, she continued seeking employment, finally finding another part-time job selling fruit from a barrow in Darlinghurst.

One morning whilst eating breakfast at a café, Nellie noticed a man seated at the table to her left was smiling at her. She shifted uncomfortably in her seat and looked out the window to show her disinterest. Without invitation, he picked up his plate and cutlery and sat down at her table opposite her.

"Excuse me miss, do you remember me?" the stranger asked.

"You seem familiar, but I don't know where from," Nellie replied in her quiet and well-educated voice. "I prefer to eat alone if you don't mind."

"I'm the tram driver that picked you up in Surry Hills." He smiled as he ignored her brush off.

"Oh, I wouldn't have cause to remember you. I was too excited about coming to the city to take notice of the people around me."

After settling into a comfortable conversation, Nellie no longer feared the man. He was very gentlemanly and easy to converse with and she wondered if he could be the key to her future.

Nellie smiled and told him she was pleased to meet up with him again. She had learned the hard way what men wanted, and right there and then in the café, she decided that sex being such a strong inducement in making a man happy, she would use it to her advantage. She would not let the rapes destroy her. The teenager decided to take ownership over her body and move beyond her sexual assaults.

Nellie didn't know how to have sex properly, but she was sure that her new friend would teach her. After almost an hour of chatting and accepting his generous offer to pay for her breakfast and several cups of coffee, Nellie invited him back to her room at the boarding house.

That afternoon and throughout the night, William made love to Nellie. He was as gentle as she thought he would be. At first, she cringed when his hands touched her skin, and became nauseated when they explored her intimate recesses. However, ignoring the soreness she still felt from the rape, she relaxed knowing that her body could become a weapon used to disarm men and get what she wanted out of life.

Two weeks into their relationship, William revealed that he was married. He told Nellie that he no longer loved his wife but still had strong feelings for her. Nellie didn't care that he was married. To her the tram driver was a mere steppingstone to her future. So, when he asked her to move into a terrace house in Woolloomooloo with him after he had left his wife and children, Nellie jumped at the offer.

Within a month of living together, Nellie became sick every morning. She realised that she had not had her period for at least two months. Aghast, she realised she could be pregnant to one of the rapists and definitely didn't want the baby. She visited Elsie, the owner of the boarding house and revealed her plight. Feeling sorry for her, she gave Nellie an address of a woman who could help.

The landlady had Edward, her lover, drive Nellie to the Randwick address and told him to bring her straight back when it was over. When Edith Ashton, the well-known abortionist, opened the door, Nellie became frightened and ran back to the car. There, Edward consoled her and told her he would be waiting for her until it was done. She returned to the house and knocked on the door, before following Ashton's assistant, Nancy, to a room at the back of the house.

An hour later, Nancy and Edward assisted a very groggy Nellie out to the car. Back at the boarding house, Elsie made Nellie a cup of tea and tucked her in bed for a sleep. She then sent Edward to Nellie's house to tell William that she was spending the night with her.

Nellie and William's relationship lasted almost four months. William's finances were squandered from paying his wife money, and they were living almost entirely on Nellie's wages from the dance academy and fruit barrow. She wanted more out of life than what he could offer. Nellie was accustomed to the absolute best in life and found it difficult living hand-to-mouth. Her habit of seldom bathing was also loathsome to William and they fought incessantly about her poor hygiene. He couldn't understand how she could have any pride in herself when she smelled so bad, and often told her that not even strong perfume could hide her personal odour. He couldn't stand her dirtiness anymore, nor her incessant complaints about taking care of his wife and children. Nellie arrived home late one night, and William had packed up and returned home to his family with his tail between his legs.

The lack of bathing was but one of Nellie's unconventional habits. She had started smoking and drinking at pubs until late. However, John was prepared to overlook her lack of hygiene, but the dancer wasn't impressed with her tardiness at arriving at work each morning or arriving in the same clothes she had worn the day before. After giving her several chances to get to work on time and dress neatly, John lost his temper one afternoon when she arrived four hours late and dishevelled, firing her on the spot.

Over the following weeks, Nellie's life was on a downward spiral. She was broke, homeless, and staying in a woman's refuge in Redfern. One morning, she fled the refuge after a violent fight had broken out between two women.

Nellie walked the streets hoping to find shelter at another refuge. She was sitting on a park bench when one of the streetwalkers approached her and told her that she needed to be careful as the park was a dangerous place for a young girl. They struck up a conversation and by the evening, Nellie was walking William Street opposite Polly. A well-dressed gentleman walked by and Nellie approached him: "Well, don't you smell nice, sir. Would you like to spend three shillings for a lovely time with me?" She asked with a captivating smile.

CHAPTER NINE

The Angel of Death

Whilst drinking at the Tradesman's Arms hotel in March 1927, Nellie met Norman Bruhn. Long gone was the innocent and naïve Ellen Cameron. In her place was a hardened young woman who had a penchant for bad men… the badder the better. And there were not many gangsters as bad as Bruhn. The violent gangster was totally smitten by the teenager. He set her up in a flat and within weeks had talked her into working as a prostitute in Tilly Devine's Palmer Street brothel.

It had been some time since Nellie had sold herself for sex. She had only worked William Street with Polly for just over a month when she met a man named Stewart who had taken her in. But when he started to talk about marriage, Nellie lost interest and soon found another man to get her claws into. That's how Nellie lived before meeting Bruhn.

When Nellie walked into the brothel looking for work, Tilly saw pound signs in her eyes. She knew the attractive freckled, petite redhead would be popular amongst her clients.

It was not long before Nellie became Sydney's most popular working girl. Men lined up to see the vivacious redhead and at three pounds per client, she was the most expensive prostitute in the state.

Tilly enjoyed the company of the educated, well-spoken, and bubbly young woman. She was a pleasant change to the dowdy and brusque women who had become emotionally detached after working as street prostitutes for so long.

Nellie, with her flame red hair, ripe figure, and provocative china-blue eyes, attracted men of the social class in which she was raised, bringing in a greater income than all the women working in her brothels. Tilly nurtured the young woman, who she lovingly nicknamed, Kanga Ruby, even sending her to Ireland for a month's holiday to recover from a miscarriage when she was pregnant to Bruhn.

Nellie often took a couple of weeks off working in Tilly's brothel to travel to Queensland with Bruhn when he trafficked cocaine to dealers in Brisbane. Whilst in the northern state, she made good money working in different towns as a prostitute.

It was in Queensland Nellie learned the art of gingering. Whilst performing her sexual deeds, a local unemployed or homeless man Bruhn had hired would sneak out from under the bed and steal the client's wallet from his pants or jacket pocket. Bruhn would wait until Nellie spoke the words, "Oh my, what a big boy you are," and hammer on the door with his fists.

Nellie would then put on an award-winning act and spring from the bed in feigned panic, claiming that either the police or her husband was at the door. She would then quickly start dressing, urging her client to do the same, before sneaking him out the back door.

One time when she returned from Queensland, Aggie, another prostitute who usually worked the streets in Kings Cross had taken ownership of William and Palmer Streets and was extorting rent from the girls. Nellie often worked the streets part-time and didn't take this effrontery lying down. She, and the heavyset Polynesian, 'Black Aggie', took to battle. The women stripped to the waist whilst hundreds of people eagerly watched on. Bookies from the nearby pub rushed to the backyard fight and fervently began taking bets on which woman would win the fight.

Nellie concentrated her blows on Aggie's stomach, and within minutes sent her sprawling to the cobblestones with a surprise uppercut. She stood above her opponent, staring down at her bloodied and bruised face. "Those two street blocks belong to anyone who wants to work them and you're no longer fuckin' welcome!" Nellie then picked up a handful of dirt and threw it at Aggie's face before kicking her in her side.

Defeated, humiliated, and battered, Aggie accepted the help of several women as they raised her to her feet. One of the women helped her put on her blouse and drove her to the hospital.

The disappointed crowd that was baying for blood at the beginning of the fight began to walk away, except those who'd backed Nellie—they crowded the bookmakers, waiting for their winnings.

Aggie left town the following week.

7

Nellie's affair with Bruhn was one of crime and passion. She knew he would never leave his family. Her nights were lonely with Bruhn spending more time either at home with his wife and kids or with his gang and Nellie's eye began to stray.

In May 1927, she met Frank Green, a violent gangster addicted to cocaine. Green, was known as both 'the little gunman' and 'Scarface' due to an unsightly L-shaped scar on down his right cheek to his mouth from a razor attack. He worked as a hired gun for Tilly Devine, protecting both her and her brothels. Taking an immediate liking to Nellie, Green paid her five pounds to have sex with him. Over the following months, Bruhn became jealous of the amount of money and gifts Green was showering on his lover and forbade her from seeing him again, threatening Green's life.

Even though his life was under threat, Green continued to see Nellie in out-of-the-way motels. He often picked her up at a railway station and they'd spend the day or night together whenever Bruhn was busy.

On the 22nd of June, Bruhn was killed after being shot several times in a Darlinghurst lane. The police, knowing about their troubled relationship, questioned Green over his involvement in the shooting, but he had an alibi. The police then questioned both Nellie and Bruhn's wife, Irene, and both women denied any knowledge of his killer.

Nellie had also fallen under the watchful eye of Australia's second policewoman, Lillian Armfield, a policewoman. She, along with welfare workers, attempted to reform the young woman, pleading with her to leave the criminal life and return home to her worried parents. Nellie, however, enjoyed her life with the gangsters and remained loyal to them and their values.

In late 1928, she became involved with Guido Calletti. A Sicilian born standover man who was often hired to stand over other standover men. Short, thickset, foul-mouthed, and illiterate, Calletti made up for his stature with his penchant for violence. He'd led the life of a criminal since he was nine years old committing countless assaults and robberies. He was so unruly that the courts labelled him an uncontrollable child.

Calletti was also the leader of a violent street gang known as the Darlinghurst Push. He was an immaculately dressed and arrogant man, and everyone knew not to take his threats lightly. He was also an expert shot and exceptionally quick with a knife and straight razor. Adept with these tools of violence, Calletti preferred to use his bare hands and took every opportunity to do so.

One night after a night of drinking at the Tradesman's Arms hotel, Frank Green became a little too friendly with Nellie. He was still in love with her and tried several times to steal her away from Calletti. But that night, Guido had had enough and punched Green in the mouth. The ensuing fight tumbled out into the street and lasted forty minutes. Their clothes tattered, and face and fists bloodied, the exhausted men shook the other's hand, ending the fight without a victor, but with their honours intact. However, the rivalry between the men continued.

In early1929, Nellie and Calletti moved into a terrace house in Darlinghurst where they set up a nice home with money made from their criminal activities. Nellie filled her new wardrobe with the latest fashions, lingerie, and shoes. Due to her relationship with Tilly, she had also developed a fondness for hats.

Nellie had befriended a new girl at Tilly's brothel, Dulcie Markham. The women became close, which was surprising because Calletti was sleeping with both women at the same time. As their friendship grew, Nellie, so enraptured by her friend's hair colour, dyed her hair the same shade of blonde.

Nellie and Dulcie made an impact on prostitution in Darlinghurst. They were the preferred prostitutes in Tilly's brothels, which at times caused catfights in front of stunned clientèle. Tilly, not wanting to lose clients or girls, scheduled Dulcie, and Nellie to work separate hours, and those hours were in her usual downtime. A smart business move—she almost doubled her income.

Nellie also attracted the attention of young naïve pastry cook, Ernest Connolly who worked at the Newtown Bakery. She playfully flirted with the lad who was very keen on her. Nellie, however, considered him nothing more than a mere plaything.

While returning home from the Darlinghurst pub on the 17th of February, Calletti believed that Connolly was walking too close to his girl and an argument ensued. The group began swearing and shouting at one another, causing several homes in Womerah Avenue to become ablaze with light as their inhabitants wondered what the commotion was at two thirty in the morning.

Calletti and Connolly were face-to-face in a heated argument. Spittle flew from Calletti's mouth as he screamed at Connolly as he pushed his fist into his chest. Connolly shoved Calletti away, causing him to stumble to the ground. When the irate Sicilian rose to his feet, he pulled out his revolver and shot Connolly in the stomach.

The group ran off as soon as the shot rang out. Two men remained behind and helped Connolly down the street. John Humphries, a local resident, woken by the gunshots, leapt to his bedroom window, and watched several men ran past his home. He then observed two men helping a wounded man along the roadside. He quickly changed out of his pyjamas before jumping into his car and drove down to offer aid to the men.

As Humphries was checking Connolly for a pulse, he was surprised to see six other men standing along the fence. Two of the men placed Connolly into the front seat and told John to drive them to the hospital. When he stopped at the St. Margaret's hospital entrance, the men jumped out of his car, leaving him alone with Connolly.

A doctor rushed to Connolly's aid. He was losing a lot of blood and was in a serious condition. One of the nurses rushed to the admittance desk and called the police, hoping that they would arrive before he died. While the doctors worked on Connolly, a police constable took his dying depositions. He told the police that he was shot by Guido Calletti.

The following morning, twenty-year-old Calletti was charged with maliciously shooting Ernest Lyall Connolly with the intent to murder him. He was also charged with being in the possession of an unlicensed weapon.

At his hearing, the police prosecutor advised the judge that Connolly had made considerable progress with his health since the shooting but was still in the hospital. The judge remanded Calletti on bail of five hundred pounds which he was unable to pay. He was then remanded in custody until the 6th of March.

Without any witnesses to the Connolly's shooting, Calletti was acquitted at his subsequent trial. He returned home and straight to Nellie's bed.

The following month, after a day of snorting cocaine and drinking beer, Calletti left to carry out his usual con. Using his normal banter while befriending a mark at Sharland's Strand pub, he invited John

Forster, a visiting grazier from the bush, to join him to search for feminine enjoyment elsewhere.

In a darkened laneway just off William Street, Calletti, walked behind his companion as they chatted about farm life. He waited until they were far enough away from the pub and then king-hit the unsuspecting man. However, unlike his previous robbery victims, Forster steadfastly stood up to his quarry.

Calletti had taken on the wrong man. The grazier was a skilled bare-knuckle boxer who battered Calletti with his left, his right and then knocked him to the ground with an uppercut. Each time Calletti fell to the ground, John would drag him back up to his feet again, before converging on him with another series of blows. Forster then dragged the unconscious Calletti down the street and into the Darlinghurst police station.

Forster waited patiently at the police station until Calletti regained consciousness and his wounds were treated. He laughed and joked with the arresting officers over how the notorious criminal had fared so badly in the fight. Once Guido was cleansed and bandaged, he was escorted by two police officers to attend his committal hearing for assault with intent to rob and released on ten pounds bail.

The grazier's friends warned him not to go ahead with testifying against Calletti, but the farmer remained resolute. He told his concerned friends that he intended to see the court case through to make sure the ruffian got what he deserved.

At the subsequent trial in late April, Forster was a solid witness. Calletti was sentenced by Judge Curlewis to Long Bay gaol for two years hard labour, which Guido immediately appealed. However, after attempting to pervert the course of justice with a dishonest alibi, the Chief Justice dismissed the appeal and Calletti was sent to gaol.

Lonely and without a man, Nellie took up again with Frank Green and severed all association with Tilly Devine. Green, an alcoholic and cocaine addict, was hot-tempered with a short fuse. Green told Nellie that it was him or the Devines' after they had fallen out after a shooting that he was involved in at the Strand pub.

Almost out of their heads on cocaine on the 16th of June 1931, Green and one of his associates, William Hourigan, planned to rob the Devine's Maroubra home. Nellie told the men that Tilly always attended the hairdressers on Tuesdays and returned home around one o'clock in the afternoon. She also revealed that Jim usually attended one of the gambling dens until late into Tuesday night.

After catching a cab to the Maroubra house and asking the driver to wait, the trio entered through the back door. Nellie noticed a diamond tiepin on a hall table next to a pistol and some coins. She pointed them out to Green who then put them in his pockets. Hourigan started sifting through the drawers of an Edwardian cabinet in the living room while Nellie made her way to the larder where she knew there was a tin that Tilly hid money in.

The trio were somewhat surprised when Jim thundered into the living room naked and brandishing a pistol minutes later. One of Tilly's prostitutes followed closely behind, quickly returning to the bedroom when she realised what was happening. A confrontation ensued with obscenities being hurled by all in the room. Jim aimed his pistol at Green and the pilferers fled from the house. Devine chased them outside and let off a hail of bullets, accidentally killing the waiting taxi driver.

Consequently, on the 11th of July 1931, Nellie, Green and Hourigan were charged with robbery under arms. They were also accused of assaulting Jim Devine whilst armed with a revolver and robbing him of a diamond tiepin valued at fifty pounds. Unfortunately, due to the police not having enough evidence against Nellie and Hourigan, their charges were dismissed.

Green and Nellie then went through a bit of a rough patch in their relationship. Green was angry because his solicitor said he would do time for the Devine robbery and was high on cocaine almost every day of the week. Cocaine made him more violent than usual, so when he returned home early on the night of the 26th of October and found Nellie on the couch kissing Charles Brame, a local musician, he pulled out his razor and lunged toward the man. In self-defence, Brame pulled a pistol out of his pocket and shot Green in the stomach. Green slumped to the floor bleeding. Nellie jumped to her feet and rushed to his side and covered the gunshot wound with her hand in an attempt to stop the bleeding.

"What the hell have you done! He wouldn't have done anything to you!" Nellie exclaimed in shock. "We have to get him to the hospital!"

"Bullshit! I know what that bastard's like. He would've cut my fucking throat! We can't take him to the hospital, we'll be seen."

Blood was pooling on the floor as Green lay dying. "Don't let me die, Nellie," he gasped.

Brame raced to the bathroom and returned with a towel. His hands were shaking violently as he handed it to Nellie. "I'll bring the car closer and we'll leave him at the hospital entrance."

"Just hurry. He's dying!" She screamed.

Nellie soothed Green as best as she could, promising her lover that she wouldn't let him die as she held the towel tightly against his wound.

Brame returned and carried Green to the car. Nellie jumped in the back and cradled Green's head in her lap as they sped to the hospital. When they arrived at St. Vincent's hospital, Brame waited until no-one was around before leaving Green inside the hospital entrance. Nellie placed Green's hands on the towel and kissed him before she and Brame fled the scene.

Green was rushed into surgery. A bullet had passed through his stomach and was lodged at the base of his spine. After a lengthy operation, the surgeon successfully removed the bullet.

7

Brame drove Nellie back to the flat and took off as soon as she left the car. She was still trembling in fear, anxious that the police would turn up at her flat and immediately began cleaning the blood from the floor.

A few hours later the police knocked on Nellie's door. They told her that Frank Green had survived his injuries and was in a critical condition. Nellie put on an act of absolute surprise, falling to the couch upon hearing of his shooting.

Despite her melodramatic histrionics, the police constable asked Nellie if she knew who had shot Green and for what reason. She denied knowing anything and told the constables that she had first heard about it when they knocked on her door.

The investigation was at a standstill until Green was coherent enough to speak with police. The senior detective on the case asked him if he knew who had shot him, and Green immediately replied, "That bastard Charlie Brame."

On the 10th of November 1931, the police arrested and charged Charles George Brame with intent to murder Frank Green and having carried an unlicensed pistol. His solicitor applied for bail citing that his client acted in self-defence upon seeing Green rushing towards him with a razor held in the air. He added that Brame was not part of the underworld and was only carrying the revolver because he had been shot earlier that year. His solicitor said that Brame had made a full confession to the chief of detectives and that he came from a respectable family.

The charges were later dropped against Brame when Green refused to assist the police.

Nellie spent the day with Frank at the hospital on the 16th of November. During the visit, Green asked her if she had been seeing Brame. Nellie told him she hadn't, vowing that she had remained faithful.

Later that night while she was walking home with her friends, Billy Ralph and Ivy Rasmussen, Nellie spotted Jim Devine driving past them. The vehicle suddenly stopped, and Devine jumped out and approached the trio. Nellie stood frozen to the spot, too afraid to move.

"You fuckin' thieving bitch!" Devine roared. He pulled his pistol out and shot Nellie in the shoulder, thigh, and abdomen, and then turned and raced to his car before speeding off. Her friends flagged down a passing motorist who rushed her to hospital. After regaining consciousness, she was able to be questioned by the police, Nellie, a woman who would never break the criminal code, refused to name her attacker. A week later after receiving a series of threats, Nellie signed herself out of the hospital and returned to her flat.

Nellie was unable to control her addiction for tough gangsters and engaged in several short-term affairs with underworld figures while Green remained in hospital. However, her promiscuous bed hopping ended abruptly when she learned that Calletti had been released from prison. She patiently awaited Calletti's arrival. After he had not shown up within two days of his release, she went looking for him. While at the Tradesman's Arms hotel, she was told by one of the gang members that Calletti had moved in with Dulcie Markham.

Seething, Nellie immediately visited Green in the hospital. Playing the role of the dutiful partner, she told him that they should open a sly grog shop and compete against Devine and Leigh. Green agreed and told her that he would get the money together when he was released from the hospital. Nellie didn't want to wait that long. She worked longer hours on the streets to make as much money as she could before Green's release.

Two weeks later, Green was discharged from hospital and returned to his standover way extorting money from racketeers, gambling houses and brothels. While he was out and about plying his trade, he kept an eye out for a suitable property in Surry Hills to operate the groggery.

Nellie had thought her illegal activities had gone unnoticed by the police after not being arrested or cautioned in months. Unfortunately, her run of luck came to an end when on the 12th of March 1932 at the age of twenty-one, she had the distinction of becoming the first woman to be charged with habitually consorting with reputed criminals. Her partner, Frank Green was mentioned as one of the criminals in the charges. She was sentenced to two months gaol at Long Bay women's prison.

As she alighted the prison tram, Nellie caught sight of her old rival, Black Aggie. She was a little leaner, and certainly older and more scarred than the last time she'd seen her.

Aggie and her fellow prisoners watched as the new inmates entered the main area of the prison. Her look of disinterest turned to anger upon recognising her nemesis.

Indignation, hatred, and bloodlust raged within as she glared at the woman who had humiliated and dishonoured her a couple of years before. Her brown eyes narrowed as she stared at Nellie and ran her finger across her neck in a throat cutting gesture. Nellie just smiled and winked toward her adversary, showing her no fear, yet knowing that another battle between them was brewing.

Four days later, Aggie made a pistol gesture toward Nellie in the recreation yard during a work break. Nellie wove her fingers together and flexed them outward… letting her adversary know that she was ready whenever she was.

"Just you fuckin' wait, you bitch. I'll get you when you least fuckin' expect it." Aggie threatened.

"I'd hear you a mile away, you fat old trollop." She had beaten Black Aggie before, and she was determined to do so again.

Nellie remained in the centre of the courtyard, cautiously waiting for Aggie to make her move. The women around them, knowing a fight was about to start, took a few steps back, not wanting to be placed in isolation for being a part of the affray. Nellie held herself with easy confidence, assured in the superiority of her fighting skills and patiently waited for Aggie to make the first move. The autumn sun beat down, and Nellie wiped the sweat from her forehead with her hand. A dormitory door slammed, momentarily breaking the tension-filled silence.

Aggie seized upon those few seconds of distraction and lunged toward Nellie with a sharpened stick. Nellie jumped out of the way, but Aggie turned around and lunged for her again. Nellie instinctively reached for the weapon in her rival's hand, but Aggie was too quick, and deftly slashed Nellie across her forearm. Bleeding from her wound, Nellie ran at Aggie, dodging as she lunged at her again with the stick.

Aggie suddenly lost her footing and fell to the ground, dropping the weapon in the process.

Nellie jumped on top of Aggie, straddling her as one of the other prisoners kicked the weapon out of reach of the fighting duo. Nellie brought both her elbows down on Aggie's chest, winding her for a few moments. However, Aggie was determined not to lose this fight and grabbed Nellie by the hair, before rolling over and slamming her head into the dirt. She then jumped up and kicked Nellie in the stomach. Nellie was strong and had a high resistance to pain. She never uttered a word. But when Aggie's foot came in for the second kick, she grabbed hold of Aggie's ankle, twisting it, unbalancing her enemy, and toppling her to the ground.

The women wrestled each other for a few moments before Aggie caught a moment and jumped to her feet, quickly followed by Nellie. The two started circling, each waiting for the other to make the next move.

The prison officers stood along the perimeter wall, each eagerly waiting to see who would win in the hope of winning a quick bet. The other prisoners were in a frenzy, screaming at both opponents to kill the other.

Nellie went in for the take-down. Body slamming Aggie, she knocked her to the ground. Quickly recovering, Aggie punched Nellie's cheek. As she swallowed the blood filling her mouth, Nellie grabbed hold of Aggie's arm, twisting it up her back and slamming her against a bystander.

One of the women threw Nellie a length of wood that she had broken off a nearby bench. In an uncontrollable rage, Nellie turned and smashed the plank along the back of Aggie's legs, felling her to the ground. Aggie let out an agonised scream and tried to roll over when she saw Nellie approaching but was not fast enough. Nellie brought her timber weapon down hard across her legs, and raised it again, bringing it down a third time. The sickening crunching sound and the agonised guttural scream emanating from Aggie's throat was enough for three guards to rush in, one to hold Nellie back and two to tend Aggie.

"Run and get the fuckin' nurse. Now!" A guard yelled out.

The nurse ran to the injured prisoner and told two trustee prisoners to bring the stretcher immediately. Two male guards carried Aggie to the infirmary while Nellie was taken to the bathrooms to clean herself up. Nellie and Aggie were told by the guards to keep their mouths shut or they would spend three months in isolation. They knew only too well what two weeks confinement in the 'hole' did to a woman… three months would have them sent to Callan Park Mental Hospital.

7

When he was discharged from hospital, Green was charged for habitually consorting with criminals, which included residing with Nellie Cameron. On the 23rd of May, he first entered a plea of not guilty against the charges, but later changed the plea to guilty. He then undertook an agreement with Mr. Shepherd SM to leave the State for two years upon paying a twenty pounds good behaviour bond.

Before leaving for Queensland, Green visited Nellie in prison and told her that he would make as much money as he could so they could start a new life up north. Nellie told him that a new start in another state was just the tonic she needed.

The month before she was due to be released, Nellie attended court on an accusation of gingering one of her regular clients, Frank Ward. She appeared before a judge known to be a hard-arsed dispenser of justice. Nellie pleaded not guilty. Her solicitor warned her about Curlewis' reputation and told her to be prepared for a long gaol sentence.

On the stand, Ward claimed that he was drinking in the Courthouse Hotel on Oxford Street and Cameron walked over and sat down beside him. He said at around nine o'clock, Cameron invited him to join her at her nearby flat and he agreed. Upon leaving the flat after midnight, Ward said that he hailed a taxi to take him home and when he reached into his vest pocket to pay the driver, he noticed his wad of pound notes was missing.

"I had only been with Nellie Cameron that night and the fifteen pounds was in my pocket when I paid for my drinks before her arrival and gone when I left her flat," he testified.

Curlewis looked toward Nellie who was sitting beside her solicitor, wearing prison garb. He studied her for a few moments. Nellie took the opportunity to put on her most innocent and frightened face when she looked up at the judge.

"Please take the stand, Miss Cameron," Curlewis directed.

When the prosecutor asked if she had stolen the money, Nellie replied: "I'd like to know how in heaven's name I could have stolen anything from Mr Ward." She stopped speaking and looked toward

Frank Ward, smiling as she continued, "We were entangled on the bed the entire time, so how could I have stolen his money without him seeing me?"

Curlewis was reeled in hook line and sinker by Nellie's prize-winning façade of innocence. Before sending the jury out to decide her fate he advised them to take their time and think well before reaching a verdict: "It's quite easy for men like Mr. Ward to make these sort of charges, and sometimes it's convenient to make an accusation against this class of woman. You know that not all married men are saints, but most of them, when a thing like this happens, have got the sense to keep it to themselves, but Ward publishes it."

Nineteen minutes later, the panel returned, and the foreman advised that they had found Miss Cameron not guilty. Nellie smiled toward the jury and thanked them. However, she saved her most salacious smile for the judge as the prison guards escorted her from the court.

Before Nellie and Green were able to leave New South Wales, Nellie was arrested and bailed for stealing. However, she absconded from bail and headed to Newcastle by train with Green, a fellow prostitute, Maisie Allen and her boyfriend, Colin, on the first leg of their journey to Queensland. The night before they were due to leave, Nellie collapsed on the hotel floor and started haemorrhaging. An ambulance was called, and she was rushed to Newcastle hospital where she gave the admitting nurse the assumed name of Mrs. Russell.

Nellie was miscarrying and was admitted to hospital due to complications. The doctor visited her after her surgery and told her that she would be spending at least a week in hospital. Though she didn't know she was pregnant, Nellie was upset over the loss of her baby.

A police officer who was visiting his mother in a nearby ward became suspicious when he saw Green standing outside Nellie's room. He advised his supervisor that he was sure that Frank Green was visiting a woman at the hospital. The sergeant sent Lillian Armfield, to the hospital to discreetly watch the patient and her visitors and determine her identity.

Upon her arrival, Lillian didn't need to investigate into the identity of the female patient. She recognised Nellie immediately.

She reported Cameron's true identity to her sergeant and a warrant for her arrest was issued. Fortunately, Nellie had caught a glimpse of Armfield and realised that her jig was up. She made her way down to the public telephone and rang the hotel. Green wasn't in the room, but Maisie answered the call and told Nellie that help was on its way.

Two Consorting Squad police officers stationed at the hospital entrance to arrest Nellie watched as, during a vicious thunderstorm, Green and Colin whisked Nellie away, hiding her under an overcoat to a car Frank had stolen the previous night. Due to the heavy rain, a woman being covered by an overcoat in the heavy rain, didn't raise their suspicions.

The escapees drove to Pyrmont where they abandoned the car and made their way back to Woolloomooloo. Nellie and Green then sought shelter at Dulcie Markham's house.

On the 12th of April 1933, as Nellie was going to see Tilly at her Palmer Street brothel, she noticed a police car crawling the kerb as she crossed the street. She made a run for it to a nearby house but was apprehended by a Consorting Squad detective before she was able to open the gate. Another detective spotted a man running from the back door of the house but was unable to catch him. The detectives asked Nellie who the man was, but she declined to answer.

The following morning, Nellie appeared in court and was sent to Long Bay Women's gaol to await sentencing. Two months later, she appeared before Mr. Shepherd S.M. who took Nellie's miscarriage and subsequent depression into consideration and fined her twenty pounds for stealing and released her without further imprisonment.

Nellie and Green left for a sojourn of six months in Brisbane. Whilst there, they continued to ply their illicit trades until they had finally accumulated the five thousand pounds that they needed to establish their sly liquor business.

The couple returned to New South Wales and moved into a large house in Lansdown Street in Surry Hills and set up the backyard garage as their groggery. The rented property was perfect. The house was situated near the main street and sat in between two alleys with a short laneway behind them. It was private enough to conduct their business, and they had an easy escape route if the need arose.

7

In December 1933, with Frank Green back in hospital recovering from yet another bullet wound, Nellie moved in with Guido. Unbeknownst to Nellie, it was Calletti who had shot Green.

On the 7th of February 1934, Calletti received word from one of his bent police constables that his flat was about to be raided for drugs and stolen goods. They also revealed that he and Nellie were about to be arrested on outstanding warrants. Neither Nellie nor Calletti wanted to spend time in gaol again, so they packed up what belongings they could and fled to Victoria.

On the 19th of February, Calletti proposed marriage to Nellie while they were dining at Mario's Italian restaurant in Melbourne. Nellie immediately accepted, hugging him in front of the restaurant full of diners, weeping as he placed a diamond ring on her finger.

The following day, Nellie using the name Ellen Kelly, married Calletti at the Fitzroy registry office.

When Frank Green learned of the marriage, he was beside himself with grief and told his informant, Jack Clarke, that he would do all he could to win Nellie back. The following November, the Callettis were extradited to New South Wales.

7

Violence again erupted in a Woolloomooloo street between Frank Green and Guido Calletti in June 1934. The bloody brawl was over Nellie. Hundreds of cheering people crowded around the men as they fought. Nellie stood by, not attempting to stop the affray in any way. She enjoyed violence, especially when it was men fighting over her.

Tiring from the wounds he had sustained, Calletti pulled out his razor and slashed Green across his lower arm, almost severing his wrist. The fight ended and Green was rushed to Sydney Hospital for surgery.

Green didn't have to wait too long to win back his heart's desire. Calletti was charged with unlawfully wounding Frank Green and making threats to further injure him. At his subsequent trial, Calletti was found guilty of the offence and sentenced to two years gaol. Within two weeks of her husband's imprisonment, Green moved in with Nellie.

However, when Calletti was released from prison within eight months of his sentence, he bumped into Nellie in Darlinghurst. Their passion for one another reignited, they began seeing each other behind Green's back.

In early July, the pair decided to leave the criminal life behind, and purchased a fruit and vegetable shop in Paddington. However, negative press written when the *Truth* newspaper learned about their enterprise adversely affected the business, sending them almost into bankruptcy. Nellie returned to the streets and Calletti to his life as a standover man.

7

The following years brought many more arrests for Nellie. She was also kidnapped, stabbed, and shot. However, none of the violence she suffered slowed her down. She continued her life of crime and love of gangster bedfellows on her never-ending quest in finding the man whose touch and kiss would make her settle into a normal family life.

In early June 1937, after learning that Calletti had moved in with her friend, Dulcie Markham, Nellie went on a drunken tirade. Never being one able to hold her liquor, she became embroiled in an argument with Harry Roper, a man who was drinking next to her at a local bar. Nellie turned and punched the unsuspecting man in the mouth and when he leapt from his chair to defend himself, she shot him in the ankle. She was charged for maliciously wounding Roper and released on forty pounds bail. However, due to the police being unable to locate the victim within a reasonable timeframe, the charge was dropped.

On the 24th of June 1938, Nellie was again found in the company of several known criminals and was charged with consorting for the second time. She was sentenced to two months imprisonment by Mr. Scobie S.M., at the Central Police Court on the 27th of June, and appealed against the severity of the sentence. On the 1st of July, Judge Curlewis entered Nellie into a bond of ten pounds. He also ordered her to remain of good behaviour for two years conditionally upon her leaving New South Wales and not returning to the state for three years.

Nellie returned to her flat and immediately packed her belongings. Three years was a long time for her to be away from Darlinghurst where she was protected, but she didn't want to run the risk of going against the judgement. Nellie was Queensland bound.

After arriving at the Kuranda airport in North Queensland, Nellie headed to a waiting taxi. She told the driver that she was from New South Wales and wanted to be taken to the best local brothel.

"A beautiful woman like you will make plenty of money in one of the Sachs Street houses. For a quick suck, I'll take you to the place that's always busy."

"See these fuckin' lips? They make more money in a day than you make in a fuckin' week. Keep your fuckin' dick in your pants and let me off here!"

The driver stopped the taxi and demanded two shillings for driving less than a mile. Nellie reached into her handbag and brought out her pistol, telling the cabbie that it was either a free ride or a bullet before jumping out of the car. The driver drove off without looking back.

Nellie caught another taxi and was taken to on the long drive to Cairns. The driver pointed out the Sachs Street brothels and Nellie thanked him before rewarding him with a pound note tip.

She sat across the street at the bus stop and watched men as they entered and left the houses. One grey house in particular seemed to have more visits from respectably dressed gentleman. She knocked on the green door of the establishment.

When she told the security man sitting inside the front door what she wanted, he took her into a room out the back where a slim woman with long black hair was sitting on an expensive velvet settee.

"You can leave now, Simon," she said, and waited for him to close the door before speaking again. "Now, tell me about yourself, sweetheart."

Nellie told the woman her name, age and where she was from. She then listed the brothels where she had worked in Sydney and Queensland. The Madam listened as Nellie relayed her work history, already knowing that she would hire her. She liked Nellie's articulate speech and assured manner. It was something she had never heard before from a working girl. But she had to almost hold her breath from the moment Nellie had entered the room due to her body odour.

"It's a pleasure to meet you, Nellie. I'm Gladys. I run Primrose House." The Madam introduced as she rose from her chair and opened the door and took Nellie on a tour of the house. Nellie was impressed that the brothel was well-furnished and clean. The bedrooms were beautifully furnished, and the mattresses were comfortable.

"To be able to work in such a high-class establishment, I charge sixty percent of your earnings," Gladys explained.

Nellie was surprised by the large amount but remained quiet. *'I'll just use Primrose House as a steppingstone,'* she thought to herself.

"After travelling so far, I'm sure you need to rest and take a bath. If you go to this address the landlady there will give you a room at a special price. You won't have to pay her until after your first shift, which will be tomorrow at three o'clock."

Nellie gratefully accepted the note and told the madam that she would be there the following afternoon.

"I look forward to seeing you again. Ask Simon to escort you to the address. It's not far away."

At first, working in the classy brothel was a good jaunt. It was the first time Nellie had worked with Chinese and Japanese women and she found them interesting. She also learned the art of eastern massage, a talent that gave her extra opportunities to ginger the clients. As in Sydney, Nellie had become the number one girl in the brothel, which caused jealousy and cattiness from the women who were left to service the late-night drunks and the dregs of society.

Tiring of Gladys taking a large cut of her earnings, Nellie decided to cut her shifts down to three days a week and work for herself from a room at the Albert Hotel.

In mid-September Green arrived and moved into the motel room with Nellie. He had plans to make contacts in the Cairns underworld and was reliant upon Nellie for money until he could find a niche in the local crime scene.

Nellie tried to keep her private work life discreet but what she didn't know was that she had been discovered. Two of the hotel's night cleaners, who also cleaned at Primrose House, had a clear view into her room at the hotel. When she turned up for her shift on the Wednesday morning, Gladys was waiting.

"I hear you're working from the Albert."

"Yes. I didn't know that was against the house rules," Nellie politely replied. "I need to make more money for myself. I'm not stealing any clients and have no intention of doing so."

"It's not something I generally allow. My girls work for me and nowhere else unless they quit. However, I'm willing to turn a blind eye if you change your shifts here to Wednesday through to Saturday and I will only charge forty percent of your takings. These are my busiest times and you have already built up a steady clientèle. I don't want them to go searching for you and cause a grievance between us. This way our relationship remains symbiotic."

"Agreed. Tell me, how did you find out I was working? I've only entertained no more than a dozen clients."

"I've been operating here for many years, darling, and have numerous contacts. The Valley is only a small place, and news about a good-looking new girl working in the area travels fast."

"Obviously. Can I start my shift now?"

"Only after you take a bath. There have been a few complaints about your personal hygiene. How you operate your personal business is up to you, but while you work under my roof, you will be clean, perfumed and wash after every client. Is that understood?"

"I'll be ready in half an hour."

7

Heartbreaking news reached Nellie in August 1939 when she received a telegram from the Darlinghurst Police Department. Her husband, Guido Calletti, had been killed in a shooting at Kings Cross. Distressed, she rang Frank. Apparently, Guido had been shot twice in the stomach at a party hosted by the Brougham Street Gang that he had gate crashed. "He was high on cocaine and pushed his way into the house and told the gang leader that he was taking over their turf. What a fuckin' stupid move. Calletti died in the hospital. He never regained consciousness."

Before making her way down to Sydney, Nellie rang a local florist and arranged for a wreath in the shape of a four feet high cross to be sent to the funeral home. Grieving for her husband, she wrote a heart-wrenching message to be attached to the wreath. She then contacted Gladys and told her that she was leaving for a few days and explained what had happened.

When she arrived in Darlinghurst, she headed straight to the Maroubra home of Tilly Devine. It had been a few years since she had had any contact with Tilly, but Nellie hoped that under the circumstances, her previous madam, friend, and confidante wouldn't turn her away.

Tilly placed an arm around Nellie and guided her into the living room before sitting her down on the settee and leaving for the kitchen to make a pot of tea.

"There you go, lovey. Get this warm tea into ya. The scones were made fresh this morning." Tilly smiled as she placed the tray of refreshments on the coffee table.

"Thank you, Till. It's so good to see you again. I'm sorry for what happened in the past. I've missed you." Each word dripped with the guilt she felt of turning against the woman who helped her when she had no-one.

"The past is in the past. This isn't the time for self-recrimination. It's a time for you to grieve for your 'usband. I'll take your bag through to the spare room and leave you alone for a while." Tilly gently patted Nellie's hand before leaving the room.

After nibbling on a scone and finishing her cup of tea, Nellie looked out of the living room window and wished she could have seen Guido just one more time so they could say their goodbyes.

The following morning Nellie woke at the cock's call. She wept as she put on her black clothing. She didn't apply any makeup. It wasn't a day for her to step out looking her best. She turned to the bedside table and picked up her black hat and ran her fingers softly along the long black plume as she remembered back to the last time she saw Guido. It was the day they had said their farewells at Circular Quay. They'd sat on a bench on the wharf eating a pork sandwich. The last words Guido said to her were, "I'll see you in three years, Red."

When she arrived at the Catholic chapel, Nellie was surprised to see a huge number of people attending the viewing. She spotted a few of his enemies standing in the shadows of the doorways for a quick exit if police showed up.

She joined the line-up of people but when one of Calletti's gang members recognised her, he took her to the front of the line. Nellie placed her black lace gloved hands on the side of the maple and silver coffin and laughed when she saw the tawdry suit her husband was dressed in. She disliked the suit and was with Guido when he bought it. She made him promise never to wear it when they were in public together. A promise he had kept until his funeral. She reached in and straightened his tie and whispered her love to him, thanking him for loving her for who she was. A hand gently touched her shoulder. She turned around and looked straight into the eyes of her husband's lover, Dulcie Markham. "Guido will be at peace now that you've come to see him off, Nellie. I'm sorry we have to meet again in such tragic circumstances," Dulcie whispered.

Nellie could see how upset Dulcie was. Her eyes were red-rimmed and puffy, the weary slope of her shoulders showed her that Dulcie was grieving over Guido as much as she was.

Nellie had loved Guido. He always accepted her restless wandering spirit and promiscuous ways. He knew she loved him and understood that her soul still searched for the man who could take away her insecurities and teach her to trust again.

The two women stood side-by-side, supporting each other as they sobbed over the man they both loved. Each kissed Guido's forehead and made their way out of the chapel, allowing the thousands of mourners to pay their last respects. Nellie and Dulcie rode in the same limousine to the Catholic section of Rookwood Cemetery. When they arrived, they were overwhelmed by the respect shown to Guido when they saw the number of wreaths surrounding his gravesite. However, the one that took pride of place in the centre of the floral tributes was Nellie's four feet high cross.

Nellie attended the wake but didn't stay long. She didn't want to be a target for the police and be arrested at her husband's farewell in front of his family and friends. She gave the first toast of the wake and spent time with Calletti's son before returning to Tilly's house.

7

After the police received information from Peggy Patterson, the nurse whose birthday party was the scene of Calletti's murder, they broke the door down of a house hidden in Bushland at Cowan Creek. Robert Branch, who was named as one of Calletti's shooters, leapt from a chair and attempted to grab a pistol from a nearby table. But the swift actions of Detective Dimmock averted a shootout when he tackled him to the ground. George Allen, the second man who was named as a shooter, dropped to the floor as soon as the police broke through the door.

After the shooters' arrests, Peggy, who had been granted full immunity, was placed in a room at the Moss Vale Guesthouse. The police knew how dangerous the men and their associates were and wanted to protect Peggy from the threats to her life she had been receiving if she didn't change her testimony.

However, the criminals had an ace up their sleeve and could get into places the police thought they couldn't. With a financial inducement of fifty pounds, Nellie Cameron visited the guesthouse and told the landlady that she was Peggy's sister and was granted entrance.

Peggy answered a knock on her door thinking it was someone sent by the police and let Dulcie into her room.

"Are you giving evidence against the Brougham Street gang members for killing Guido Calletti?" Nellie asked.

"Yes, I am" The nurse nervously replied.

"I'm here on behalf of the gang to let you know if you go ahead with your testimony, they will kill your sisters and then you. If you want, I can negotiate a financial agreement with the gang leader to pay for your silence. Then you and your family will be safe."

"But I've already given a statement to the police. I can't say that I lied and go to gaol."

"Tell them it was a mistake. Two of the men are outside now. I can tell them you will forget what you saw and say so in court, and you'll be paid handsomely for your memory loss."

The sobbing witness agreed. Nellie told her that one of the Brougham boys would meet her at her flat after the trial and she would be rewarded for her silence.

Nellie left the guesthouse and joined the men who were waiting in their car on the opposite corner. As soon as she told Mick, the gang leader who replaced Guido, that the nurse would keep her mouth shut, he handed Nellie the fifty pounds.

"Tell me, Nellie, why did you go against Calletti? He was our enemy. What did he do to you for you to hate him so much?" Brian, the gang's lieutenant asked.

"Hate him? I still love Guido. It's also none of your fucking business! Guido's dead and nothing can bring him back. He knew the life we led was one where we lived by the sword, and like me, he was prepared to die by the sword. Death is part of our life."

7

World War II broke out two weeks after Nellie returned to Cairns. When she went to her room and saw Green on the bed, time suddenly stopped, and a rush of sadness and guilt enveloped her. She hadn't realised the depth of her grief until she saw Frank. She asked him if he could stay in another room for a few days as she needed time to herself after Guido's death.

Alone in her room, Nellie thought back to the times she and Guido had spent together. There were barely any words ever spoken in anger between them. Tears burned her eyes as she finally let herself properly grieve for the man she loved in her own unique way.

The years fell away, and she was drawn back to the past when she first met Calletti—the polite manner, the gentleman so different to the vicious and callous person he was renowned as. A sudden, visceral ache flooded her body and constricted her throat as she remembered their most intimate moments. She recalled his sweet smile and gentle touch when they made love, tender moments far removed from the violent outside world they were a part of. She dabbed at her eyes with her cornflower blue handkerchief realising there was no going back when someone dies.

Four days after arriving back in Queensland, Nellie ended her relationship with Green and returned to Primrose House for her shift. Gladys welcomed her warmly, embracing her as she walked through the door, and guided her to her office.

"Sit down, sweetheart. I'll call for a pot of tea or would you prefer something stronger?" the Madam offered.

"A cup of tea would be nice thank you."

In 1940, while on a night out, Nellie met greyhound trainer Charles Francis Bourke, a notorious Sydney criminal and gunman. Enamoured by Nellie, Bourke remained in Cairns a week longer than he'd planned. Just six weeks later, after many phone calls and telegrams, Nellie returned to Sydney and married Bourke using her married name of Ellen Kathleen Calletti. One week later, not wanting to be arrested for breaking her bail conditions, she caught a train to Brisbane and started working in a brothel at Wren Street, Bowen Hills.

Unfortunately, Nellie's new marriage was a rocky one. Even though Bourke allowed his wife to continue working as a prostitute, he often became jealous and turned up unannounced at her Brisbane flat to make sure she wasn't seeing anyone when not at work.

Once, when Nellie visited Bourke in Sydney, he caught her talking to a man at a bar in Surry Hills. He stormed into the pub and struck the man after accusing him of sleeping with her. Both Nellie and the man, a taxi driver she'd met just ten minutes before, denied the accusation, but Bourke was insistent, pulling out his pistol and firing. Fortunately for him, the bullet had only grazed the cabbie's shoulder. With some quick talking from Nellie and financial remuneration from Bourke, the taxi driver left and didn't report the matter to the police.

Life from then on was one of brutality for Nellie whenever she was with Bourke. At times she was unable to work due to a fat lip or black eye. Once, when she returned to Wren Street covered in bruises, Veronika, the Madam, offered to send Gary, her bodyguard to teach Bourke a lesson. But Nellie, ever strong and independent, told her boss that she would handle it.

During the Second World War, Nellie made a lot of money with punters lined up outside the Wren Street brothel to see her. Due to Brisbane's shortage, in July 1942, Veronika and several other brothel owners arranged for a trainload of seasoned Sydney prostitutes to Brisbane to work.

Nellie's exile from New South Wales had been over for a year, so she decided to return to her husband and take advantage of the profitable Sydney wartime trade. She was fortunate to have retained her good looks and figure even though she had been a drug user and alcoholic the previous fifteen years and bore the scars of countless razor fights and bullet wounds. These scars she wore proudly. Many women who'd lived a life like Nellie's generally looked much older than they were and retired from prostitution early. Once the looks were gone, so was the money.

By 1940, Nellie was tired of living such a public life and ached for some peace. She also ended her violent marriage and moved into a flat in Surry Hills. She continued working as a prostitute, preferring to work the streets of Darlinghurst than compete against younger girls in brothels.

In 1945 in an attempt to leave prostitution, she started selling grog from her flat. Two weeks later, an undercover cop rocked up at her door in the wee hours and asked for a bottle of whiskey. At court that morning, in lieu of a fine, she was forced to surrender thirty bottles of whiskey and one hundred and sixty-eight bottles of beer. There ended Nellie's sly grog sojourn.

In March 1947, Nellie's alcoholic neighbour, Sandra, arrived on her doorstep with her five-year-old daughter, Janice. She asked her stunned neighbour if she would take her daughter and raise her as her own, or she'd drop her off at the nearest orphanage.

Nellie looked at the frightened, underweight little girl and her heart almost burst with pity. She took hold of Janice's hand and had barely finished telling the mother that she would take the child before Sandra bolted. She was never seen again.

Enjoying the role of motherhood, Nellie lavished love and gifts upon her adopted daughter, treating her as though she were her own. She relocated to a nicer and larger flat in Taylor Square and decorated Janice's room like the princess she thought her to be. The little girl loved her new mother almost immediately and often climbed into bed with her for comfort after a nightmare. Nellie would hold her frightened child close and promise that no harm would ever come to her again before singing her to sleep.

The following November, Nellie became Janice's legal guardian and promptly adopted her, much to the little girl's glee.

In 1950 Nellie met an Irish wharf-labourer named William Francis Donohue. The pair hit it off and Nellie and Janice moved in with him the weekend after they had met. William warmly accepted Janice, often bringing home sweets, a doll or jigsaw puzzles. Nellie had finally met *the* man and was living the life she had always dreamed of.

However, it didn't take long before Prince Charming revealed his true colours. When drunk, Donohue was just as violent and jealous as Bourke. Believing that Billy was the best she could find so late in life, Nellie resigned herself to staying in the relationship.

On the 31st of March 1952, Donohue assaulted Nellie in a drunken rage. As he kicked her as she lay on the kitchen floor, Nellie screamed out to Janice, telling her to climb out her bedroom window and go to Grandma Anne's. Frightened and upset, Janice arrived at her adopted grandmother's flat and tearfully told her that Uncle Billie was hurting her mother.

When Nellie attempted to escape through the front door, Donohue shot her in the back. Shocked by what he had done, he immediately called the ambulance and Nellie was admitted to St Vincent's Hospital in a critical condition. Surgeons later discovered that the bullet was lodged in her liver. They also discovered that Nellie had several healed bullet wounds in her abdomen from when she was shot in 1931. Unfortunately, two of those wounds had become cancerous and were too advanced for the surgeons to operate on.

In shock at what he had done, the repentant Donohue asked their neighbour to take care of Janice. He kissed the little girl on her cheek and promised she would see her Mummy soon. After checking on Nellie, Donohue surrendered himself to police at the Darlinghurst police station and confessed to the shooting. Two days later when Nellie was conscious enough to answer police questions, she refused to co-operate and the charges against Donohue were dropped.

In the months after the shooting, life for Nellie and Janice was a happy one. Donohue had sworn off alcohol and had stuck to his word. Janice, enrolled at a private school, was doing well. The family spent weekends at the beach or in the country. Life was finally peaceful and filled with the love Nellie thought she would never experience.

In 1953, Nellie began suffering constant pain in her lower abdomen. After walking Janice to school, she went to her local doctor's surgery and was referred to a surgical specialist the following day.

Several days after undergoing x-rays and blood tests, the specialist told Nellie that she had inoperable liver cancer. Nellie almost fainted in the chair. The doctor asked his nurse to bring in a glass of water and after Nellie had calmed down, he asked if he could contact someone to drive her home.

"No thank you, doctor. I'd rather walk. I have a lot to think about."

Nellie slowly walked to her daughter's school, wondering what would become of Janice after she died and if she would remember her. Tears rolled down her face as she waited on the seat near the gate for the three o'clock bell to ring.

"I lived a life of death, drugs and horrors that brought me to this end. Why couldn't I leave this earth with a bullet like Guido?" she whispered to herself as her body shuddered in a sob.

The ringing of the school bell brought her out of her thoughts. She quickly dried her tears and straightened her clothing, making herself presentable for her daughter. Upon seeing her mother, Janice rushed over, hugged her, and started talking excitedly at top speed about all she had done that day at school. Nellie tried to concentrate on what she was saying, but all she could think of was that she would soon die, and Janice would become an orphan. Her heart broke as she held back the tears, pondering how life could take such a cruel turn when she finally had all that she'd ever wanted…

The following months Nellie fell into a deep depression and was suffering with a great deal of agony. Billy brought her home cocaine and heroin to help ease the pain, but it wasn't keeping her comfortable for long. She spent almost every day in bed and refused to bathe or eat.

Tilly visited the flat every morning and prepared breakfast for Janice and placed a fresh packed lunch in her school bag before walking her to school. Then after cleaning the flat, Tilly would spend a few hours with Nellie, and leave her with a cup of tea or scones, biscuits, or a slice of fruitcake, depending on what she had baked the night before.

Nellie spent most of her days going through photos of her life with Janice, over and over again. They brought her comfort. She had almost completely disconnected socially, except for speaking with Anne, her neighbour, and of course her guardian angel, Tilly.

Using a line from Raymond Chandler's *Farewell, My Lovely*, Tilly would often remind Nellie that she was 'a smooth shiny girl, hard-boiled and loaded with sin' and she'd beat the cancer…

On the 1st of November, Janice received a birthday party invitation from one of her school friends. She was excited about attending. Not wanting to let her daughter down, Nellie forced herself out of bed and went shopping with Tilly for a new party dress, hair ribbon, and party shoes.

That week, Nellie was almost back to her old self. She was smiling and staying out of bed. She accompanied Janice and Tilly to and from school each morning and also helped prepare the meals. At night she read stories to her daughter until she fell asleep. When Billy arrived home from the wharves, she always had a pot of tea and cake waiting for him when he walked through the door.

On Sunday the 8th of November, the morning of the party, Nellie had a difficult time keeping Janice from bouncing off the walls with excitement. An hour before she was due to leave, Nellie fixed her daughter's hair, tying the plaits with new pink ribbons. She then dressed her in the pretty pink and white floral party dress, white socks, and black patent leather shoes.

Nellie then took several photos of her husband and daughter together. Billy then took a few of Nellie with Janice, and then their sweet old neighbour, Anne, took photos of them all together.

When the time came for them to leave, Nellie held her daughter close and told her how beautiful she was and how much she loved her. She then caught hold of Billy's hand before kissing him and holding him close. Then, smiling at the top of the steps Nellie waved her family goodbye.

The loving mother and wife waited until she could no longer see their car and walked back inside. She closed the door and drew all the curtains throughout the flat. Then, after rolling up several bath towels, she closed the doors leading to the kitchen and tucked the towels in the gap between the doors and floor. Tears rolled down her cheeks as she walked towards the gas stove and turned on all the jets before opening the oven door.

Calmly, Nellie removed the cooking trays, placed a folded towel on the floor of the oven and then laid her head upon the towel. She whispered her husband and daughter's names and apologised before deeply inhaling the gas.

While the oven hissed and the gas's toxic odour filled the room, Nellie sang her favourite nursery rhyme from when she was a child.

"Mistress Mary, quite contrary, how does your garden grow? With Silver bells and cockle shells, And pretty maids all... in... a... row..."

Nellie's chest tightened, her nose started bleeding and her heart began racing. She closed her eyes from the dizziness and vomited. For a split second, she sat up and reached up to turn off the gas jets, but she remembered the agonising pain of cancer. A moment later, a sudden feeling of euphoria overcame her, and she felt like she was floating. Then, a peaceful sensation overcame her soul. She smiled as she whispered her daughter's name before falling asleep.

7

Billy returned home several hours later and detected a strong odour of gas as he approached the flat. Alarmed, he took Janice to Anne's.

As soon as he opened the door to the flat, he was almost overcome. He took off his jacket and placed it over his mouth and nose, and then discovered the rose-coloured body of his wife laying on the floor in front of the stove. He quickly turned off the gas jets before opening the windows and doors.

When he returned to Nellie, he knew she was dead. He sat beside her body sobbing for several minutes before calling an ambulance.

Janice was inconsolable. She cried for her mother constantly, confused as to why she was dead. Tilly and Billy explained that her mummy was sick with a disease and the doctors were unable to make her better. He said that God had called her to heaven, so she didn't suffer anymore.

"Can God call me too, Aunty Tilly? I want to be with my Mummy, please."

Her eyes welling with tears, Tilly held Janice close.

"You have such a long life to live, my little darling. God won't call you until you have your own children and grandchildren."

"I can't wait until then, Aunty Tilly! I want to see my Mummy now!"

Tilly held the heartbroken child close while she cried for her mother.

7

At the age of forty-two, Nellie Cameron-Calletti-Bourke who had been arrested seventy-five times and involved in four shootings. Two of her lovers had died from gunshots, she had been shot several times, kidnapped, stabbed, and slashed by razors more than thirty times.

On November the 10th 1953, more than a thousand mourners including Tilly Devine, Kate Leigh, and her ex-lover, Frank Green, crowded the Darlinghurst Chapel for Nellie's extravagant funeral. Local police and the Consorting Squad detectives mingled in the crowd, hoping to nab any criminals wanted for serious offences.

Nellie was buried as Ellen Katherine Bourke in the Botany Roman Catholic Cemetery. William, Janice, and Tilly Devine were grief-stricken as they stood by her graveside.

She was survived by her de facto husband William Donohue, estranged husband Charlie Bourke, her mother, Mrs. Lillian Cameron, and her adopted daughter, Janice.

The *Sun Herald* wrote: 'She had exceptional sex appeal: she had the nerve to carry a gun for her love; and she could be trusted with secrets. She was completely loyal to the criminal scale of values.' An epitaph Nellie would be proud of.

Chapter Ten

Dulcie Markham

Dulcie May Markham came into the world on the 27th of February 1914 at Crown Street Women's Hospital. Her mother, twenty-year-old Florence Millicent Markham. Her father was twenty-one-year-old John Allen, who aspired to become an actor. On Dulcie's birth certificate he registered himself as a 'Theatrical Artist'. However, dreams of stardom never eventuated, and he was employed as a dock worker.

Early childhood was a tough but happy one for Dulcie. She was raised in a federation style home in Salisbury Street, Waverley, a budding residential area at the time. Her parents raised her lovingly, but cracks in the cement of their marriage began to appear in 1918 when her father rarely came home, and her mother started seeing another man.

On the 13th of July 1920, Florence gave birth to a second daughter and named her Florence Ena. Dulcie was six years old. She was excited to have a sibling and doted on her little sister. By this time, Dulcie's father had moved out of the house and she seldom saw him. Raising her daughters as a single parent, Florence took in washing and ironing to supplement the family's governmental income. She had not heard from her husband in some time, nor was she receiving any financial support from either father.

As the girls grew, so did the cost of raising them. There were only so many hours in the day that Florence could work, and she didn't want to leave her girls with babysitters for more hours than she was able to spend with them. She contacted both her daughter's fathers but learned that her husband was unemployed and young Florence's father had died in a drowning accident in the Hawkesbury River.

Later that year, Florence's brother, Robert, showed upon her doorstep. As she was brewing a pot of tea, Robert told her that he had fallen on hard times after being retrenched from his job in Cairns and was homeless. Florence invited him to move into their home until he found employment and could afford his own accommodation.

This is when Dulcie's life irrevocably changed.

One night, Dulcie was awoken by a hand across her mouth. Terrified, she tried to pull the hand away until she saw her Uncle Bobbie. He told her to keep quiet before he started touching her private places. A few moments later, he placed her hand on his penis and told her to play with it for a while. Dulcie had always been told to obey and respect adults, so she touched it. He then placed his hand over hers and moved it up and down and asked her to lick his special toy like an ice-cream. Dulcie obeyed. She never questioned if what her uncle had done was wrong, she was young and thought that's what uncles did…

The following night, he returned to her bedroom, but this time he started kissing her on her lips. Dulcie couldn't breathe. She closed her eyes and laid on her bed as still as a corpse. When he stopped, he told her not to tell anyone because it was their 'special secret' and she was his 'special little girl'.

On the third night, her uncle pulled off her nightie. Embarrassed by her nudity, Dulcie tried to cover her groin area, but he pulled her hands away. "It's time for you to make Uncle Bobbie very happy," he whispered as he removed his pants and laid on top of his ten-year-old niece.

Dulcie squirmed underneath her uncle's weight and when she tried to tell him that she couldn't breathe, he placed his hand across her mouth and told her to be quiet. Several seconds later, he used his legs to separate hers and slowly thrust himself inside her. The terrified child tried to scream from the pain, but her uncle pressed down harder until he was finished.

"Remember, this is our special secret. You must never tell anyone."

Over the following months, Dulcie isolated herself from her family and friends and at night she woke up screaming from nightmares. Her schoolwork suffered because she was easily distracted, and she had trouble concentrating in class.

The sexual abuse continued after her uncle moved to a flat in Newtown. He would often ask Florence if Dulcie could come over so he could take her to a movie. As a treat, he would take her to the ice-cream parlour before returning to his flat and abuse her again.

At fourteen years old, Dulcie's body started changing. She didn't understand why she was sick in the morning. A couple of months later, her mother noticed that Dulcie's clothes were becoming tighter around her stomach. Thinking she needed to alter the waistband she started measuring her daughter's waist, but her hand suddenly stopped upon a prominent bulge. "*Is Dulcie pregnant?*' she thought to herself. Florence placed breakfast in front of little Flo and told Dulcie to go to her room.

Florence closed the bedroom door and looked at her teenage daughter, attempting to find the words to say.

Dulcie knew something was wrong. "What's wrong, Mama?"

"Dulcie, you're pregnant! Who have you been having sex with? I can't believe you would do this to us!"

"What? How can I be having a baby? I don't even know what sex is! What is sex?" Dulcie naïvely asked.

Confused by her daughter's questions and denials, Florence asked if she had been naked in bed with a boy. When she saw the blush and shameful look that crossed her daughter's face, she realised the truth. "Who is he? Is it one of the boys from school?"

Dulcie just shook her lowered head, too ashamed and afraid to speak.

"Well, who is it then?"

"He said I'm not allowed to say. He said I was a *good* girl for making him happy." Dulcie almost whispered.

"Who said this Dulcie? Who? Please, you must tell me."

Tears welled in Dulcie's eyes. "Uncle Bobbie." She rasped.

Florence almost vomited—her own brother was having sex with her daughter.

"Uncle Bobbie? Are you sure, Dulcie? Darling, don't be afraid to tell the truth about who did this to you. Don't blame Uncle Bobbie. He loves you kids very, very much."

"Mama, it *was* him. I'm not lying! He came to my room almost every night when he lived with us and he does it every time I go to his home. He told me it was a game all girls play with their uncles to make them happy."

Florence needed to sit down. "We can't tell anyone about this. We'll get rid of the baby and you're not to tell anyone what happened. And you won't be spending time alone with your uncle anymore. Do you understand?"

"I never wanted to play those games with him!" Dulcie cried as her mother held her close and wishing she could take her pain away.

Florence kept Dulcie home from school and raided the secret tea tin where she hid her emergency money and went to see Janet Wright, an abortionist, she had used herself. She made an appointment for her daughter and paid the five pounds fee before rushing back home.

At eleven o'clock the following day, Dulcie and her mother arrived at Wright's home on Kippax Street, Surry Hills.

An hour later, Dulcie, traumatised by the experience, returned home with her mother to rest. She sobbed all the way to their house, upset upon seeing the five-month-old foetus of her aborted son. Wright was known to show aborted babies to teenagers in hope it would deter them from becoming pregnant again.

Things were never the same between Dulcie and her mother. Her Uncle Bobbie tried to convince his sister to allow Dulcie to attend movie matinees with him on weekends, but Florence always had an excuse for why she couldn't go.

Over time, Dulcie became despondent at home and was up to mischief. She was brought home by several shopkeepers for shoplifting food, cigarettes, and clothing. The school principal sent letters home informing Florence of her daughter's constant truancy, stealing from fellow students and disruptions in class. But more worrying for her mother was that Dulcie was having sex with men she had met at the local pubs and was often paid for the deed.

In April 1929, Dulcie was drinking at the Marrickville Hotel with a few men during their lunchtime break. Just after midday, she saw her father walk in with three men. One of the men was her Uncle Bobbie.

Already intoxicated, Dulcie finished the whiskey in her glass, walked over to her uncle and punched him in the mouth. She then began screaming that he was a rapist who had gotten her pregnant. Her father, absolutely dumbfounded and distressed by his daughter's outburst and allegations, grabbed hold of Dulcie, and pulled her still screaming out into the street.

"Be quiet Dulcie! You're causing a scene!" He whispered as he dragged her into his car. All the way back to the home that he had left many years before, Dulcie was yelling obscenities at him, telling her father that he was a bastard and a loser for leaving his family. Once they arrived at his wife's house, John dragged his daughter inside.

"What the hell is all this about Florence? When was Dulcie pregnant and when did your brother rape her?"

Dulcie, who was past keeping the secret, pointed at her panic-stricken mother, and screamed, "Tell him, Mum!" before running to her bedroom. As she packed her clothes and shoes in a suitcase, she heard her parents arguing before a loud thump was followed by her mother crying. Her father had no right to drag her home. He was nothing to her anymore. As she climbed out of her bedroom window, she heard her father threaten to kill her uncle before hearing his car speed off down the street.

Not knowing where to go, Dulcie caught a tram which she alighted in Darlinghurst.

7

Homeless and not knowing what to do, she sought refuge in the Salvation Army Young Woman's Hostel. When the man in charge asked her name and her age, she stuttered before answering, "D…Dulcie Wilson. I… I'm seventeen."

In the shelter, she met the best and worst of Sydney's humanity. She knew Dulcie Markham, the loving daughter and sister, would never cope with such a lifestyle. But Dulcie Wilson, the runaway, was tough and independent. The new Dulcie would conquer her new life and leave the dark memories of her childhood behind.

On the second night she was fortunate enough to meet Vera Purcell who told her where she could get food, and the shops that were easy to lift clothes from. She told Dulcie that she used to be a leader of a gang of girls who robbed shops until they were all caught and convicted and how she'd done six months hard labour in Long Bay…

Dulcie liked Vera—she found her a bit rough around the edges, but she also knew street life and how to survive it. When Dulcie revealed that she was only fifteen years old, Vera became even more protective of her. They spent almost every day and night together, becoming partners in crime, stealing food and clothing from stores around the area. They made good money from selling their stolen goods to local fences.

Vera became embroiled in a fight in a Darlinghurst pub one night and was razored across the face, arms, and chest. She was rushed to hospital where she required over one hundred stitches and remained in hospital due to the severity of the wounds and massive blood loss. When she and Dulcie were alone, Vera told her to get out of the hospital as one of the nurses had phoned the police and she didn't want them questioning her. The following morning Dulcie returned to the pub where she had left her hat and coat and stopped to have a whiskey to calm her nerves. She had never seen someone attacked so violently before or seen so much blood.

Needing fresh air, she walked across the street and sat on a brick wall, trying to think of what she would do. All she felt like doing was crying and for the first time since running away, she thought about returning home to her mother. Moments later, a well-dressed lady approached and gently touched her shoulder.

"Oh 'ere, 'ere lovey, what's the matter with a beautiful young woman like you? Are you all right?" the woman asked.

"My friend was attacked by a razor and I don't know anyone else or where to go."

"There, there, now sweet'art. There's always somewhere to go around 'ere. Don't you worry about that."

"But I don't know anyone, and I can't go back home," Dulcie said.

"Well, you know me now, lovey. I'm Tilly Devine. Maybe I can 'elp you," she smiled as she gently patted the frightened teenager's hand to reassure her.

Within a week of meeting Tilly, the svelte teenager with long blonde hair, was working at her Palmer Street Brothel. Dulcie, with her piercing grey eyes, full lips and model looks, became the most popular girl in the brothel. One client was so charmed by the brothel starlet, that he purchased a silver bracelet and gave it to her during one of his regular weekly visits. Having already received several bracelets from other clients, Dulcie placed it around her ankle, and it soon became a fashion statement for most of the working girls in Tilly's brothels.

Tilly was raking in at least eighty pounds a night, helped by Dulcie working eighteen hours a day to keep up with the clients wanting to see her. Dulcie was elated. She had a purse full of pounds earned by selling something that she had mostly given away.

The young prostitute's beauty was intoxicating to the men and envied by other workers in the brothel. One woman of equal beauty,

Nellie Cameron, befriended her and helped her with advice on what to do with the clients throughout the first few weeks. The pair were almost inseparable during the first few months of their friendship. Nellie guided her through the labyrinth of life in Darlinghurst and helped her become a stylish dresser to accentuate her spectacular figure. They visited the hair salon together where Dulcie had her first perm and enjoyed having her fingernails manicured and polished. After they'd finished their beauty regime, they walked down the street and men would literally stop their cars and watch as they crossed the road.

With Dulcie looking more like a Hollywood movie star than a prostitute, she attracted even more clients so several of the girls left Tilly and went to work for Kate Leigh, hoping they could capitalise on being the new girls. But none of them could compare or compete with Tilly Devine's two most-prized prostitutes.

Within three months, and with Nellie's assistance, Dulcie rented a flat in a nice area of Darlinghurst. They spent days purchasing furniture, pots, and pans, manchester, and all that was needed when setting up a first home. On the Sunday after Dulcie had settled in, Tilly and Jim arrived with a baked a leg of lamb and vegetables for a housewarming celebration.

7

Dulcie was happy in her new life. Her thoughts often wandered to her mother and sister. She missed them. She would occasionally take a cab and park down the street from her childhood house and watch little Flo playing in the yard. Sometimes of a weekend, she would watch as her mother tended to the garden. It broke her heart that she was so close but unable to touch or speak to them. It hurt Dulcie to see her family enjoying life without her and knowing their life of innocence continued and she would no longer share their peace and love. She knew she couldn't go back—she was no longer the frightened little girl needing a mother's protection. But nothing could silence the longing or the internal screaming and the void in her heart that begged her to just go home.

She looked towards her bedroom window and a shiver ran down her spine as she remembered back to the nights her uncle would steal into her room and shred away her innocence and trust, stroke by terrible stroke. Her uncle had stolen a little of her soul every time he raped her. As far as she was concerned, her uncle was the devil, but she would not let him define her. He would not leave his mark. From then on, the only devil she would dance with, was herself.

7

With her looks, style, and engaging personality, it didn't take long for Dulcie to become a highly prized adornment of Sydney gangsters. She had a zest for life that seemed unquenchable, she could charm the stars, and had a spontaneous sense of humour which attracted men to her like moths to a flame.

In April 1931, the seventeen-year-old moved in with twenty-one-year-old Alfred Dillon who was still living with his mother in her Woolloomooloo home. Dillon was also Guido Calletti's partner in a Darlinghurst fruit stall. The pair had met at the Tradesman's Arms hotel several weeks prior. The problem was that Dulcie had also been stepping out with twenty-one-year-old violent gunman, Cecil "Scotty" McCormack, who had intentions of marriage, but the relationship ended when McCormack was sentenced to six months gaol for consorting with criminals.

When McCormack was released from prison, he hoped that he and Dulcie would resume their relationship. His first stop was the Tradesman's Arms hotel where he found Dulcie drinking at the bar. After a few whiskies, they left together, and she spent the night with him. Dillon had been told about her liaison with McCormack and quickly put a stop to it when he arrived home and presented Dulcie with a pearl necklace and a silver watch.

Due to her prostitution lifestyle, Dulcie had become somewhat materialistic. She found McCormack to be a good lover, but he was cheap and never bought her anything, save an occasional drink at the pub. Dillon won her affections.

During the evening on the 13th of May, McCormack approached Dillon and his mate, Matthew Foley, on the corner of Bourke and William Streets in Kings Cross after leaving the Fifty-Fifty Club. Words were quickly exchanged. McCormack was enraged over Dillon's relationship with Dulcie, and Dillon fired back with accusations about McCormack stealing ten pounds from his mother two weeks beforehand. McCormack told him to prove it.

"I don't have to prove anything to a bastard like you. I've already shown that I am the better man. Dulcie chose me over you!" Dillon boasted.

A violent fight ensued and minutes later, Dillon pulled a lawyer's bodkin from his belt and stabbed McCormack several times in the left side of his chest. The final stab pierced both his lungs. McCormack fell back through the plate glass window of a dress store.

Dillon and Foley fled the scene hoping McCormack would honour the code of silence. However, they had nothing to worry about. McCormack would never fizgig to the police. He was dead.

Mark North, an acquaintance of McCormack's was questioned about his death. He told the police that he didn't know who had stabbed him but told them that he thinks it may have been a bloke named Dillon who was going out with McCormack's ex-girlfriend, Dulcie Markham. When the police arrived at Dillon's flat, they were told by a friend that Dulcie was at the pictures. The police then went to the local theatre and called out Dulcie's name. When they informed her of McCormack's death, she calmly accompanied them to the morgue and identified his body, saving his mother the ordeal of seeing her son dead.

Later that night, Ruby Reardon, a casual lover of Dillon's, walked into the police station and told Detective Sergeant Kennedy that she had been speaking with Dillon and Foley not far from where McCormack's body was found. Kennedy and his partner, Detective Wilson, drove to both men's home and brought them in for questioning. They denied being involved in the murder.

Reardon was brought into the Darlinghurst Police Station to pick the men she saw out of a line-up. She pointed straight to Dillon. When Kennedy returned to his desk, the Glebe municipal collector was waiting for him. The man handed him a bodkin that was sucked up by a pump in a storm water channel one hundred and fifty yards from where McCormack was killed.

Dillon was charged with feloniously and maliciously murdering Cecil McCormack and was remanded in custody.

Dulcie visited Dillon every day he was in remand. She brought him food and told him what was happening in the world outside, often bringing in newspapers so he could read the reports about his arrest and trial. When Dillon asked her why she was wearing a black wig, she told him it was a mark of respect for McCormack.

At his subsequent trial, Dillon was found guilty of manslaughter and sentenced to thirteen years at Long Bay gaol. As the police led him from the dock, he turned towards Dulcie and shouted that he would always love her. Dulcie waved back at him and told him that she loved him too. Tears rolled down her face as she turned and left the courtroom.

However, Dulcie wasn't prepared to wait thirteen years for Dillon. She did love him, but thirteen years is an awfully long time. She had visited him several times but stopped going to the gaol after sixth months. To quell her heartache, she returned to Tilly's Palmer Street brothel and worked as though nothing had happened.

7

In Brisbane on the 4th of March 1934, at the age of twenty, Dulcie married sideshow worker, small-time thief and extortionist, Frank Bowen. Her husband considered himself an Al Capone style mobster.

Their life over the following years was no bed of roses. As 'carnies', they moved from town to town and state to state for the first two years of their marriage. Bowen operated a roll-down table at carnivals as a sideshow attraction. Dulcie found the lifestyle unsettling and in her state of depression, became more and more addicted to cocaine and alcohol.

In May 1936, Dulcie and Bowen, under the aliases of Jim and Dulcie Lewis, travelled the sideshow circuit in Queensland. Frank had not researched the working requirements in some of the rural towns in the state, like the Kingaroy Show Society, where out of state 'carnies' could only set up an attraction if they were free of a criminal record. Bowen explained that he had a letter from the police stating that he had no criminal convictions but said that he had left it at a hotel in Toowoomba where he and his wife stayed overnight. The secretary of the show society allowed Bowen to set up and told him that he had to provide the letter within the following seven days.

Bowen, concerned about lack of money, pleaded with Dulcie to help him forge a letter from the Queensland Under Secretary stating that he wasn't a criminal. Dulcie wanting to get out of the State and back to NSW, used her womanly wiles and wrangled her way into another carnie's caravan. While her host was busily preparing a pot of tea, she slipped his telegram of permission into her pocket.

After politely sharing a pot of tea and biscuits with the carnie, Dulcie returned to the caravan and showed her husband.

"Good work! You didn't have to fuck him, did you?" he asked.

"Of course not! *He* was a gentleman and made me a pot of tea!"

145

The following morning, the Bowens left for Brisbane, stopping at several post offices to grab a few telegram request forms. They found a room at a hotel in Fortitude Valley and Dulcie set to work on her forgery skills. While her husband snored in bed, she spent most of the night attempting to replicate the Under-Secretary's signature. By dawn, there were crumpled papers strewn across the floor, but lying on the oak coffee table was a forged telegram request form from the Queensland Under Secretary.

On the April the 22nd of April, Dulcie handed the forged telegram to Reginald Poulton, the counter officer at the Brisbane General Post Office. He looked at the telegram addressed to "J. Lewis" at Kingaroy and read the words, "Showman permit issued for a roll-down show April 22 to April 28" aloud to Dulcie to ensure that the telegram was worded correctly.

"This is from the Under Secretary of Justice, Madam?" the postal officer asked.

"Yes sir. It is to be sent as soon as possible please. It is of great importance."

On closer scrutiny, the officer noticed the telegram hadn't been endorsed and handed it back to Dulcie explaining that he couldn't send it without endorsement. Dulcie signed the back with her name, Mrs. D. Bowen, and returned it to the officer and paid the one penny fee before leaving the post office.

Later that afternoon when the officer read the outgoing telegrams, he was suspicious when he noticed the signature of a George Arthur Carter, Under Secretary of the Department of Justice, a name he was unfamiliar with. He took it through to his supervisor, who recognised it as a forgery, and immediately contacted the police.

Two days later, Dulcie was questioned by Plainclothes Constable Croneau from the Criminal Investigation Branch in Brisbane. He accused her of forging the telegram, which she denied. She told the constable that a showman she knew by the name of Jim Lewis had given her two pennies to send the telegram to him. Constable Croneau then asked her if she was aware that she had no right to send an unauthorised telegram using the name of the Under Secretary for Justice and that it was a crime. Dulcie denied knowing that it was illegal and thanked the constable for advising her of such information.

"You should have known," Croneau remarked. "You've been following shows long enough to know it was fake. This Jim Lewis was apparently going to run a roll-down show at Kingaroy and was going to use your telegram as a permit. You should have known there was something suspicious about it. It's unusual for a man to send a telegram to himself, isn't it?"

"Dinkum constable, I didn't know. I never even gave it a thought," Dulcie replied, her blue eyes gleaming with feigned innocence.

"Are you sure there's even a man named Jim Lewis?" the constable asked. "From what I hear, your husband is in Kingaroy awaiting a permit and he's using the name Lewis, the same name you used at a motel in Toowoomba…"

Dulcie almost swallowed her tongue in shock when she realised just how much information Croneau knew. "No sir, not to my knowledge."

The constable didn't believe her and despite her denying any wrongdoing, he arrested her for falsifying a telegram on behalf of her husband.

Following her arrest and the subsequent charges, Dulcie was released on ten pounds bail and ordered to appear in court again the next week. However, Dulcie didn't turn up to court and an immediate police search began. Several days later, the police discovered she was in the hospital with a head wound after being struck with a bottle during an altercation at a Brisbane pub.

With the finesse and artistry of a seasoned actress, Dulcie stood in the dock, fluttering her long eyelashes, and demurely brushing back her platinum blonde curls as she pleaded her innocence. She said she had no interest in a sideshow at Kingaroy and she didn't forge a permit for a man known as Jim Lewis. Knowing the best way to lie is to make statements as close to the truth as possible, Dulcie admitted when questioned by the police prosecutor, that she had been known by several names and had been convicted for consorting with criminals, prostitution, and offensive behaviour, but flat out denied that she had forged a phony telegram. She admitted that although it was her writing on the front and back of the telegram and that she had endorsed it, she vowed she was unaware of any wrongdoing.

Magistrate Burne said, "I was sending you to gaol. The court is convinced that you had rigged the permit for the Kingaroy sideshow and, therefore, you must pay a penalty. He fined her ten pounds in default of three months' imprisonment and allowed her fourteen days to pay the fine.

The arrest and subsequent court case were the beginning of the end of the Bowens' marriage. Angered that her husband hadn't stood up for her or taken any responsibility for the forgery, Dulcie returned to Sydney. He followed six weeks later.

7

One night, a woman named Jean Patten arrived at the doorstep of Dulcie and Frank's flat. She told Dulcie when she answered the door, that she was Bowen's ex-fiancée and demanded money to buy clothes for their children. Dulcie was surprised to find out that not only had her husband been engaged before, but he also had two children. Not wanting to leave the children and their mother outside in the bitter cold and rain, Dulcie invited them inside to sit by the fireplace. Bowen had still not returned home several hours later, so she made dinner for everyone in the hope that he would arrive before it got too late.

By nine o'clock, Bowen still hadn't returned home, so Dulcie went to the wardrobe where she hid her secret stash of cash and retrieved twenty pounds before handing the money to the woman.

"Please, I can't take your money. I'll come back in a few days to meet with Frank." Jean politely declined, surprised to be handed such a large sum from someone she didn't know.

"Please take it. I'm sure Frank would have given you the same amount. I hope it helps you and the kids."

When Bowen arrived home, he wasn't prepared for the roasting he received. In fact, he was surprised Jean turned up to their home, especially with the children in tow. One of the reasons he left her was because she was so soft-spoken and shy.

Frank's dishonesty and gambling debts finally took its toll, and Dulcie walked. The only person she could think of going to for comfort was Tilly Devine. When she arrived at the Palmer Street house, she told Tilly what had happened and temporarily moved into her Maroubra home.

By happenstance, two weeks later, Dulcie ran into Guido Calletti at the Tradesman's Arms hotel. She asked after Nellie and he told her that she was in gaol. Later that night, after consuming a lot of alcohol, the pair ended up in bed together and started an on again off again relationship.

Tired of working in Sydney, Dulcie longed for a change of scenery. In mid-1937, she packed her bags and flew to Melbourne. It didn't take long to find work in a local brothel, and like in Sydney, with her glamorous movie star looks and dazzling personality, she became the most popular prostitute in the brothel.

Within weeks of her arrival, Dulcie had several Melbourne underworld figures to be hot on her trail. Arthur "The Egg" Taplin, a Sydney standover man who was on the lam from the Darlinghurst police, was the first to garner her attention. That night she and twenty-two-year-old Taplin became lovers. Over the pursuing months, the two were inseparable, and Taplin, to ensure his woman was safe, became her pimp and protector.

At the Cosmopolitan Hotel on the 15th of December, Taplin and two of his mates decided to have some fun with Harcourt Lee. They suspected that he was a homosexual due to his employment as a hairdresser. Taplin began standing over him to buy them drinks. Harcourt, more of a pickpocket than a hairdresser, knew the men were gangsters through his own criminal affiliations, and was aware of Taplin's violent temper. In fear for his life, Lee paid for the trio's drinks until late into the night.

Taplin left after a barman told him that Dulcie needed him to pick her up. Feeling that the threat of danger was gone, Harcourt refused to continue buying drinks for Taplin's mates who had remained at the pub. The men left soon after his refusal and later returned with Taplin, who was in a rage.

"You're a fuckin' bright bastard. Why wouldn't you buy my mates a drink? I've a good mind to blow your brains out here and now. I've got a rod on me," he roared before grabbing a pot of beer from a nearby table and smashing it over Harcourt's head.

Taplin then put his hand into his pocket where Harcourt knew he always carried his gun. Dazed and bloodied, the hairdresser stumbled to his feet and quickly withdrew his pistol, shooting Taplin before he had a chance to point his weapon.

The other patrons ran for cover as Taplin fell to the floor with a wide-eyed look of shock frozen on his face. While the barman phoned the ambulance, Harcourt ran from the pub and hid his pistol in a hole in the wall at the rear of the hotel before returning to his Carlton home. He was arrested several hours later.

Taplin died on the 21st of December. Dulcie maintained a vigil by his side. Grief-stricken, she attended her lover's funeral before returning to Sydney. From that day onward, the police christened Dulcie with the sobriquet, 'The Black Widow', a name also adopted by the underworld.

On the 7th of January 1938, after no more than three hours deliberation, the jury found thirty-eight-year-old Harcourt Lee not guilty of murdering Taplin.

Dulcie resumed working in Tilly's main brothel and quickly regained the title of the 'belle of the brothel'. One night, while drinking at the Bell's Hotel, Dulcie stole twenty pounds from an American tourist with whom she had spent the night. The tourist reported her to the Darlinghurst police and Dulcie was arrested. When she appeared in court, the magistrate sentenced her to one month's gaol at Long Bay Women's prison.

With her friend and rival for Calletti's affections, Nellie Cameron, living in Queensland after being ordered by the court to leave the state, Dulcie began visiting Calletti in gaol after her release. She always arrived with her cane basket filled with cigarettes, biscuits, coffee, and often a cooked chicken or two. She also bribed the guards with a few pounds so the pair could spend some time alone for sex. When Calletti was released the following April, he asked Dulcie to move into the flat he'd shared with Nellie, hoping it would make his wife jealous enough to return home.

Dulcie and Calletti lived the high life. They spent most nights partying and kicking up their heels at the Fifty-Fifty Club. Not wanting to return to work at the brothel, Dulcie started working privately, renting rooms under the aliases Tosca de Marquis and Tasca Damarene. She hoped the sobriquets would not attract the attention of one of Bumper's boys and be forced to pay him a cut out of her earnings. She was already paying the motel owners ten percent of her takings, but Bumper demanded thirty percent and if she could get out of paying him a penny, she would.

The relationship with Dulcie seemed to be a good one for Calletti. He had gained weight and was a lot more relaxed. However, his complacency ended abruptly after she convinced him that he was losing the respect and fear of his fellow gang members and other associates. Spurred on by Dulcie's need for money and possessions and to maintain the respect of his criminal peers, Calletti made a play to gain control of the SP Booking protection rackets in Darlinghurst and Surry Hills.

Several violent fights ensued between the gangs who quickly ceded Calletti their turf when most of their men were either hospitalised due to their injuries or were severely incapacitated. Another violent brawl broke out between Calletti's mob and the Brougham Street gang who were still selling protection to several SP Bookies. Calletti told his gang members to keep a watch on several members of the Brougham members and relieve them of their takings when the opportunity arose.

Numerous battles took place on the Woolloomooloo wharves and again on Butlers Stairs in the Domain, where several gang members were seriously injured, mostly from the Brougham Street mob. Over the following weeks, the Brougham leaders scaled down their rackets to almost nothing. Calletti bragged around the town that he had defeated the mob.

At thirty-seven years of age, Calletti was once again the king of Darlinghurst, and for several months no-one was brave enough to challenge him.

After attending his beloved grandmother's funeral on Sunday the 6th of August, Calletti met with Dulcie at the Tradesman's Arms. After a few drinks, his brain started ticking over about the money he was missing out on from the Brougham Street gang's new standover venture they had started with cabbies. With a little prompting by Dulcie, they made their way to 'the Cauldron' the name the sinister neighbourhood of Brougham Street was known by, where a birthday party for Peggy Patterson, a local nurse, was in full swing.

An uncomfortable silence overcame the partygoers when they saw who had disrupted their night. Several of the women, fearing a fight, stood behind their lovers, while others attempted to stare Dulcie and Calletti down.

"I 'ope you're not 'ere to cause a fuckin' blue," one of the gang members remarked as he took a few steps toward Calletti.

"Nah mate, I'm only here for a few friendly drinks."

The mob leaders cautiously called a truce and the party continued. However, the more booze he consumed throughout the night, the more boisterous and nastier Calletti became.

Unfortunately, the crime king made the mistake of bragging about how he was going to take over the gang's taxi standover business before threatening one of the Brougham gang members. A fight ensued. The sound of breaking glass interrupted the party-goers fun and the room fell into silence. Three shots then rang out causing everyone to drop to the floor. A few moments later, the shrill scream of a woman pierced the air. Peggy, the birthday girl had discovered Guido Calletti on the floor in a pool of blood.

One of the guests called for a taxi to take Calletti to the hospital. However, when the cabbie arrived and saw that he was expected to convey a wounded criminal, he refused. The driver had heard plenty of gossip about Calletti and he wasn't keen on getting involved in a police investigation.

He left the Brougham Street address and drove to a nearby police call box and reported the shooting. When Detective Sergeant Dimmock and a young constable arrived at the house to investigate the reported shooting, they saw Calletti cradled in a blonde woman's arms. One of the uniformed officers knelt to check if he was still alive. "He's unconscious and bleeding badly."

"What's your name, Miss?" McCarthy asked.

"Mary Eugene, Sir." Dulcie replied not wanting him to know who she was.

"Do you know this man?"

"Yes, he's a friend of mine. Guido Calletti. We came to the party together."

"You better go call an ambulance, Paul. This man's almost dead." McCarthy directed the constable.

An ambulance arrived twenty minutes later and conveyed Guido to St. Vincent's Hospital. The doctors did all they could to save Calletti. During surgery they removed two bullets from his abdomen and told the detectives that he was in a critical condition and not expected to live. Dulcie remained by his side in intensive care, holding his hands as she waited for him to regain consciousness. Unfortunately, Calletti succumbed to his wounds just before ten o'clock. He died in Dulcie's arms.

Detective Sergeants James and McCarthy led a group of detectives through the Brougham Street house to question the other men and women who had remained after the shooting. But they met a wall of silence and found not one firearm when they searched the premises.

7

Dressed in black, Dulcie attended the church service and sat on a pew five rows back from the altar. She watched as Guido's brother placed his prized football blazer across the coffin. She listened as a man bent over the coffin and in a voice raw with emotion, cried, "He was my mate and they shot him."

Before leaving the church, she went over to pay her final respects to Guido. Leaning across, she hugged her lover and kissed him on his cheek, openly weeping as the police stood nearby.

Dulcie caught sight of Nellie Cameron. And as her friend approached, she told her how Guido would appreciate that she was there. She offered Nellie her sympathies as she reached out and held her hand. Then both women in turn, returned to the coffin and kissed Calletti on his forehead and turned to leave the chapel.

They turned and made their way up the aisle when Dulcie was stopped by one of the detectives: "Excuse me, I'd like to ask you a few questions."

"What kind of cold-hearted bastard are you? Leave me alone and let me mourn!"

Nellie hugged Dulcie when they reached the footpath and offered her a ride in her waiting limousine.

As Guido's coffin was lowered into the ground, Dulcie and Nellie stood side by side, each sobbing into their handkerchiefs. Opposite them, Guido's mother openly wept beside her husband and surviving three sons.

7

Not wanting to attend court and give evidence at the inquest into Calletti's death, Dulcie fled to the mining town of Lithgow where she resumed working as a prostitute. She was aware the police would still be looking for her, so she continued using the name Mary Eugene.

However, one night she was arrested in the Lithgow Hotel and charged for ransacking and stealing from a motel room whilst a young couple were attending a wedding. Drunk, she abused the arresting officers and was charged for stealing, being drunk and disorderly as well as using indecent language. A policeman at the station recognised her from a photo on an outstanding warrant and asked her what her name was.

"Mary Eugene."

Not one to be easily fooled, the constable waited a few hours for his prisoner to wake up and then called out, "Dulcie!"

She looked up and asked what he wanted.

"A trip to Sydney, Miss Markham and that is exactly what you and I are about to take." He smirked.

When she appeared in court, she admitted to the stealing charges and was sentenced to one month in gaol and fined for being drunk in a public place and using indecent language.

Upon release from prison, Dulcie, tired of Sydney, packed her bags and again hopped on a train to Melbourne. John Abrahams, a small-time criminal, and heavy gambler was the first to fall for Dulcie's charms. Why she chose to keep company with such a lowlife was beyond most people. However, like all her relationships with men, her union with Abrahams didn't last long.

Two months into their relationship, Dulcie learned about the death of her estranged husband, Frank Bowen, who was also known as 'the prettiest boy in gangland', due to his handsome features. He had become embroiled in a gang dispute and was killed in a shootout in Kings Cross. Not ready to return to Sydney, she sent a wreath that said: 'We loved, we lost touch, we moved on. Rest in Peace, Frank. Love Dulcie'.

While out at the Rob Roy Hotel one night, a man well known to Abrahams, Frederick James Anderson, an underworld crime figure with a penchant for violence, took an immediate liking to Dulcie. She laughed when Abrahams told her that Anderson was also known by the name 'Paddles' due to his extraordinarily large feet as well as 'Big Doll' due to his height and looks. Dulcie took an instant liking to him and the two began secretly dating behind Abraham's back.

Anderson promised Dulcie the world and financed her setting up a brothel. When Abrahams found out about the joint business venture, he became enraged and told Dulcie that she couldn't see Anderson again. A fight broke out between the two, and after Dulcie threw a glass of beer at Abrahams, he retaliated by punching her in the face before throwing her across the room. Abrahams left her lying barely conscious on the floor.

Bloodied and bruised, Dulcie caught a taxi to Anderson's house. When he opened the door and saw the state she was in, he went into an immediate rage and threatened to kill Abrahams. She pleaded with him to stay with her, explaining that her live-in lover attacked her in a drunken fit of jealousy over their brothel plans. Anderson poured a whiskey for Dulcie and sat beside her on the settee fighting hard to control his temper.

On the 14th of June, when Anderson was driving Dulcie to a store, he passed the two-up school and spotted Abrahams climbing out of his car. He pulled over to the side of the road and ran toward him. A brawl between the two men erupted. However, outmanoeuvred by his larger adversary, Anderson lay humiliated, battered, and defeated on the footpath.

The following night, Anderson and Dulcie met a few friends at a Melbourne nightclub. Abrahams was also there. The two men stayed away from each other most of the night, however, as he was leaving the club, Abrahams called Anderson a 'fuckin' thievin' bastard' as he walked by his table. Not putting up with his effrontery, Anderson and two of his companions followed him through to the carpark and the sound of gunfire interrupted the patrons several minutes later.

Abrahams miraculously dodged the volley of bullets before furtively making his way to his car. When he opened the car door, he was surprised when he saw Anderson standing outside the opposite car window. His rival raised his pistol in front of him and fired one shot, hitting Abrahams at close range in the throat. Abrahams died before the ambulance and police arrived.

Several weeks later, Dulcie was picked up by police and charged with vagrancy. She had given the brothel to one of the women, not wanting to be involved in anything remotely close to Anderson. Dulcie spent two weeks in prison and upon her release, returned to Sydney and began working in Tilly Devine's Palmer Street brothel once more. She later learned that Anderson had been acquitted of Abraham's murder and was planning on returning to Sydney. She sent Anderson a letter and told him that she wasn't interested in continuing their relationship.

One night, a man looking for company contacted the brothel and was fortunate enough to speak with Tilly. He told her that her business came highly recommended and requested an attractive and well-spoken lady to spend an hour or two with. It was Nellie's night off, so Tilly waited for Dulcie to finish up with her client and told her to freshen up because she had a fine gentleman to meet in his room at the top-notch Wentworth Hotel.

"The punter sounds like a bit of an old fuckin 'stiff. Easy fuckin' money I reckon. You probably won't even get to fuck 'im. 'is cock will explode in 'is pants when 'e sees you naked."

"I hope you're right, Till. I'm about done for the night."

Just before nine o'clock, Dulcie knocked on the dark, lacquered door of room forty-six. She was surprised when it was opened by a distinguished looking gentleman dressed in a well-tailored black suit.

"Good evening, sir, I'm Dulcie. I've been sent to take care of you."

The man opened the door wider and let her through. His appreciative gaze followed her as he closed the door. He looked her up and down and lusted for her like no other woman he had met before, and there had been many. He didn't need to pay for sex, he could get that anywhere. But after hearing others talking about a few of the educated blonde prostitutes in Sydney and their sexual treats, he wanted to try it for himself, even if it was just the once.

"Good evening, Miss, I'm Hugh, and I must say I am both surprised and impressed with you. Would you like a glass of wine? I have a sweet Shiraz just wanting to pass by a beautiful lady's lips."

"Yes, please," Dulcie replied with a sultry smile.

Hugh handed her a glass of wine and Dulcie walked over to the bed, took a sip of wine from the crystal glass before placing it on the bedside table. She smiled toward her client as she began to undress.

For Hugh, there was nothing more enticing and exciting than watching a woman undress. Dulcie played her siren part well. She let her dress slink slowly down her body, revealing her long stockinged slim legs and sexy white silk French underwear.

Dulcie stopped and wagged her right index finger playfully toward Hugh as he walked toward the bed. "Not so fast, sweetheart. A little bit of cash needs to caress my hand before we get down to the tickety-boo."

"Oh yes, right. It's my first time with a lady such as yourself. I don't know the proper etiquette." Hugh blushed as he handed Dulcie thirty pounds.

"Proper etiquette, how gallant of you, sir." Dulcie smiled. "Thirty pounds, I see? Do you want me to stay the night?"

"You can stay if you like. I have no other plans," Hugh replied as he removed his double-breasted dinner jacket and began to unbutton his shirt. "That's if you're not otherwise en…en…engaged," he stuttered breathlessly as Dulcie removed her camisole, revealing her pert breasts.

He quickly closed the gap between them and took her chin gently in his hand. "You smell delightful, seductive, and alluringly… lovely," he gasped before kissing her.

After their time in bed, Dulcie searched through Hugh's wallet while he was taking a shower. She pulled out one piece of paper that had the NSW government insignia on the letterhead and was surprised to read that her client was a prominent politician from the United Australian Party. Dulcie had never taken an interest in politics. She had never voted in her life. But Hugh suddenly became of great interest to her.

Over the following months, Dulcie and her senator met almost weekly. Hugh would look for reasons to visit Sydney and spent more time away from his wife and children, which started to cause problems in his home life. He showered gifts of furs, pearl necklaces and perfume upon his lover, who had stopped charging him for their time together.

Eleven months into their relationship, Dulcie realised she was pregnant. After undergoing several abortions and suffering two miscarriages, she was both surprised and elated to be carrying this child. She hadn't planned on falling in love with the senator. But he was the first man to treat her so respectfully and made her feel like a feminine woman, not the gangster moll she had become. He wasn't as dangerous or exciting as her former beaus, but his down to earth attitude, gentlemanly manners, and his eagerness to pleasure her in bed, instead of her having to do all the pleasing, had shown her a different side of life, a life she now desired.

It was a miserable and foggy Monday evening when Dulcie's cab arrived at the Wentworth Hotel. The receptionist knew her by name and gave her the room key without being asked. He knew she was there to spend time with the senator, but also knew that many of their political and rich clients used the prestigious hotel to romance their mistresses whilst in Sydney on business. He also knew that their clients appreciated the discretion of its management and staff, most of all.

Dulcie glanced around the room to make sure all was perfect for Hugh's arrival. It felt so cold and uninviting being so well lit up. Wanting to make the atmosphere romantic, she turned off all the lights except a floor lamp in the corner and sat on the settee. Suddenly becoming nervous about breaking the news about her pregnancy to the senator, she fidgeted with the tassels of a doily on the armrest. She knew Hugh was deeply in love with her and had promised that they would be together soon. Dulcie hoped that the news that they were expecting a baby would be the catalyst for him to finally leave his wife and they could set up a home together in Canberra as he had promised.

After ordering a bottle of champagne and two steak meals to the room for nine o'clock, Dulcie changed into a sexy long white silk lacy nightdress and matching gown she had purchased that afternoon. She brushed her hair and freshened her perfume, wanting everything to be perfect for Hugh's arrival.

The champagne and meals were wheeled into the room, but the senator was oddly late. Dulcie went to the bay window again and checked to see if his black Oldsmobile was parked across the road and was disappointed to see that it wasn't. She walked over to the table and picked the silver dome off one of the meals and felt the plate. It was still warm, but she knew if Hugh didn't arrive soon, the meals would be cold and inedible.

It was almost ten o'clock when the senator finally arrived. He had been held up with family problems. Although she was disappointed that her dinner plans were ruined, Dulcie put on a smile and offered to massage Hugh's shoulders to relax him.

"Nothing can relax me at the moment. I hate to do this to you, but after tonight, I can't see you anymore. My wife and children are arriving tomorrow. Margaret's pregnant and wants us to tell her parents tomorrow night at a family dinner at their Vaucluse mansion." Hugh sighed as he sat slumped in an armchair.

Dulcie felt suddenly faint and nauseous. She slowly walked backward until her legs touched the bed. She sat down, staring into the nothingness as she tried to gather her thoughts. The words 'I can't see you anymore' and 'Margaret's pregnant' played over and over again in her mind like a broken gramophone recording. She walked over and kneeled beside the senator and touched his hand with her trembling fingers. He flinched at her touch before he stood and walked toward the window, staring out into the darkness. She followed him and stood beside him. Never in her life had she felt the need to be with a man like she did with Hugh. He was all she wanted in a man and she loved him deeply.

And he knew it.

He turned and took her in his arms. "You are such a beautiful creature. Any man would be proud to have you by their side," Hugh whispered. Instantly her heartbeat quickened as she hoped he was going to tell her that he couldn't be apart from her. His lips were so close to hers that she ached to kiss him and tell him that she too was carrying his child.

For a few moments, he looked at her longingly before letting go and he shook his head slowly, taking a few steps backward. "But it can't ever be. It's impossible for us to keep seeing each other. With Margaret being pregnant, the newspaper reporters will keep an eye on everything we do. I can't afford the gossip or to lose my status within the party, especially now with the current upheaval and the wave of distrust against Menzies."

"How far along is she?" Dulcie asked quietly.

Hugh took an intake of breath while he looked Dulcie in the eyes and replied, "Four or five months."

The words cut through Dulcie like a knife. Her trust in him completely shattered with those few words. He'd told her that he wasn't sleeping with his wife—they had separate bedrooms. She felt betrayed. She held back the tears as she gathered her clothes before walking to the bathroom. She held back the anger and hurt as she changed into her clothes and shoes before sitting on the toilet for a few moments to gather the strength to walk away.

For what seemed like hours, but were mere seconds, Dulcie stood with her hand on the bathroom door handle. Swallowing hard, she opened the door and walked the few steps to the hotel room's door. Without looking back, she turned the knob and walked out of the senator's life.

When she arrived home, Dulcie walked to the kitchen and put the kettle on the stove before going to her bedroom and stripping off her clothes. She sat on the bed sobbing as the reality hit that she had lost her dream lover, her dream future, and was in a worse position now than when she'd first met him.

She placed her hands over the small bump of her belly, and for the first time considered aborting the baby. She was almost five months pregnant, the same duration as Hugh's wife. Almost as if the baby could read her thoughts, Dulcie felt the first niggle of movement inside her womb.

She broke down crying. Her baby was alive.

She couldn't kill it.

She wiped her eyes and lay back on the bed, tracing her stomach with her fingers and softly whispered, "We'll be right sweet pea, we'll be right."

The Rudderless Direction of Life and War

When Japanese submarines attacked Sydney Harbour, Dulcie, who retired from prostitution due to being heavily pregnant, desperately wanted to contact Hugh and ask for money to leave the state to protect their unborn child. But she could not. She had been a headliner in the papers enough and did not want to subject her child to the ridicule and attention it would receive being the bastard child of a prostitute and a cheating politician.

Dulcie was fortunate to have Tilly in her life. The brothel Madam had spent a fortune on baby necessities and ensured that the pregnant mother ate plenty of fruit and vegetables and took proper care of herself. Dulcie knew how much Tilly still missed her son, so she asked her if she would like to be the baby's Godmother. Tilly accepted the honour and was so proud of being the Godmother that she offered to buy Dulcie a cottage in Surry Hills to live in rent-free for as long as she wanted. Dulcie was appreciative of her generous offer but told Tilly that she wasn't planning on remaining in Sydney in fear of running into the baby's father. Tilly had tried to find out who the father of the child was since learning of the pregnancy, but Dulcie vowed to take her secret to the grave.

As the due date neared, Dulcie began to worry about the responsibility of bringing a child into the world. She knew that nothing would ever be the same for her again and her life of careless abandon was over. Overwhelmed by hormones, she had a sudden urge to see her mother. She had not seen her family in years. She'd heard that her sister had married, and she now had a niece. News that did surprise her, was that her mother had also remarried. But the last time she spoke with her sister, she told her that her mother and stepfather were embarrassed by the constant headlines in the paper about her life of crime and prostitution and would not welcome her if she were to visit. Dulcie closed her eyes and wiped away the tears, cursing the pregnancy for her melancholy thoughts.

On the 29th of February, Dulcie was woken by a dull backache. She got out of bed and made herself a cup of tea. The pain wasn't constant, so she put it down to falling asleep on the settee the previous night. However, two days later while taking a shower, she felt a cramping pain in her lower abdomen. Knowing that the time for the birth of her baby was just days away, she called Tilly, who rushed over. After feeling her tightening abdomen, Tilly told her that she was probably in early labour and more than likely had some time before the baby would come. She told her to rest and call her when the pains were ten minutes apart.

The contractions strengthened around two o'clock and Dulcie was unable to get comfortable. No more than an hour later, she phoned Tilly. The pains were ten minutes apart.

Tilly attempted to keep Dulcie comfortable with back rubs and placing warm towels on her lower back and abdomen. However, later that night when her contractions were a minute apart and much more intense, Dulcie became aggressive and told Tilly not to touch her. She felt like she had been in labour for an eternity and the baby would never find its way out. She rolled on the bed as one contraction tore through her abdomen, "Ohhh my fuckin' god!" Dulcie screamed, "this baby is going to tear my insides apart!"

"It'll be all over soon, sweet'art. We just need those waters to break," Tilly cooed as she wiped Dulcie's face with a cool cloth.

Twenty minutes later after an ear-piercing scream during a long and hard contraction, Dulcie's waters finally broke. "That feels so nice and warm." She sighed. "Is the baby coming yet?"

"Not yet darlin', it'll be here soon."

Dulcie's contractions suddenly became so close that it felt like they were never ending, and her abdomen was tied in one huge knot. She complained that her hips were aching, and the back pain was unbearable.

Tilly told her to raise herself up and pushed the bed pillows underneath Dulcie's abdomen. "Now, 'unch yourself over. 'opefully this will relieve the pressure."

"This baby is fuckin' taking fooorreeevveerrr to come!" Dulcie yelled as another long contraction ripped through her body.

After assisting Dulcie to squat in the bed, Tilly told her to use the bedhead to anchor her through the contractions. Tilly could see how tired Dulcie was and told her that if the baby wasn't born soon, she'd ring for an ambulance.

Dulcie pushed and pushed until her face was crimson. Tilly told her to slow down or she would tear herself. She slowed down the pushing a little before screaming out that she could feel something between her legs. She turned to watch Tilly as the pain slowly subsided.

"That's the wee baby's 'ead!" Tilly replied excitedly.

Dulcie felt a stronger urge to push and she pushed long and hard as Tilly squealed that the baby's head was out. "Really! You can see it?" Dulcie excitedly asked between panting.

"Yes, a 'ead full of fuzzy blonde 'air just like yours! Now get ready to push again."

"No wonder it fuckin' hurt!" The soon to be mother half laughed.

Then after two more pushes, Dulcie delivered her baby into the world.

"You 'ave a daughter, darlin'!" Tilly exclaimed. "Oh, the sweet little mite already 'as 'er eyes open."

"A little girl. I have a little girl?"

Tilly clamped the cord before gently picking up the newborn, who immediately let out a loud and healthy cry. She looked at the perfect baby and smiled as she placed her in her mother's arms. "She's slippery and warm!" Dulcie smiled as she looked down upon her daughter and smiled. "All that bloody agonising pain and look what I have. A perfect little angel."

"She's a corker alright." Tilly lovingly smiled. "What's 'er name sweet'art'?"

"Amelia Mary Louise Markham. Mary in honour of her Godmother." Dulcie smiled not taking her eyes off her daughter.

"Thank you. I feel very 'onoured. A beautiful ending for the last day orf February."

"Isn't she just beautiful?" Dulcie gushed as she looked upon her daughter with the pure love. "She's much smaller than I could ever have imagined."

Dulcie started crying. She was overwhelmed with emotion that she could finally see her baby after carrying her for nine long months. She had never felt such overpowering love for anyone in her life until she looked into the innocent eyes of her daughter.

With the financial assistance of Tilly and the girls from the brothels, Dulcie didn't need to return to work. But when Amelia was five months old, the owner of her rented flat told her she needed to find somewhere else to live as he had family arriving from England and they needed the flat. Dulcie and Amelia moved in with Tilly who cared for the baby after Dulcie returned to work at Palmer Street. However, her stay at the Maroubra house was short-lived when Dulcie met Arthur Williams and relocated to Queensland, moving into his Newfarm house.

7

In 1943 with the influx of soldiers on the South Coast of Queensland, (now known as the Gold Coast after a name change in 1953), Dulcie thought she could capitalise on being the new blonde in the area. She rang Tilly and asked if she could come and get Amelia and look after her for a while. Tilly was on the next train to Queensland. Three days later, Dulcie promised her one-year-old daughter that she would be down to pick her up very soon. And then with one last kiss and hug, Tilly drove off in a cab with Amelia to the train station.

Using the pseudonym "Tosca de Merene" Dulcie worked in several brothels along the coastal strip. She had worked almost twenty hours a day for the first few weeks and made less than half of the money she made in Sydney because prices were lower, and the house cut was higher. Arthur, to supplement their income, began selling illegal liquor that Tilly was sending him through a smuggler. His share was forty percent of the sales. The remaining money he had given to the smuggler.

Between Dulcie's and Arthur's illegal activities, they were making a fair living and were able to move out of the Sea Haven Guest House and rented a fully furnished two bedroom flat at Main Beach for £6/6/ a week. Two weeks after settling in, Dulcie caught a train to Sydney to pick up her daughter. When she arrived at Central Station, she saw Tilly and Amelia waiting on the platform. Dulcie couldn't believe how much her little girl had grown in the six months she had been away.

Life on the coast was a happy one for the family. Dulcie often spent the warm days at the beach with Amelia, or they went fishing with Arthur on a nearby wharf during his time off work.

Alas, almost a year later, their idyllic life took a turn for the worst when Arthur overcharged a group of American soldiers for whiskey and they sought revenge. One night while the family was sleeping, four American GIs broke down the front door of their flat and dragged Arthur from bed. One of the men held Arthur's hands behind his back while another man punched him in the jaw and abdomen several times. When Arthur fell to the floor, two more soldiers joined the fray in kicking him until he lay in a pool of his own blood.

Grabbing her daughter from her cot, Dulcie ran out in the street hysterically screaming for help. Two men who were drinking beer on a verandah of a house opposite asked what had happened. When they heard that one of their own was being attacked by Americans, both men bolted into the house to help. Upon the arrival of reinforcements, the Americans fled by the back door and through an open window in the kitchen.

The neighbours rushed Arthur to the hospital where he was treated for a fractured arm, four broken ribs and a broken nose. Also suffering two black eyes, extensive bruising, and abrasions, Arthur spent four days in the hospital.

Afraid for the safety of both her and her daughter, Dulcie and Amelia stayed in a local motel until two of Tilly's minders arrived. Now with protection, they returned home where the bodyguards remained until a week after Arthur's discharge.

Arthur's recovery took longer than expected, and with the meagre income made from the brothels, Dulcie fell behind in the rent. She worked as many hours as she could, but still didn't make enough money to pay for rent, food, and taxi fares. It wasn't long before the family was evicted.

Homeless and broke, Dulcie and her family returned to Sydney where Tilly put them up in her Maroubra home. Dulcie resumed working at the Palmer Street brothel while Tilly shared the care of two-year-old Amelia with her trusted friend, Olive.

Arthur resumed selling sly grog for Tilly, but not without threats from Kate Leigh and her gang members. While speaking with one of Tilly's buyers at a Newtown gambling house one afternoon, Kate arrived. When she saw Arthur, she immediately assumed he was there to usurp her grog and cocaine trade and sent John, one of her henchmen after him.

The gangster pushed Arthur against the wall and was pressing a pistol up against his nose when Ray Kelly walked in. If it weren't for the intervention of the crooked detective who was there to collect his monthly protection money, Bruce, the owner of the gambling den, would have been wiping Arthur's brains off the wall.

Dulcie was happy being back at Palmer Street. She made more than the other women because she wasn't averse to servicing the Negro men when the Aboriginal girls weren't available. The African American men loved Dulcie. Her blonde hair, slim legs and natural beauty attracted them in their droves and most of the GIs tipped her generously for her first-class service. Dulcie made up to sixty pounds extra each week just from tips seeing her 'black fellows', as she affectionately called them.

Within months of working for Tilly, Dulcie had made enough money to set up her own brothel. She told Tilly what she was planning, and she told her to be careful and if she could help in any way, to let her know. Two weeks later, Dulcie was operating her own brothel in Riley Street, Surry Hills.

On the 27th of November Dulcie got into some difficulties when one of the regular clients arrived at her home banging on her door. She angrily answered and asked him what the fuck he wanted.

"What the fuck do you think I want? How much to fuck the brothel madam?"

When she refused to let him in, he became violent and pushed his way past her and dragged her to the bedroom. When Dulcie tried to escape, he slapped her across the face and threw her onto the bed.

Fearing for her life, Dulcie reached for the revolver she kept in the bedside drawer and shot him. Not wanting to be charged with attempted murder, she drove him to St. Vincent's Hospital and told the nurses that she had found him injured in the Domain. When questioned by the police, the soldier told them it was Dulcie who had shot him and gave the police her address.

When the detectives arrived at Dulcie's home, she answered their questions and allowed them to search the house. One of the detectives found bloodstained bedding in the bathroom and asked how the blood came to be on the sheet. Dulcie told him that it was her 'ladies time' and she hadn't gotten around to washing it. Appalled the policeman dropped the sheet back onto the floor and they left, satisfied with her answers.

7

On Christmas morning 1945, Bing Crosby's *White Christmas* was playing on the gramophone as Dulcie and Tilly fussed over Amelia. The little girl, wearing a pretty red frock and red patent leather shoes, sat cross-legged next to the presents under the well-lit Christmas tree. The blonde ringlets that usually haloed her face were held back by red hairclips and ribbons. Amelia was glowing with the childhood innocence of expectancy and excitement as she patiently waited to open the brightly wrapped Christmas gifts.

"Can't I just open one please, Mummy?" Amelia asked as she eyed a present topped with a shiny red bow.

Jim chuckled at the little girl's pleading eyes, "You only want to open one Amelia? I think Santa brought you more than one surprise."

He got up from his chair and stood beside Dulcie. "I think you should open this one first." Jim said picking up a rectangular parcel topped with a small tag signed from him and passing it to her. Amelia ripped into the paper and squealed in delight when she saw the Clementine doll.

Dulcie handed her another gift, and again the paper was torn apart in glee as Amelia unwrapped a yellow teddy bear with moveable limbs. She hugged the soft toy close and kissed him before placing him in the floor beside her as Tilly and her mother piled more gifts in front of her.

It was a hot day, and Amelia was red-faced and sweaty as Jim and Arthur watched her ride her new red two-wheeled scooter up and down the garden path. Dulcie called them in for lunch, handing Amelia a glass of cordial with ice to cool her down.

After washing her daughter's hands, Dulcie and Amelia joined everyone at the table for roast pork and redcurrant jam sandwiches. The adults enjoyed their meal with a beer or two, while Amelia drank an entire jug of iced cordial. Tilly could see her Goddaughter was tired and fussed over her like a mother hen before gently carrying her to the bedroom that she had decorated specially for her. She placed her on top of the bed and started to read Amelia her favourite book, Fuzzy Wuzzy Rabbit. Before she had reached the fourth page, her little angel was dead to the world. She smiled and kissed Amelia's forehead and left the door ajar before returning to the living room.

That evening after enjoying a Christmas dinner of roast duck, chicken, and lamb with all the trimmings, Dulcie put Amelia to bed. When she returned to the living room, everyone was seated around the shortwave radio, listening to King George as he addressed his Empire with his Christmas message.

"Once more, on Christmas Day, I speak to millions of you scattered far and near across the world. As always, I am greatly moved by the thought that so vast and friendly an audience hears the words I speak from this room, where the Queen and I with our daughters are fortunate enough to be spending a Christmas at home...

7

Unfortunately for Dulcie, her bad luck continued. In January 1946, she realised with dread that she was pregnant again. When Arthur left to do a pickup for Jim, she caught a taxi to Woolloomooloo leaving Amelia with Olive. She continued on to Victoria Street, Darlinghurst where she met with Ivy Collins, a recommended abortionist. Collins was busy, but her daughter took the forty-five pounds fee and made an appointment for Dulcie the following Friday evening.

Returning to her brothel, Dulcie noticed several men standing at the corner, and a further two were parked in their cars opposite her house. She turned on the lamp and covered it with a red scarf at the front window signalling that the brothel was open for business. Her girls, Caroline, May, and Eileen were immediately run off their feet.

Late Friday afternoon, Dulcie had a taxi drop her off at the corner of Downs and Liverpool and Forbes Streets, Darlinghurst. From there she made her way on foot toward Victoria Street for her appointment when she was stopped by Constable Niall who knew Dulcie and her habits quite well.

He asked her why she was out so late at night and she told him that she just needed a walk out in the fresh air. The policeman noticed she didn't carry a purse and arrested her for having insufficient lawful means of support. Dulcie pleaded to the police officer to release her, telling him that she had to return home to her daughter. Niall, who was accustomed to her lies, ignored her.

Appearing in Darlinghurst court the following afternoon as Dulcie Williams, she pleaded not guilty to all charges. When questioned about her abode, she told the court that she was living with Arthur Williams and her four-year-old daughter at 361 Liverpool Street, Darlinghurst. She lied and said they had been living together for six years and her husband supported both her and her daughter financially. When the magistrate asked why she was found without any money or a handbag, Dulcie explained how she'd gone for a walk and didn't realise how far she had gone. The magistrate gave her the benefit of the doubt and dismissed the charges.

That evening, she again made her way to Ivy Collins' with twenty pounds in her handbag in case she was questioned by the police again. After midnight, Dulcie staggered out of a taxi and made her way inside her home, no longer pregnant.

The relationship between Dulcie and Arthur started to corrode several months later and they went their separate ways. Although she had worked for Tilly for many years, Dulcie didn't pick up on the brothel Madam's entrepreneurial skills and was broke within six months of opening her brothel's door.

One October afternoon while she was drinking at the Tradesman's Arms with a couple of GIs, she was introduced to Donald "The Duck" Day. An ex-jockey, Day made his money as a racketeer and standover man whose pistol made up for his miniature four feet one height. He also sold bootleg grog to the American soldiers.

Donny had an electrifying, magnetic personality. Dulcie also considered him an attentive and magnificent lover. She once joked to one of her friends, "The bastard may be short, but his cock is fuckin' ten inches long and it stands at attention all night!" Dulcie knew that Day was still in involved with his long-term, common-law wife, thirty-nine-year-old Rene Day and that he also had another lover on the side, twenty-year-old blonde, Joyce Cusack. He was a bit of a Casanova, but she was a seductress herself. Adultery or being a mistress was never a concern to her.

Dulcie's relationship with Day ended when his wife's lover, Keith Kitchener Hull, shot him four times in self-defence at their brothel above a fruit shop at 428 Crown Street, Surry Hills.

It didn't take long for the newspapers get hold of the 'Angel of Death's' relationship with Donald Day. The Perth *Mirror* ran an editorial where they named her 'Pretty Dulcie' and stated she had a 'death curse' hovering around her like a shadow. They said that 'in the palm of her beautiful white hand, men dance to the tune she calls. And the tune she calls is DEATH! Year in, year out, it seems, this glamorous siren of the underworld dawdles on Death's doorstep. And one after another the men who have loved her have met a tragic end.'

7

Single once again, Dulcie left Amelia in Tilly's care and headed off to Melbourne under the alias Tosca de Marquis. In her handbag, she carried over eight hundred pounds in cash. Not long after alighting from the bus, she entered a local real estate office in St Kilda seeking a house to operate a brothel from.

Dulcie was surprised when she saw one of her past clients sitting behind the large oak desk. "Eddie? Fancy fuckin' seeing you here. I'm sure you remember me, sweetheart."

"Yes, yes. Of course, I do Miss, miss…" Edward stammered as he nervously looked toward his wife.

"de Marquis, Tosca de Marquis. I'm in search of a house to run a business from. Do you have anything available?"

"I think there's a vacant house in Brighton Road," Mrs. Pitman interjected as she approached them.

"Thank you, but I was thinking more about the Acland Street area."

"Oh, we don't have anything available in *that* location."

"I wasn't fuckin' talking to you anyhow, you fuckin' arrogant fat bitch!" Dulcie snapped. "Do you have any houses or not, Mr. Pitman?"

"Edward, get her out of here now. We don't want the likes of *her* in our office!" Mrs. Pitman snipped before storming back to her office.

Edward walked over to Dulcie as she spat a few more insults towards his wife and asked her to leave, whispering as they headed to the door, "Meet me at 56 Acland Street at midday. The place is yours and it's off the books."

Later that evening to celebrate her new enterprise, Dulcie caught a cab and asked the driver to take her to a place that had good music and food. He drove her to the Plaza Café on the corner of Barkly Street. She gave the cabbie a two-pound tip and entered the café, finding herself a table toward the back.

Dulcie found herself mesmerised by the female blues singer whose voice seemed to touch her soul. Molly Byron, who wore her curly hair cropped short like a man's and dressed in black trousers, a man's shirt, and a tie, started playing a trumpet, backed by her all-woman jazz band. Dulcie remained at the café until closing, filling herself upon the delightful food and Italian coffee enjoying the music.

The following week, Dulcie had her brothel up and running. Acland Street was a dodgy, run-down, drug-infested area in a shady part of St Kilda. Wanting to ensure a safe working environment for herself and her girls by seeking out a protector for the brothel, she made her way to the

Court House hotel, aka the 'blood house' where the barman introduced her to several rough looking men.

There she met Leslie 'Scotland Yard' Walkerden, a violent criminal who was the type of man Dulcie fell for. He was hard-nosed and bad to the bone, a potent aphrodisiac for the gangster moll. The feeling was mutual. The pair left the hotel before closing time after Dulcie suggested that they would find more privacy at her house where Leslie became another notch in her garter belt.

The Scarlet Room brothel was very profitable for Dulcie. She enjoyed being a Madam and hostess, directing men to a dimly lit room where the girls would introduce themselves before serving their quarry a glass of whiskey or beer.

Walkerden and his men often dealt with the bullshitters who tried to touch the girls up before leaving for a wank up the street, or the young men who came in, chose a girl and when they entered the room and were asked for the money, had empty pockets. A tough lesson, but the bullshitters learned not to fuck with Dulcie Cameron.

One night when Walkerden was taking care of business elsewhere, Dulcie was in her bedroom and heard one of her girls arguing with a client. She didn't bother getting dressed and arrived in the room wearing her lingerie. The man refused to pay Sharon, who had made the mistake of servicing him before taking the money. Dulcie demanded the five pounds be paid and the man laughed at her before walking out the door. The enraged Madam rushed to the linen closet and retrieved an axe before chasing the man down the street threatening to kill him. The police arrived, and after one of them covered Dulcie with his coat, he asked her what happened.

"The bastard insulted me about my price!" She spat.

The relationship between Dulcie and Walkerden was a happy one. They never fought or argued. He wanted to marry her and told her that he would welcome Amelia with open arms.

Life was perfect once more for Dulcie. In early September, she sent a telegram to Tilly advising her that she would be arriving to pick her daughter up to bring her back to Melbourne on the 20th of the month.

Fate decided it was time for another gangster to leave the earth. On the 12th of September Walkerden left the Baccarat club in the early hours of the morning and noticed that one of his back tyres was flat. He retrieved the jack from the back of the car and set about changing the tyre. Three armed men jumped from a nearby Morris and began shooting at Walkerden as he made a run for it across the street. Not able to outrun the spray of bullets, he was hit by a hail of buckshot from the shotgun in his left arm and abdomen. The shooters took off in their car as Walkerden staggered along the footpath, calling for help. A man from a nearby house answered his call and rushed him to hospital. When the nurses removed Walkerden's clothing, they saw that his left arm was almost severed, and his stomach had been shot out. Surgeons did the best they could but due to the extensive injuries, they were forced to amputate the arm.

Two days later, when questioned by detectives, Walkerden refused to name his attackers. "Don't waste your time. I'll fix it my way."

He died half an hour later.

Dulcie was devastated by her lover's death. She closed her brothel and turned to drugs and alcohol, believing the newspaper reports that she was the 'angel of death'. She flitted between Melbourne and Sydney.

When in Sydney, she enjoyed a few dalliances whilst working as a prostitute in brothels throughout Surry Hills, Woolloomooloo and of course for her close friend and benefactor, Tilly Devine. Due to drugs, alcohol and her stressful lifestyle, Dulcie's beauty was fading, and she was unable to make the amount of money as before.

In April 1951, Dulcie returned to Melbourne where she rented a house in Fawkner, St Kilda. She returned to working in brothels and keeping company with gangsters. She also spent time reminiscing with her thirty-one-year-old sister, Flo.

Dulcie, Flo, and her brother-in-law, George had something else in common—they were all criminals. Flo and George weren't involved in anything major, just petty crimes like stealing and shoplifting. One night after imbibing a few too many beers, they left Flo's house in St Kilda with a plan to break into a local department store. However, on their way they stumbled across a business van parked down the street. Ensuring that no-one was around, they stole four rolls of material and other items, hiding the stash under floorboards in a vacant house two doors down from Flo's. However, their early morning shenanigans were witnessed. A woman who lived in a nearby house, told police she saw a neighbour with two other people standing near the van earlier in the night. She pointed to Flo's house.

The police continued their surveillance of Flo and George's home, and when one of the constables recognised Dulcie, he told his partner that she was involved in prostitution and was also a gangster moll.

"Could be a crime ring!" His partner enthused.

"I don't think so with those other two. They look more like paupers than organised criminals."

After a few hours, Dulcie, Flo, and George walked up to the vacant house. The constables waited a few minutes before entering the building.

"We're here to conduct a search for stolen goods." Constable Garrett stated. "Which one of you own the house?"

"I'm watching the property for the owner until he returns." George replied.

"Keep your mouth shut George!" Dulcie snapped.

"Criminals keep their mouths shut when they have something to hide." Constable O'Brien said as he began searching the room.

Moments later he discovered the stolen items under the floorboards in a bedroom and arrested the family members.

In court O'Brien said that the stolen goods were hidden under a hinged door which had been covered with carpet and a wardrobe. Dulcie and Flo denied knowing anything about the trapdoor. George told the magistrate he checked the property a couple of times a week while the owners were away in England, and he'd never set eyes on the stolen goods before…

"There is no evidence of actual possession against any of the accused. This case is dismissed. The defendants are free to go." The magistrate ordered.

In May 1952, while drinking at the Court House Hotel Dulcie met twenty-three-year-old former professional boxer, Gavan Walsh. Gavan boxed under the name 'Young Stenner'. Walsh dabbled in some minor criminal activities, but nothing of the calibre of Dulcie's usual boyfriends. The young man fell hard for Dulcie, but to the thirty-eight-year-old, he was just a fling.

During a drinking soirée she hosted at her Fawkner Street home on the 25th of September, Dulcie met the redheaded, suavely dressed Leonard 'Redda' Lewis. She was immediately smitten with the cheeky petty criminal and flirted with him.

Later that evening, Charles Mills and Ernest Martin turned up at the house in search of Gavan. They found him and his brother, Desmond Walsh, chatting with Dulcie, who was sitting up in bed. Mills started yelling and demanding money Gavan had stolen. Desmond tried to explain to the men that his brother wasn't the man they were looking for, that he was the one who had stolen the money. They ignored him.

Afraid that the interlopers were about to shoot one of the brothers, Dulcie tried to escape. The deafening crack of a pistol echoed in the confines of her bedroom. Dulcie's face was a mask of shock and fear. Her scream broke through the suffocating tension as the searing heat of the bullet burned into her flesh.

Gavan leapt to her aid, but both Mills and Martin fired at him shooting him in the leg and stomach. Desmond reached down to help his brother and was shot in the hand by Mills. Before leaving, Mills shot Gavan in the stomach again. Both gunmen then fled. One of the guests called an ambulance before also taking flight.

Arriving before the ambulance, the police found Desmond in the bedroom trying to help his younger brother, who lay unconscious on the floor. When the medics entered the room, they kicked the empty wine and whiskey bottles out of the way so they could tend to the wounded. The ambulance attendants dressed the bullet wounds as best they could and rushed the victims to the Royal Alfred Hospital.

When the police spoke to the doctors, they were told that Dulcie was in a serious condition, Desmond was bleeding from his shattered hand, but Gavan was critical. The three were rushed into surgery. The bullet was removed from Dulcie's shattered hip and she was plastered from her ankle to her thigh. The bullets were removed from Gavan's leg and stomach, but the doctors held grave fears for his survival. The bones in Desmond's hand were shattered and after several hours in surgery, the doctors mended the hand the best they could.

Gavan later died in the recovery room during the early hours of the morning, having never regained consciousness.

While she was recovering, Dulcie received regular visits from Redda Lewis. The two became lovers upon her release from hospital and Lewis moved into the Fawkner Street house. In December, just three months after Gavan died, Dulcie and Lewis married in the very bedroom she and the Walsh brothers were shot.

On the morning of her fourth wedding, Dulcie sat on the side of her bed with her plastered leg resting upon a chair. Redda, ever considerate of his lover, had roped off the room to protect her leg. Dulcie looked like a virgin bride dressed in a fitted white skirt suit, her coiffed platinum blonde hair was topped with a white halo veil covering half her face, and her lips were coloured with her signature red lipstick.

Lewis was smartly dressed in a black suit with a black and red striped tie. In the presence of more than sixty guests who were squeezed in throughout the house, Dulcie and Redda traded 'I dos' before sealing their vows with a kiss.

When a *Truth* reporter who had attended the wedding asked Dulcie if she had any qualms about mixing marriage and violent death, she replied: "Not a fuckin' one."

7

At the murder trial for Mills and Martin, Dulcie, still recovering from the shooting, was carried to the witness box by her husband. When the solicitor for the defence asked her if she and the Walsh brothers had been shot by the men sitting beside him, she denied seeing either man at her house.

The jury retired and a few minutes later returned with a verdict of not guilty.

When Dulcie had recovered enough, she and Redda travelled to Sydney. They had just sat down to a cup of tea when they were interrupted by a knock on the door. Redda answered the knock and found two uniformed constables standing outside.

"Is Mrs. Dulcie Lewis here?"

"Yes." Redda answered.

"Your name please sir?"

"Leonard Lewis. What do you want with my wife?"

"Mrs. Lewis? You are to accompany us to Darlinghurst Police Station where you will be charged with consorting with the known criminal, Leonard Lewis. You will appear before a magistrate this afternoon."

"What? He's my fuckin' husband! You can't arrest me for being with the man I am married to! Fuck off out of here!"

"Please come with us without any further use of indecent language or I will charge you. Come along quietly please."

"Go with them, love. I'll see what I can do."

The magistrate was cold and straightforward when he told Dulcie that he didn't care that she was married to Leonard Lewis. She had broken the law being in his company and the charges would stand. He then sentenced her to seven days in gaol.

The week after Dulcie's release, the Lewis's set up house in Liverpool Street, Darlinghurst. However, their marriage soon began to unravel. Dulcie wanted money to furnish a room for her daughter, so she could live with them. Lewis wasn't interested in children, especially someone else's bastard and told her so. From then on, the pair fought incessantly.

The Lewis's no longer shared a bed. Redda also stopped sharing his criminal earnings with Dulcie. Having no other choice, she began working in several of the local brothels. But Dulcie found pickings were grim with the younger and prettier girls that were available. She was still attractive, but she walked with a limp which caused the men to think that she was handicapped.

Sex with clients didn't fulfil Dulcie's carnal needs, so she sought out other men to liaise with while her husband was sniffing out lovers for himself. She became involved in several flings but none of the men held much fascination for her. One night at the Ziegfeld Club, she met Ernest Martin who had been arrested for shooting her former lover, Gavan Walsh. The pair became an item.

On the 4th of July 1947, Dulcie and Martin returned to her home in St Kilda. Ernest invited his twin brother, Charles to dinner one Saturday night and during the meal, Charles brought up "The Duck", whom he knew Dulcie was once involved with. She told him that they had only met a few times and that was only for fucking. Charles told her that he would like to see Hull dead in revenge for killing Day. Dulcie told him that she wasn't interested in becoming involved in any more violence

Charlie returned to Dulcie's house on the 27th of July with a man named George Barratt. They banged on the front door so hard that Ernest, fearing trouble, opened the door armed with a pistol. The men pushed their way inside and told Dulcie and Ernest that if the police turned up, they were to say they had been with them all day.

"Why? What the fuck have you bastards done? I told you I want to keep out of fuckin' trouble, Charlie!" Dulcie fumed.

Barratt admitted shooting Hull while he was sitting in the cab of a truck and they didn't know whether he was alive or not. Dulcie rang the hospital giving the name Diedre Hull and asked after her 'cousin' Keith. She was told he was resting comfortably and had been wounded in his chest and both wrists.

"You stupid fuckin' cunts! Dulcie said to leave it alone Charlie! You know this will bring the fuckin' cops to our door!" Ernest raged. "We'll alibi you and not for you fuckin' idiots, but to keep the cops at bay!"

On the 31st of July, at the behest of his brother, Ernest and Dulcie visited the boarding house owned by Valma Hull, the wounded man's wife. They wanted to ask about her husband's shooting. Valma, thinking she was about to be killed, rang the police, and gave them the description of the people at the door. "The woman said her name was Dulcie," she said before ending the call.

During their investigations, the police were told that friends of Donald Day were furious that the murderer had got off. They said one man in particular, Charles Martin, often raged about revenge. The police were already aware of Martin's reputation of being a gunman and made sure they were heavily armed before leaving to question him. Charles gave Dulcie and his brother as an alibi, saying that he and George Barratt had spent the entire day with them drinking and playing poker. The police then visited a nervous Barratt who had a slightly different version of events—he said that he had gone to the movies with Charles, Dulcie, and Ernest.

CIB officers were suspicious when they heard Dulcie Markham's name mentioned and immediately set off to question her. When they arrived, both Dulcie and Ernest told them the same story as Charles had. They each said that they didn't understand why George would say they went to the movies.

"George was so fuckin' drunk that it's a wonder he didn't think that he was in the fuckin' movie with the amount of grog he drank," Dulcie joked. One of the detectives then point-blank asked Dulcie if she attended the boarding house owned by Valma Hull on the 31st of July. Dulcie said she went around to make sure that she was alright as she had met Hull once or twice in Sydney. When the other detective asked Ernest if he had accompanied Dulcie, he admitted that he had as she couldn't drive anymore with her bunged-up hip.

On the 4th of August, Martin and Barratt were charged with the attempted murder of Keith Hull. Ernest was also charged with the attempted murder of Valma Hull. They appeared in St Kilda court and entered a plea of not guilty. Bail was refused for the men and they were remanded until the 12th of August. Only Ernest was allowed bail.

The following Saturday, after hearing rumours she was about to be arrested, smartly dressed Dulcie walked into Russell Street Police Station and banged on the sergeant's desk.

"If there is any charge waiting for me, I am here to answer for it." She was arrested for conspiring to murder Valma Hull and was released on bail.

When Keith Hull refused to name his assailant, the case fell apart. The magistrate had no option than to dismiss the charges against all defendants.

7

In mid-April 1952, after falling off the bed in a Surry Hills brothel, Dulcie required further surgery on her hip. Whilst in hospital, she and Lewis decided to go their separate ways. Lewis returned to Melbourne and moved back into his parents' home in Prahran.

Upon answering the doorbell on the 22nd of April, Lewis was shot three times in the stomach and fell to the floor. As he called out to his parents for help, the coldblooded gunman shot him a further three times. His distraught mother called the ambulance and then the police. Following a frantic rush to the hospital and extensive surgery, Lewis survived.

After he woke from surgery, one of the detectives pushed hard for him to name his assailant. Redda coolly replied: "I'll cop it sweet."

Dulcie didn't travel to Melbourne to see her husband. She didn't send him a card, flowers or even call him. She didn't want a man in her life who refused to accept her daughter.

7

Plagued by reporters after exiting a local shopping centre, Dulcie allowed them a few minutes. The first reporter to ask a question was from the *Daily Mirror*. "Dulcie, how do you feel about your husband being shot?"

"I've had enough. I don't want to be involved in any more shootings and I don't want to talk about any shootings."

"Who shot Redda, Dulcie? Was it one of your lovers in a fit of jealousy?"

"All I know is that my husband returned to Melbourne on business. I have no men friends who would be jealous."

"What's it like being the angel of death?" Another reporter asked.

"Has anyone told you to fuck off today?" Dulcie sneered as she climbed into the passenger seat of Tilly's car.

Dulcie's primary concern was Amelia. Tilly had found a flat for them and Dulcie finally settled down into being a mother to her daughter. She was concerned about how the constant news stories about her would affect Amelia's life. One morning she was shocked to find a reporter standing at her gate when she was about to walk her to school.

"Dulcie, you've been pretty quiet of late. Any new man on the scene?"

"Look here, mate. Every time my name hits the headlines, I have to move my ten-year-old daughter to a new school. It's not fair on her. She deserves a good life away from the newspapers that want to print about all the heartbreak that happens in my life. How could anyone be interested in me anymore?"

7

Life was pretty quiet for Dulcie over the following years. She returned to work in brothels whenever she was desperate for money. However, time was not her friend. A lifetime of drinking, drug taking, shootings, stabbings, and every heartbreak showed upon her face.

Amelia was a calming anchor for her mother. She was raised well by both Tilly and Olive and had all the manners and integrity of a child raised on the uppity North Shore of Sydney.

7

During 1954 and 55, Dulcie was still seeing several regular clients each week. They provided money for little luxuries and private school fees. In 1955 during an argument with one of her clients, the irate mongrel threw Dulcie over the balcony, twenty feet to the ground.

In hospital and under the influence of morphine due to suffering fractured ribs, internal injuries, and a punctured lung, Dulcie maintained the underworld code and refused to answer any of the detective's questions. "I was going down to get the washing and I slipped down the stairs. There's nothing sinister. It was an accident."

Facing Central Police Court once again in 1957 for soliciting, Dulcie hobbled up the courthouse steps wearing a mauve frock, her hair professionally coiffed, and carrying a bright red handbag. She smiled and waved at the newspaper men, friends, policemen and detectives as she made her way through the building. All of whom nodded their head in return. One of the *Daily Mirror* reporters who admired her tenacity, wrote that it was just like having a celebrity enter the room. Dulcie received a five pounds fine when the magistrate who knew of her past, felt sorry for her. She then vowed before the court that she would retire from prostitution.

In January 1959, it was Dulcie's turn to face the taxman when she was called to appear before a special Federal Court. She had been charged for not filing a tax return during 1957. She told investigators she had forgotten and had been suffering with memory loss since her fall in 1955. She was found guilty and fined fifty pounds and ordered to pay one pound in court costs.

The 1960s was the decade that reformed Dulcie. Her daughter had grown into a well-educated young woman and was working as a secretary in a law office. The partners of the firm knew of her mother's past but were willing to give the well-spoken young woman a chance. They were not disappointed. Overjoyed that her daughter had found lawful employment with career advancement, mother and daughter celebrated at a nearby Italian restaurant.

One night in March 1964, Tilly decided to play matchmaker and Dulcie up with an Irishman named Sean. Her scheme worked. Six weeks after meeting, Sean moved into Dulcie's Bondi flat.

Unfortunately for Dulcie, even though the insurance salesman had no criminal friends, he was a compulsive gambler. She started selling sex again to buy groceries or to pay the bills because Sean had gambled away their money. Often, when the police caught Dulcie soliciting in Darlinghurst, they felt sorry for her. Instead of charging her for prostitution, they would arrest her on the lesser offence of vagrancy where she would be released after a stern talking to by the magistrate.

Amelia was living in her own flat and was engaged to a pleasant young accountant named Michael. She became concerned about her mother after visiting her several times and discovering no food in the cupboards or refrigerator. During one visit, Dulcie broke down and wept, revealing that because of her partner's gambling habit she was on the verge of being evicted. Amelia advised her to break it off with him. Dulcie asked Sean to leave and to never darken her doorstep again when he arrived home that afternoon.

The following morning, Amelia paid the outstanding rent and both she and Michael filled her mother's cupboards and refrigerator with food.

While playing the poker machines at the Bondi Surf Club in February 1967, Dulcie met a sailor named Martin Rooney. The pair hit it off immediately. However, Dulcie had finally learned from her many tragic relationships to take it slowly. The pair enjoyed spending time together reading under a large sun umbrella on the beach and going to the movie theatre or watching television at home. She had learned to enjoy the simple things in life at last!

In 1969, Dulcie moved into Martin's Moore Street home, a short distance from her flat and in 1972 the happy couple married.

After all the tragedies, oceans of tears, broken hopes, and unrealised dreams, 'The Black Widow', 'Angel of Death' and 'Australia's most beautiful bad woman' had finally found her prince. Martin adored her and lovingly called her his Princess Cinderella.

Unfortunately, Dulcie's life of bliss tragically ended on the 20th of April 1976, when she fell asleep while smoking and caught her bedroom alight. She succumbed to the smoke and died from asphyxiation.

Martin was inconsolable. Her husband told everyone, including the newspapermen, that he had lost the love of his life. During an interview, he told a reporter: "I loved the woman. She was a wonderful housewife and we both wanted to forget the past. I knew all about her. She was Mrs. Rooney, not pretty Dulcie Markham, and that's how she'll be buried."

Dulcie had outlived most of her criminal friends and enemies from Sydney's violent and tumultuous razor gang era. She had outlived most of her prostitution friends and the criminal men she had met or been involved with over the decades. She had also outlived her adopted mother, friend and Amelia's Godmother, Tilly Devine.

Her funeral was held at St Patrick's Catholic Church, Bondi which had standing room only. Martin remained by her open casket throughout the service and eulogies. He refused to leave his beloved's side. Dulcie was dressed in her favourite lilac dress and black shoes that she had kept from the 1940s. Her blonde hair was styled the way she liked it. Her lips were coloured in her signature red lipstick and her nails were polished to match. Martin spared no expense to ensure Dulcie was the most beautiful woman at her funeral.

Wreaths sent from almost every state in Australia lined the graveside. The floral tributes were from judges, magistrates, policemen, detectives, and friends. Dulcie may have been called 'completely incorrigible' by the late Lillian Armfield, but she sure garnered a lot of respect from the court and constabulary.

The eulogy was read by Detective Frank 'Bumper' Farrell, who had himself arrested Dulcie on numerous occasions. He had a deep affection for Dulcie and Nellie Cameron. He enjoyed it when both women went along with jokes he often played on new recruits.

Dulcie was cremated at Eastern Suburbs Memorial Park.

During her life as a criminal, Dulcie accrued one-hundred convictions in New South Wales, Victoria, Queensland, and Western Australia for prostitution, consorting, vagrancy, assaulting police and the public, keeping a brothel, drunkenness, and drunk driving. She had also spent time in gaol.

She was a true princess of crime.

CHAPTER TWELVE

Kathleen Beahan: The Beginning

Kathleen Mary Josephine was born on the 10th of March 1881. She was the eighth of twelve children born to Timothy and Charlotte Beahan. Her father worked as a boot and shoemaker and her mother was a tradesman's daughter.

Although her father was a hardworking, honest man, Kathleen Beahan and her family lived in poverty in a dilapidated house on the outskirts of Dubbo. Her brothers often stole food amongst other things, and the punishment their father meted out was severe. He knew firsthand where a life of crime could lead: his friend, Andrew—Captain Moonlite, was hanged for his crimes.

When Kathleen was eight years old, the headmaster dragged her home. She had taken her father's gold watch to school to show her friends. She didn't want everyone thinking they were poor, and to her, the watch was proof that they had money. But the school bully snatched the watch and ran off behind the toilets. He laughed as he told her that she would never get the watch back. In a fit of anger, Kathleen hit him over the head with a paling she had pulled from the school fence. She walloped him several times before he threw the watch at her and ran away, screaming for help.

The headmaster visited the Beahan home and handed Tim the watch, explaining what had happened. After the he left, her father beat Kathleen so hard that her mother, had to pull him away, screaming, "Tim! No more! You'll kill her!"

However, a mere flogging—she'd had many, was not enough to quell the rebel in Kathleen Beahan's soul.

At the age of ten, she was caught shoplifting a pair of socks. The shopkeeper dragged her home by the ear and complained to her father, who had only arrived home from Tenterfield an hour before. Tim belted her with his leather strap and sent her to her room without food for the rest of the day.

Hardly a week went by that Kathleen was not in trouble. Not knowing what else to do with his unruly daughter, Tim made a brutal decision on the 26th of November 1891. He was going to teach Kathleen a lesson she would never forget.

"Come with me," was all he said.

He and Kathleen walked hand in hand down Macquarie Street past the sandstone courthouse building, and then along the twelve feet high red brick walls that surrounded the gaol. They stopped when they reached an area where the death cart picked up bodies of prisoners who had died. Tim's mate, Michael Connolly was waiting for him.

"Are you sure you want to do this?" He asked gravely.

"If this doesn't work, nothing will…" Tim sombrely replied.

"Follow me, but you must be quiet, or it'll be my job."

Father and daughter followed Connolly to a room under the Dubbo police station and stopped in a small area that had an iron grill window.

Tim knew that nineteen-year-old Harold Dutton Mallallieu was to be hanged that day and with a heavy heart he looked down at his unsuspecting daughter.

"Look through there." He said as he pointed to the grill. Through the bars, Kathleen watched as a frightened man wearing loose grey clothes walked up the gallows stairs. A looped rope hanging from a beam above the platform was swaying in the breeze from a nearby window. While the man stood in front of the rope, she listened as the Archdeacon, whom she often saw at her school, asked him if he wished to speak.

"No sir. I have nothing to say. Goodbye sir. I am very much obliged to you." He shakily replied.

The Archdeacon nodded before making his way down the stairs.

"What's happening Da?" Kathleen innocently asked.

"Watch and stay quiet."

Kathleen watched as a white hood was placed over the man's head, and the knotted rope was placed around his neck. The next minute she saw another man, dressed in black and wearing a white hood that only showed his eyes, draw a bolt across the scaffold. She then watched in horror as the man dropped to his death.

Kathleen let out a loud scream. Tim quickly placed his hand across her mouth before grabbing her hand and rushing up the stairs.

"We'd better go, Nosey Bob doesn't like any noise while he's working." Connolly said. "I wouldn't have his job for all the gold in the world."

"Da, Da! What happened to that poor man?" Kathleen asked, visibly shaken.

"Kathleen, do you *really* want to know what happened to that man?" Tim asked when they stopped by a tree down the street from the police station.

"Yes Da, I do."

"He was hanged by the neck until he was dead because *he did wrong things*. That's what happens when you steal things. Do you want that to happen to *you*?"

"He's dead? He's really dead, Da?"

"Yes, he is. He can't get another chance and you won't either if you keep your nonsense up!"

When they returned home, Charlotte was livid when she saw the state her daughter was in. Tim ignored her ceaseless questions and went to gather up his farrier tools before leaving for work.

When Charlotte learned what had happened, she held Kathleen close and told her that she would never be hurt that way. She then made her some warm milk with honey and laid down beside her on the bed Kathleen shared with two of her siblings, holding her until she sobbed herself to sleep.

Unfortunately, witnessing the hanging death, didn't teach Kathleen a lesson nor curb her rebelliousness. She remained taciturn and held her insatiable curiosity and wont for adventure at bay for the following weeks. But the horror of seeing Harold Mallallieu's twitching body gave her nightmares for the rest of her life.

During the following two years, Kathleen continued either getting into trouble or causing it. One morning she received another beating from her father for constantly truanting from school and stealing a pencil from her teacher's desk. However, no matter the harshness and painfulness of the punishment, there seemed to be no deterrent.

When she hit her teen years, Kathleen would often sneak out of the house at night, spending time with the worst people of Dubbo, roaming the streets, and drinking alcohol by the river. It was a dangerous time for young girls. They often became prey to the 'girl hunters' within the local prostitutes, or men travelling through country towns looking for young girls to traffic to the brothels in Sydney. Dubbo police had already received fifteen reports from distraught parents who had a daughter go missing.

Tim resorted to setting traps to stop her from escaping of a night. But the wily Kathleen was never caught by them. She had seen her father set the first one, and from then on escaped through her brothers' bedroom window instead of her own.

On the 3rd of May 1897, Kathleen again snuck out of the house and had not returned home by nine o'clock that night. Her parents were forced into making the heartbreaking decision to surrender their daughter to the police. They were both at their wits end over her behaviour and were concerned about what further influence she could be on their other children.

Tim made his way to the Dubbo police station, but it was unmanned. He walked next door to the police residence and spoke to the young constable. He told him about the problems he and his wife were experiencing with Kathleen's uncontrollable behaviour.

"It breaks our hearts to do this, but we have eleven other children we must think about." He almost wept.

The Constable went in search of the wayward teenager, combing all the known haunts used by teenagers around the village. Just before midnight, he happened upon Kathleen with a local prostitute at the Dubbo train station. They were about to board a goods train to Wellington. Upon seeing the policeman, Kathleen turned and ran toward the end of the platform but was caught by the second police officer who had arrived after receiving a report that Kathleen was going to be sold into prostitution to a Sydney brothel owner. Kicking and screaming, she was dragged to the police station where she spent the night until the courthouse opened the following morning.

The prostitute was arrested and charged for procuring a woman under twenty-one years of age. She was sentenced to two years with hard labour.

On Monday the 4th of May, Kathleen appeared in Dubbo court. Her father told the magistrate he was unable to control his daughter. He explained that she sometimes spent two to three days away from home after sneaking out through the window at night. Even though it was breaking their hearts, as parents they had to think of their other children and place Kathleen where she could receive proper control.

"I find the minor child, Kathleen Mary Josephine Beahan, to be a neglected and uncontrollable child. I hereby order that this child is to be taken from this place to Parramatta Girls Home where she will learn instruction and behavioural compliance. She is to remain at the institution until the day of her eighteenth birthday."

Kathleen tried to run across to her mother but was held in place by the police officers. "Please Mama, take me home. I promise I won't sneak out anymore. I'll go to school. Please Mama…"

Charlotte was beside herself in heartbreak, but she knew she must protect her other children from Kathleen's wilful ways. She tearfully looked away from her daughter as Tim placed his arm around her and led her from the courtroom.

Terrified, broken-hearted, and missing her family after spending four days alone in a cold prison cell, Kathleen was escorted by police on a five-hundred-mile train journey to Parramatta. On arrival, she was handed over to a further two policemen who carted her off to the home.

When the diminutive five-feet tall Kathleen arrived at the gates of the imposing building, she shuddered at its size and bleakness. She could hear girls screaming to be let out and wished she were back at home. The matron of the reform school met the policemen at the door and took custody of Kathleen after they unshackled her. She was left alone in a small room for some time before the door suddenly opened and a man told her to follow him. She did as she was instructed and followed closely behind the man to a large shower room that had no doors on the shower recesses.

"Undress and get in the fuckin' shower. I haven't got all fuckin' day!" He growled.

Kathleen looked at the large cockroaches crawling in and out of the drain and up the wall, then looked behind her: "Can I just wash may face and hands please?

"Get undressed and shower before I fuckin' rip your clothes off you myself!"

The teenager faced the wall and removed her clothing. She was embarrassed to be undressing in front of the man.

"Nice arse." He said, laughing as he watched the terrified teenager as she showered.

When she had finished, the warder handed her underwear and a tunic. He then took her back to a small cell. Kathleen noticed a pair of black shoes, a pair of white socks and a white apron stacked on a stool.

An hour later, the door opened again, and a woman told her to follow her and not to speak to any of the other girls or she would be placed in isolation. "And you don't want to go down to the punishment cells. Terrible things happen there."

"Can I have something to eat please? I haven't had any food since last night."

"Yeah, at breakfast," the woman snapped as she turned around and slapped Kathleen across the face. "Don't open your mouth again! Next time you'll get a dozen strikes."

Kathleen put her hand over her cheek where the sting of the slap still smarted. She was suddenly very homesick for her parents and siblings. At home, she knew what to expect from her father. But not here. She walked behind the woman with a feeling of doom in the pit of her stomach.

Weeks into her confinement, Kathleen befriended an Aboriginal girl named Julie, who preferred to be called Jules. Her new friend had been at the home since she was eight years old and was due to leave in two months. She showed Kathleen the way of the home and advised her to stay out of trouble. She warned her that several of the warders would try to have sex with her, and when they did, not to fight them otherwise they would all rape her. She said she'd been pregnant a couple of times, but she was kicked or punched in the stomach both times until she miscarried.

Kathleen asked her why the matron didn't protect the girls from the attacks. Jules laughed, saying that she also sends the girls to the dungeon to be taught a lesson knowing they would be raped.

"Is there any way to escape the home?"

"Girls that tried were beaten while they were shackled. Those that had escaped were brought back and drugged for weeks and were given water and no food for two weeks as punishment."

Not wanting to be raped or beaten, Kathleen kept her head down and concentrated on her work in the laundry and kitchen. She stayed clear when arguments and fights broke out. In her sewing and cooking classes, she followed directions as well as she could. She wasn't adept at sewing, but cooking came easy to her—she had been taught by her mother and older sisters.

There wasn't any school at the home. Education wasn't important to the management of the home, only labour and teaching the girls useful skills to become a dutiful wife or factory worker.

Whenever one of the male guards sought Kathleen out to spend time in the dungeon, Jules came to her rescue and offered herself instead. But it didn't always work. Kathleen had only been at the home for twenty-two days when she was targeted for a job—matron's orders. There was no job. It was a ruse to get her down to the dungeon. When she realised what was about to happen, Kathleen fought, kicking, and screaming and begging for the men to leave her alone. Her pleas fell on deaf ears.

The day Jules was released, she told Kathleen to stay alert and try to conform to what the warders wanted: "It will make your life easier."

Kathleen asked if they could meet again when she was released in two years. Jules explained she was returning to her people at Lake Wallaga, seven hundred miles away. The girls embraced before one of the female guards led her friend out of the building and through the front iron gates.

Like Jules, Kathleen tried to offer the newer girls' advice when they arrived at the home. And like the other older girls, she tried to protect the younger arrivals from the rapes and assaults. Girls as young as eight years old also fell prey to the paedophilic attentions of some of the male warders. There were some good ones among the male and female guards, but they never lasted at the home long. They were either driven out or the matron gave them long shifts for weeks in a row, weakening them so much that they quit and found employment elsewhere.

Kathleen lived her time in the home in fear, pain, and impatience. She had endured sexual abuse time and time again. She had felt the cane and strap from the female guards whenever they felt she had done something wrong or had stood up for someone.

Unlike most of the other girls, Kathleen didn't receive visitors. Her parents couldn't afford the long trip to Parramatta to see her. She received a letter from home every six months or so letting her know how they were and any news they had to share. During the last year of her incarceration, mail was held as punishment after Kathleen refused to hold a twelve-year-old girl down for the guards to watch as two older girls forcefully had sex with her—a punishment regularly meted out.

There wasn't a day during the years she spent at Parramatta home that Kathleen didn't hear one of the inmates screaming out for help, or pleading to one of the warders to stop, or for one of the women guards to stop beating them.

Many of the girls had what was called a 'Matta'—a female lover. The girls would carve each other's name or initials into the skin of their arm to prove their love for one another. This relationship was the only love and solace girls found in the home. Kathleen never had a Matta, she had friends, but didn't form a close bond with any of the girls except for Jules.

The 10th of March 1899 was the day that Kathleen had dreamed about for three years. She was leaving the place she referred to as the 'hell-hole'. It was her eighteenth birthday, and she was old enough to start a life of her own. That night she lay in bed wide awake staring at the ceiling until she was summoned to the matron's office at five o'clock in the morning.

The matron handed her three pieces of paper. One proved she had served her time in the reformatory. The other was an address of a government funded boarding house where she was to live until she could afford her own accommodation. The third piece of paper had an address for the factory where she was to start work the following Monday.

The matron also warned her, while two male warders stood by the door, that if she ever told anyone anything about life in the home, the warders would ensure she would never walk again. Kathleen never said a word publicly, but she revealed certain acts of violence that had occurred at the home to several friends throughout her life.

7

After her release, Kathleen worked at the factory. She lasted there four months, but got fed up with the owner, who happened to be the brother of one of the warders, and his continual harassment for sex. For the following year, she worked from factory to factory and shop to shop around Surry Hills and Glebe. Soon, boredom with the mundane life of working, eating, and sleeping saw her venture out to look for excitement.

In one of the Surry Hills speakeasies, she caught up with another young girl her age who was part of a gang which welcomed Kathleen to join them. The girls called her Kate, so Kate forever it was.

From then on, Kate dived headlong into a reckless and promiscuous lifestyle. One of the gang members she had sex with was James Lee, he was a year younger than she. He was mesmerised by Kate's piercing blue eyes. James was born to a Chinese father and an Australian mother. He was known around the streets and by the police as 'Jack', a small-time petty criminal and illegal bookmaker who operated in Sydney's underworld. Jack, like his father, was also an opium addict and lived in the Chinese community near the city's vegetable markets.

Unmarried and living the life of a petty criminal, Kate discovered she was pregnant in late 1899. Excited and wearing the glow of pregnancy, she vowed that her child would enjoy the privileges of life that her parents were unable to provide her and her siblings.

She obtained employment in a low wage factory and continued her involvement in Jack's criminal activities, albeit in a small way by shoplifting. Kate mainly lifted baby items and food, luxuries that she was unable to afford on her meagre wage. Jack preferred to steal items of value that he could sell on the black market to feed his opium addiction and pay his rent.

Kate had spent the last months of her pregnancy alone. Jack had taken off on one of his interstate jaunts. No longer having the small weekly income from Lee, she scrubbed floors and cleaned houses to survive.

Immeasurable joy came to Kate's life in June 1900 when she gave birth to a daughter with the help of two ladies' who also lived in the boarding house. She named her Eileen May. Lovingly gazing into her newborn baby's eyes, she promised her child that she would give her the best life she could.

On the 28th July 1901, when Kate was walking home from the job she had in Surry Hills, two policemen on bicycles stopped and asked her what her business was and for her address. She told them she was returning home from the grocery store in which she worked and that she was living at Lily's boarding house. Jack, who had returned, was looking after Eileen. Upon hearing her voice, he walked out to the street carrying their daughter.

When one of the Constables saw that he was Chinese, he promptly arrested Kate for vagrancy. During the 1920s, police used the *Vagrancy Act* to arrest women living with or associating with a Chinese man.

"Why arrest me? Men have a Chinese mistress or visit them in the Chinese opium dens and brothels!" She complained.

"Keep your Chinese loving mouth shut, or I'll charge you for resisting arrest!" One of the constables sneered.

The law, as it often does when pertaining to women, was hypocritical. Upper class Australian women were permitted to keep a Chinese houseman or gardener. These elite women of society were safe from prosecution due to their wealth or their husband's status. However, the poor and those the police or the wealthy disliked, could be gaoled for up to three months.

The police, disgusted that an Australian woman would shack up with a Chinese man, let alone give birth to his mixed blood child, placed Kate's charge sheet at the bottom of the court schedule. She endured three days on remand in the cold and filthy cells until she was called to appear in court late in the afternoon on the 1st of August. Standing before an unsympathetic magistrate, Kate was sentenced to fourteen days hard labour in Long Bay Women's gaol.

Unable to remain at the boarding house to care for their daughter with Kate in gaol, Jack left Eileen with the older woman who lived in the next room. Also named Eileen, she and Ada, her friend who lived down the hall, cared for the infant until Kate was released.

Kate, disappointed that he had left their daughter, searched for Jack, and finally found out he had moved to Melbourne and joined a Chinese gang. She heard that he had learned from the local Chinese vegetable traders that there was plenty of money to be made at the port of Melbourne collecting illegal caches of opium arriving on ships and selling it through the city streets and pubs.

Determined to provide a good life for her daughter, Kate continued working in the grocery shop, as well as picking up odd house cleaning jobs. Eileen was her priority, and she did all she could to save enough money to rent and furnish a flat for the two of them.

One night, cashed up and bearing a diamond engagement ring, Jack turned up at the boarding house and proposed. Surprised and delighted, Kate immediately accepted. She and Jack found a suitable flat in Surry Hills. Kate was elated that she and Eileen could live respectably as a family.

Raised as a Roman Catholic, Kate was turned away from the local Catholic priests when they learned she had given birth to a child out of wedlock. She was disappointed but understood the strict doctrines of her religion. She and Jack continued to canvass churches around the city, and finally came across a priest at the Independent Presbyterian Church in Hunter Street, Sydney, who would marry them.

Kate tried to contact her family by telegram to let them know of her happy event, however in those days, it was much easier to contact someone in Britain than in outback New South Wales. Jack was able to contact his parents, who told him they would be proud to attend the wedding and meet their granddaughter.

Dressed in a cream frilly blouse, corseted cream skirt, an off-white wide-brimmed hat with a flower and feather arrangement that a bird would be proud to call home, Kate married Jack on the 2nd of May 1902, at the age of twenty-one. They were surrounded by a small group of family and friends who celebrated their marriage with a small party at their flat.

At last Kate had what she hoped for, a husband, a beautiful daughter with stark blue eyes like her own, and a lovely home to upkeep. She was extremely houseproud after being raised in a hovel with a dirt floor and kept her flat spotlessly clean and the furniture dusted and polished.

Just four months later, due to Jack's opium addiction, the Lees found themselves broke and soon to be homeless when he had used his savings as well as Kate's household and rent money to buy his drugs. Desperate to stay off the street with their daughter, they broke into the Mary Street home of Willie Ping, a man Kate knew from the store. They left twenty minutes later loaded with jewellery and valuables.

On the 24th of July, the police knocked on their door and searched the premises, finding an item similar to one missing from Ping's home. Both Kate and Jack were then arrested and charged for breaking and entering a dwelling and stealing items to the value of two pounds ten shillings.

After the police prosecutor put forward his case against the Lees, the magistrate commented that he was suspicious of Kate's relationship with Willie Ping and hoped there wasn't anything untoward happening between them. Shocked by the magistrate's inference, Kate reminded him that she was a married woman with a child and only knew Mr. Ping from whenever he had shopped at her workplace.

The following month, the Lees' stood side by side at trial. They were subsequently acquitted when Kate produced a receipt from the shop in Darlinghurst where she had purchased the item they had been accused of stealing.

Following the backlash after the newspapers printed details about their trial, Kate and Jack were concerned about the racism being directed at them by using the surname 'Lee', so they altered their name to the more Anglicised spelling of Leigh.

One afternoon, Jack arrived at the flat desperate to buy opium and asked Kate for money. When she refused an argument ensued and he began demolishing their flat in search of money. A neighbour rode his bicycle to the police station, concerned that either Kate or her husband would kill the other. The police entered the premises and found broken furniture and glassware throughout the flat. They came across Kate on the bed and Eileen in her crib playing with a wooden elephant pull toy. Jack was nowhere to be found.

When one of the constables asked Kate why her home was in such a bad state, she told him to 'fuck off out of her home so she could clean up her husband's mess'.

The police, disgusted by Kate's use of foul language in the presence of her infant, told her to present herself at the police station the following morning to face a charge of using obscene language.

When Kate arrived at the station with Eileen on her left hip at ten o'clock the next day, she was charged and fined one pound.

Over the years Jack disappeared for several months off and on but would always turn up out of the blue. After a vicious beating meted out by her husband in November 1903, Kate gathered hers and Eileen's personal belongings and travelled by train to Narromine where she moved in with her father. She enjoyed spending time with her family, but city life beckoned and in May 1904, she returned to Sydney. With money given to her by her father and three of her siblings, Kate rented a small flat in Glebe where she found employment in a local dress shop and again advertised around the city for housecleaning jobs.

Life was extremely difficult for Kate as a single mother. Paying local women to babysit Eileen took a fair share of her income. She reverted to her old ways of selling items she had stolen from shops and houses she had cleaned to fences who often spent their time in pubs waiting for 'clients'.

In October 1904, Kate returned home from one of her cleaning jobs and found Jack sitting on the couch. He didn't ask about his daughter.

"How the hell did you find me?"

"You're not that hard to track down." He smugly replied.

Jack wasn't the same man she had married just three years before. He had become more violent, aloof, and hardly spent any time with Eileen. He spent most days away from the flat, returning during the early hours of the morning, only to disappear again whenever he woke up.

One afternoon when she returned home from work, Kate found an eviction notice nailed to her door, citing rental arrears. Jack had been continually stealing her money no matter how often she found a new hiding place in the flat. When he returned the following morning, they packed up what they could carry and rented a room at the Tradesman's Arms Hotel.

Jack's behaviour worsened. His drug addiction had almost completely taken over his life. He had lost so much weight that he resembled a skeleton. He barely slept and was becoming more and more antisocial and violent toward Kate.

On the 27th of January 1905, Patrick Lynch, the licensee of the Tradesman's Arms Hotel was collecting rent from the hotel's tenants. Jack invited him into his room on the pretence of inspecting mouldy wallpaper. While the landlord was standing on a chair examining the wallpaper, Jack pushed Lynch down with such force, he hit his head on the iron leg of the bedstead and was knocked unconscious. Jack then stole the money from the landlord's pockets before stealing what cash he could from the money box on the shelf under the bar downstairs before fleeing.

When Kate returned to the room, she found Eileen alone on the floor playing with her toys, and Patrick unconscious on the floor bleeding from a gash on his forehead. Jack was nowhere to be seen. She cleaned the licensee's wound as best she could. When he regained consciousness, Lynch immediately searched his pockets, and discovered his money gone.

Seeing only Kate and her daughter in the room, Patrick assumed that Kate was responsible for attacking him. He made his way downstairs where he told the cook to go and quickly fetch the police.

Kate carried Eileen down to the bar and offered to clean the entire hotel and any other jobs he needed done until she had paid him in full for any money Jack had stolen. She told Lynch that she was sorry that her husband had attacked him and explained about Jack's opium addiction. The landlord didn't believe her and told Kate to leave the premises.

After finding a bed at a local women's refuge, the following morning Kate was questioned by the police about her involvement in Lynch's assault and robbery. Her responses were in line with the landlord's, except for her involvement in the crime. The police told her that they would return after they spoke to the person whose house, she said she had cleaned to check her alibi.

Kate sat on the bed at the shelter worrying about where she and her daughter could live. She didn't want Eileen surrounded by the filthy drug addicts and drunks living in the refuge. She knew she couldn't work anymore than her four jobs, as she would have to pay too much in babysitting costs and she rarely saw Eileen as it was.

The police arrived at the shelter two days later and told Kate she was no longer a suspect in the attack on Patrick Lynch. She was relieved, but still worried for her husband who had been found with some of the stolen money still in his possession and had admitted to the robbery during a drug-fuelled stupor.

That afternoon, Kate met with Jack in his cell and together they concocted a story that he had attacked the landlord in a rage after finding her in bed with him "paying" for their rental arrears. And that story is exactly what Jack said when he was called to the stand to give testimony before Chief Justice Sir Frederick Darley. The prosecution took him to task on his testimony, accusing him of lying and put forward Lynch's version of the assault and robbery as the truth.

"I went into an upstairs room at 14 Little Hill Street and saw Lynch in bed with my wife. Lynch was asleep and I pulled my wife off the bed, waking Lynch who then yelled out, "What's your game?" and got up and struck me. I fought back in self-defence. I told him that I would have him charged and contact the police for his assault. I then ran downstairs. I did not steal his money or watch and chain."

Outbursts of shocked gasps and hushed whispers rose from the gallery upon hearing a husband malign his wife with accusations of immorality and disrespect. The Chief Justice demanded silence from the court, again and again, ordering those present to be quiet or leave. When order was restored, the crowd waited for an indignant Kate to call her husband out for the lies that would tarnish her character.

Kate was asked to take the witness stand and swore the oath. Those in attendance went as silent as the night as they waited for her to vehemently deny her husband's disparaging evidence. Mouths dropped open and audible gasps of disbelief filled the stunned courtroom as her testimony almost echoed that of her husband's. The only difference was that she added that she and James were so broke that she felt she had no other option than to have sex with Mr. Lynch to pay the rent. She wept and dabbed a floral handkerchief at her eyes as she relayed her story.

But Chief Justice Darley would not have deceitful shenanigans occurring in his court. He charged both Kate and James Leigh with perjury. In a subsequent appeal against the charge, Kate was acquitted. But her reputation was sullied after publicly admitting to being in bed with a man other than her husband.

Jack's charge of stealing the watch and chain was discharged. The watch wasn't found on his person when he was arrested. However, he was sentenced to five years gaol for the monetary theft due to the large amount of cash found in his possession.

Regardless of their unity in court, Kate only visited Jack in gaol for several months at the beginning of his sentence. She was tired of him begging for money or demanding she smuggle opium in whenever she visited. The last time he saw her, Jack told Kate that he needed at least ten pounds to pay one of the inmates for opium. When she refused, he abused her, threatening to send men to the shelter to collect his dues. Kate stood, slapped him across the face and walked out, never to return to the prison again.

Concerned that her husband would come good on his threat, Kate left the women's shelter and rented a flat in Surry Hills, using the little money she had saved.

After more than two weeks of walking the footpaths of East Sydney in search of employment, she finally found work as a waitress at the Senatorial café. It wasn't an ideal job for Kate with her brusque manner, but it was better than begging for pennies on the streets. Her employers, Mr. and Mrs. Kiely were impressed by her punctuality and cleanliness and often praised her for being quick to clean the tables once the diners had left and keeping the floor sparkling clean in their busy café.

One evening Kate was in the kitchen washing dishes after a busy lunchtime. Mrs. Kiely came into the kitchen and asked if she could make a Chinese man a cup of tea as she was busy adding up the bill for a large table of diners.

Kate looked up at the clock. It was after seven o'clock, past her knock-off time. She made the cup of tea and placed it in front of the man, who immediately pushed the cup and saucer away, sending it crashing to the floor. "I don't want it now. You take too long!"

"Go on, you can get the hell out of here now!" Kate spat before turning around to collect the mop and bucket from the kitchen. He followed Kate, and when she was within reach of a broom, she grabbed hold of it, spun around and held it in front of her, ordering the man out of the kitchen. But he seemed oblivious to what she was saying and continued heading toward her.

Not wanting to become involved in what seemed like was going to become a violent confrontation, several customers fled the café. Kate looked the man straight in the eyes and recognised the same look she had often seen in her husband's eyes when he was high on opium.

A young man Kate often made sandwiches for, tackled her accoster, dragging him out onto the footpath. When the Chinese man got to his feet, he ran at the customer brandishing a knife in his outstretched hand.

Not wanting to lose his life, the young man fled up the street. When Kate saw the knife, she told Mrs. Kiely to get down behind the counter. Kate remained where she was, hoping that Mr. Kiely would soon arrive and help diffuse the situation.

"Get the fuck out of here with that knife, you stupid bastard, before you hurt someone!" Kate yelled. Terrified customers huddled together at the back of the café hoping the crazed man wouldn't turn on them.

"Please leave, and we'll forget this ever happened," Mrs. Kiely called from where she was crouching behind the counter.

Enraged and drug-addled, the man wasn't going anywhere. He approached Kate, knife in hand, threatening her. She backed slowly toward the counter and felt behind the jars of sweets for the pistol Mr. Kiely had hidden there if they were ever robbed. Her boss walked into the café and when he saw what was happening, he grabbed a chair and smashed it across the intruder's back. The crazed man barely reacted.

"Oh, for God's sake man! What the fuckin' hell is going to stop you!" Kate roared.

Mr. Kiely rushed at the man again but was distracted by a woman's scream. His momentary distraction gave the Chinese man the opportunity to attack the café owner, stabbing him in the wrist, chest, and shoulder. Falling to the floor bleeding, he pleaded with Kate to keep the madman away.

Kate whispered across to Mrs. Kiely for her to run out the back and bring her in the axe. Moments later, she was holding it in her hand. The man rushed at Kate and she ducked out of his reach causing him to plunge the knife into thin air.

"Come any closer and I'll split your fuckin' head in two!" Kate threatened as she wielded the axe like a pro. The drug-crazed man ignored her and lunged at her again. Kate brought the axe down across his arms, cutting deep into his flesh, but he came back for more as blood gushed from his gaping wound.

Changing tactics, Kate waited for the man to come closer and when he was about a foot away, she swung her foot across, tripping him over. Drawing on the strength of the teenager who had survived reformatory life, Kate punched her assailant about the head and pinned him to the floor.

A male customer walked into the café, saw what was happening and immediately rushed to Kate's assistance. His chivalry brought more men forward and within seconds, five men were able to finally keep the psychotic Chinese man secured until the police arrested the assailant five minutes later.

Mrs. Kiely continued to care for her husband until the ambulance arrived while Kate ushered the remaining customers out through the back door of the café.

Kate made headlines in the papers two days later. While she and Eileen were eating breakfast at the kitchen table, Kate smiled as she read the editorial aloud, "Miss Leigh fought on with a power which she said she never before knew herself to be possessed of."

"I know where your strength comes from Mum. You look after us without any help. No better woman could do what you do," Eileen proudly stated.

CHAPTER THIRTEEN

Kate Leigh—the Criminal, the Madam, the Matriarch

Kate tried to toe the straight line over the years. She'd worked in cafés, shops and even laboured in dirty, sweaty factories to make ends meet and pay for Eileen's private school education. But the long hours, dreadfully low wages and lengthy times spent away from her beloved daughter took its toll and she returned to a life of crime.

At the beginning of 1911, her landlord raised the rent of her modest home in the slum area of Foveaux Street, Surry Hills, to eight pounds a year. The area was steeped in unimaginable poverty, crime, and violence. Kate had planned to leave the destitution and filth as soon as she could, but the rise in rent filled her with such utter wretchedness that she would never escape the slum.

Kate barely slept as she added up her expenses over and over again in her head and always came up short. She was working as a waitress as well as cleaning the odd house or three, but even with the extra income, she could barely make ends meet. As she watched the sky glow in shades of orange and pink with the rising of the sun, the answer to her plight came to her…she would sell her body along Campbell Street.

Working for herself was more convenient for Kate. She found she could leave home after Eileen left for school and be home before school was out. It wasn't long before she found more streets to work. Overjoyed by the money she was making, Kate and Eileen dined at expensive restaurants and shopped at high-end boutiques.

It was during one of these shopping excursions that Kate found a beautiful wide brimmed black hat adorned with three long ostrich feathers. She bought it as soon as she caught sight of it. This was the beginning of Kate's millinery addiction.

By 1913, Kate had saved enough money to establish her own brothel. She scoured the streets searching for young, attractive women with good figures to kick-start her bawdy house enterprise. Once the rented house was furnished, she placed a lamp in the window of the living room and covered it in a red shawl to let men know the ladies were ready and waiting. She also offered a finder's fee of a shilling to barrow boys and the homeless for every paying man they brought to the brothel. Her marketing plan worked a charm and within the following month, she had clients turning up at her front door and women looking for work lining up at her backdoor.

During a night out at the Cambridge hotel, Kate was introduced to the ruggedly handsome Samuel 'Jewey' Freeman. Jewey's original career was a bootmaker until the call to the dubious glory of a life of crime seduced him. Freeman began robbing people at gunpoint and quickly earned a reputation in Sydney of being tough, cold-hearted, and well on his way up the criminal ladder.

After whiling away the hours drinking whiskey and listening to Freeman boasting about his plans to establish a criminal empire, Kate was impressed enough to arrange for a neighbour to look after Eileen so she could spend the night with Samuel. Home can be such a disingenuous word at times… Sam's dwelling was more of a one-room shack built in the vermin-infested, foul-smelling rookery of Frog Hollow where toxic effluent flowed constantly down the airless alleys.

Kate knew Jewey was nothing but a small-time criminal with big dreams that would never come true, but she felt he would make a solid steppingstone to the crime empire she planned to establish. Freeman, however, was smitten by his Katie, so much so that he had her face tattooed on his inner right arm. He wasn't abusive toward her in any way and was congenial toward Eileen. He often took the teenage girl to the cinema to watch the latest movie or to local dances where he played the role of an overprotective stepfather.

One evening at a dance, he had punched a sixteen-year-old boy so hard that he knocked him out cold. The only sin the lad had committed was to offer Eileen a glass of lemonade and request a dance without asking for Freeman's approval.

Both Eileen and Freeman were asked to leave the hall and never return. Kate turned up at the boy's home the following day with a new jumper to replace the one Freeman had wrecked and five pounds as an apology.

In early May 1914, after drinking beer for most of the day, Freeman and Ernest 'Shiner' Ryan came up with a plan to rob the Eveleigh Railway Workshops. They drew a mud map of the workshops and the driveway. Ryan, a frail-looking man who had made a name for himself as a safecracker, counterfeiter, and thief, told Freeman that it would be one of the easiest jobs he'd ever be involved in.

"You know the factory employs fuckin' hundreds of workers, so payday will be best time to hit. Can you imagine how much loot will be in those fuckin' chests!" Freeman exclaimed.

Freeman knew a man named Norman Twiss (no relation to Tilly) who worked at the Eveleigh Railway factory. Norman also owed him money. "I can't make any plans without inside help. This bastard owes me a bit of money. It's time for him to pay the piper. Drive me over to his house and I'll let him know what's what."

"I walked here. My car's back home," Shiner replied.

"Use my fuckin' car and it better come back in one fuckin' piece or you'll both fuckin' know it." Kate warned.

When they arrived at Twiss's home, he offered them each a beer before they sat around the kitchen table. At first, the factory worker was reticent about becoming involved in the robbery. Twiss had never been in trouble with the police and he was aware that he would be sent to gaol if they were caught. However, when Freeman sweetened the offer with a promise of one hundred pounds and writing off his four-hundred-pounds gambling debt, he eagerly agreed.

In a hushed tone, Twiss revealed that the next payroll would arrive on the 10th of June. He said that the paymaster, would have two cashboxes loaded with the factory wages in his carriage.

"How much do you think will be in the boxes?" Freeman asked.

"Should be around five thousand pounds."

Freeman's and Shiner's eyes widened with greed and glee when they heard the amount. They knew the money would have to be cut three ways and a hundred pounds thrown Twiss' way. But all in all, they considered a little over two thousand pounds was a good return for a few minutes work.

Freeman and Shiner returned to Kate's and the three continued their planning.

"How do you and Ryan plan to get away from the factory without being caught?" Kate asked.

"We'll have to check the place out and see." Shiner replied.

"You don't need to. I know the place from picking money up from Twiss." Freeman remarked.

"I have an idea," Kate piped up as Jewey was drawing a map. "You can use my car to get away in. I can disguise myself with a scarf, goggles, and a blonde wig and drive you there. You can chuck the cashboxes into the car, and I'll take off and meet you in the 'Loo somewhere. My car's fast enough."

"That's a fuckin' good idea, Katie. Ya know I only love ya for your brains don't you." Freeman smirked as he pulled her towards him. "But I don't want you anywhere near the place. The police know your car and we'd be in the lockup in minutes. I know of a mechanic with a car who could do with some extra cash. I'll go see him tomorrow."

At eight o'clock the following morning, Freeman and Ryan drove to Arthur Tatham's home in Castlereagh. The mechanic was surprised to see Freeman at his door offering him six hundred pounds to do a job. Freeman placed a bottle of whiskey on Arthur's kitchen table, pushed an empty glass toward him and smirked. "This is just a sweetener for the job."

"You've got Buckley's if you think a bottle of fuckin' whiskey and a promise of six hundred pounds is enough to use me car for a fuckin' robbery. If you bastards get caught, I'll go to prison with yas. I want a thousand fuckin' pounds upfront!"

"Where the fuck am I gonna get that much money from? Out of my arse?" Freeman asked, nettled by Tatham's demand.

"I don't care where you fuckin' get it from. No cash, no car."

By the time Freeman and his henchman left Tatham's home, they had arranged a time for Ryan to 'steal' Tatham's car and for him to report the car missing to the police.

During the return trip home, Freeman told Ryan that he would need to find a place that was easy to rob before the Eveleigh Railway holdup. "I need cash to pay Tatham."

They discussed different businesses that would have enough cash on hand and decided on the Darlinghurst post office. Freeman would carry the robbery out himself.

Kate was pleased to hear their plans were almost airtight. Freeman hadn't told her about the post office heist though. He wanted to keep that under his hat. She did have concerns however about using a car that could be traced to a person that was known to Freeman. But her lover shrugged it off saying that the police couldn't prove they knew one another.

"I still say it's better if you use a car that you steal yourself. There's plenty of them parked in the streets. It would only take minutes to nick one." She said, not impressed that her concerns were so quickly brushed aside.

"God in heaven Katie! The fuckin' plans are done. We've got the car we're gonna use!"

"Pardon me for fuckin' living!" Kate fumed before storming out of the room.

The following morning, Freeman, armed with a revolver, secreted himself in a nearby alley. Veiled by the pre-dawn darkness he waited for an opportunity to break into the Post Office. It was five o'clock and Oxford Street was already busy. Several carts were unloading their produce outside shops and cafes. Street cleaners were sweeping the streets and the aroma of fresh bread baking in the local bakeries pervaded the area. Freeman watched Michael McHale, the local night-watchman as he patrolled the footpath opposite the Darlinghurst Post Office.

A few minutes before six o'clock, Freeman crept across the road while McHale's back was turned. A young paperboy towing his newspaper cart, noticed Freeman picking at the lock on the Post Office door and immediately alerted McHale. When the watchman arrived at the building, he found the door ajar, and the padlock on the top step. Cautiously, with his pistol pointing in front of him, McHale pushed the door open with his foot and quietly entered the building. He slowly proceeded to the mail sorting room at the back of the post office. As he quietly made his way down the hallway, the watchman heard a noise coming from a room behind him. When he turned around, he was confronted by Freeman aiming a pistol point blank at his face.

"What the hell are you doing here?" His question was answered by a report from the revolver. McHale felt a sharp pain in his right cheek and fell against the wall.

Outside, a sudden agonised scream tore through the quietness of the cold winter morning. Freeman looked past McHale and saw tram conductor, Edward Heagney, clutching his side and calling out for help. Freeman realised the bullet he fired at McHale had passed through his cheek and wounded the conductor. Aware the police would be on their way, Freeman fled down Liverpool Street clutching a handful of stolen cash, with the wounded watchman in close pursuit.

The pain and loss of blood slowed McHale down, giving Freeman the chance to lose him when he jumped the fence of a nearby house. A man in a passing car stopped to help the watchman and drove him to the hospital.

When Freeman arrived at Kate's house, he found her boarder, Raymond Moore sitting at the kitchen table eating a sandwich.

"What happened to you? You look half fuckin' dead."

"Shut your fuckin' mouth. Where is she?"

"At the brothel." Moore replied as he rose from the table and left the house by the back door.

Kate was furious when Freeman showed up at her Surry Hills brothel and told her about the robbery and shooting. She threw an ashtray at him, berating him for coming to her house. "The last thing I fuckin' need is the police storming the fuckin' brothel!"

"I shot him in the face. I'd be fuckin' surprised if he remembers what his own fuckin' mother looks like!" Freeman replied in his defence. "All that trouble and all I got was twelve fuckin' pounds!"

Pissed off that he was interrupted before obtaining the one thousand pounds demanded by Tatham for the use of his vehicle, Freeman sent Shiner to steal the car the night before the planned robbery.

On Wednesday morning the 10th of June 1914, Freeman and Ryan sat in the car while they waited at Eveleigh Railway Factory for the paymaster to arrive. Ten minutes before midday, he and Ryan donned their driving goggles and tied their respective handkerchiefs across their faces. They didn't have to wait long for the carriage.

Frederick Miller, John Henry his junior assistant, and the driver, Albert Andrews, pulled up at the railway factory in their horse-drawn carriage. Hodge and Twiss waited for Miller to give them the nod, and then carried the larger cash box to the main office.

As Twiss removed the second cash box from the carriage, Ryan, wearing a green handkerchief across his lower face, placed his foot on the accelerator and skidded to a stop alongside the horse and carriage. Freeman, with his mouth and nose covered with a black handkerchief, opened the passenger door, and leapt from the car. He pointed a revolver at Miller's head, and yelled, "bail up" in true bushranger style. Wanting to get the robbery over and done with, Freeman knocked the paymaster to the ground before pointing the pistol at Twiss' head, demanding that he hand the cashbox over.

Twiss, as planned, offered no resistance, and calmly lowered the cashbox which Freeman grabbed before racing back to the car. Robert Hodge lunged toward the cash box knowing he could take care of himself if the need arose. However, he thought better of his heroic act when Ryan aimed a pistol at him: "Is your boss's money worth dying for?"

After loading the cashbox onto the back seat of the car, Freeman jumped into the front passenger seat and Ryan accelerated off down the road. Albert Andrews, Miller's driver, bravely took off after the getaway car, but his horse wasn't fast enough. He turned the cart around and headed back to the factory.

Shiner sped through the streets, almost crashing into several pedestrians as he made their getaway. They headed toward Ultimo where they parked the car along Bulwarra Lane, making sure the street was deserted before removing their handkerchief and goggles. Both men sat back and laughed, relieved that they had made it safely away. Freeman threw the revolver on the floor of the car before he and Shiner placed the cash bags in one of Kate's old, battered suitcases they had secreted in the back before leaving that morning. They then made their way to Kirk Lane where Kate had left her car for them to return home.

At three thirty that afternoon, two loud bangs on her door brought Kate to her feet and sent a shiver down her spine. She straightened her frock and boldly answered the door, prepared to face the police. Instead, she was surprised to find Freeman and Shiner standing on her doorstep.

"Is that bastard Moore here?" Freeman asked as he rushed through the door, closely followed by Shiner.

"No. He's gone up the Hollow to the dog meet."

"Where's Eileen?"

"You know where she is. She's staying at Vera's for the night. Now stop with the fuckin' questions and tell me how it went!"

"We'll show you how it fuckin' went!" Freeman grinned.

Kate rushed and locked the back door before racing around the house closing all the curtains before joining the men in her bedroom. When she entered, Ryan was removing the money bags from the suitcase while Freeman sat on the bed and sorted the cut.

After the equal shares, including Twiss and Tatham's slice into piles on top of the bed, Freeman threw some notes and coins into one of the cash bags. "Take this over to Twiss at the Tradesman's Arms. Don't fuckin' tell him anything!" He instructed Shiner.

After tossing Tatham's share in a bag, Freeman looked across the bed at Kate. "If that bastard thinks he's gonna get a thousand quid, he's in for a shock. He's getting two hundred quid and he can fuckin' lump it if he doesn't like it!"

"Just shut up and hurry up and get this money out of here. I don't want the fuckin' cops banging my door down finding it fuckin' here and dragging me off to the cells."

"I've got just the place to hide it. I'll take it there before going to Tatham's. Here's a few hundred for you." Freeman said as he planted a kiss on Kate's lips before leaving.

Unfortunately, Freeman and Ryan were unaware their 'clean getaway' had been observed. A quick-thinking bystander witnessed the robbery and had written down information about the car. He then alerted the police to its make, colour, and registration number. The police were able to trace its ownership through the registration number 10297 to Arthur Tatham, who, as planned, had reported the car stolen the previous day. Two detectives questioned him about the disappearance of his car and about his associates. The mechanic put on a good show of acting surprised and irate when the police told him his car had been used in a daring daylight robbery. However, the detectives were not fooled by his performance. They were certain Tatham knew more than he was letting on.

Meanwhile, around four thirty that afternoon, Police Commissioner, Frederick John Hanson, chanced upon the getaway car. He found the empty cash box on the floor of the car and a revolver under a cushion of the driver's seat with all five chambers still loaded.

Just after seven o'clock that evening, Freeman drove Kate's 1910 Napier past the dilapidated houses in Frog Hollow. Stray cats and rats skirted out of the path of the car's headlights as he turned off Riley Street and parked in a nearby alley. With his cut-throat razor gripped firmly in his right hand, Freeman made his way through the sparsely lit laneways stinking of urine and faeces until he descended the steep sandstone staircase as he headed to the cock pit.

The excited cheers and curses from men urging their cocks to fight echoed into the night. Freeman made his way down the stairs and nodded to the man at the door as he entered the fighting pit. He saw Tatham leaning against the rear timber wall. The mechanic looked ill at ease and out of place among the dog fighting riffraff. He tipped his hat with his right index finger when he spotted Freeman and walked towards him.

"Thank fuck you're here. I was about to go to Kate's house. Give me the money so I can get the fuck out of this hell hole."

"Kate would have chased you with a tomahawk if you showed up with this fuckin' attitude. Take it and go."

"Let me count it first."

"You're a fuckin' stupid bastard, aren't ya. Show that cash bag in here and you won't make it to the end of the lane alive. It's not what you fuckin' asked for, but the fuckin' cashboxes didn't hold what we were expecting. Now get out of here."

Tatham knew better than to argue with Freeman, especially in his own territory. He shook his head in disgust and left. Freeman waited a few minutes and followed him out to make sure he wasn't robbed.

When he returned to Kate's house, Freeman found Moore and Shiner sitting in the living room drinking beers and Kate in the kitchen cooking sausages and potatoes.

"What the fuck is Moore doin' here?" Freeman whispered. "We've gotta get rid of him."

"Are you off your kadoova? He fuckin lives here! What do you want me to do, kick him out?" Kate angrily replied. "Give him some fuckin' money and send him up to the sly groggery for a few hours."

Moore refused to go at first, but when he saw Kate make a move toward the back door, knowing her threats of burying her enemies behind the chook house, he grabbed the money from Freeman and bolted.

Freeman sat on the chair opposite Shiner and the two discussed the money.

"The next few months we won't be spending a fuckin' quid of that money until we're out of the state. We need to act and live as normal and not take a step out of turn. The last thing we need is to have the fuckin' cops askin' us questions."

"I'll stay at my flat and poke me head in at the Arms every now and then. There's no way we can stay here in Sydney." Shiner remarked.

"You won't be fuckin' hangin' around here, I know that!" Kate grumbled as she handed the men their dinner. "And I wouldn't be tellin'

Ettie anything about the robbery either if I were you Ernie. The fewer the people that know the better!"

7

When the detectives arrived back at the station, Frederick Miller, the Eveleigh Railway paymaster was waiting. Miller was there to voice his suspicions about one of the factory's employees, Norman Twiss. He told the detectives that the more he went over the events of the robbery in his head, the more he was sure that Twiss was involved.

"What makes you say that?" Detective Moore asked.

"He was too calm for a man that had a gun held at his head during a robbery."

The heist caused such a hullabaloo in the newspapers around Sydney, dubbing it the 'most sensational exploit of the criminal fraternity'. The media were also excited about it being the first time a getaway car was used. Reporters crowded the local police station vying to be the one to scoop the arrest when it happened. Others questioned employees at the factory, hoping to discover unknown information. Newspaper sales skyrocketed as the public hungered for every morsel of information they could read about the 'motor bandits who had pulled off one of the most daring daylight highway robberies ever perpetrated in the history of the State'.

Reporters tailed the police as they investigated their lines of inquiries throughout Sydney, Melbourne, and Hobart. They were relentless in their pursuit to be the first to send a telegram to their editor of any breaks in the case.

Three days after the heist, front pages of the papers screamed with headlines that the police had offered a four hundred pounds reward for the armed offenders. They released a description of the men involved in the robbery and added that one of the robbers had a tattoo of the Australian flag on his arm.

It didn't take long for the Darlinghurst police station to be crowded with do-gooders wanting to assist the police in apprehending the felonious miscreants. However, even with the influx of people stating they had information about the robbers, the police were unable to glean any new or valid information.

Meanwhile, Ryan and Freeman continued making plans to leave for Melbourne where they would meet the ship that would take them to America. Freeman remained at Kate's house, not daring to leave in case he was recognised. He had become highly suspicious and paranoid, which left Kate and her daughter walking around the house as if on eggshells.

Two days after the reward announcement, the police upped the ante and added a further forty percent of the stolen money as an added incentive. The twelve hundred pounds inducement still attracted storytellers, but it also brought in one man who had invaluable information about the robbers. He named Freeman as the person who had orchestrated the heist. The attractive monetary reward had nothing to do with his community-minded conscience, of course.

Freeman was placed under surveillance. The Inspector General of Police sent telegrams to the newspapers stating the police were close to making an arrest of those involved in the robbery. He hoped his announcement would make Freeman nervous and push him into making a mistake.

The police also became suspicious when they discovered that Tatham was a long-standing friend of Freeman's. They paid another visit to the mechanic's home and brought him in for questioning.

During the interview, Tatham revealed more knowledge about the Eveleigh robbery than had been released to the newspapers. The police accused him of being involved in the heist, which he denied. He would much rather face prison time than Freeman and his gang if he fizgigged on them. However, even without his confession, the police felt they had enough to charge him with being an accessory to the robbery.

On the evening of the 23rd of June, a young constable showed up at Kate's door asking to speak to Freeman. She told him that he was down at the pub and would be back later that night. "Mrs. Leigh, I have information that will help Freeman. It will cost him twenty pounds." The recalcitrant constable offered.

"It bloody better be worth twenty quid if you know what's good for you." Kate snarled before leaving to get the money.

The constable revealed that the police were planning on arresting Freeman for the Eveleigh Railway workshop hold up. He told her that from that afternoon, they would be watching the house. Kate thanked him for the tip-off and paid the money. She then watched after him until he left the street.

Freeman was sitting in the living room and heard everything. "I've gotta get out of fuckin' Sydney!" He went to their room and started packing all that he could fit into a suitcase. "I'll stay with Phil until I can leave the fuckin' country."

"Are you sure he'll take you in? You know those guys will fizgig for a few pounds!"

"Yeah, he owes me for giving him an alibi for the jewellery shop robbery. It'll be right."

"How will you let me know when we're leaving for America?" Kate asked, suspicious Freeman would take off without her and Eileen.

"I'll send a message through one of the boys. We have to be fuckin' careful of the cops now."

On the morning of the 24th of June, Kate drove to Strathfield Railway station with Freemen secreted under a blanket on the floor in the back of her car. She stopped a few hundred yards from the station and dropped him off a little way down the tracks.

However, the police were ten steps ahead.

Fearing a shootout, the police preferred to arrest Freeman out in the open and the train station offered them the perfect cover. Superintendent Childs positioned himself across the street from the station. His men were dressed in casual clothes and strategically placed around the platform.

Freeman's hand trembled as he paid for a ticket to Melbourne. Then, ticket in hand, he pulled his hat down and stood at the end of the platform. When the Melbourne Express train approached, Freeman picked up his suitcase and went to board the train. As he was about to step onto the train, he was grabbed from behind by two burly detectives.

At the police station, Freeman protested his innocence. He told the detectives they had the wrong man, saying he had spent that morning at the races. "The races don't run of a morning." Detective Robertson challenged. Freeman quickly replied that he must have mixed his days up and tapped his index finger on his chin before 'remembering' that he was in bed with Kate Leigh that morning.

Robertson sent one of the constables to bring Kate into the police station and sent Freeman down to the cells. When Leigh arrived, Robertson asked her to take a seat. As soon as she sat down, he asked her where she was on Wednesday morning the 10th of June.

"How the hell would I know where I was two weeks ago? I'm lucky to remember what I did yesterday!"

"I'm sure you'd remember if you were involved in the Eveleigh Railway payroll robbery, Mrs. Leigh. We have received information that indicates you were." Robertson warned.

Katie nearly spluttered out her reply. "The bloody Eveleigh robbery? You cops brought me in for that? Are you bloody mad or just bloody stupid!"

Robertson ignored her sarcasm and continued. "We've got Samuel Freeman in the cells. He tells quite a different story. Are you sure you don't have any information to tell us?"

As far as Kate was concerned, she wasn't anybody's fool. She had dropped Freeman off at the station and he was on a train to Melbourne. She knew the cops were trying to trap her and wasn't having any of it.

"Well, you cops may like wasting your time, but I don't like wasting mine. Have a pleasant afternoon." She smiled, then promptly stood up and left.

Later that afternoon while she was sitting down to an afternoon tea of scones and jam, an agitated Shiner rushed through her back door. "Why the fuck didn't you tell me that Jewey got arrested!"

"What the fuckin' hell are you on about? He's on a train to Melbourne! I dropped him at the station meself. Comin' in here and scarin' me half to fuckin' death!"

"Haven't you read the papers? He was arrested at Strathfield this morning!"

"Fuckin' hell! I walked out on the cops a couple of hours ago! They told me he was in the cells and I called them liars! They said Sammy had told them that I was involved in the robbery!"

"I've got to get out of fuckin' Sydney! I tell ya, there's no fuckin' way in hell I'm goin' back to gaol. Sam wouldn't open his mouth to the cops. He knows what will happen to him if he did!"

"Better watch your back at the railway stations. Now get out of here in case the police are watching!"

After Shiner left, Kate walked through the house and cautiously peered through the windows for any strange cars or men standing on the street. She didn't know what to do about Freeman being in gaol. She sat down at the table and finished the scone, drank the last of her tea and went into her bedroom to get changed. "If the cops think they can play a game with me… I'll show them I can play the game just as well," she said to her reflection in the mirror as she adjusted her hat.

"Eileen, c'mere now!" She called out.

When her daughter came out of her bedroom, she immediately saw her mother was nervous. "What's happened, Mum?"

"Bloody Sammy's gone and got himself bloody arrested. I've gotta to go to the police station. You stay inside and don't open the door to anyone, you hear?"

Kate arrived at the police station with sandwiches and scones for Freeman. But when she was taken to his cell, he looked at her as if he had never seen her before. "Who's that ginger cunt?"

"She says she's your girlfriend," the policeman said.

"Get her the fuck out of here. I've never seen the bitch before in my life!"

Kate knew Freeman only said what he did to protect her. But she was going to stand by her man and help him any way she could.

7

Four days after Freeman's arrest, Shiner sent his remaining share of the stolen money by train to Walter Falkiner, who was a criminal friend of long standing. He retained eight hundred pounds for himself.

After leaving the station, Ryan became worried about entrusting so much money to his mate. He headed straight to the local chemist and purchased a bottle of peroxide and returned home to transform his looks. He then cut his hair short before applying the peroxide. As he nervously waited for the liquid to bleach his hair, he searched through Ettie's wardrobe for one of her wigs, clothing, and shoes. After packing them and his own clothes into two suitcases. He then returned to the bathroom to wash the peroxide out of his hair and give himself a shave as close to the skin as possible.

When Ettie arrived at his flat unexpectedly, she saw his transformation and the packed bags on the kitchen table.

"What the hell have you done to yourself and where are you goin'? She asked.

"I have to go to Adelaide on business. I don't want to be recognised." He hastily replied.

Ettie knew there was no point in asking if she could join him. After a quick kiss goodbye on her cheek, he handed her fifty pounds before leaving for the train station.

On the way, Shiner stopped at a park and used their toilet facilities to change into his female disguise. Dressed as a woman, he then awkwardly hobbled back to his car wearing Ettie's high heeled shoes.

When he arrived at Central Station, he noticed a large contingent of detectives and police officers patrolling the platforms and carpark. He adjusted Ettie's black hat on his head, straightened his frock and cardigan before taking a firm grip on his luggage. He then approached the ticket office as confidently as possible and purchased a ticket in the name of Edna Johnson.

During the hours he awaited his train, several policemen passed by him. Every now and then he would look away, hoping that his five o'clock shadow had been kept at bay with his late shave. Shiner was extremely relieved when the station master announced the imminent arrival of The Adelaide Express and he boarded the train without incident.

His mother was waiting for him at the station when he arrived. She kissed her son on the cheek and hugged him close before pushing him away to look at him.

"What have you done this time Ernie to bring you scampering home with your tail between your legs?" She asked.

"Now there's a nice welcome for a son that's travelled almost a thousand miles to see his sweet mother. I've done nothing wrong. I was worried about you with this threat of war and wanted to make sure that you're safe." He smiled as he hugged his mother again for good measure.

Becoming concerned when several telegrams he had wired to Falkiner remained unanswered. Shiner packed his small leather bag and told his mother that he needed to attend a business meeting in Melbourne, before heading to the train station.

Upon his arrival in Melbourne, Shiner caught a taxi to the address in Albert Park he had been sending the telegrams to but found it vacant. He began to sweat as he realised his suspicions about his friend were valid. He knocked on the door of one of a neighbouring house and was told that Falkiner had left for Davenport in Tasmania the previous week.

Ambling aimlessly along the street, Ryan came across a house that looked to be uninhabited. He waited until night and using his safe breaking skills, picked the lock on the back door. Upon entering, he saw that the furniture had been covered with white sheets. He walked into the main bedroom and opened the wardrobe and draws and saw they were full of clothing. He then noticed mail piled up at the front door, and surmised the homeowners were away. That night Shiner secreted six hundred pounds in a jar in the chimney of the house before falling asleep on the comfortable bed in the main bedroom.

Early the following morning, he crept out and ate breakfast at a nearby café as he waited for the post office to open. When the post office opened, Shiner rushed over and wired Ettie to buy a train ticket immediately out of the money he had left her and gave her the address of the house where he was squatting.

When Ettie arrived in Melbourne, she expected to be sailing to America. Instead, she learned that Shiner only had left six hundred pounds of the money and they wouldn't be leaving for America until he found Falkiner and his stolen money in Tasmania.

Feeling tricked into coming to Melbourne, and aware that without the stolen money, she would be stuck in Australia and never see America. She told Ryan that she was going for a walk and would be back after she had her land legs back. As she walked, her anger grew. She wasn't interested in chasing Falkiner all over Tasmania and knew whatever money Shiner had left from the robbery, would be used up during the farcical search. Every step she took she thought about the reward money which would cover a trip to America and more. She stopped a man and woman who were walking their black and tan spaniel and asked them for the address of the police station. They gave her the directions to St Kilda police station and advised her to catch a taxi.

Twenty minutes later, she hailed a passing cab and asked the driver to take her to the police station. She walked in as bold as brass and asked to speak to a detective about the Eveleigh robbery.

During the hour-long police interview, Ettie recounted her knowledge of the events that had transpired since the Eveleigh holdup. She told the excited detective that she went out to dinner with Ryan at the Lonsdale Café the night before the robbery. She told him about the money and pistol he had pulled out of his pocket the night of the robbery and the subsequent shopping spree.

Early the following morning, fourteen detectives and five uniformed police officers surrounded the Albert Park house. Ryan yelled out that he was armed and prepared to shoot his way to freedom. But when he saw the heavy police presence, he threw the gun out through the front door and walked out with his hands raised in the air. Two detectives grabbed Ryan and handcuffed him as the other police entered the house and searched for firearms and the remainder of the holdup money. Within twenty minutes the six hundred pounds enclosed within the glass jar was discovered by a uniformed officer.

The next day, Ryan faced the Melbourne magistrate charged with participating in the robbery at the Eveleigh Workshops. The judge ordered that he was to be extradited to Sydney that evening and would be remanded in custody until the New South Wales detectives arrived.

"While awaiting the arrival of Detective Robson, the Melbourne detectives brought Ryan in sandwiches and a pot of tea for dinner. They sat inside his cell with him chit-chatting while he ate. It was then they learned the means in which Shiner had eluded the police in Sydney. The men laughed heartily as they listened to how he had disguised himself as a woman and even more so when he described how he had hobbled past the police officers wearing his girlfriend's high heel shoes.

"Don't laugh too hard. My masquerade helped me evade arrest by the detectives you had watching out for me at Spencer Street Station in Melbourne." Ryan sniggered.

"Yeah, one of the constables found two wigs at your house. Someone will be in shortly to cut a lock of your hair to compare it to the few hairs found on the wigs." One of the detectives countered.

An hour later, Robson accompanied by two fully armed detectives arrived to escort Shiner to Sydney. Robson thanked his Victorian counterparts for assisting them in his arrest and wished them luck in catching Falkiner.

The arrest of Shiner's scarpering friend was imminent. The Melbourne police had set up operation "Will-o'-the-Wisp" where they rode around as passengers on Tasmanian trains to aid in capturing Falkiner. Melbourne detectives' luck changed when they intercepted and deciphered coded telegrams and traced Falkiner's movements around the state.

After Falkiner's arrival at the Orient Hotel in Hobart, the detectives knocked on the door of his room: "Are you Walter Ormond Falkiner?" Detective Barr asked. Knowing the game was up, he admitted to his identity. Upon searching him, the detectives discovered fifty-seven five-pound notes and thirty-one sovereigns in his pockets. Money, they assumed was from the holdup. Falkiner was arrested as an accessory to the Eveleigh factory robbery.

During their investigations, the detectives uncovered enough evidence to link Freeman to the shooting of Michael McHale, the night watchman at the Post Office. They were confident enough in his guilt for them to charge him with intent to murder. Freeman knew he would go to gaol for a long time and could possibly face the noose.

When Kate met with Freeman the following afternoon, he told her to establish an alibi for him. She promised her lover that she would look after him. And she most definitely gave it her best attempt.

When she arrived home, she noticed Moore was laying on the settee with empty bottles lying around on the floor.

"Haven't you got anything better to do? You're fuckin' lucky Eileen is spending the night at Ethel's and not here to see this fuckin' pigsty!"

"I'll clean it up before I go to fuckin' bed."

"That's good, you useless cunt. I'm not here to be your fuckin' housemaid!"

"Better than that bastard you're with. He can't even rob a payroll without getting caught!"

"He's a lot more useful than a lazy cunt like you that gets sacked from a job every month! In fact, you can make yourself fuckin' useful. If the cops come 'round, tell them that Sammy was here all night at a party on the sixth of June."

"Fuck off. I don't owe that bastard anything!" Moore snapped in reply.

Kate didn't say a word. She gave him a look that would terrify the devil himself, then turned around and walked out to the backyard. When she returned, Moore almost soiled his pants when Kate walked toward him with a tomahawk axe raised above her head.

"I'll cut ya bloody head off you bastard if you don't tell the police Jewey was here all night!" In a fury, Kate brought the axe down on Moore's forehead cutting him above his right eye. Not satisfied that Moore didn't get the message, she slammed the blunt end of the axe on his arm, breaking it in two places as he tried to protect his head.

Fearing for his life, Moore picked up two empty bottles of beer and threw them at Kate before escaping through the open back door. Kate screamed after him, but the terrified and bloodied Moore kept running without looking back. The last thing he wanted was to be buried behind the chook shed in the backyard.

When he arrived at the hospital that night, he told the nurses that he had fallen off the roof while replacing some tin that had blown off in the storm. He wasn't too smart, but Moore was canny enough to know that reporting Kate for assault would result in death.

7

After reading about the Eveleigh heist arrests, Francis Gilbert, a railway labourer at the factory, arrived at the Darlinghurst police station and offered information about Norman Twiss. He had been acquainted with Twiss for ten years, having met him in Dubbo. He told the police about a conversation between Twiss and himself one night at Flanagan's pub about five weeks prior to the payroll heist. Twiss had said it would be quite easy for anyone to get at the payroll money. The police asked if Twiss had said anything about a plan to hold up his workplace, and Gilbert replied that he hadn't, but he wouldn't put it past him.

Detectives Roche and Pattinson furthered their inquiries at Flanagan's Hotel in Oxford Street. The owner told them that they'd best talk to his barmaid, Molly Butler. She had her suspicions about Jewey and Norman and the Eveleigh robbery and she told the police she had seen both men with Paddy several times before the robbery.

"Who's Paddy?" Pattinson asked.

"Oh, that's what I call Arthur Tatham. But what got me suspicions quiverin' was Jewey and Paddy meetin' 'ere the same day as the robbery. The boys ain't never in 'ere on a Wednesday!"

After leaving Flanagan's Hotel, the detectives met with Freeman in his cell and relayed the information they had been given. Jewey's reply was short and sweet, "I wish to state that I know absolutely nothing at all about this robbery."

The police had enough evidence to charge Freeman, Ryan, Twiss, and Tatham, and as expected, all four men pleaded not guilty to the robbery. Freeman also faced charges of feloniously wounding with intent to murder Michael McHale but felt confident enough of Kate's alibi to get off on the charge if he pleaded not guilty.

Unfortunately, the court case didn't pan out as the men had expected.

Ryan denied participating in the robbery and when questioned about leaving town, he stated he'd only left after seeing an illustration in the newspaper that looked like him, and he didn't want to be arrested for a crime he didn't commit. The jury and the judge didn't believe him, and he was sentenced to ten years at Parramatta Gaol.

Twiss was acquitted because of a lack of evidence. He was so excited at the verdict that he kissed Ryan and wished him luck before rushing out of the courtroom, waving goodbye to the jury and the judge. He was dismissed from his job at the Eveleigh factory and returned to Dubbo, where he remained out of trouble and was never seen by police again.

As she had in the past for other men, Kate perjured herself and stated under oath that she and Freemen were together all night on the fifth of June. She told the court they had spent the first half of the night at a skating rink and had stopped on the way home and bought a pie. She said her daughter was staying at a friend's house for a few days, so she and Freeman stayed in bed until late into the afternoon the following day.

However, the prosecutor was several steps ahead of Kate. The police had spoken to the owner and manager of the skating rink and both men had signed an affidavit stating that the rink was closed at the time Kate said she was there. That was not the only problem with her story. Both Ettie Kelly and May Bragg, friends, and former lovers of Freeman's, signed statements that they were with Freeman that night and Kate wasn't with them. Then when it came to Detective Robson and Constable Hooper's time to testify, they swore under oath that Freeman had told them that he did not know Leigh when she visited him in gaol after his arrest.

Kate stood up and started screaming at the top of her lungs that the cops were nothing but dirty liars. "Sammy said he didn't know me to protect me from getting involved in his troubles, as any good man would do."

Justice Sly was livid over Kate's behaviour. He told her to sit down or he would throw her in gaol for contempt of court. She immediately sat down swearing under her breath as she gave Hooper a death stare.

The evidence and witness accounts offered by Joseph Clifford and Michael McHale, was strong enough to secure a conviction. However, Raymond Moore slammed the final nails in the men's coffins, testifying that Kate had tried to coerce him into providing an alibi for Freeman on the night of McHale's shooting by attacking him with a tomahawk.

The jury returned with a guilty verdict with a recommendation that Freeman be executed.

Kate let out a deafening shriek and burst into tears when she heard the jury pronounce the death sentence. Then, shocked into silence, she fell back onto the wooden bench and wept into her handkerchief.

The Judge sentenced Freeman to ten years in Parramatta Gaol for his role in the robbery and commuted his death sentence to life, which was to begin once the ten-year term was served.

When she heard the lengthy sentence her lover was given, Kate screamed across to the judge that he was convicting an innocent man, and then thanked him for not hanging him. The judge ignored her outbursts and nodded toward Senior Constable Charlton, who promptly walked across the courtroom and arrested Leigh for perjury.

Freeman turned around and told Kate to forget about him and not to bother to write as she was being led from the court. Turning back to the judge, Jewey spoke, "Your Honour, I reckon I am the makings of a good soldier. I ask you, instead of sending me to gaol, please send me to the front where I can fight for the freedom of Australia."

Ernest Shiner Ryan requested the same.

Justice Sly seemed to hold the men in some esteem after their offer to go to war. He replied respectfully and courteously to their courageous proposal: "I believe you are perfectly right. Both of you are bold and apparently afraid of nothing and you would make particularly good soldiers. Still, I cannot send you to war. This is the boldest case I have ever tried."

7

Kate hadn't emerged from the Eveleigh Robbery fiasco unscathed. On the 29th of March 1915, she appeared in court to face the perjury charge. Detectives Robson and Turbet were the only witnesses summoned by the court to give evidence, such was the strength of the case the prosecution had against her.

Turbet began his testimony by reading out an extensive list of offences from Kate's charge sheet. They included offences under the *Vagrancy Act*, prostitution, using abusive words, shoplifting, and being the holder of a house frequented by prostitutes. Robson testified that Leigh was a woman who had no respect for the law and she often bailed out criminals and gave them false alibis. He added that there was also a long list of complaints made to police by neighbours at each of the houses Kate had 'resided' in during the previous eight years.

Robson stated that Kate was an extremely dangerous and shrewd woman, who was always prepared to assist criminals and at times, for a price. He said she would continue to resort to any violence necessary for revenge or to maintain the lifestyle she had become accustomed to unless she was imprisoned for a good number of years.

The magistrate perused the numerous charge sheets and asked the defendant if she had anything she would like to say to the court. Kate knew the odds were stacked against her. She jutted her chin out and held her head high, and replied, "I'm not guilty, Your Honour. I reserve my defence." The magistrate then questioned her about several dubious statements she had made in the Eveleigh case, and for supplying a false alibi for Freeman. She declined to comment. It took the jury less than twenty minutes to return a guilty verdict. The magistrate noted Kate's aloof and unconcerned demeanour in court and sentenced her to five years at Long Bay Gaol.

She couldn't hide her astonishment and anger about her sentence. She looked at the judge and slammed both her fists on the table, yelling, "Five years for stickin' to a man! I'll swing before I stick to another!"

The newspapers revelled in printing stories of Kate's life as a brothel madam and criminal associate. Her relationship with Samuel Freeman had cost her dearly. Her beloved daughter, Eileen, was sent to live in a Catholic convent while she did her time in gaol. She gave everything up to protect the man she loved, and he hadn't the decency to even send her a letter from prison.

On her arrival at Long Bay Gaol, Kate wasn't treated with the fear or respect her presence usually demanded. The prison guards didn't care who she was, to them she was just another criminal. She underwent the demoralising strip search, was showered in cold water and then had delousing dust thrown over her, just like every other woman endured during their induction to the prison.

Kate, dressed in a grey cotton tunic, grey socks, and black leather shoes, followed the guard along the stone walled corridors to her cell, defiantly meeting the glance of every inmate she passed. Leigh knew she would be targeted as fresh meat in the gaol, but she would show them that she was a woman who could stand up for herself.

As soon as she finished her breakfast the following morning, Kate slipped five pounds into the pocket of one of the guards in the dining hall. Ten minutes later, she was called out of muster by the female prison officer and asked what she expected for the money. Kate simply replied, "kitchen duty".

The women soon learned she was a force to be reckoned with, a sentiment augmented when two of her working girls joined her in prison. Kate maintained the regime of being polite to the other women, participating in callisthenics, maintaining the pretence of high spirits while doing so. However, Kate gritted her teeth through the enforced attendance at church and the required kneeling in prayer on the cold stone floor of the chapel every Sunday. She kept to herself as much as possible, reading acceptable ladylike books, her censored letters and grinning and bearing the cold showers during winter that were supposed to assist in building self-control and strengthen her character.

Four years later, Kate's good behaviour was rewarded when she was released from gaol on parole. Her heartbeat quickened when she heard the loud clang of the gates closing behind her. She didn't look back. Kate held her head high and climbed into the waiting cab.

She was surprised at the many changes that had occurred in East Sydney during her confinement. The war had ended. Germany had formally surrendered and signed the Armistice. Australians were still celebrating the recent cessation of hostilities, whilst also mourning the loss of almost sixty thousand of their sons, brothers, and fathers. Within the grief, jubilation, and uncertainty, being the criminal entrepreneur that she was, Kate saw financial opportunities.

7

After her relationship with Freeman, Kate decided she would never again be a man's patsy. She thought it was about time she ran her own criminal empire instead of filling a man's wallet. She met Eileen at a café in Darlinghurst and enjoyed corned beef and pickle sandwiches and two pots of tea. Later that afternoon, Kate and Eileen were sitting in the real estate office again, this time signing a contract for the purchase of 109 Riley Street, Surry Hills.

Within the following twelve months, Kate had re-established her illegal activities and then some. She used the two back rooms at her new home as headquarters for an illegal gambling den, selling sly grog, and allowing men to remain drinking at the roughly set up bar after six o'clock. Only those who knew the password of 'mum' were allowed entry.

Six months later, Kate purchased a fruit and vegetable shop at 212 Devonshire St, Surry Hills. There she established a second sly grog shop in the flat upstairs. This address offered the veil of darkness needed to conduct such a clandestine business with a dimly lit alleyway at the rear offering a private entry for customers.

In 1921, Kate purchased 2 Lansdowne Street, Surry Hills which became her principal place of residence. She finally had a house she could call home. She and Eileen spent a fortune on furnishing their new abode. Kate also employed local seamstresses to run up curtains for every room, whilst paying two local women to clean her house twice a week.

It was here that Kate's philanthropist side appeared. She began holding birthday parties for disadvantaged children and living her life as normally as she could for a brothel madam, standover woman, gambling den owner, fencer, and sly grog seller.

Leigh had made a name for herself as a tough-as-nails woman within the criminal sector. However, the local Catholic church and school saw her as a saint due to the amount of money she donated. Her neighbours saw her as a benevolent saviour knowing that if they were ever hungry, Kate would buy them food.

On the 26th of September 1922, Kate married petty thief, fellow sly grogger, and one-time musician, Edward Joseph 'Teddy' Barry. However, Teddy found out the hard way that Kate wasn't a woman to deceive and use as a sugar-mummy. Five months later, he was on his way to divorce court.

Over the years, Kate ran a lucrative criminal operation and was often described as 'the most evil woman in Sydney.' People living in East Sydney knew who she was, and many, expecting trouble, went into hiding whenever they saw her black 1925 Studebaker cruising the streets. She was known to force those who owed her money or had done her wrong into the rear of the car for a 'chat'. Before the reticent passenger entered the car, her driver, whether it was Bruce Higgs, Herbert Corliss, or Walter Tomlinson, would lay down the folding seats in the back, and close the car blinds as their quarry watched on, shitting themselves knowing their grisly end was probably nigh.

Between the properties she owned, her illicit activities, and the sly groggeries and brothels at 25, 27, and 31 Kippax Street, Kate's wealth increased substantially. Concerned for her life, and that of her criminal empire, Kate hired thugs from Sydney gangs, like her nemesis, Matilda Devine, with whom she had a long-running conflict during their criminal duopoly.

During the late 1920s, Sydney police were fed up with the growing cocaine problem, which exacerbated local crime and violence. They made a beeline to Kate's brothels and houses. They were prepared to do whatever was needed to shut the cocaine queen down.

With the prohibition on prostitution, selling cocaine through chemists and the pubs being closed at six o'clock each night, the police had plenty they could pin on Leigh.

One police officer on her books, advised her that she was under surveillance. Kate was smarter than the police gave her credit for and soon found alternative avenues to sell her cocaine shipments.

Glass shattering in the dead of night at her Riley Street residence on the 27th March 1930, alerted Kate to uninvited visitors entering her home. Thinking it was an opposing gang come to kill her, with lightning speed, she leapt across the room and raced through to the kitchen, grabbing her loaded shotgun.

There, she came face-to-face with John Prendergast, known in the criminal world as 'Snowy'. With him was Joseph Prendergast, Albert Runnalla and Frederick Lee, all employed in legitimate and well-paying jobs but also engaged in petty crime. She knew they were there to rob her of her cocaine.

"Get the fuck out of my house, you fuckin' cunts, or I'll fuckin' shoot you where you stand!" Kate threatened. High on cocaine, Prendergast lunged forward to unarm Leigh, fearing that he was armed with a razor, Leigh shot him in the stomach. The others legged it from the house as soon as they heard the shotgun blast, unaware that one of their mob had been wounded.

When the police arrived, a blood trail led them to a lane behind Kate's house, and to Prendergast who was bleeding profusely from his wound. When asked for his name, he told the officer he was Jack Bennett. He was recognised upon his arrival at the hospital but died half an hour later. When the coroner emptied his pockets, he found a cut-throat Bengall-style straight razor.

Later that afternoon, Kate was arrested under the surname Barry and charged with murder. The magistrate released her on three-hundred pounds bail to reappear on the 30th of March. At her hearing, the police officers were questioned and told the court that they considered John Prendergast a dangerous criminal. The magistrate stated that it was his belief that Mrs. Kate Barry was in fear for her life and had acted accordingly. She was released without charge.

7

Luck finally ran out for Kate. On the 1st of July 1930, Kate's policeman informant was on leave and she had not heard any warning whistles from lookouts she had planted around the streets. When Detective-sergeant Wickham knocked on the front door of 104 Riley Street, in the company of Detective Thompson and the New South Wales Drug Squad, Kate made a run for it. Leigh was found in possession of cocaine and was arrested by Lillian Armfield.

Four men who were found sitting at the kitchen table were searched for drugs, but none were found on their person. Scratching like a cat, screaming like a banshee, and fighting like a street brawler, Kate was carried out to a police car by no less than seven police officers, much to the entertainment of the neighbours who crowded outside to watch the fray.

Three days after her arrest, Kate's eighty-one-year-old mother, Charlotte, died in her home at 41 Hall Street, Bondi. Devastated that she was unable to reclaim her mother's love, her death came as a double blow.

Mr. Moseley re-appeared in Central Police Court without his client. He declared to Mr. Perry S.M. that Kate Barry was unable to appear before him to answer to her possession charge due to collapsing during the graveside funeral of her mother at the Rookwood Cemetery the day before. Moseley said that the defendant was in bed at home before offering the magistrate a doctor's certificate stating his client was suffering with 'shock and neurasthenia'.

"I don't care for a doctor's certificate. They can be written out by any forger or quack. I want the doctor to appear before me immediately!"

"With respect Your Honour, it would not be difficult for me to have him here by two o'clock this afternoon."

When court resumed, the doctor wasn't sitting at the defendant's table, but sitting dressed in black with red swollen eyes, was Kate Leigh. She was the epitome of a deeply grieving daughter. Kate was unable to concentrate on or follow the court proceedings. She trembled, constantly wiped her eyes with a handkerchief, and cried aloud throughout the hearing.

Mr. Perry S.M. realising that no-one could put on such an act, granted a two-week adjournment on compassionate grounds.

When her trial began two weeks later, Leigh's solicitor, Mr Moseley, entered a not guilty plea, stating that the police had framed his client and denied that she had ever been involved in the drug trade in all her life

Detective Sergeant Wickham stood in court and accused Kate of being the most dangerous criminal he had ever come across. "I have known this woman for almost twenty years. She is a principal in the cocaine traffic in this city. Not only does she peddle it herself, but she is one of the biggest suppliers to other peddlers. She is the uncrowned Queen of the Underworld and there is no doubt that she wields a powerful influence in the Sydney underworld. She boasts about her privilege of obtaining preferential treatment over other prisoners in the gaols and of her influence with high political and legal people. I regard her as a menace to the community. She is a low moral type, a most dangerous type, who is capable of committing any crime in the criminal calendar."

After evidence from Lillian Armfield, several police officers, and witnesses, the magistrate berated Kate for breaking the *Dangerous Drugs Amendment Act* and told her she was the worst of her kind in Australia. He sentenced her to twelve months in gaol for possessing cocaine and tacked on another twelve months for consorting with known criminals, namely Walter Tomlinson and Frederick Dangar. But due to a shortage of gaol cells, Leigh was offered a fine of two hundred and fifty pounds in lieu of the twelve months, which she paid.

7

Age, as it does, began catching up with Kate. Through several marriages and even more relationships, she clocked up one-hundred and seven convictions and had served thirteen gaol sentences. She lived through the Great Depression, two world wars, and charges that ranged from vagrancy, prostitution, indecent language, and assault, to attempted murder, murder, cocaine dealing, and shoplifting. Changes of strength in the criminal underworld finally unseated Kate from her high and mightiness as the Queen of Surry Hills when new age criminals cockwalked the footpaths. The taxation office also knocked the wind out of her sails when it demanded payment of her back taxes.

On the 1ˢᵗ of October 1954, Kate attended a bankruptcy hearing. Her statement of affairs showed assets totalling almost two-thousand pounds, which included furniture and three properties in Surry Hills. Unfortunately, her liabilities were shown as around seven-thousand two-hundred pounds.

The gap-toothed stockily built brunette Queen of Surry Hills who trotted around the city draped in diamonds, pearls, enormous hats, and furs, became a pauper after losing her money, houses, and possessions.

On the 31ˢᵗ of January 1964 at the age of eighty-two, Kate was rushed to St. Vincent's Hospital after suffering a stroke. The following day she slipped into a coma and died on the 4ᵗʰ of February.

Her funeral was held on the 7th of February at St Peters Church on Devonshire Street, Surry Hills. It was well-attended by family, criminals, neighbours, and police.

A surprise mourner sat on the back pew dressed in black and wearing a wide-brimmed veiled hat. When she raised her head from prayer, Tilly Devine stood up and left the church. She didn't want to sit and listen to the hypocritical testimonials and eulogies of the woman many despised. She laughed toward the heavens as she walked down the church stairs, "Kate, I 'ope you're not listening to the fuckin' bullshit they're going on about in there."

Author's Note:

Unfortunately, Kate's plot at Eastern Suburbs Memorial Cemetery has no marker. It's just a grassy area without a headstone. No matter her behaviour, she deserves more respect than to be disregarded by society. I hope to be able to remedy the situation in the future.

CHAPTER FOURTEEN

Lillian Armfield

A female police officer with a penchant for wearing a pearl necklace and carrying a handbag, Lillian May Armfield was Australia's first female detective. Dressed in a frock or a tailored suit because the department didn't provide a uniform, and carting her signature black handbag, she fearlessly took on the most violent criminals of Sydney's Eastern suburbs.

Lillian was born in Mittagong, New South Wales, on the 3rd of December 1884 to George Armfield, a labourer and his wife, Elizabeth. Educated at the local school, she fared well with mathematics, was proficient at reading and spelling, and her penmanship was clear and distinct.

Upon leaving school, Lillian trained to be a nurse. After graduating, she worked as a nurse at Callan Park mental asylum. There she cared for the female inmates and treated them with respect and compassion. The superintendent of the hospital often praised Lillian for her competence and kindness to patients.

After witnessing a robbery whilst purchasing groceries at a Rozelle corner store in 1913, she was shocked at how long it took for police to arrive. From that day on, Lillian decided to become a policewoman.

In 1915 the police service expanded under the command of Inspector General James Mitchell. World War I had markedly changed everyone's life in Sydney. Crime, drugs, prostitution, and welfare problems had increased and with it came the need for a mightier police force incorporating both men and women.

Almost five hundred women answered the advertisement placed by the New South Wales Police Department for the two available positions. The successful applicants were Maude Marian Rhodes, who was previously employed as an inspector for the State Children Relief Department, and thirty-one-year-old Lillian May Armfield.

On the 1st July 1915, they were sworn in as Probationary Special Constables whose primary duties were to direct traffic and control the behaviour of juvenile girls. They were also required to carry out interrogations on women and children, strip search women or question women who felt uncomfortable in the presence of a male officer. Dressed in casual clothing, the policewomen also patrolled Sydney's streets, railway stations, parks, and wharves.

During an interview with a local newspaper reporter, Inspector-General James Mitchell, who received a lot of backlash from within the police force and the community at large about hiring the women, made his intentions clear to why he had appointed special constables Lillian Armfield and Maude Rhodes: "Female officers will be the frontline of preventative measures to reduce the numbers of young women decoyed into prostitution, charged with public drunkenness, or assaulted late at night in parks. Their main beat will be the poor neighbourhoods of Eastern Sydney around Woolloomooloo, Darlinghurst, Surry Hills, and Paddington."

The appointment of both Rhodes and Armfield was heartily welcomed by women's organisations around Australia. They also had the authority to make arrests. They found that women and children in those areas were treated more compassionately by policewomen and were better served on both sides of the law.

Lillian refused to use handcuffs on women and children, unless it was necessary. This practice was frowned upon by her superiors, but she wanted to work with the same level of compassion as she had while nursing. She had made a promise to herself to do all she possibly could to avoid sending women to gaol. To her, using compassion, kindness, and positive instruction was an alternative to rough treatment and imprisonment on petty and frivolous crimes and misdemeanours.

Lillian also refused to take women through to the cells when arrested, preferring to take them to headquarters. When she brought in first offenders, she often sent for their relatives or friends to be with them and spoke to them in a private room to alleviate the necessity of arresting them and going through the courts.

She found the light work offered to policewomen was not her cup of tea. Intelligent, direct, and using language that would make a shearer blush, her goal was to help women and stop them from joining brothels or selling themselves on the streets.

She and her fellow female police officer were forced to work unarmed in one of the most violent areas of New South Wales. The policewomen were paid seven shillings sixpence a day and were not permitted to collect an allowance for any expenses incurred in the line of duty or be paid overtime. They were also on call day or night. Lillian travelled from Sydney to other stations around the city and rural areas whenever a policewoman was required. Even though men treated them like they were the weaker sex, they worked eight hours a day, with one day off each week and twenty-eight days holiday throughout the year, the same as their male counterparts.

However, unlike her male colleagues, Lillian wasn't granted permission to carry a baton, or even a gun. The department had only furnished her with a warrant card. Upon joining the police department, she was required to sign an indemnity agreeing that the department was not responsible for her safety and welfare whilst in their employ, she would never marry, she would relinquish her rights to superannuation, and that she alone was responsible for the cost of her clothing.

Following her twelve months' probation, Lillian finally became a fully-fledged special constable. The slum streets of East Sydney became her beat. Often, on her days off, she would visit her favourite families, taking them pots of soup or stew, and sometimes a rabbit or two to keep them from starving. The children delighted in her visits, especially when she played skip rope with the girls or billy-cart racing with the boys. More than once she had returned home with laddered stockings and skinned knees.

Some women wouldn't allow Lillian into their homes as she had been banned by their husbands. It worsened when rumours began circulating that she was a lesbian. The homes where there were daughters often didn't allow her admittance, some men even threw rotten fruit at her and called her out for being a single woman in the police department.

Lillian's rough manner, swearing, stocky build and penchant for tackling and using her fists when the need arose, didn't help dissuade the rumours. The city police stations were often full of gossip about her sexuality. Fellow police officers also placed bets to see which of the male police officers could get Lillian into bed first. None were successful.

Armfield kept her private life to herself. Her sexuality and proclivities were the business of no-one but her. She did have a lover, whom she met clandestinely a few hours out of town, but she wasn't sharing that information, it was private between her and the other person.

In 1916, a case she was involved in brought her to the attention of the high-ranking officers in the police department. Parents from Orange in the central west of country NSW, had contacted Central Police Station reporting their daughter as a runaway and said that they believed she was on her way to Sydney. Knowing instant action was required with the teenager being over one hundred and fifty miles from home, the station sent the girl's description and photograph to all city stations, as well as pinning a missing poster in Central Police Station.

After a call was placed through to Detective Sergeant Tom Mankey, he immediately called Lillian into his office where she was handed a photograph of the teenage girl. Lillian studied the photo and was concerned that the young girls' attractive looks and blonde hair, would put her at risk of being preyed upon by prostitutes and pimps. She was also aware that a naïve country lass would be an easy target for the lowlifes of the city.

"Don't concentrate on her clothes. She's more than likely changed out of them by now. Patrol and scour every inner-city street. Ask the homeless, ask the street girls. Check the bus and train stations. Leave no stone unturned!" Mankey ordered.

"I'll walk the streets day and night if I must until she's found." Lillian replied before placing the girl's photograph on the detective's desk and leaving.

She stopped by her desk and removed an apple and an orange from her drawer and dropped them into her handbag. She then made her way through the crowded street and briskly walked toward Circular Quay. She eyed every tram, motor car, and horse-drawn carriage that hurtled along the street, checking to see if the young girl was a passenger.

Lillian assumed the runaway would stay away from the main streets as possible. The neighbourhood streets where the impecunious and indigent lived in their overcrowded terrace houses filled with mould, vermin, and cockroaches, were her everyday beat. They were the Eastern Sydney streets she called the devil's playground. She knew every nook, cranny and hideout between Darlinghurst and Surry Hills. She knew of the hovels where runaways hid in Woolloomooloo, Redfern, and Darlinghurst. She knew where the brothels and the drug houses were. She especially knew where the scourge of society frequented that liked to prey on young girls. These were the streets that the locals warily ventured into. No outsiders would brave the back streets and narrow alleys of the roughest suburbs in East Sydney.

Lillian considered this her territory. She didn't care that smoke from the surrounding factories polluted the sky. Nor did the smell of yeast and hops from the local breweries and urine and faecal odours from lanes and alleyways keep her away. These were her streets and these people needed her.

Three days a week Lillian would drop by the bakery, the butchers, and the local vegetable and fruiterer, collecting baskets of damaged food to leave at the doorsteps of the poorest of families. This was how she earned the trust and respect of the tenants and the homeless. They knew she cared for their wellbeing and they often gave her information about crimes or drug peddlers. She hoped they would have information about the runaway girl.

She headed towards Riley Street in Surry Hills. Frog Hollow housed the most slimy and despicable criminals of the worst kind. She wasn't advised whether the runaway had money or not and she wasn't going to leave anything to chance.

As she walked toward one of the slum houses, she was sure she had seen a girl that resembled the photo of the runaway, a few yards down the street. She took off after the teenager and wondered why on earth runaways always turned up in the most dangerous areas of the city. When she had caught up with the young girl, in one deft movement, Lillian had her arms around the wayward teenager. The girl fought tooth and nail to escape the constable's grip, but she was no match for the policewoman, who had learned how to quickly restrain women whilst working in Callen Park.

"Do you know how worried your parents are about you? Be still and behave!" Lillian chided. "You're lucky to be still alive as it is!"

The teenager could care less. She had one aim and that was to escape and run as far away as she could. However, at 5 ft 7¾ inches tall and weighing 12 stone 10 lbs, Lillian was much taller and stronger, and the runaway soon gave up the struggle.

Lillian dragged the recalcitrant runaway alongside her as she fought her way through the gathering crowd to return to Central Police Station.

She was in an ominous situation where both she and the girl could be hurt or killed. Lillian was forced to stop when more than one hundred people thronged around them. Knowing that being a police officer offered her no safety among the mob of menacing faces, she held the girl close. Threats and spittle were cast toward her, but she wasn't going to let the runaway free.

A sudden pain hit the side of Lillian's face when someone from the crowd threw a broken bottle. Warm blood trickled down her cheek and neck, but she maintained her firm grip on the girl. With her heart racing and blood dripping onto her fitted beige suit, Lillian scanned the crowd for a friendly face. The teenager was terrified and screamed out for the constable to let her go.

Several men joined the fray, fighting against the surge of violent women pushing forward to attack the police officer. They could care less about protecting Lillian and the teenage girl. Their concern was that their wives and neighbours would be thrown into gaol and their kids sent into institutional care.

Lillian tried not to panic when she recognised several of the men as members of violent gangs. She wavered in her thoughts whether to hold the teenager's hand and make a run for it or remain steadfast and look the bastards unfalteringly in the eye. She chose the latter.

"Fuck off outta here the lot of you. I'll remember your faces and will be watching every fuckin' move you make from now on!"

As the women in front of Lillian spat at her while trying to pull the girl from her arms, a whistle sounded in the distance, followed by a choir of the shrill sounds. More than thirty police officers shunted their way through the unruly crowd, roughly pushing people out of the way. When the officers reached Lillian and the young girl, the crowd had already started to disperse.

The runaway was taken to a children's shelter to await the arrival of her concerned parents. Lillian was both pleased and relieved they had both survived. However, the brouhaha had angered her. She had been unable to effectively protect herself using only her wits as a defence.

For the first time since becoming a police officer, Lillian was furious about the no-weapon rule for policewomen.

From that day forth, Lillian's excellent work in expeditiously solving the runaway girl case earned her involvement into investigations involving murder, rape, theft, and drug-running, to white slave trafficking and prostitution.

A problem that caused Lillian angst and distress occurred in November 1919. She had become the superior to Special Constable Maude Rhodes. In her position of authority, she ordered Maude to patrol Central Railway Station. She refused. Lillian lodged a complaint and Rhodes was sacked for refusing to obey a legitimate order from a superior officer. She received fourteen days' pay and was discharged from the police force.

Lillian's next prominent case was her involvement in the arrest of Eugene Falleni. This was an interesting case for the detective as Falleni was transgender. Eugene was born a female in Livorno, Italy. She changed her name from Eugenia to Eugene whilst living in New Zealand and from then on was known as Harry Crawford.

On the 5th of July 1920, Harry was arrested on suspicion of murder after a body was found in bushland off Mowbray Road at Chatswood. It had been identified as Annie Crawford. Her charred remains were found three years previously, behind the Cumberland Paper Board Mill along the Lane Cove River.

It took the police three years to identify Annie's remains by dental records and her son's confirmation that the jewellery and clothing found on the body belonged to his mother. Harry Crawford also resembled a distressed male witnesses had seen near where Annie's body was found.

After being arrested by Detective Sergeant Robson, Constable Walsh, and Detective Constable Watkins, Harry packed clothes and toiletries into a suitcase before they drove him to police headquarters. Robson took him down to the cells and when Harry saw the rough types on remand and the lack of privacy, he asked the detective if they would put him in the women's cells. When Robson told him that only women are allowed in the women's cells, Harry admitted what he had spent his life avoiding: he was a woman.

This news stopped Robson in his tracks. He took Harry by the arm and escorted him into a private room before asking Detective Constable Lillian Armfield to accompany him to question a murder suspect.

"You say you are a woman?" Robson asked as soon as he and Armfield entered the room.

"Yes,"

"What's your name?" Robson shot towards Harry, not believing his claim.

"Eugenia Falleni. I changed my name in New Zealand."

"I'm leaving the room. Armfield, strip search him and let me know if he's a man or a woman."

"Remove your pants please, sir."

Harry slowly stood up and slid down his trousers, turning his face away in embarrassment. Stunned at seeing that he was indeed a woman, the Detective Constable waited until Eugenia was respectable again before opening the door and calling her superior into the room.

"She's a woman. I'll remain here during the interrogation."

During questioning, a young constable knocked on the door telling the detective that a woman named Elizabeth Crawford wanted to see her husband. Eugenie told the constable that she didn't want to see her. However, Elizabeth refused to listen to him and began crying hysterically not believing her husband could have murdered anyone.

"Go out and speak with her, Detective Armfield. Tell her the truth about her… husband." Robson directed before turning back to Falleni. "How the hell did you fool two women into believing you were a man?" the detective asked.

"Look in my suitcase. You will find it. There's something in there that I have been using," Eugenia said as she looked down at her hands.

"What is it, something artificial?"

"Yes, but don't let her see it."

"Do you mean to say that she doesn't know *anything* about this?" Robson incredulously asked as he held the wooden dildo in the air.

"No. My first wife knew nothing about it either. Not until the latter part of our marriage, at least."

When Lillian told the distraught wife the truth about Harry Crawford, she just stared blankly at her in disbelief for a few seconds. "Harry's not a woman. I think I'm pregnant."

"I can assure you, madam, the man in there is a woman. I have seen the nether regions personally. I'm sorry, but if you are indeed pregnant, you aren't pregnant by her."

Elizabeth still refused to believe that she had married a woman. She thought she was pregnant because her period was late. She didn't consider that at her age she was going through menopause.

Robson came out into the main area of the station to see what was taking Armfield so long. He was then forced to reaffirm to Mrs. Crawford what Armfield had told her. She still refused to believe him, pleading with the detective to let her see her husband.

"Armfield, show her what's in his suitcase."

Upon seeing the wooden phallus, Elizabeth almost fainted. The young detective rushed to her side and helped her to a chair.

"I'm sorry, Mrs. Crawford, but Harry is a woman. Her name is Eugenia Falleni and she's from Italy, not Scotland," Lillian explained.

Falleni's trial started on the 20th of October 1920 and only lasted two days. The prosecutor knew he would win the case, not only in proving that Eugenia was the last person to see Annie alive but to portray her as a homosexual and a deviant. He had a number of witnesses who testified to the Crawford's tumultuous relationship and how distressed Falleni was in the weeks following Annie's disappearance.

Eugenia, who was dressed in men's clothing, continued to deny the charges, stating; "I do not know anything at all about this charge. I am perfectly innocent. I do not know what made Annie leave our home."

But under oath a witness testified that she spoke with Harry after Annie disappeared and was told: "I had a jolly good row with her and gave her a crack on the head and cleared off."

Two hours later, the jury returned a guilty verdict and sentenced Falleni to death.

During a State Cabinet meeting in October 1920, the death sentence was commuted to life imprisonment. Prison reform workers worked tirelessly and constantly petitioned the court for Falleni's release from gaol. In February 1931, the Minister for Justice spent an hour with Eugenia before granting her release due to her being almost sixty years old and not of robust health. Eugenia was also ordered not to live as a man.

Falleni changed her name to Jean Ford and lived as a woman until her death in 1938.

7

Detective Constable Armfield was involved with many high profile and dangerous criminals over the years. Cocaine dealer, Botany May Smith, chased her down the street with a red-hot flat iron when Armfield turned up at her residence to arrest her for cocaine running.

For over thirty years Armfield investigated drug traffickers, sex offenders, pimps, madams, and prostitutes, and the most dangerous of all that were involved in the razor gangs—Tilly Devine, Kate Leigh, and their gangsters. It was a miracle she survived. She was the first female police officer that arrested a suspect with a pistol in the 1920s and the first woman police detective allowed to wear a service revolver.

In 1947 Lillian Armfield was awarded the King's Police and Fire Service Medal. She was the first woman in the Commonwealth to receive such a high honour. At the age of sixty-five, Lillian retired from the police force after almost thirty-five years of service and was awarded the Imperial Service Medal.

Upon retirement, she was presented with an illuminated address and two-hundred pounds by the Lord Mayor of Sydney. The hierarchy in the Police Department allowed her a payment of four hundred and fifty-five pounds, six shillings and five pence in lieu of an extended leave of absence. Even after so many years of commendable service, Lillian still didn't receive a superannuation or pension payment because of the agreement signed when she joined the police service.

Lillian May Armfield lived her final years in the Methodist Hostel, Leichhardt and died on the 26th of August 1971 at Lewisham Hospital.

CHAPTER FIFTEEN

Razor Gang Wars

Late January 1929 whilst doing her daily food shop, Tilly stopped by her local butcher and was served by a new lad. She ordered a brisket of beef and the boy went out the back and retrieved a good-sized cut of the meat, then wrapped it in paper and handed it to Tilly. She paid him the three shillings for the beef, and after giving the boy a sixpenny tip, she made her way home to cook the roast for dinner.

When she began unwrapping the brisket, Tilly noticed a peculiar odour and was shocked to discover the meat was rancid. Angered by being sold odious meat, she returned to the butchery, flung open the door and roared that she had been sold stinking rotten meat and she wanted her fuckin' money back!

The owner, William Ashcroft, attempted to calm her down, explaining that the boy had taken the brisket from the wrong pile. Tilly wasn't so easily placated. She shoved the meat under the noses of the other women in the store and asked them if they would cook meat that smelt so fuckin' vile. Some of the women fled the butchery in fright, while others remained and sympathised with her outrage.

Tilly threw the beef at Ashcroft and grabbed hold of a long-bladed butcher's knife from the counter. Then, thrusting it within a hair's breadth of his chest: "You fuckin' give me back my three shillings, or there'll be more than pig's blood on the fuckin' floor!"

One of the women left the store and hightailed it to the local police station where her constable husband was on duty. She explained what was occurring, both he and another constable hastily made their way to the butchery. When they arrived, Tilly was still irate but was no longer holding the knife and was standing calmly against the wall. Constable Peters asked her to accompany him back to the police station. She was charged with demanding three shillings by menace from William Ashcroft.

On Wednesday the 4th of February, when the magistrate questioned her about her actions, Tilly responded with her usual shades of grey, and blamed everyone but herself for the violent confrontation. Frustrated by her malignancy to the law, he committed Tilly for trial and released her on twenty pounds bail.

7

On the 27th of January, two of Tilly's girls, Phoebe and Maureen gingered Robert Powell, a regular at Tilly's many brothels. He had noticed after a previous visit that his wallet was considerably lighter. Suspicious that the girls were fleecing him, he paid another visit to the Palmer Street brothel two days later. This time he was prepared.

Powell had torn a corner of each note of the fifteen pounds he had tucked inside his wallet. He booked an appointment for his usual double act with Maureen and Phoebe, for their normal three-hour session. As sure as death and taxes, the money was missing when he checked his wallet before leaving the room.

Powell wasn't a married man and had nothing to fear about reporting the theft to the police. He lodged a complaint at the Clarence Street Police Station in Woolloomooloo for the theft. Constable Nolan wrote down the complaint and told Powell that they would investigate the matter.

Tilly was livid when the police turned up at her Palmer Street door and accused her of stealing money from Powell. She angrily denied the allegation: "Now bugger orf and find someone else to annoy. I make a lot orf fuckin' money and don't need to steal a few pounds from some punter!"

Constable Nolan didn't give up so easily. "We need to question two of your girls Mrs. Devine…Phoebe and Maureen."

Tilly sent one of her girls off to fetch them. When the women arrived, they could tell by the look in Tilly's eyes that she wasn't impressed. "If you bitches 'ave stolen 'is money, you'll never cross my threshold again!"

Tilly didn't give two shits about the girls gingering the clients, however, wealthy clients like Robert Powell who hired her girls almost every night of the week, she treated like gold.

The women knew that as soon as they spoke with the police, their working days with Tilly were over. They were angry with themselves, as none of the other brothel madams around East Sydney were as good to their girls as Tilly was. Phoebe immediately admitted to stealing the money and sharing the loot with Maureen. They were arrested and appeared in court for the theft and released on thirty pounds bail.

The following month, the magistrate was lenient on the prostitutes for their early guilty pleas and sentenced them to three months in Long Bay Women's Gaol.

7

Being the brothel Queen of Woolloomooloo and Darlinghurst, Tilly aspired to become the top dog of the Eastern Suburbs. To accomplish this, she knew she would need to be more aggressive and tougher than the men. She'd had enough of being dominated by men in her life. Jim's violence toward her and the bashings she'd received by pimps and other prostitutes during her life had taught her that people fear might over respect. Tilly had the guts, the fists, and a straight razor to prove that she would take no shit from anyone who stood in her way.

Her first target was Kate leigh. Tilly seethed whenever she heard that her long-standing rival had opened another brothel or sly grog shop.

By May 1939, their dissension had become so heated that both women hired thugs to protect themselves and to harass or assault anyone they perceived as enemies. For several months it was a tit for tat game of Tilly's gang mutilating Kates girls with razors, and in retaliation, Kate's thugs would shoot at Tilly's girls from nearby rooftops when arriving at one of her brothels.

However, unbeknownst to the women, storm clouds were gathering on the horizon, and the faint rumble of a coming thunderous rage was already growling in the distance.

Aware of the profit her husband was making selling cocaine, Tilly wanted in on the action and began selling the drug from her Palmer Street brothel. Initially, her clients were her girls. She offered them the cocaine at no cost and continued supplying it without charge until they were addicted. Once the girls became dependent, she used them to peddle cocaine to their clients, offering them ten per cent discount on their snow as an incentive. Her new business venture saw Tilly's profit margin soar.

However, within months of using Jim's cocaine, her girls began to resemble skeletons and suffered with skin infections. She immediately stopped supplying them with the drug and told them to pour whatever they had left into the outside toilet. Feeling responsible for her workers' ill health, she told them to take time off until they were healthy again, helping them with food and rent money until they had recovered.

"That snow shit that you've been orf loadin' to me girls is making them sick. Where the fuck are you gettin' it from?" Tilly angrily quizzed Jim.

"Fuck woman, I just got out of bed and you fuckin' start. It's the Jew's coke. Go fuckin' ask him."

"The bastard's probably cuttin' it with that boracic acid shit again. My girls look like death warmed up!"

Needing more girls and money to cover the financial loss of seven girls off work due to their cocaine ailments, Tilly hired eight more women to work from her brothels.

7

It seems Karma took a hand in Tilly's favour. Jim Taylor, leader of the small time Woolloomooloo Gang and drug dealer, caught up with Phil Jeffs on the 7th of May and challenged him to a face off at Eaton Avenue in Darlinghurst. Jeffs took up the gauntlet and the fight was set for ten o'clock that night.

'Blood Alley' where the fight was scheduled to take place, was thus named due to the countless razor fights and muggings that had left the area stained with blood almost every day of the week.

Just after ten o'clock, Jeffs, his friend William Archer, the proprietor of the Hot Bath House, and the rest of his men entered the seedy dimly lit lane and came face to face with their rivals. Jeffs, and Charles Sorlie, the leader of the opposing gang, looked each other up and down.

The Jew clenched his fists as he waited for the fight to start. "Are we going to stand here all fuckin' night or are my men going to teach yours a lesson in manners?"

Seconds later, a brick thrown by one of Jeffs' men hit an opposing gang member in the face and the brawl began. Shrouded by fog and smoke, for more than thirty bloodthirsty minutes, men armed with bricks, bottles, clubs, razors, and pistols fought each other with everything they were worth. Finally, the police arrived with more than enough manpower to shut the bloody fight down. Those who weren't seriously wounded were arrested, while those suffering bullet wounds, razor slashes and other injuries were taken to hospital in one of the many ambulances that arrived at the scene.

At Darlinghurst Police Station, the detectives investigating the melee were met with a wall of silence. Not one of the men broke the criminal code of silence.

Jeffs and several other gang members managed to escape over a fence when the police arrived. But later that night when he turned up at the police station to bail his mate Archer out, a constable told him that he was in hospital and immediately placed Jeffs under arrest. He was charged with inflicting grievous bodily harm upon Charles Henry Sorlie and Frederick Edward Johns.

"I don't know these men. How the hell can you charge me for their assault?" Jeffs angrily disputed. The police ignored his statement and locked him in a cell. Two constables then left for the hospital where they also charged Archer with assaulting Johns and Sorlie.

At two o'clock in the morning on the 8th of May, Jeffs was released from the cells on one hundred pounds bail. He returned to his Rainbow Street mansion in Kensington. Later that morning, he was awoken by the sound of his front door being kicked in. Fearing an attack by Sorlie's gang members, he leapt from his bed to look out his bedroom window and saw a maroon Ford Model A Tourer parked across his driveway. When he turned around to fetch his pistol, Jim Taylor barged into his bedroom demanding money for the bad drugs he had bought the week before. Jeffs grabbed hold of his bedside lamp and smashed it over his assailant's head and then lunged toward his bed, retrieving the revolver that he kept under his pillow. When he turned around to fire, Taylor was faster on the draw and shot Jeffs in the shoulder, knocking him backward, a second shot hit him in the chest.

Taylor fled the house and jumped into the waiting car. He and his accomplices sped off down the street, almost sideswiping a mother pushing a baby in a pram. Critically wounded, Jeffs managed to crawl down to the street in search of help. He managed to make it several hundred yards before collapsing from loss of blood. He lay on the footpath groaning in pain as he weakly called out for help. A milkman doing his morning rounds chanced upon him. "Milko, I've been shot," he rasped. "Please take me to the hospital."

At St. Vincent's hospital, where Jeffs was under police guard, Detective Keogh and Constable McLachlan arrived to take his dying deposition. When asked for his employment details, he told the police that he was a pastry cook.

"Are you the leader of an international crime syndicate? Detective Keogh asked.

"You've got to be kidding, right? Jeffs laughed, flatly denying the accusation.

Keogh continuing his line of inquiry, asked him who had shot him. Jeffs denied knowing who had shot him and refused to answer any questions about the Eaton Avenue fracas when asked, other than saying "There will be no dying deposition from me, sir. I'm not going to die." He then inquired about the health of his mate, William Archer. Keogh told him that he was in a critical condition after his gunshot wound had become septic.

Constable McLachlan, knowing William Archer was a close friend of Jeffs' told he that he had undergone further surgery to remove more bullet fragments from his body, his prognosis was poor.

Pissed off over the prospective loss of a close friend and ally, Jeff rasped one word to the police, *Sorlie*.

"Sorlie is the one that shot you?" Constable McLachlan asked.

"No, the fuckin' bastard shot Bill." Jeffs rasped.

"Who shot you, Phil? C'mon man, make it easy on us. You've already given us one name, what does another matter?" Keogh encouraged.

"Taylor, that cunt Taylor and that fat bastard Clark!"

"I need you to confirm their names. Sydney is full of men with the surnames Clark and Taylor."

"Jim Taylor and Bill Clark. Them bastards," Jeffs spat.

That afternoon, thirty-eight-year-old Charles Sorlie was arrested and charged with maliciously shooting with intent to do grievous bodily harm to William Archer. When he appeared in court, Mr. McMahon, S.M. remanded Sorlie until the 22nd of May, on ten pounds bail.

The police had almost pieced together the cause of the 'Blood Alley' melee and Jeffs' shooting. They were unsure of the validity of the claims made by Sorlie and Johns that they were innocent bystanders, but they were backed up by witness testimony, which the police suspected was paid for. Without opposing evidence there wasn't much they could do.

They were still on the hunt for Taylor and Clark, both of whom seemed to have disappeared into thin air. Jeffs later negated his statement about Taylor being the shooter and refused to testify in court. Nonetheless, the police obtained information from other sources confirming that Taylor was indeed the shooter. They also learned from police informants that Jeffs was selling overcut cocaine and the Woolloomooloo gang wanted their money back after buying crook cocaine.

They had gleaned from several sources that Taylor was unable to settle the matter with Jeffs about the money at the gang fight. He then sent Clark along to the Kensington house to demand its return. They were told that Taylor had broken into the house after he was unable to rouse Jeffs from his sleep and when he entered the bedroom, an argument ensued when Jeffs refused to give them the money and he was shot.

Dressed like a peacock in a purple suit, green shirt, long blue coat and yellow socks, Phil Jeffs cut a colourful figure when he took the stand at Taylor's trial. But he was suddenly overcome by amnesia when questioned by the prosecutor about the man who shot him.

Under oath, he swore that he had never told the police that Taylor was his assailant. He also denied that Taylor or Clark were at his home on the morning of the shooting and accused the police of lying.

The prosecutor then asked if he recognised the shooter. "I've never laid eyes on him before in my life, sir."

Due to the lack of evidence from their star witness, the judge had no alternative than to dismiss the charges and release Taylor.

Jeffs escaped to his hideaway beach house in Woy Woy, where over the following months, the locals were treated to constant visits from sly, rugged, scar faced criminal types.

7

On the 14th of July, caterers were busily preparing and cooking food in the Devine's Malabar kitchen. Tilly was fussing after the cleaners she'd hired to clean the house before her guests began arriving to her soirée that evening. Tilly made sure they had cleaned every surface, polished every stick of furniture, and swept up every particle of dirt from the floor.

Tilly loved entertaining. It gave her a chance to show off her fancy home and finery, as well as spoil her friends with good food and plenty of alcohol.

The dining table was set with fine china, silverware, and Edwardian champagne glasses. Buffet tables lined the living room wall laden with silver trays stacked with hors d'oeuvres, sliced meats, roasted chickens, and a variety of hot vegetables. Not one to shy from displaying the extremes of wealth and decadence, Tilly also had three crates of imported French champagne, gin, whiskey, and vermouth in the car garage for a night of endless drinking.

Late that afternoon, flashy motor cars rolled down Malabar and Torrington roads, parking wherever they could find a place close to the house. No-one ever knew what would happen when visiting the Devine's and having your motor car parked close by was always advisable in case the need arose for a quick getaway.

As the guests arrived, two valets dressed in tuxedos took the men's coats and the women's furs and handbags, while a woman dressed in a maid outfit handed each female guest a glass of champagne, and a second offered the men a glass of whiskey.

Elegantly dressed in a shimmering black and gold dress and dripping with diamonds and pearls, Tilly glided hospitably between her guests as music played softly from her Rexonola Gramophone.

Every time she waved her hands in conversation, Tilly's rings sparkled, but none more so than the platinum diamond and sapphire diamond ring Jim had bought her the day before as an early anniversary present.

As he watched her from the corner of the room, Jim found his eyes inexorably gliding over the curves of his wife's body. He had to admit that she looked fantastic with her new hairstyle and figure-hugging dress. A smile curled at his lips as he remembered the hours spent making love the previous afternoon after he had given her the ring. As if she could sense his thoughts, Tilly flashed him a devilish smile before returning to her conversation with one of the local councillors.

Even though Jim could be cruel, violent, hot-headed and was seldom demonstrative of his warm-hearted side, at times he preferred to keep Tilly on side and found giving her gifts and a little bit of loving every now and then kept her happy.

Unfortunately, his wife wasn't the woman who was generally in receipt of such sentiment, it was usually one of his many lovers, one predominately more than the others—Dulcie Markham. He and Dulcie were able to keep their affair quiet. Not even Calletti, who Dulcie was also seeing at the time, was aware of their relationship.

Surprisingly, the night went off almost without a hitch. The only drama that caused a ripple during the dinner party was when a guest's husband was caught having sex with another man's wife.

Craig, a friend of Jim's, went in search of his wife and opened the door to the guest room. He found her on the bed with her legs hooked over some man's shoulders as he was furiously fucking her. In a rage, Craig pulled the man off his adulteress wife and dragged her from the bed by her hair into the living room naked, embarrassing her in front of all the guests.

The wife of the errant husband calmly walked up to him and threw a glass of champagne in his face. Not finished with her woman-scorned style revenge, she reached into his left trouser pocket, retrieved the car keys, and kneed him in the balls. A round of applause emanated from the guests as she smiled and nodded before walking out of the house.

Adding insult to humiliation and injury, Craig grabbed hold of the unfaithful husband by the shirt as he was hurriedly dressing and began pounding his face with his right fist until blood poured from a pulpy mass of flesh that once was his nose.

The disgraced wife raced back to the bedroom and gathered her clothes before dressing in the bathroom. When she returned to the living room, she pleaded with her husband to drive her home. He turned his back on her and continued throwing back glass after glass of Jim's best whiskey, ignoring her.

"And I thought we'd make it through one night without a fuckin' shooting or fight!" Tilly laughed. "Cheers everyone." She smiled as she raised her champagne glass into the air.

The following morning while the cleaners were tidying up after the dinner party, a loud banging sounded at the front door. One of the maids answered the knock and was pushed out of the way by armed police. A further six policemen carrying pistols barged through the back door.

"What the fuckin' hell is going on here?" Jim roared as he thundered into the living room. Tilly followed close behind, still tying up her cream silk dressing gown.

"We're here to search your premises, Jimmy. We received information that you have firearms and ammunition in your house."

"There's nothing here. Fuck! When will you cops learn that Leigh bitch likes to cause trouble and waste your fuckin' time!" Jim spat.

"That fuckin' fat sow! 'ow dare she do this to decent living people minding their own fuckin' business." Tilly chimed in.

"No matter if it is a crank call or not, we have orders to conduct a search."

Jim paced the hall nervously as the police upended furniture, pulled down drapes, emptied out drawers and searched every nook and cranny in every room of the house.

"I 'ope you bastards clean this mess up or I'll be sending the cleaning bill to the fuckin' Darlinghurst Police Station." Tilly warned.

A detective remained in the dining room with Tilly and the cleaners making sure they didn't touch anything or leave the house. Jim sat on the settee in the living room, trying not to sweat.

"Would you like a cup of tea, Detective?" Tilly offered. "I promise not to poison ya. The only arsenic we 'ave 'ere lovey is on the fly paper!"

"Yes, a cup of tea, thank you, Tilly. Two sugars and a little cream please." The detective replied with a laugh.

When Jim saw one of the constables open the gramophone lid, he stood up and walked across to the record player and started a conversation with him in an attempt to distract him. But his actions only made Detective Sergeant Matthews suspicious.

"Leave that constable. You search the settee Mr. Devine has been keeping warm for the past twenty minutes."

Jim knew the jig was up and remained in the centre of the living room waiting to be arrested.

"Well, what do we have here, Jimmy?" The detective held up a box of bullets. "I must say I'm a little disappointed."

"Here, Detective Sergeant, it's a pistol. I found it pushed under the settee backing," the young constable said.

"You know what happens now, Jimmy. I'd like you to accompany me to Darlinghurst Police Station where you will be charged with having an unlicensed automatic pistol in your possession."

"I've got nothing to say until I face the courts." Jim said with a sigh.

"Yes, Jimmy, we know your drill."

"I'll see you in court in the mornin' Jimmy," Tilly called out. "They'll fuckin' pay for this!"

Once Jim and the police were gone, Tilly looked about her vandalised home and summoned her cleaners. "You girls get stuck into this mess. There's an extra ten quid each if the 'ouse is done when I get back 'ome."

After dressing, she drove to Guido Calletti's flat and banged on his door. Stretching and yawning, Dulcie Markham opened the door.

"Where is 'e? I need 'elp with that fuckin' Leigh slut!" Tilly fumed.

"He's still in bed, Till. It's eight o'clock in the fuckin' morning."

"I don't care if it's fuckin' midnight. Get 'im out 'ere or I'll pull 'im out orf bed meself!"

Dulcie could tell Tilly was fit to kill and knew better than rub her the wrong way in the mood she was in. Ten minutes later, she and Guido were dressed and following Tilly to her car.

"Where are we going Tilly? And what the fuck's goin' on?" Guido asked.

"We're going to rattle that Leigh bitch's chain! Jimmy's in the lock up for possession orf a fuckin' pistol and bullets! That bitch is still runnin' the show from gaol!"

"Stop by Green's fuckin' flat 'cos him and Sid will be up for this too." Guido advised.

"Where do you think I'm fuckin' drivin' to, London?"

After picking up Green and McDonald, Tilly drove straight to 27 Kippax Street where she knew Kate still had a few girls working. Upon their arrival, she and her companions set about throwing bricks, rocks, and bottles at the house. Minutes later, Bruce Higgs, one of Leigh's casual lover and driver, appeared at the door holding a rifle aimed at Dulcie.

"Get the fuck off this property or I'll shoot the fuckin' lot of you!"

"You and who's fuckin' army?" Green scorned as he pulled out his revolver. He saw the fear immediately show in Higgs' eyes. Green's reputation as the 'Little Gunman' was known far and wide, and Higgs knew he didn't stand a chance against him.

"Me for one!" Screeched a woman's voice and Tilly laughed when she saw Leigh's sidekick, Vera Lewis, standing beside Higgs aiming a pistol at her.

"That'll knock ya on your fat arse, ya fuckin' daft trollop! C'mon boys. No gun play today. Leigh will get the message when 'er little fledglin' visits her today." Tilly said as she turned and headed back to the car.

The following morning Tilly waited for Jim at the Central Police Court. He was set to appear before Mr. Laidlaw, S.M.

"Are you Mr. James Edward Devine?" the magistrate asked. "A shearer from Maroubra?"

"Yes, Your Honour." Jim replied.

"Thank you. I'll hear from the prosecutor now and then I'll return to you, Mr. Devine."

"Yes, Your Honour." Jim replied.

Sergeant Thomas, the police prosecutor relayed Detective Sergeant Matthews' sworn statement to the court. Jim listened intently and every now and then whispered to his solicitor. However, when the prosecutor referred to the presumed vendetta between the Devines and Kate Leigh, the magistrate rebuked him and told him to stick to the facts of the charges, not gangland gossip.

When Thomas finished reading the statement, Mr. Laidlaw turned to Jim and asked if he had anything in answer to the allegations. Devine stood and told him that he had.

"Well, tell me your side of the story, Mr. Devine."

"Your Honour, I purchased this pistol and cartridges ten weeks ago in Newtown. You see, I was assaulted and robbed of a diamond pin and ten pounds a few months back. On another occasion, several doors in my house were smashed open. When I was living at Kensington, my home was also broken into. I live in fear of molestation, sir."

"You may sit back down Mr. Devine. Sergeant Thomas, do you have anything to say in answer to Mr. Devine's claims?"

"Yes, Your Honour. The defendant has numerous convictions against him for riotous behaviour and assault. He is known to be part of the drug trade and is also involved in prostitution."

"Please stand, Mr. Devine. Sir, it is a serious offence for a man with such a diverse criminal history to possess an unlicensed firearm. I have no alternative but to sentence you to four months imprisonment, or fine you fifty pounds in default of gaol."

"I'll pay the fine, Your Honour."

As Jim paid the fine at the nearby court office, an altercation was taking place in the yard of the Central Police Court.

Constable Dawson rushed to the disturbance and found two women wrestling one another on the ground. Tilly had come upon Vera Lewis, who just happened to be attending court on a matter of her own. The brothel Madam was biting down hard on Lewis' finger and refused to let go, while her opponent was punching her in the face and chest. Dawson pulled the fighting femmes apart and asked what the fight was about.

"This fuckin' bitch blames me for her husband being fined!"

Tilly remained abnormally quiet and went along with the police without putting up her usual fight. That afternoon, both women were charged with riotous behaviour. The magistrate remanded Tilly for trial until the 22ⁿᵈ of July. Lewis, who pleaded guilty, was fined three pounds in default of twenty-one days' imprisonment.

7

On the evening of the 17ᵗʰ of July, Frank Green rang the Devines' using a Kings Cross shopkeeper's telephone. He told them that he and Sid McDonald had been attacked by Leigh's gang members. He said that Sid had taken off, but he was shot in the shoulder by Leigh's enforcer, Gregory 'Gunman' Gaffney. He told them that a crowd had quickly gathered forcing Leigh's men to hotfoot it back to the hollow.

Tilly and Jim jumped into their car and made their way to the Cross. As they drove down Seaview Street, Jim suddenly stopped the car and Green jumped in the back.

"Leigh's men are out to fuckin' kill us tonight. They fuckin' shot me! I thought I'd be attending my own funeral! The bastards said they were coming back to finish the fuckin' job!" Green growled as they drove off.

"We'll be ready for them! 'ere, put this towel on your shoulder, keep it there until we get 'ome. I'll dig the bullet out then!" Tilly advised.

"The bullet went straight through, Tills" Green replied.

"Easier for me to fuckin' fix."

"I reckon they'll turn up at Maroubra to finish what they started," McDonald warned.

"I'll make a stop on the way to make sure we're ready for them." Devine declared.

Unperturbed, when they returned home, Tilly served the men up a meal of corned beef and cabbage that was simmering on the stove before they left. She then armed herself with a straight razor and placed a pistol on the table.

"You concentrate on eating while I mend your shoulder." Tilly said as she busied herself cleaning Green's wound with disinfectant before wrapping a bandage around his shoulder.

"You'll be good as new in no time!" Tilly remarked when she finished.

"Thanks Tilly. You should have been a nurse." Green gratefully replied as Tilly sat down to eat.

"Keep an ear out for those bastards. I've heard Gaffney was a crack marksman in the AIF." Jim warned.

249

"If 'e comes near my 'ouse, 'e'll leave with a cracked 'ead!" Tilly snarled.

After they finished eating, Jim dimmed the inside lights, making it impossible for anyone from the street to see into the house. Just after midnight, Tilly's Pomeranians started barking from the front veranda. Jim stood beside the front window and carefully peered through the side of the curtain watching and waiting. He didn't have to wait long. A tan 1926 Model T Ford car rolled to a stopped outside his garage gates.

Green and McDonald stationed themselves by the back door, while Tilly stood by the side entrance to the house, her pistol pointed and ready to shoot. Jim watched as the men stood along the fence line of the property. Gaffney seemed to be high and was acting extremely hostile, while the other men stood behind him waiting for him to make his move.

"Open the fuckin' door and come out here ya fuckin' cowardly cunt! I'm out for blood you bastard!" Gaffney roared as neighbouring veranda lights started switching on and the occupants of the homes watched on from behind their curtained windows.

"That's fuckin' close enough. Don't come into my fuckin' yard you cunts or I'll start shooting," Jim roared, waving a military rifle in warning.

"Go on, shoot, ya fuckin' bastard. I have heaps of mates that'll fuckin' come gunnin' for ya!" Gaffney yelled out before letting off a shot that hit a brick on the veranda. He then leapt over the fence and stomped towards the house.

Jim fired a warning shot, but Gaffney pulled out his revolver and pointed it at the living room window. The other men leapt the fence and stood behind the rival gang member. Jim offered one final warning. In response, Gaffney raised his gun and aimed it at Jim. Fearing he was about to be shot, Jim pulled the trigger of the rifle and Gaffney fell to the ground.

Green and McDonald made their way slowly along the back and the side of the house as Gaffney's accomplices began shooting. Tilly raced to the front door and fired back, felling Tomlinson moments later. The remaining men, realising they were outgunned, fled to the car, and raced off.

"Who's that laying on the footpath?" Green asked when he saw Gaffney's body.

"I don't fuckin' know." Jim replied as he poured himself a glass of brandy.

"I'll check." Green said as he also poured a brandy for himself.

"Stay inside," Tilly snapped. "You don't know whether the fuckin' bastard is kiddin' or not. It could be a trap!"

Green, brandy in hand, ignored Tilly's warning. Outside, he found Gaffney gasping for breath as blood seeped from a wound to his chest. Kneeling beside him, Green offered him a sip of the brandy. Gaffney declined. "I won't tell the police who shot me. I'll be solid."

Alarmed by the gunfire, terrified neighbours had rung the Daceyville police station reporting the gunfight. Sergeant White and Constables Harper, Head, and Dumack sped to the Torrington Road intersection. When they arrived, they discovered Gaffney unconscious and lying in a pool of blood. An automatic revolver lay by his outstretched right arm.

Sergeant White followed a trail of blood several yards down the street and found Tomlinson moaning and bleeding profusely from a bullet-shattered right arm. He called out to Constable Dumack and told him to summon an ambulance immediately.

Constables Head and Harper questioned the Devines, Green and McDonald about the shooting. Tilly angrily showed them the bullet holes in her living room walls to prove that they had acted in self-defence.

Gaffney was holding on to life just one slow heartbeat to the next as the ambulance attendants attempted to stem the bleeding. Sergeant White who accompanied Gaffney in the ambulance, tried to question the gang leader, but he refused to answer any questions.

After Head and Harper finished taking down their statements, they followed the Eastern Suburbs Ambulance as it hastily conveyed the wounded men to St. Vincent's Hospital.

Upon arriving at the hospital, the physician on duty found a bullet had shattered Gaffney's breastbone, penetrating both his lungs, and exiting under his right armpit. He told the police that Gaffney's wounds would more than likely be fatal. A magistrate was called to the hospital to witness a dying deposition. However, Gaffney was a man of his word and refused to speak.

Tomlinson was also questioned and like Gaffney, refused to offer a statement. The doctor told police that the men needed to be operated on as soon as possible or it could be too late to save them. The detective nodded his approval, and the men were hurriedly wheeled through to theatre. Although the doctors did all they could, Gaffney died on the operating table at four thirty that morning.

Tomlinson survived after shattered bone particles and a bullet were removed from his forearm. Unfortunately, he sustained too much muscle damage and he never regained proper use of the arm.

Head and Harper returned to the Devines to question them and their boarders once again. Jim voluntarily, after speaking with his solicitor, admitted that he had shot at Gaffney because he was in fear of his life. He explained that Gaffney had shot Frank Green earlier in the night in Woolloomooloo and was concerned that the gang would arrive at his home armed with pistols, and because of the current gun laws, he had nothing in his home to protect himself. He told the constable that he borrowed the rifle and cartridges from a friend, and only intended on using the firearm as a warning if and when needed. He said that when the dogs started barking, he saw that a car had pulled up outside his house and fearing that it was Gaffney and his gang, he went into his bedroom and retrieved the rifle, loaded it and returned to the living room.

Devine then gave a complete account of the shootings, omitting Tilly's involvement, stating that he shot both men after they fired upon him and his home. "Those other mugs with Gaffney fired at the house as they took off like cowards to their car. I fired two shots back at them but didn't think that I hit anyone."

"Green went out and checked on Gaffney after I told 'im not to go near 'im in case 'e was kiddin'. But 'e ignored my warning. Jim was trying to settle 'is nerves before driving Gaffney to the 'ospital, but you police arrived before 'e could." Tilly added.

Constable Harper told the Devines, Green and McDonald that they would return later that morning if there were any further questions. Jim handed the rifle and cartridges to the constable as they headed toward the door: "I think you'll be needing to take these with you."

On the 19th of July, the recognisable police knock resounded through the Devines' house. Tilly answered the door wearing a skimpy negligee: "What can I do for you Constables?" She asked with a smile.

"We're here to arrest James Devine, Frank Green and Sidney McDonald." Constable Harper sternly replied.

"They 'aven't done anything wrong. Why don't you go after real criminals?"

Jim was standing in the living room with the boarders: "What the hell? I fired in self-defence. Why the hell are you arresting me? You expect me to stand unarmed in my own home while those bastards came to kill us? Those bullets came so close to me that I heard them whizz pass my ears!"

"Why are we under arrest? We weren't involved in the shootings." McDonald demanded to know.

The officers arrested Devine for Gaffney's murder, before arresting McDonald and Green for vagrancy. All were released on bail. Jim was told to return to the coroner's court on the 2nd of August 1929, for an inquest into Gaffney's death.

CHAPTER SIXTEEN

People with Power Understand One Thing—Violence

oroner, Mr. E. A. May, S.M. presided over Devine's hearing for the murder of George Gaffney. Mr. R. D. Meagher and Mr. Sproule were again representing Jim.

Sid McDonald was called as the first witness. He gave evidence stating that he and Green were walking along Bourke Street, Woolloomooloo around seven thirty on the night of the 17th of July, but when they reached the corner of Nicholson Street, a car stopped beside them, and two men jumped out. He stated that Gaffney and a man unknown to him, charged at him and punched him across his ear, knocking him to the ground before kicking him in the stomach. McDonald further testified that while he was lying on the ground, he heard a gunshot and got up and ran up Bourke Street to escape being shot. He said he passed Frank Green standing near a fence, but when he returned, Green and the two men were gone.

"Jim Devine came along with his missus in the car. Green was sitting in the back. I got into the car and Frank told me that he had been shot and said the blokes threatened that they were coming back to finish the job."

"And what happened then?" the coroner asked.

"Devine said, 'That's bad luck for us if they do, we have nothing out there.'"

"What did you take that to mean?"

"That he had no guns to fight them off. When we got near Jim's place, he stopped at a friend's house and borrowed his rifle. Then we went to Jim's house, put the wireless on and had some supper. At about midnight, everyone was getting ready for bed when the dogs barked. Jim switched the lights off because he thought it could be Leigh's gang coming to shoot us."

McDonald then explained how he walked out to the veranda and saw a car pull up opposite the house and watched as three or four men got out. He said that Jim was holding the rifle in his hand. "When the men reached the fence, Jim called out asking them who they were. A shot was fired, and Jim told them if they came any closer, he'd shoot them."

"What happened then, Mr. McDonald?"

McDonald went on and told the court the events that followed. His testimony was pretty much the same as Devine's at the hearing about him finding George Gaffney bleeding out the front of the house and offering him a drop of brandy: "He said he didn't want it as it would make him cough. I then went inside and called for an ambulance."

Tomlinson was the next to be called. He limped up to the witness box with his left arm in a sling. He was still recovering from the shooting. He testified that he knew nothing about the shooting. He said he could not remember whether he was at Maroubra or not on the night of the shooting. The crown then excused him from the witness box.

The next witness, George Gibson, testified that he saw Green in Bourke Street at seven thirty on the night of the 17th of July. He said Green had said that he'd been shot. "I took him to his house and washed his wound before driving him to Kings Cross and dropped Green off outside a shop. On my way home, I met Gaffney in William Street, he asked me if I had seen Green, and I said no. He said, 'I shot the bastard tonight and I'm going out to go on with him and Devine tonight.' He appeared to be half drunk. Later I saw Jim in his car in Oxford Street and told him what Gaffney had said. Jim said that they wouldn't go out there and I told him that they would. I told him that he's got an automatic, and he means business. Jim then told me that Gaffney knew he had no protection because the police had taken his gun."

Florence Smith, Gaffney's common law wife, dressed in black for mourning, gave evidence next. She handed her expensive fur coat to a woman sitting beside her and walked to the witness box. She said at four o'clock on the afternoon of the shooting, Gaffney told her that he was going to look for Green. She testified that he had placed a revolver in his pocket that was like the one produced in court. "He told me to wait up for him, as he might have to go away and for me to have his clothes packed for when he got back home."

Tilly, wearing a fancy brown dress, mink coat and her customary diamonds and rubies, was the next witness to be called. Whilst being questioned, she played with the rings on her fingers, or disinterestedly examined her well-manicured nails.

"What was the state of your nerves during the shooting?" Mr. Sproule asked.

"I was excited more than frightened."

The next witness to be called was Alfred Matheson. When he didn't answer the summons, Detective Matthews told the Coroner that he had been informed that Matheson was in New Zealand. He then tendered a statement in evidence which the errant witness had made to the police.

When there were no more witnesses to be called, Sproule rose from his seat and began his closing for the Coroner.

"In a lonely locality, with his wife relying on his protection from bandits or murderers outside with deadly weapons, what else was James Devine to do?" asked Mr. Sproule. "He killed the aggressor, which was justifiable homicide," he said, answering his own question.

"I have listened carefully to the arguments, and I think Devine is to be congratulated on the presentation of his case by Mr. Sproule," the Coroner complimented. "However, I do think it is a matter for a jury to say whether or not the shooting was justifiable. I find that George Gaffney died at St. Vincent's Hospital, on the 18th of July, from the effects of a bullet wound inflicted on him by James Edward Devine, and that the defendant did feloniously murder George Gaffney. I therefore commit Devine for trial commencing September, next month."

He granted Jim bail of four hundred pounds on the condition that he report to the Darlinghurst police station three times a week.

7

Tired of the constant police raids due to Leigh's lies to have her closed down and gaoled, Tilly was ready to put an end to it. And God help anyone that got in her way. It was time to teach the woman a lesson and what better way to send her a message than to obliterate her gang.

Tilly wanted to show Leigh, that unlike her, she didn't kiss the copper's boots by being an arse-licking lackey. She didn't grovel or play toesies with the police to get what she wanted. She often gave the odd report to the police… some may have even been in regard to Leigh's illegal activities… she much preferred bribery over fizgigging. However, at times the latter better suited her purpose. The brothel Madam also used a large portion of her illicit earnings to pay bribes to police, council members and fines. To her, the payoffs were an investment, and one that was generally returned one hundredfold.

Unfortunately, in spite of all the bribes and social visits with her Berwick House ladies, Tilly was still unable to shut down Leigh's operations. If those in power didn't have the balls to get rid of the bitch, she would wipe East Sydney of Leigh and her gang, herself.

Making her move on the 6th of August, Tilly sent Sid McDonald with a message to Wally Tomlinson, Leigh's lover. "Tell your fuckin' whore boss that Tilly is taking over the sly grog and cocaine business."

"She ain't my boss or whore! Do you think that Devine bitch will get away with anything even with Katie in fuckin' gaol? You stupid skinny cunt!" Tomlinson retorted.

Just after midnight, a message with the words, 'fuck off' written in pencil on a piece of paper and tied to a brick, was thrown through the front window of Tilly's Maroubra home. She understood Leigh's response loud and clear.

Violence begets violence, and on the 7th of August, Tilly hatched a strategic plan in her quest for domination over East Sydney. She called her gang together to prepare for battle. Frank Green, Guido Calletti, and Sid McDonald, and a sundry of other criminals not afraid of letting a little blood, even if it was their own, assembled at 193 Palmer Street. The place and time for the meet was written on paper in pencil and in a reciprocal response, delivered by a brick thrown through the front window of Leigh's Surry Hills house.

At the designated time of nine thirty, Tilly's men departed Palmer Street prepared for battle. Guido nuzzled his chin into his jacket braving the icy winter wind as he led Tilly's gang members armed with guns, razors, and knives, through the shadowy labyrinth of alleys and backstreets to Kellett Street, Kings Cross.

Kate's gang, some of whom had been snorting cocaine and drinking beer most of the evening, waited for the war to begin. They were also armed to the teeth with bottles, razors, pistols, rocks, and knives.

Just after ten o'clock, from street gutter to street gutter, the two groups taunted and threatened each other. When Green and Calletti reached the middle of the street, two shots suddenly rang out. One of the bullets whizzed right past Calletti's head. Incensed, he stormed across the street and slashed the face of the first man that stood in his path.

Parked two hundred yards up the street, Tilly sat in her car shivering from the cold as she waited for the brawl to commence. Her heart almost stopped when she heard the gunshots. A chill ran down her spine as she watched the men fearlessly fight in her name and honour, trusting that she should be the person to run Sydney's underworld.

Forty-seven violent gangsters ripped into each other with whatever weapon they had in hand. Cutthroat razors slashed through flesh and bones, spraying the street and footpath with blood and tissue. Gang members were slammed up against brick walls as their attacker beat them to a bloodied pulp. Agonised screams, swearing and pistol shots resonated throughout Kings Cross.

Green spotted Tomlinson cowardly sitting in Leigh's 1927 Morris Cowley across the street. He whistled to Calletti and nodded toward the car. Tilly's two top men stormed over and pulled him out onto the road. Guido held Tomlinson's arms behind his back, while McDonald slashed his face and arms with his straight razor.

The manager of the Palais Royale, J.C. Bendrodt, a resident in a nearby block of flats, bravely yelled out the window for the men to stop fighting and to leave the street. A barrage of empty bottles were thrown at him in reply. Unperturbed by the gang's reaction, he returned to the window with a pistol and fired several bullets down to the lane. Annoyed by his interference two gangsters returned fire. One bullet missed Bendrodt by a whisker as he threw himself to the floor out of harm's way.

Tilly, aware the police wouldn't be too far away, returned home and made herself a pot of tea. She placed a plate of scones on a side table and cautiously checked the street through her living room window. With the scene was set, she made herself comfortable on the settee and turned the page of the new issue of a *Woman's Budget* magazine, looking busy in case the police showed up at her house.

Meanwhile, back at Kellett Street, police cars started to arrive. The officers stepped over broken shards of glass as they followed numerous blood trails, leading them to the battle victims lying on the side of the road or in a nearby alley. Those gang members who were still able escaped into the darkness. Others, who were not so nimble footed, were rounded up by police and arrested. Gang members who were severely injured were rushed to the hospital.

Twenty-two-year-old Bruce 'Doubleday' Higgs arrived at St. Vincent's Hospital in a taxi, drenched in blood and suffering eight major facial lacerations, a large cut across his left ear and another across the palm of his right hand. The next person to be dropped off outside the hospital was thirty-five-year-old Percy Lennon. He had almost lost his left eye when his face was slashed five times during the brutal battle. Twenty-three-years-old Patricia Wilson arrived next suffering razor cuts to her left hand. Two men also showed up to the hospital after midnight and refused to identify themselves to the staff. They left as soon as their wounds were treated.

A broadcast was sent to the police wireless patrol in the Sergeant Hill area to attend to Kellett Street victims that were currently at the hospital. Several of Leigh's gangsters were questioned by the police when they arrived. They refused to answer any questions.

"Mr. Higgs, the doctor tells me that you have received multiple injuries that were sustained by either a razor or knife. How did you come upon these injuries?" Constable Wallace asked.

"I was slashed with a fuckin' razor, you daft fool!"

"Can you tell me the name of who attacked you?" Wallace asked ignoring Higgs' hostility.

"Fuck! I can live with the fuckin' scars, copper, but I can't live with me heart being cut out or being shot down by fifty fuckin' bullets! I've got nothin' to say to you!"

It would seem Tilly's gang were the winners in the Kellett Street battle. Both sides received serious injuries, Kate's gang most of all. Most of her men needed recuperation time before they could return to guard their 'grog queen'. Whereas Tilly's men who were also injured, some serious that Tilly, or their wives tended to, returned to normal duties the following day.

The police, who were looking into strategies to quell the panic from the public, offered protection for any gang members to come forward and expunge the wall of silence that surrounded the violent clash.

The weeks following the fray, the underworld was quiet. Nonetheless, suspicion and planning between the two factions stepped up a few notches behind closed doors. Green learned through one of his gang affiliates that Leigh had put a hit out on Tilly and Jim. She wanted the

Devines dead to avenge the death of George Gaffney. Tomlinson and Dalton offered to carry out the murders.

Green left straight for the Devines' Maroubra home and informed them about the threat to their lives.

"Tomlinson couldn't hit a dead fuckin' rat with a drainpipe!" Jim scoffed.

"It's either the quick or the fuckin' dead in this business," Tilly spat." And I don't plan on dyin."

Concerned that there would be more gunfire at their home, Jim and Tilly devised a plan to take Tomlinson and Dalton down. Green and Calletti were the best shooters in Tilly's gang, and both men volunteered for the task. The underworld watched and waited in suspense for Judgement Day for either the Devines' or Leigh's men. They knew one way or another, someone was going to pay with their life.

7

Discontented with the violence perpetuated by the medley of Sydney gangs, and the threat of warfare to erupt once more between Tilly's and Kate's gangs, NSW Parliament drafted the *Vagrancy Amendment Act 1929* with a consorting clause.

Eight months beforehand, the *Truth* newspaper had run an editorial stating: 'Labouring under a lax Crimes Act, Sydney has degenerated into a violent lawlessness in a ruthless underworld bid to demoralise orderly civil life'.

Two weeks later they ran another editorial and reported that an intrinsic transformation had occurred within the Sydney underworld: 'Crime in Sydney has become an organised profession'. They also demanded the government to act on the rising violence perpetuated by the razor gangs.

The contentious Consorting Clause was adopted by Parliament with bipartisan support in early December 1929. Labor had bitterly opposed the offence on the ground that it unacceptably impeded the liberty of the defendant. It was specifically brought about to assist police with the eradication of the razor gangs. Under the new law, those who habitually consorted with reputed thieves, prostitutes, or persons who have no visible or legal means of support would receive more egregious penalties. Parliament also endorsed auxiliary clauses to the act, offering the police the ability to offer prima facie evidence of illegal activity which would be strong enough to bring about a conviction. This gave New South Police almost immeasurable powers to gaol any person they deemed associated with criminals.

It was one of the most tyrannical and effectual policies adopted to fight organised crime that had ever been passed in a Western democracy.

7

Stripling underling, Paul Richards decided to become a police informant. He was a new member of an amateur Newtown gang who was aiming high. Richards thought if he reported the proposed battle between Tilly and Leigh's gangs to the police, he would receive a favour in return.

He'd heard about a copper by the name of Collin Summers whose reputation was well-known within crime circles. The fledgling gang member thought that if he could get him onside with good information on criminal activity, Summers would turn a blind eye to his gang's petty crimes.

When he told Summers about the revenge war and asked him to ignore any crimes committed by his gang in return for his information, he received a swift clip across the ear and was told to get out of the police station before he got his arse booted out.

The police, aware that with the word already on the street, it would also mean the Devines would also know. In an attempt to head off a second violent gangland war, they raided the Devines' Maroubra home on the 5th of September. During the surprise blitz, they confiscated a small cache of rifles, pistols, and bullets.

But Tilly was ahead of them. Fearing a raid on her brothels, she had rented a hotel room in the name of Karen Lee at the Strand Hotel in Woolloomooloo. She then told Green and Calletti to move the firearms and ammunition that she'd hidden under the Palmer Street brothel to the hotel room.

Over the subsequent weeks, the Devines kept a low profile. Jim phoned his bets through to his bookie, and Tilly arranged for Calletti and McDonald to collect her earnings from her brothels. She stationed her men at the front and rear of each establishment, armed, and prepared for trouble.

7

The trial for the murder of George Gaffney was heard at the Central Criminal Court before Mr. Justice Stephen on the 15th of September. The Senior Crown Prosecutor, Mr. McKean, K.C. represented the Crown and Mr. R. D. Meagher appeared for Devine.

In opening the case, Mr. McKean stated that the tragedy was the aftermath of a warfare in the underworld. He said that James Devine had shot and killed George Gaffney, and it was a question of whether it was murder or self-defence.

Devine repeated his previous statements about the shooting from the dock, before turning to face the jury and stating that he did not fire with any deliberate intention to take a life.

At the close of the Crown case, Mr. Meagher requested that his Honour should take the case from the jury. However, Mr. Justice Stephen stated that it was a question of degree which must always be left to the jury before sending jury to deliberate.

Jim and Tilly sat nervously outside the court waiting for the decision. "They can't get you for this Jimmy. It's self-defence. Any goose can see that!" Tilly hypothesised, hoping to offer her husband some hope.

Twenty minutes after retiring, the jury returned with a not guilty verdict, thereby acquitting Devine of murder. Jeers and gasps of disbelief emanated from Gaffney's family and friends. Cheers and shouts of congratulations filled the room from the Devines' friends and associates. Mr. Justice Stephen asked the gallery to quieten, and when silence returned, he discharged the charges against Jim.

On the 9th of November, the sweet taste of revenge was on Frank Green's mind and his trigger finger was pretty fucking itchy. Devine had put out a contract on Leigh's boyfriend Tomlinson, and Frank told him that he would be the one to kill the squealing bastard. Jim gave the nod, and Green spent the night in Tilly's rented hotel room opposite the Strand Hotel. Later that afternoon, he watched the streets below for Tomlinson and Dalton, knowing they drank at the Hotel every Saturday afternoon to collect SP bets.

Almost like clockwork, the men arrived just before two o'clock alongside two other criminals, Edward Brady and Charles Connors. Green knew to be alert for Connors. He was well aware of his reputation with a razor.

On his arrival at the hotel, Green ordered a whiskey at the bar. As he sat on a barstool shooting the breeze with the barman, he could feel the eyes of Leigh's gang members burning into the back of his head.

After ordering a second whiskey, he turned around and faced them, smiling broadly, and tapping his left inside coat pocket: "I'm happy to accommodate any trouble if anyone cares to give me any." The bar suddenly went so quiet that you could hear a mouse piss on cotton. Tomlinson put his head down staring at the glass of beer in front of him. Connors returned a noxious smile as he played with his Bengall razor. "Furthermore," Green smiled, "Big Jim Devine is outside ready to back me up."

Leigh's men were visibly disturbed by Green's brazen admission. Connors returned the razor to his pocket and they turned their heads away from the bar. Green let out a laugh and left.

After the six o'clock swill ended, the pub patrons were told to leave. Connors left first and looked around before nodding. Tomlinson and Dalton followed him outside once they saw the signal that all was clear.

As they walked along William Street, Green rushed out from behind a car and shouted, "Cop this you bastard!" before taking aim and firing his revolver. Three gunshots splintered the air, shooting Dalton at point blank range. Screaming and clutching his chest, he staggered a little, and then collapsed to the footpath.

Throwing caution to the wind, Tomlinson rushed to his mate's side shaking him when he saw the blood speckled spume running from the side of his mouth. Green stepped forward and snarled, "Your turn!" as he aimed his long-barrelled revolver and fired, hitting his mark in his left arm. Tomlinson, never knowing when to keep his mouth shut, looked up from where he had fallen and rasped, "Have another go you fuckin' bastard!" Green obliged his request. Standing stood over Tomlinson, he aimed his revolver and shot him once in the chest.

The footpath outside the hotel resembled a bloodbath as petrified onlookers remained where they were, too afraid to move or utter a word lest they be shot. Another man named Brady cried out in shock that he had been hurt when he saw blood on his hand.

Thomas Kelly, a known criminal, just happened to be passing by the hotel moments after the shooting. When he saw Dalton lying on the footpath, he stopped and jumped from his vehicle and ran across to check the men. Upon seeing that Dalton was still breathing, he picked him up and carried him to his car, before returning to retrieve Tomlinson. He rushed the men to St. Vincent's Hospital and pulled up outside the hospital entrance. Kelly then charged through the hospital doors carrying Dalton and told the nurses that there were two dying men needing help as he laid Dalton on the floor before going back out for Tomlinson.

The doctors hastily examined Dalton, however, he died within minutes of his arrival without regaining consciousness.

Thinking Tomlinson was dead, Green fled the scene and met Jim at their checkpoint before making their way to Devine's car that was parked two blocks away. As soon as they arrived at the Maroubra house, Green threw the revolver over the back fence and Devine changed into more casual clothes, before sitting at the kitchen table reading a newspaper.

McDonald, fearing the arrival of the police, drove Green to a nearby hotel room where they both remained in hiding.

Back at the hospital, Tomlinson had been rushed into surgery. The doctors discovered that a bullet had punctured his right lung, and another had shattered the ulna in his left arm. He was in a critical condition.

The police questioned bar staff, customers, and witnesses of the shooting. Those who were brave enough to speak to the police said they saw a man with a gun disappear down a lane opposite the hotel, but all refused to make a statement. The police, aware that the witnesses feared retaliation from the gunman, promised to ensure their safety, but to no avail, they feared Devine more than they did the police.

Upon hearing Tomlinson had survived the shooting and knowing Leigh would be fit to kill over the attempt on her lover's life, Green and McDonald did a runner from the city and went into hiding.

Driving along the Princes Highway the day after the shooting, Jim became suspicious that he was being followed. When he reached the Waterfall stretch of the highway, police driving a Morris Cowley, pulled him over and he was arrested.

He was taken to the Darlinghurst Police Station where he was questioned by two detectives who asked him about his involvement with the Dalton and Tomlinson shooting.

"I'm not involved with any gangsters! I come from a respectable family." Devine asserted.

"Did you know that there was going to be a shooting?" Detective Pierce asked.

"I heard some rumblings…" Jim replied. That statement was enough to implicate him in the crime and he was arrested for the attempted murder of Tomlinson and denied bail.

Meanwhile, a police all-points bulletin was put out for Green. The police checked all his known hangouts and came up empty. It was as if he had disappeared into thin air.

7

Over two hundred mourners arrived at St. Mary's Cathedral in Sydney to attend Barney Dalton's funeral on the 12th of November. Kate Leigh arrived in her chauffeur-driven Studebaker and walked arm-in-arm into the church with Tomlinson. Several of Dalton's former teammates from the Eastern Suburbs Rugby League Club also turned up to pay respects to their former winger. During the Eulogy, one of the players spoke of how Dalton was integral to their team winning their first premiership, and again in 1912 when they took their second title.

After the service, the funeral cortege left for Botany Catholic Cemetery where Dalton was laid to rest. Kate Leigh paid for the funeral.

7

Knowing Green was involved with Nellie Cameron, the detective in charge of the case, Detective Sergeant Lynch, put an officer on detail to follow her in hope she would lead them to their quarry. Nellie's shadow followed her everywhere. After she had been tailed for several weeks, the police started thinking she didn't know where Green was.

However, on the morning of the 3rd of December, the young constable parked a few yards up from her house and watched as Cameron carrying a suitcase and climbing into a waiting taxi. He followed the cab to Redfern Train Station and stood close by when Nellie purchased a train ticket.

Overhearing her asking for a ticket for one to Cronulla, he waited for a few minutes before buying a ticket for himself. The constable then stood several feet away from Nellie on the platform and sat behind her on the train. When she left Cronulla station, Nellie looked around for police cars before catching a taxi which stopped at the side of the road a few miles out of town.

The policeman following in a cab behind her, asked the driver to continue up the road as he kept an eye on Cameron through the back window. When she was out of sight, he asked the driver to turn around and to stop where the woman was let off. "Wait here until I return. I'm here on police business." He directed, showing the cabbie his warrant card.

Cautiously, the constable followed Cameron as she rushed through the dense sandy scrubland, stopping when he caught sight of a timber cabin. He hastily made his way back to the waiting taxi and asked the driver to take him to the local police station where he reported his finding to his superiors.

That night, the constable led Detective Sergeant Lynch and several policemen through the undergrowth to the dimly lit shack. Lynch placed his index finger to his lips telling the men to remain silent, then all six feet and five inches of him stood up and banged on the cabin's door: "Open up, It's the police!"

"Please, don't shoot. We don't have any guns!" Green called out. McDonald slowly opened the door, and in a matter of seconds, he, Green and Cameron were arrested and handcuffed.

At the police line-up, Tomlinson broke the usual gangster Omertà, and pointed the finger at Green, almost shouting that he was the one who had shot Dalton. Not content with fingering Green, Tomlinson also said that there was one man missing from the line up… Jim Devine.

Opening his mouth and singing to the cops, Tomlinson earned himself the wrath of the underworld and was on the outer. To gangsters, you betray one, you betray them all and then you watch your back. While Green was being transported to Long Bay Gaol, he was seated beside one of his old mates, Kelvin Dowling. The men chatted about the old days, and when Kelvin asked what he was in for, Frank replied: "That bastard Tomlinson picked me out of a line up today. It's a pity I didn't get him as well as Dalton."

The following day, Detective Sergeants Miller and Lynch, aware of information linking Devine to the Tomlinson and Dalton shooting, sent out an all-points bulletin after learning the Devines were holidaying at Port Kembla.

A solo police officer patrolling the streets caught sight of Devine in a maroon Studebaker. He advised the station of his whereabouts by two-way Morse transmission while he followed the car. Realising he was being tailed, Jim told the driver to speed up and lose the cop. The policeman was led on a dangerous high-speed chase for fifteen miles, but the Studebaker was abruptly stopped by a police blockade at a Bulli intersection.

Devine was arrested immediately and charged with Dalton's murder.

"I didn't bloody shoot or kill anybody!" He yelled, protesting his innocence when he arrived at the Darlinghurst Police Station.

"Mr. Devine, we have here Walter Tomlinson's dying depositions. His statements differs somewhat to yours." Detective Sergeant Miller smirked.

"I don't care what that lying mongrel said. He'd lie on his mother's deathbed if Kate bloody Leigh told him too!"

Miller began narrating excerpts from the depositions, raising his voice a little when reading, Tomlinson stated that "when Frank Green fired the shots at close range, 'Devine was standing at the corner and had his revolver drawn'. Mr. Devine, these depositions are enough for us to arrest you."

Jim appeared before Mr. Geddes, S.M. at the Central Police court on the 5th of December and was charged with having feloniously and maliciously murdered Bernard Hugh Dalton. Sergeant Napper, the Police Prosecutor applied for a remand until the following day due to further inquiries that were still taking place.

Mr. Tracey, under the instructions of Messrs. R. D. Meagher and Sproul & Co. appeared on behalf of Devine and applied for bail.

"Some time ago, my client was arraigned on another murder charge, and he had answered on all occasions to his bail. It is not anticipated that the defendant would fail to answer to bail now. If necessary, he will report daily to the police." Mr. Tracey declared.

Mr. Geddes granted bail of fifty pounds.

7

Trouble hadn't ended for Tilly either. During a hot summer evening on the 30th of December, she was hauled into the Darlinghurst Police Station and locked up. Police patrolling the area had seen her talking with a streetwalker in Kings Cross and nabbed her for consorting with a known prostitute. Tilly used her old trick of offering the constables her customary five pounds bribe, but they would hear nothing of it and threatened her with bribery charges if she tried again.

Out on bail, Tilly returned home and found Jim sitting on the settee drinking a whiskey and reading the racing guide.

"I got done again by the fuckin' cops today. Fuckin' consortin' with me own girls! I won't be put in fuckin' gaol again. I'm goin' to 'ave to think about what I can offer the court!"

"They'll be putting us in prison for fuckin' pissing in the alleys soon." Jim growled.

"At least that will keep the fuckin' streets cleaned and get rid of that awful fuckin' piss smell!" She retorted.

Tilly met with her solicitor, Mr. Berne to discuss a plea bargain offer with him. She told him that she had been longing to return home to England for some time to see her parents and her son she had left behind. Her solicitor told her that he would put the offer before the court and hoped they drew a sympathetic magistrate.

On the 6th of February, Tilly appeared before Mr. Laidlaw, S.M for the consorting charge. Mr. Berne told the magistrate that his client was willing to leave the state for two years and return to England.

"If the application is genuine it might be the solution." Laidlaw replied.

Mr. Berne assured the magistrate that if he adjourned the hearing for a week, that his client would appear before the court and show her ticket to England as well as her passport.

"If I can be satisfied she bona fide intends to leave for England within a month, and if I can be satisfied that she intends to behave herself, I don't know how that would not be a very fair way out of it." The magistrate declared.

The police prosecutor, Sergeant Dennis, said that he would agree to the adjournment for the week. He added that there were other charges against Mrs. Devine for assaulting police and riotous behaviour. The magistrate bailed Tilly for the week on the consorting charge and told her that within the following week, the police would decide upon what action to take in the other pending matters.

At breakfast the following morning, Tilly asked Jim if he'd look after the money coming in from the brothels if she were granted leave to England. Entrusting her husband to oversee her finances was a huge risk for Tilly, he wasn't half the man she was, nor did he possess her business acumen. But to Tilly, seeing her son again after so many years was more important. Her mother's health was failing, and she wanted to spend time with her before she died.

As promised, Tilly went to the shipping office to purchase a first-class ticket to England. However, to her dismay, the clerk recognised her from the many newspaper articles and refused her request, offering her a third-class ticket instead.

"My money is just as good as anyone else's! You don't 'ave the right to refuse *ME* first class passage!"

The clerk didn't utter a word. Behind the protection of the stainless-steel grill, in all his bravado, the man pointed to a sign on the wall behind him that stated that he indeed had that right.

Defeated by the shipping company's law and not prepared to break her bond with the magistrate, the renowned brothel Madam paid for third class passage.

The following Monday, Tilly and Mr. Berne fronted court and waited for Mr. Laidlaw to become available. Catching him between hearings, Tilly produced her ticket and visa, proving she would be sailing to Britain in February 1930. The magistrate dismissed the consorting charges and told Tilly if he heard that she was back in Australia before the two years was over, she would be sent to gaol for six months.

CHAPTER SEVENTEEN

Society Prepares the Crime; the Criminal Commits It

At the beginning of the new decade, the five feet four inches tall and one-hundred-and-ten-pound Matilda Devine was the most powerful female gangster in Australian history. She wore that toughness loudly and proudly. Tilly never left home without her straight razor or the small backup revolver secreted in her garter belt or within the folds of her newest fur coat.

Tilly owned a network of thirty brothels throughout East Sydney that were open twenty-four hours a day, earning her at least seven pounds a day from each prostitute. The police didn't have the experience or the manpower to keep up with Tilly's entrepreneurial skills of maintaining her well-organised prostitution empire. For a poorly educated woman who emanated from a poverty-stricken, working-class background, to become the Queen of the Sydney Underworld and one of the richest women in Australia, was never heard of before. Tilly had finally become a 'Top Dog' in a world that was built for men.

Due to her brothel conglomerate and Jim's cocaine enterprise, the Devines had risen pretty high in the world and Tilly was living her dream at last. They often dined at the most expensive restaurants, Tilly owned a fleet of cars and held numerous properties in her real estate portfolio. She wore the absolute best of fashionable clothes and expensive jewellery, but most of all, she was able to afford the best legal defence that money could buy.

Tilly could also afford to look after her prostitutes, gang members and henchmen, and she paid the latter well. As a brothel madam who started at the grass roots of the business, Tilly knew how tough it was. She helped her new working girls out as much as she could by providing mothers with food, and shelter for the homeless girls until they were making enough money on their own. She never asked for the money back.

She was also well known for helping the poor in her area, donations to the Catholic Church and schools, and local hospitals. Tilly's 'Bail Soirees', the glitzy dinner nights she often hosted at hired halls or her Maroubra home, were also legendary.

However, as benevolent as she was, Tilly was also was known for her violent and eruptive temper. Those in her employ were aware that if they ever betrayed her in any way, the punishment would collectively come with a good solid left from her heavily bejewelled fist, or a razor swiftly pulled from the furrow in her fox fur stole and shoved toward their face along with a string of violent threats.

Tilly's pride and joy was her elegant and stately Maroubra residence that boasted a candelabra in the living room, a state-of-the-art wireless and a grand piano. Australian bushland paintings hung along the walls. A mirrored Edwardian hall stand welcomed guests at the entrance, a chiffonier in the living room was lined with paraphernalia from the Royal Family. Royal Doulton and crystal was proudly displayed in the dining room, and an oak sideboard lined with spirits, wine and whiskey filled decanters enticed visitors into a second living room.

Her home and brothels were always spotlesslesly clean. Tilly couldn't stand a speck of dirt, dust—or blood tarnishing her home or anything out of place. Whenever the police raided her home or brothels, she wouldn't rest until everything was put right. At least once a day she would scold somebody with "Cleanliness is next to Godliness, and by the fuckin' Jesus Christ, you bastards will keep my 'ome clean!"

An avid royalist, Tilly often purchased souvenirs through a catalogue from the United Kingdom. On display in her chiffonier were Minton's Queen Victoria Golden Jubilee sepia mug and a King Edward VII Coronation souvenir plate which she showed proudly to every visitor.

Tilly's second pride and joy was her pack of Pomeranians. She took her precious pets almost everywhere she went, treating them like royalty and were fed only the best cuts of meat. "And god 'elp any bastard that 'urts my babies!" was a threat anyone who knew Tilly had heard time and time again.

7

Spectators from the underworld and public arrived as early as they could to grab the best seats in the gallery for Barney Dalton's Inquest on the 21st of January 1930. Those who arrived too late crowded along the passageway or outside windows hanging onto every word that was passed down the lines.

Mr. E.A. May, S.M. presided over the Inquest as the Coroner. Mr. Kemmis, of the Crown Law Office, conducted the prosecution with Detective Sergeant Lynch who assisted the coroner. Mr. R.D. Meagher appeared for Jim Devine. Mr. C. H. Moseley represented Frank Green; and Mr. G. K Osborne appeared for the relatives of Dalton.

Devine and Green were seated at the defence table with their backs to the impatient reporters eagerly waiting to hear any sensational details during the proceedings. Jim's stress about the trial had triggered his bacteria folliculitis to flare—his neck was covered in unsightly boils and his tea tree oil treatment generated an overwhelming odour at the front of the courtroom.

The morning seemed to drag on as Mr. Kemmis read summaries of the events that had occurred during, what he called, 'the long running war of the underworld'. Throughout the proceedings, McDonald sat across the gallery from Tomlinson seething over his smug facial expressions whenever the prosecutor emphasised Devine's name whilst listing his endless crimes. To McDonald, Tomlinson wasn't anything more than a sap who sucked from Leigh's tit for protection and money, and a canary that broke the criminal code of not singing to the police.

Tilly was dressed resplendently in a green floral frock, her platinum blonde hair was stylishly curled, bright red lipstick coloured her lips and a dozen dazzling diamond rings glittered from every finger. She purposely sat behind Tomlinson. Every now and then she leaned forward and whispered to him that his goose was cooked, or warn him that canaries can lose their voice, and other colourful threats.

Tomlinson was nervous, but he felt compelled to give Dalton a voice from beyond the grave.

Dressed in black and looking every inch the mourning and melancholy widow, Mrs. Bertha Emily Dalton was the first to take the witness box. Everyone in the court cupped their ears and listened intently as the bereaved woman whispered throughout her testimony. She told the coroner that her husband was a sober person and drank little after being questioned about his drinking habits.

Bertha testified that on the day of the tragedy, she and Barney had arranged to spend the following Sunday at Port Hacking. She also stated how her husband and Charles Connors, came and went from the house several times that day until about four thirty in the afternoon.

"Did you see your husband after four thirty that afternoon?" The prosecutor asked.

"He was dead," she sobbed. "I didn't see him after that. Mr. Connors came back and told me he was shot. That was after six o'clock. Connors said that my husband was in St. Vincent's Hospital. I asked him who had shot him, and he said it was Frank Green. I went down to the hospital then, and a Sister told me that my husband was dead."

After Bertha's testimony had finished, the prosecutor called a doctor who testified that Dalton had died without regaining consciousness.

Whilst on a luncheon adjournment, McDonald caught sight of Tomlinson while he was waiting to be served at a pie van. Unable to control his temper, he grabbed hold of him and told Tomlinson if he didn't keep his mouth shut, he would shut it permanently.

"Fuckin' sing to the coppers! I'll shut your mouth for you!" He roared before punching Tomlinson in the mouth and began pummelling until he fell to the ground. The police arrived and pulled him away from Tomlinson and arrested McDonald for assault. A second officer helped Tomlinson to his feet.

Recovered from his ordeal, all eyes were on Tomlinson, still wearing his blood splattered fawn suit, as he nervously made his way to the stand.

Under Green's intense and threatening glower, he testified: "My name is Walter Tomlinson. I'm a labourer and live in Ink Street, South Kensington. I was with Connors and Dalton in the hotel on the 9th of November and we had a few drinks. Green was there too. Devine wasn't with him. I heard Green say, 'Devine's waiting for me up around the corner.' We had a few more drinks and then me and the others walked outside. We spoke to a few friends that were also leaving the pub, and the next thing I saw was Dalton getting shot down! I went to pick him up and got shot myself."

"Who did the shooting?" The coroner asked.

"Green. I saw a gun in his hand. He said, 'Cop this, you bastard' and then I think he fired four or five shots straight off. I saw Dalton fall on the ground. That was just before I was shot. When I came to, they told me that a man named Tommy Kelly had taken me to the hospital. Another man got shot. I think his name was Grady, but I didn't see it happen. When I was in hospital, I made a deposition and named Green as the man who had shot me."

"Where were you wounded?" The coroner asked.

"I was shot through the left arm and the right lung." He said, to gasps from the packed gallery.

Mr. Osborne asked if Dalton produced any firearms at any time. Tomlinson replied that he hadn't.

"You say that the shooting of Dalton was entirely unprovoked?" Mr. Osborne asked surprised.

"Yes, sir." Tomlinson nodded.

"Mr. Tomlinson, did you see Mr. James Devine at the hotel or in the street at all?" Mr. Meagher asked when it came his time to question the witness.

Tomlinson looked nervously toward Devine and then Tilly, before stating that he did not see James Devine at the scene.

Devine and Green remained calm throughout the inquest. They did offer the odd threatening glance toward Tomlinson, but Jim knew that Tilly would have made sure the stool pigeon would keep his big fat beak shut.

"Who was the lady that accompanied your sister when she visited you in hospital?" Mr. Meagher asked.

"I don't know her name." Tomlinson replied as he shifted a little in his seat and looked toward Kate who was sitting at the back of the gallery.

"Let me remind you… wasn't the statement made after Kate Leigh came to see you?"

"No, she never came to see me."

"Didn't she practically live at the hospital while you were recovering?"

"No!"

The coroner then joined in on the questions, following Mosely's intent of getting to the truth.

"You know Kate Leigh?" Mr. May asked.

"I know her as Mrs. Barry." Tomlinson replied.

"She was a constant visitor at the hospital?"

"Yes, I just knew her, that's all."

No matter how many times the question was asked by both Devine's lawyer and the Coroner, Tomlinson continually denied any involvement with Leigh.

Several detectives and a constable testified on the stand for the prosecution, as well as Thomas Kelly, the boxing instructor who had conveyed Dalton and Tomlinson to the hospital. He denied witnessing the shooting. The evidence given by the detectives was written evidence from a runaway witness. A constable stated that he had overheard Green bragging about shooting Dalton and throwing the revolver over a back fence. Most was at the very least, circumstantial and hearsay evidence.

After the Crown had finalised their evidence, Mr. Meagher made a plea of innocence on behalf of Devine. The coroner was surprised that no witnesses had been called to testify that they had seen Devine at the scene, but without evidence placing him at the hotel, his hands were tied. Mr. May declared that due to lack of evidence against James Devine being at the murder scene, there was no evidence for him to answer, and he was discharged.

"However, due to Mr. Tomlinson's testimony and that of the police, Francis Roland Green must stand trial for murder."

Jim smiled and punched his fist into the air when he heard the coroner's decision. A shrill squeal of delight emanated from Tilly, proud as punch to show her happiness over her husband's freedom.

Jim quietly rose to his feet and shook Mr. Meagher's hand, thanking him for a great job once again, before leaving the courtroom arm-in-arm with his wife.

In making submissions of innocence on behalf of Green, Mr. Moseley released a bitter attack on Tomlinson, calling him a liar who was doing Kate Leigh's bidding.

Mr. May disagreed with Mr. Moseley and returned a finding that Dalton died at St. Vincent's Hospital on the 9th of November from the effects of a bullet wound inflicted by Green and committed him for trial at the Central Criminal Court on the 17th of March.

An application for bail was pursued by Mr. Moseley for Green but was refused. In the other charges against him for the attempted murder of Tomlinson and his friend, Grady, Green was remanded to the Central Police Court for the 15th of April.

Green, who had been manacled throughout the proceedings, remained in his seat waiting to go to the police patrol van to arrive and return him to Long Bay Gaol. He watched as Devine left the courtroom as a free man. After was gone, he dropped his head forward shaking it, "He walks again, and I'll do his time as well." He muttered to himself.

The following day, Sidney McDonald fronted court for the assault on Tomlinson. He appeared before Mr. Laidlaw, S.M. and pleaded guilty to a charge of riotous behaviour.

Constable Ryan testified that McDonald, who was known to police, had assaulted Walter Tomlinson, the chief Crown witness at the Coroner's Court the previous day. He said that the assault had taken place outside the court during the luncheon adjournment for the inquest into the death of Bernard Dalton. "He was under the influence of drink at the time."

"He was under the influence yesterday when he was brought before this court." The magistrate interjected.

Detective-Sergeant Miller testified next saying that he had known McDonald for three years. "He is a very violent man." He stated. "On one occasion I brought him back from Brisbane for breaking and entering. He has also assaulted police on several occasions and is an associate of Devine and Green."

"The same Green who was committed for trial on a charge of murder yesterday?"

"Yes, Your Honour."

Miller went on to state that McDonald had lived in the same house as the Devines and Green. He said that he was found living in a hut with Green when he was captured on the charge of murder.

"Have you seen me in company with Devine since I was charged with vagrancy?" McDonald asked.

"No, I have not." The detective replied.

"He has a long record, Your Honour." The prosecutor said as he handed the record-sheet up to the magistrate.

"Assault police, two charges, three months and six months; 5/9/29, assault police, £2 or 21 days; 17/6/27, break, enter and steal, two years; 29/10/29, assault and robbery, eighteen months," Mr. Laidlaw read out aloud. "And there are various other convictions for assaulting police and attempting to steal from a person."

"I have paid the penalty for all those, Your Worship." McDonald responded.

"I regard this as a profoundly serious matter. You assaulted a chief Crown witness, and that sort of thing cannot be tolerated at all." Laidlaw remarked. He then fined McDonald five pounds in default of two months hard labour and ordered that he enter recognisances of fifty pounds to be of good behaviour for twelve months.

McDonald agreed.

7

On Tuesday the 29th of October 1929, the world was sent into shock and chaos when the news broke that the Wall Street stock market in New York had collapsed. In just four days, twenty-six billion dollars was wiped from the market bringing about the Great Depression.

The American stock market's losses caused a worldwide domino effect. Income made from Australian exports quickly fell to an all-time low, forcing industries to a standstill, which then caused unemployment to increase rapidly. Australia had borrowed vast sums of money from overseas banks and, due to the Depression, they knew they would struggle to repay the debts.

The New South Wales economy was also badly hit by the stock market collapse. It had already been savaged by high unemployment and the state government had borrowed a great amount of funds to help with works and were concerned about the repayments of their financial obligations. The Treasurer had talked down the disquiet about losing their budget surplus and the expectation of a deficit much greater than any other state in Australia.

7

Tilly's voyage date, the 15th of February was closing in, so she began planning a series of farewell parties before sailing to England. As usual with her soirées, she spared no expense. Her friends, acquaintances, solicitors, dressmakers, and favourite shop assistants attended three bon voyage parties, the last being on the 14th of February. Snow was blown like avalanches and alcohol ran like rivers through a myriad of glasses as her guests danced to the latest songs. Tilly showered everyone with free food and booze, reminding her gang members and all that knew her, that she was, indeed, the Queen of the 'Loo.

Every one of the guests, including Tilly and Jim, ignored the doom and gloom the newspapers and radio were broadcasting about the Depression. It was time to rejoice—to celebrate Tilly evading gaol and that she would soon be off to enjoy time with her family in Britain.

The following morning, Tilly made sure that the gifts she had purchased for her family were secured. She then checked her locked box in the smaller trunk, relieved that Jim had not discovered the five thousand pounds she had locked away. Then went to check the pockets of her coats and grinned to herself when she touched the extra ten thousand pounds she had secreted was still there.

Dressed in her salmon frock, a red beret and wearing her black leather pumps adorned with dazzling fake gems on the front of each shoe, Tilly waved to Jim, her girls, and gang members from the deck of the *Otranto*. She blew Jim a kiss and proudly waved the bouquet of flowers he had given her. When the pier was a mere speck in the distance, Tilly made her way to her mediocre cabin and sat back on the bed as she sipped a glass of champagne in celebration of seeing her Freddy and family very soon.

CHAPTER EIGHTEEN

Topsy Turvy World

Two days after his wife's departure, Jim was woken in the early hours of the morning by one of Tilly's henchmen. Tilly's classy brothel on the corner of Nelson and Darling Streets, Rozelle, had been set alight.

"Is anyone hurt?" Jim asked, alarmed.

"No, we got them out wearing what little clothing they could grab. The fire spread fuckin' quick. I reckon one of Leigh's bastards did it!" Desmond growled.

"Wouldn't put it past the bitch. While the cat's away, the rat will play!" Jim spat. "You take your car and I'll take mine.

Devine arrived a few minutes after the fire trucks and ascertained by the distinct odour of kerosene, that it was a hit job.

While the burnt sections of the brothel were being rebuilt, Jim relocated the girls throughout the other brothels. He planned to exact revenge on Leigh but decided to take it slowly to lull her into a false sense of security. He sent word through the underworld that whoever had set the house alight was going to pay for it.

A few weeks later, whilst drinking at the Tradesman's Arms, he mentioned to a few of Leigh's gang members how he'd heard that two men were seen running from the brothel after it was set alight. A couple of weeks later, at Club 400, Jim set off another rumour. He informed two cocaine dealers working for Leigh that he was told an up-and-coming brothel owner from Melbourne had set the fire…

7

Tilly's arrival at her home in Camberwell was a heart-warming event. The house was no longer the rundown dump she had been raised in. It had been repainted, repaired, and additions had been made. The front yard was neat and lined with boxwood hedges and scattered with lilacs, roses, hollyhocks, and snowberry shrubs.

With the money she sent her parents each month, her parents had turned the dilapidated hovel Tilly had left eleven years before, into the home her mother had dreamed of living in.

Freddy, now eleven-year-old, was waiting for her on the front porch. Tilly's breath caught in her throat when she saw him. Her mother had sent her photos, but for him to be standing in front of her in the flesh, and looking so much like his father, brought tears to her eyes. "Be strong you daft cow, you can't take him back with you no matter how much you want to." Tilly chided herself as she took a deep breath and walked along the cobbled path to the front door.

Young Freddy looked nervously toward his mother. Tilly smiled, trying not to show her anxiousness. Smiling the crooked smile of his father's, Freddy asked, "Can I carry your bag for you… m-m-mum?"

Tilly was unable to move. Her hands trembled, her throat became dry and she bit down on her lower lip as a sob rose in her throat. She slowly turned her head to blink away newly formed tears as she attempted to maintain a grip on her fragile control.

Her heavy breath pierced the frigid morning fog as she savoured her son's words. She had never been called 'mum' before. The word was both endearing and heartbreaking.

"Yes, Freddy, you can carry this one if you're strong enough." Her voice almost broke as she offered her son the smaller of her trunks.

When she walked into the house, Tilly was surprised when she saw the colourful streamers and a large 'welcome home' banner hanging above the blazing fireplace. A table in the centre of the room was laden with food and drinks. Her father and her excited siblings stood along the fireplace that was the laundry room when she was a little girl. She looked around and smiled, impressed with the changes.

Her family screamed "Welcome Home!" before rushing in and hugging and kissing the weary traveller.

When Tilly saw her mother sitting on a Davenport settee, her heart dropped. She looked so sick, but she smiled and reached out, beckoning her over. Tilly let the tears flow freely when she felt the warmth of her mother's arms around her.

"Mum! It's so good to see you again! It's been too long."

"A very long-time love, but you're here now. What do you think of our lad? He's growing up into a handsome young man and is doing very well in school."

"That 'e is. Spitting image of our Jimmy, 'e is." Tilly smiled as she looked adoringly upon her son.

"Am I going back to Australia with you, mum?"

Tilly's breath caught in her throat as heartbreak stabbed at her heart. She would have loved to take her son home with her, but she had promised her mother she wouldn't upset his schooling and his stable life in Camberwell. "I would love to Freddy, but you see, in Australia, it's still pretty rough with a lot orf crime. You're much safer 'ere with your grandparents."

"Could I visit you for holidays?" He eagerly asked.

"We'll see, Freddy. We'll see. Now show me your bedroom and tell me all about school and your friends…"

7

When the name 'Matilda Devine' was called out at the Central Police Court on the 12th of March, there was silence. The Police Prosecutor, Sergeant Hart stood up and stated: "I am informed that the defendant has left the country."

Mr. Laidlaw, SM. smiled and replied: "Well, I think you can safely withdraw the assault police and riotous behaviour charges, Sergeant Hart."

7

Frank Green's hearing at the Central Criminal Court in Darlinghurst on the 20th of March was heard before Mr. Justice Stephen. Unable to appear for his client due to a clash of court dates, Mr. Mosely instructed Mr. Windeyer, K.C., and Mr. E. S. Miller to appear for Green. The Senior Crown Prosecutor, Mr. McKean, K.C. appeared on behalf of the Crown.

Tomlinson again appeared as the star witness and reiterated his statements from the coroner's inquest. He was cross-examined by Mr. Windeyer and testified that he did not know of anything between Green and Dalton. He then again lied under oath when he stated that he didn't know Kate Leigh was the head of a violent Sydney gangs.

The detectives and other witnesses gave the same evidence as the previous hearing and upon not having any new evidence, Mr. Justice Stephen adjourned the case until the 24th of March.

7

The Depression was causing heartache for countless Australians. Men who were retrenched due to the downturn of the economy found it difficult to obtain employment. Many had their homes and cars repossessed due to not being able to pay their finance company leading to families becoming homeless, living on the streets, or moving in with relatives.

On the 22nd of February 1930, the *Sydney Morning Herald*, printed: 'Hunger, real hunger, is a fearsome thing … Worst of all is the bodily weakness, the nausea, the despondence, which follow a prolonged fast, and the uncertainty of when the fast is to be broken … It is hard, extremely hard to struggle around for a job on an empty stomach, weak and dizzy, and jostled by the passing throng.'

The illegal businesses around Sydney were also feeling the pinch. Some were fighting for survival. Others had already given up and lived on what little money they made from their illicit endeavours for as long as they could.

Bread and dripping and 'cocky's joy' (golden syrup), became the staple food for most city-dwelling Australians during the Great Depression. Newborns survived on diluted condensed milk, and toddlers ate arrowroot biscuits or near-rotten fruit and vegetables thrown out by grocers and at the markets. Many women, like their convict mothers before them, started keeping chickens for fresh eggs and meat. Men and women went out picking berries, fishing, or hunting rabbits and bush turkeys, to feed their families. Bakeries and corner stores sold stale bread, bruised fruit and vegetables, dented cans of food, broken biscuits, and other spoiled produce. Butchers sold cheap cuts of meat that they had previously sold as dog food.

7

Tilly's first months in Camberwell were a whirlwind of attending weddings, birthday parties, christenings, and family get-togethers. But homesickness and a longing to return to Australia had enveloped her. She was enjoying her time with her son and family, but she missed her husband and the life she had left behind. She was also concerned about the lack of brothel updates Jim had promised to send. But what was more worrying her more was the subtle dissatisfaction she read between the lines in letters that she had received from her girls. She longed to return home, but there was a small matter of being sent to gaol if she did…

Missing Bondi and Coogee beaches, Tilly asked her mother if she could take Freddy to Blackpool during the summer school holidays. When she gave her approval, Tilly purchased a motor home for the vacation and stocked it with food, new clothes for Freddy and water in preparation for their upcoming trip.

Four days after the holidays began, Tilly and Freddy arrived in Blackpool and parked their motor home under the shade of a large sycamore tree. After the long drive, Tilly felt like stretching her legs, so she and Freddy went for a walk along the jetty, stopping to watch people dancing to the music of a German oompah band. Tilly couldn't help but tap her feet to the music, and moments later, both she and Freddy were pulled into the crowd of dancers, which they merrily joined in.

Later, as they ambled along the pier, Freddy asked to stop at a phrenologist to have his character read. Tilly didn't believe in such nonsense, but she would have given her son the moon if she could. The man felt the bumps along Freddy's head and began to speak: "You will find your talent in singing. You have a determined personality. You are a young man with an adventurous streak that will take you abroad."

Tilly smiled at Freddy's enthusiastic response: "That means I'm going to Australia, Mummy!"

After a lunch of fish and chips and several milkshakes, Tilly took her son for a ride on the steam roundabout… five times. When she found it difficult to get him off the ride, she mentioned the shooting galleries, and Freddy ran swiftly to her side. Their last adventure for the day was the Blackpool Tower which Freddy promptly compared to the Eiffel Tower in France.

That night, Tilly and Freddy fell asleep before eight o'clock. Both exhausted after their first day at the seaside retreat.

The remainder of the two weeks were just as busy with sea-bathing at the open-air baths, playing and riding the myriad of sideshow events, donkey rides, and enjoying Punch and Judy shows. Tilly's favourite places were the gardens, open-air bars, and the market stalls along the wharf. The highlight for both of them, however, was a three-hour boat ride provided by one of the local families.

Tilly took her time returning home. She took the longest route possible to reach Camberwell, stopping in several villages overnight. When they arrived back at the house, she was pleased to see her mother's smiling face greeting them from the veranda.

After a large roast lamb meal with her family, Tilly settled on her bed and started sorting through her letters. Most were from friends at home, but then she saw one from Maisie, one of her girls, who had written 'important!' on the back of the envelope after her name and address.

Maisie reported that there were a lot of strange goings-on in the brothels, and the girls were sorely missing her. She apologised and wrote that she didn't want to reveal any of the shenanigans because she knew Tilly was caring for her sick mother. She wished her madam well, and her mother good health and signed off. However, she had included a snippet from an article in the *Truth* newspaper where Kate Leigh had castigated her, knowing she was out of reach of Tilly's vengeance.

Leigh had invited the reporter to her home and almost as soon as he had sat down, she began her tirade about her nemesis. She said that it was her educated opinion that Tilly Devine had ruined the life of innocent young women by setting them to work in her brothels. She then stated that she had once loaned Tilly a dog which she refused to return it. She went on to say how she did good for the community whereas Tilly took everything she could from those around her.

Incensed, Tilly took care of her mother's medicinal needs before leaving for her bedroom where she closed her door and penned a letter to the editor of the *Truth*.

On the 29th of June 1930, the newspaper printed the letter:

'Dear Sir,

I am writing this teller asking a favour to keep my name out of the papers in any connection with Kate Leigh's, as I don't wish to know her class. I never mixed in with her and never in her life did she give me a dog. Why, my dogs! I have their pedigrees, and they are a class above hers. Fancy her saying things about me now that I am out of the country! And tell her for me I don't wish to see her iron face in London, as I have my parents here and they are clean.

That woman! She could not compare herself with my mother, who is a wonderful old-fashioned lady and knows nothing of my doings in Sydney, thank God.

Anyway, I must say you gave my husband a fair go at his trial in your paper, so surely you will be fair to me. Let dying dogs die. As I say, give a dog a bad name and it sticks. Even the Police said I was not as bad as I was painted. There are lots in Sydney who will miss me, even the police as I hope never to come back to Sydney. I like it but you people did not like me because I am English. If I had been an Aussie girl there would have been nothing said. I was too straight for half of them. I spoke my mind as all Londoners do, right from the shoulder.

Kate Leigh! That thing of a virago! She is jealous of my youth and prosperity. I know too much for her, that is why she hates me, and then she has the cheek to say she doesn't mind being called 'notorious', but she hates to be called the 'worst woman in Sydney'. Well 1 think myself a class above her. The underworld all took their hats off to me and class me a lady beside her.

Men in jail know her class. Why is it she can do as she likes, and other women are dead frightened? No, she is too handy for the police. She is known as the biggest 'Top-off'! in Australia. Leigh is a white slaver and dope-pusher. Send one of your reporters around to different prisons and ask those that are doing a turn what class of a woman she is.

One well known man is doing life at Long Bay. She sent a dinner to him last Xmas and he found out it was from her. He packed it in a clothes bag and sent it right back to her, and if you don't believe me, I can tell you the man's name if you care to answer this letter.

So, I must thank God I was born of good parents. My father has never taken a drink and never been inside a police court in his life. My dear mother is very sick at the present time and I am nursing her back to health, otherwise I would put my address on this letter, it would worry them if they saw half what was in the papers about me. So, trusting you will do me this favour for once, as your paper is a class above others.

I remain,
Matilda Devine.'

7

Tilly's letter to the newspaper inspired Jim to take revenge upon Leigh for the Rozelle house fire. He contacted a bent detective at the Surry Hills police station and told him there was a cache of cocaine arriving at Leigh's Riley Street home the following morning.

The carefully planned raid on the house was undertaken on the 1st of July by Detectives Thompson and Wickham of the C.I.B. Drug Bureau. Sergeants McCleod and Russell along with policewoman Lillian Armfield, accompanied them.

In the dead of the night, Kate was taken by surprise when Detective Sergeants Wickham and Thompson silently entered the house. They made their way to the dining room where they came upon several men sitting around a table, ordering them to stand up so they could be searched. Kate, unaware of what was occurring, walked into the room to join the men, when she saw the police.

"What the hell are you doing in my bloody house!" she demanded.

"Kate, you need to calm down. We're here because a report was made that there was cocaine on your premises," Lillian Armfield explained. "I need you to accompany me to your bedroom where I can search you."

"You're not laying a fuckin' finger on me, you lesbian bitch!" Leigh roared. "Now, fuck off and get out of my house!" She then turned on the detectives and uniformed policemen, throwing a nearby bottle of ginger ale at them as she screamed at them to get out of her house.

As she swung around to attack Detective Armstrong, something fell from the pocket of her coat. Leigh swiftly bent over, picked it up and threw it into the fire. Armfield hastily rushed to the fireplace, grabbed hold of a fire poker, and retrieved a tobacco tin from the flames. The police waited several minutes for the tin to cool down before the policewoman opened it and found cocaine inside.

McCleod and Russell then frisked the men as the detectives continued to search the house. Lillian searched the combative Leigh in her bedroom and found nothing on her person. However, detectives and McCleod had located fifteen packets of cocaine in kitchen cupboards, under floorboards and nine tobacco tins filled with white powder under Kate's mattress.

Lillian told Leigh that she was under arrest, but Kate wasn't going to make it an easy arrest. She turned around and slammed Armfield against the wall. Lillian was no slouch in the defence department, she had Leigh on the ground pleading. As the police sergeants took Kate to the car, she kicked and punched them in an attempt to escape. Her protests were so loud that her neighbours gathered on the footpath outside their homes. Armfield tried all she could to calm her, but nothing would keep Leigh quiet. The detectives, tired of her carry on, picked her up and carried her to the waiting police car.

As the police wrestled with the aggressive drug dealer, she screamed out for all and sundry to hear: "It's a frame up! The fuckin' bastards are tryin' to frame me!"

At the Central Police Station, under the surname Barry, Kate was formally charged with having cocaine in her possession. The following morning at the District Police Court, she was remanded in gaol to reappear in court on the 8th of July.

Devine heard about the seizure of the snow and subsequent arrests at the Tradesman's Arms the following morning and inwardly chuckled, "I got one up on the fat cunt and now the cops owe me."

7

Tilly thoroughly enjoyed being a mother to her son. They spent a lot of time together visiting museums, playing at the parks, going to the cinema watching the newest children's movies, or just playing boardgames at home. Each weekday morning Tilly proudly walked Freddy to school which was at the end of their road. The school keeper rang the bell at 8:45 am and Tilly would stay with Freddy until the second bell rang at 9:00 am when he would rush to his classroom. Then as the bell rang at 4:00 pm, the doting mother would await her son at the school's gate to walk him home.

7

Frank Green's second trial for the Dalton murder began on the 9th of June. Prison life had taken a harsh toll on him. He was thin and pale as

287

he feebly smiled toward his wife, Dolly, in the gallery. She had taken the week off from her job at the Woolloomooloo custard factory to support him.

Tomlinson again repeated his false testimony he had given at the previous trial. Green's solicitor, Mr. Windeyer, KC. cross-examined him, indicating that the Crown's case largely depended on his testimony which was nothing more than a continuance of an old feud between himself and Green. He then looked toward Justice James and said that he found it strange that out of all the people that were in the position to see who had shot the men, Tomlinson was the only one to blame his client.

The trial was adjourned to the following day, where the jury re-heard the evidence that was previously presented to the court. The jury was empanelled and spent the night deciding if Green was guilty or innocent. The following morning, the foreman told the judge that they were deadlocked. Justice James discharged them for failing to come to a decision.

Green was again remanded to Long Bay Gaol without bail and set a date for a third trial to commence on the 12th of June.

"Is there a way we can get to somebody in the jury?" Jim asked Sid McDonald as they left the court. "If they acquit Green, the cops will most likely come gunning for me."

"I'd leave this one alone, Jim. The description they gave of the shooter doesn't fit you or Green. He'll be acquitted, that's for sure. That bitch Leigh being in court when that fuck face Tomlinson says there's nothin' between them, proves he's full of shit,"

"You better be right, or I'll be after you next." Jim retorted.

Appearing at the Central Criminal Court, Darlinghurst on the 12th of June, for the fifth time since the shooting, Tomlinson's testimony was almost verbatim to the previous hearings and trials. He seemed almost bored as he retold the events that led up to the shooting and what had transpired after.

When Green took the stand, he refuted Tomlinson's entire testimony. "On my word of honour as a gentleman," his strong words at odds with his gaunt and weakened state and trembling voice, "I don't know why Tomlinson has given this evidence against me. I don't think he knows himself. I was not at the hotel after four-thirty that afternoon. Unless it is because of a woman… a woman with whom he has lived with. A woman who hates me… Kate Leigh."

In summing up for the jury, Justice James said that it was impossible to shut one's eyes to the fact that at present in Sydney, there seemed to be a vendetta among certain sections of the community that were the cause of shootings and razor-slashings. He said he hoped those involved would meet and end the violence.

The jury returned at 3:10 pm with a verdict of not guilty. Loud cheers burst forth from the gallery. Frank Green leapt from his chair and briskly shook Mr. Windeyer's hand, thanking him for his representation. He turned and sent a black look of hatred toward Jim Devine. Dolly's white gloved hands went to her face and she openly wept in relief at her husband's acquittal. Nellie Cameron, with whom Frank had been having an affair, smiled and blew him a kiss.

After discharging Green, Justice James said that he wished the vendetta between the gangs would cease. He supposed that something was at the bottom of it, but what, he did not know. The judge looked toward the criminals seated amongst the gallery and reiterated his wish that the underworld war of the past two years would end. He passionately petitioned Jim Devine, Tom Kelly, Nellie Cameron, and Kate Leigh, who were seated in the gallery, to do something to clean up the violence. He said that if they must quarrel among themselves, to get together and settle it, using their fists if they must, but not revolvers and razors.

After the judge had finished his discourse, Green stood and stated that he always fought with his fists, which brought laughter from the crowded gallery.

Later that afternoon during the celebrations of his release at the Tradesman's Arms Hotel, the non-attendance of Jim Devine was well noted. Green ignored his absence and drank beer like it was water. Unfortunately, his revelry ended abruptly when he was arrested and taken to the Central Police Court where he was charged with having on the 9th of November 1929, maliciously wounded Walter James Tomlinson and Edward James Brady with intent to murder.

He appeared before Mr. McMahon and was represented by Mr. Moseley. His solicitor told the court that Green had recently been acquitted at the Criminal Court on a charge of murdering a man named Dalton. The shooting which Green was now charged with took place at the same time as that which caused Dalton's death. He said the jury had been asked to find whether it was Green's hand that held the revolver that killed Dalton. He stated that it followed that the same hand that killed Dalton had wounded Tomlinson and Brady.

Mr. Moseley added that Green had already been in gaol for seven months and he asked that the bail be made as light as possible. Mr. McMahon admitted Green to bail, which he fixed at two hundred pounds, and remanded him until the 20ᵗʰ of June. These charges were dismissed when Green re-appeared in court.

7

Tilly was enjoying her time with her family. She took them out on day trips around London and was surprised by the changes. She shouted her parents, siblings, and their families to meals at high class restaurants and took them on several shopping sprees.

When her mother asked her where the money came from, Tilly lied and told her that Jim was wealthy, and the farm was doing well. She didn't want her mother to know that she had continued the life she had previously led.

Sometimes at night, sentimentality pulled at Tilly's heartstrings and she silently cried into her pillow. The thought of leaving Freddy and her family again broke her heart. She and her son had built a bond, and she had her parents to thank for that. They had raised him with the knowledge that he was well loved by her and explained that her circumstances after his birth had forced her to leave him with them. Tilly had sent money and gifts and clothes for Freddy from Australia over the years and with every parcel, she sent three times the letters always telling him how much she loved and missed him.

A sob caught in her throat when she realised that once she returned to Australia, the peanuts street games they played together would stop. No longer would she be woken up on weekend morning by Freddy jumping into bed beside her as she told him stories about the 'farm', and they'd talk about school and make plans for the weekend. With all her heart she wanted to take him with her, but the threats Jim had made in the past about bringing him home, and the thought of breaking her parents' heart by taking their grandson from them after so many years, caused her confusion and heartbreak.

7

Anna, a new girl Jim had hired to work at the renovated Rozelle brothel had garnered his special interest. She was blonde, tall, curvy and could talk the leg off a chair. She was also incredibly beautiful. Jim took her to

Kate Leigh's court appearance on the 8th of July and they sat at the back of the gallery.

Leigh appeared before Mr. Perry, S.M. and was being represented by Mr. Moseley, who made a fortune from his wayward client. Moseley approached the bench and told the magistrate that two witnesses had been located in Melbourne, and as the charge was such a serious one, he had briefed leading counsel, but they had not had time to go fully into the facts.

Sergeant O'Toole, the Police Prosecutor, opposed a further remand saying: "We say that the witnesses who are allegedly in Melbourne are myths. There is a conspiracy between the defendant and other drug traffickers. A witness will come before the court and the defence will accuse the police of certain practices."

Angered by the accusation, Mr. Moseley jumped to his feet. "We don't know anything of that. It is disgraceful for him to accuse me!"

"He does not accuse you, Mr. Moseley." the magistrate corrected.

"The police have brought a witness sixty miles to attend court this morning and are ready to go on." Sergeant O'Toole stated.

"We say that the cocaine found on her premises was not put there by the defendant." Mr. Moseley stated.

Mr. Perry remanded Leigh until 16th of July on her former bail of three hundred pounds.

Jim and Anna's relationship turned into a hot romance. He no longer wanted her to work in the brothel and told her that he would look after her. However, Anna had heard about Tilly's violent temper and told him that even though she had feelings for him, she was afraid that his wife would kill her. Jim told her that he'd had affairs before, and Tilly never found out, so she would be safe.

"So, I'm just an affair? You don't love me and just want to fuck me? That's all I am to you? Well, screw yourself! I don't need to be fucked over by you when I can lay on my back and make money for myself!" Anna raged.

"Hey, calm down, Anna. Fuck, I didn't mean that. I love you and want us to live together. I told you that so you would feel safe from Tilly. I won't let her harm a hair on your fuckin' head!".

Anna moved into the Maroubra house after Jim told her that he would send Tilly a letter and tell her to stay in England as their marriage was over.

7

Tilly sat on her bed looking at her mother's garden through the window. The petals had started fading and falling to the ground. Saturday morning was the day her mother judiciously carried out her garden duty, a task that gave her immense pleasure. Tilly was delighted to be able to her help prune the dying roses to ensure a fuller flush the following spring.

The late year coldness made Tilly miss Australia even more. She had become accustomed to the heat of an Aussie summer and found the chilly and windy weather in England uncomfortable. To take her mind off Australia and her concerns about not hearing from Jim, she spent the first weeks of November Christmas shopping with her mother and sisters.

Her mother started preparing for Christmas earlier than usual, excited that at least for one year, they would be celebrating Christmas Day as a complete family. On their way home from seeing a movie one afternoon, Tilly, her mother and Freddy stopped to choose a Christmas tree. Freddy's eyes sparkled with excitement when he spotted the tallest tree laying against the cart.

"Grandma, can we please buy that tree! It almost reaches the sky!" He enthused.

"Darling, it's quite expensive. Maybe next year." She said as she gently patted her grandson's head.

Tilly, unable to bear the disappointment in her son's eyes, walked straight over to the vendor and handed him a pound note, "and 'ere's another pound if you deliver it to 57 'ollington Street, this afternoon."

The delight on Freddy's face when she purchased the tree was a memory that would remain in Tilly's heart to the day she died.

"You're spoiling him love."

"Mum, I'd give 'im the world if I could."

Upon returning home, Tilly's father told her that he put some post from Australia on her bed. After packing away the gifts and Christmas decorations she'd purchased and made her family a pot of tea, Tilly took her cup of tea and two of her mother's homemade biscuits to her room. One by one she opened the letters from her girls, none of which held any positive tidings. Maureen and Edith had written that Jim had run the brothels into the ground, and he was using cocaine and drinking more. The other two women revealed they had left Palmer Street after Jim started offering them to his mates and promising to pay them for their time, but they never received the payment. However, the letter from Dawn came as the most crushing blow. She revealed that Jim had pawned most of her jewellery and had been asking the girls if they knew whether she had any money hidden in any of the brothels…

Sitting in the privacy of her bedroom, Tilly looked out the window and sobbed over her husband's breach of trust. She had been suspicious that there was something wrong for some months having not heard from him, nor receiving any letters from him. She knew she would need to return to Australia, but she was broken-hearted about leaving her family so soon.

An excited squeal and the sound of furniture being moved around, caught Tilly's attention. She sat up and wiped her eyes and listened. Her father was giving directions in a matter-of-fact way, alerting her to the arrival of the Christmas tree. She took in a deep breath and walked to the door, stopping to straighten her dress and cardigan before entering the living room.

Freddy was already sorting through a box of Christmas decorations when she walked over to the tree. "Look Mum isn't it the tallest tree you've ever seen! It almost reaches the ceiling!"

"It is the best and tallest tree in the world, sweet'art," Tilly lovingly replied. "If you look under my bed, you'll find two boxes of brand-new decorations."

When Freddy returned, the Twiss family decorated the tree. Almost an hour later, the once bare pine tree was decorated with colourful shiny glass baubles, lights and topped with a large red bow.

That night, Tilly sent a letter off to her solicitor advising him that it was paramount for her to return to Australia earlier than legally expected. She asked him to do whatever needed to be done to keep her out of gaol. She told him if she was fined, to pay the court, no matter the amount. She also sent a letter to Dawn, letting her know that she would be returning to Sydney as soon as she could, but told her to keep it under her hat as she didn't want Jim to know she was coming home early.

The following evening, Tilly took her family out to the Savoy for tea and during dessert, she broke the news that she needed to return to Australia as soon as possible. It broke her heart when she saw the tears in her son's and mother's eyes. But she knew that to continue looking after them it was imperative that she return home to deal with Jim and restore her businesses to money making enterprises again.

"Mummy, please stay. I want to spend Christmas with you!" Freddy pleaded.

"Yes, Till, please spend at least one Christmas with us. It would make us all ever so happy." Her mother beseeched.

Not wanting to disappoint her son and parents any further, Tilly promised them that she would stay until after the New Year. "But I will need to go down to the Tilbury Docks tomorrow morning to purchase a ticket."

The following morning, Tilly's father drove her down to the shipping office where she purchased a ticket on the *SS Ormonde*. It was the earliest ship available and was due to leave on the 6th of January. Tilly smiled to herself as she looked down at her ticket, "More time with my sweet boy."

"Do you really have to leave so soon, Till, my love?" Her father asked as they drove home.

"Dad, the businesses have gone downhill since I left and without the income, I won't be able to help you or Freddy. Jim has no business sense at all. If it weren't for that, I would have stayed longer than I had planned."

"So, you don't plan on taking the lad home with you?"

"With all my 'eart, Dad, I would love to take him back with me. But… I can see that 'e is much better orf staying 'ere with you and Mum. I'll come back and see you all as much as possible. I promise."

Once she uttered the words, Tilly knew she couldn't take them back. Silent tears rolled down her cheeks as she stared out of the window. She looked at the Camberwell streets that hadn't changed much since she left. Access to water was still only available from a public tap. Washing still hung on lines across the streets from one flat to another. At least her family home, like most houses in the area were connected to electricity. However, there were more people, higher unemployment, and more poverty. Times were as tough in England as it was in Australia for the working class.

Tilly smiled inwardly knowing that her brothels kept the wolf from her parent's door and her son well fed, well dressed, and not wanting for anything. And when she returned to Australia, she will have her houses filled with girls and making a fortune again.

The two weeks leading up to Christmas was a busy time for the Twiss Family that year. With Tilly purchasing all the ingredients needed, they would be able to enjoy all the trimmings of Christmas. Tilly was in her glory as she, her sisters and mother prepared mince pies, boiled sweets, and baked sponge cake for the Christmas trifle. Freddy enjoyed cleaning the mixing bowls and wooden spoons with his fingers and tongue, always eagerly waiting for the next bowl to be placed in front of him. Her father had purchased extra ice blocks and placed them in the alcove on the back verandah. That was the 1930s version of a Camberwell refrigerator.

When they had finished cooking, they placed the sponge cakes and fruit mince pies wrapped in thick cloth on the marble slab that was sitting on top of the ice blocks. Freddy ducked behind his grandmother and filched a pie before she rolled down the makeshift sacking door to protect the food.

Freddy wasn't without his responsibilities. Tilly put him in charge of making paper chains and then helped him place them across the living room ceiling, adding more Christmas spirit to the room.

Late in the afternoon on Christmas Eve, Tilly, Freddy, and her sister Lillian, left for the shops and market stalls. It was a family tradition when they were young and extremely poor. Her mother would clean houses and take in washing all year so they could attend the Camberwell markets to buy a turkey suspended from rails outside the butcher shop, hoping the price would come down before the markets closed that night. As children, they loved being amongst the jostling crowds looking at the toys and the coloured lights. It was almost the same. The stalls were still lit by paraffin lamps and the vendors standing by their cockney barrows were still shouting out their prices, each vying to be cheaper than the other. There were still a lot of people eyeing off the turkeys. Tilly shed a tear as she watched her son's wide smile and the curious glint in his eyes as he too experienced the markets not bothered by the snow falling on his woollen hat.

"I can tell you one thing. I won't be fuckin' waiting until the last ten minutes to buy the turkey! I'm buying it now, as well as any other meat the butcher 'as! Be ready for sore arms in the morning after plucking that turkey!" Tilly smiled as she pointed to the largest turkey hanging from a hook.

That night, they plucked the turkey, goose, and a chicken, and placed them in the oven to slowly cook overnight. Tilly and her parents then spent most of the night wrapping the gifts and placing them around the tree. She was exhausted when she finally fell into bed just before four o'clock in the morning.

As it was on her birthday, Christmas Day was no different. Tilly had not received a card or gift for her or Freddy from Jim. She shook the thought from her head. "Today is a 'appy day. It's my first Christmas with my son. I'm not going to let Jim ruin this for me?!"

When she was dressed in her Christmas finery, Tilly crept out to the living room and was surprised to find the table already set with mince pies, cakes, and boiled sweets. She smiled when she saw Freddy looking up at her with a grin from ear to ear from beside the Christmas tree. The smell of the wood burning in the open fireplace, the scent of the pine Christmas tree, the aroma of pork roasting in the oven made Tilly feel like she was home.

However, nothing could beat the feeling of her son looking up at her with eyes filled with excited expectation and her family sitting around the living room waiting to open the Christmas presents. She knew it would be the best Christmas she would ever experience.

"Mum! We've been waiting for you to wake up *ALL* morning!"

"His lordship here has been out of bed since five o'clock." Her father grinned.

"Well, I can't 'old up Christmas anymore, now can I?" Tilly smiled. "Time to open the presents!"

Tilly sat on the settee as her father rose from his chair and sat beside Freddy near the Christmas tree. "Now Freddy, like we do every Christmas, we give everyone their gifts and then open our own."

Tilly saw the look of disappointment on her son's face and felt sorry for him. She knew he would have been reading his name on the Christmas tags attached to so many presents. "Just for this Christmas, why don't we all sit by the tree and pass whatever gift we pick up to 'oever it's for?"

The next twenty minutes, the Twiss Family opened their piles of gifts while Freddy's laughter and the sound of ripping paper rang through their home. When Tilly's mother got up from her chair and walked into the kitchen, she and her sisters followed. It was time to start preparing for their early Christmas lunch and Tilly couldn't wait to eat that turkey! Her father and Freddy remained in the living room, concentrating on setting up Freddy's train set. She was proud when she saw that her son had arranged his other presents, books, a cricket set, a jigsaw puzzle, clothing, a chess and draught set, and a snakes and ladders game, neatly by the side of the tree.

When it was time to eat Christmas dinner, the turkey was the prominent centrepiece, surrounded by a goose, a chicken, pork, roasted vegetables, a jug of bread sauce, two trifles, a large leg of ham, cranberries, and pudding. Never had the Twiss' had such a full table on Christmas Day.

After they had cleaned up after their meal, the family played parlour games, as was their tradition. Tilly nearly wet herself laughing when during charades, Freddy was trying to get everyone to guess a book he had read at school before the holidays…The Tale of Mrs. Tiggy-Winkle.

During the afternoon, everyone grazed on the leftover food. There was no meal served that night, everyone was too full. But at 7:00 pm, they ended Christmas Day with a game of Hunt the Thimble, before everyone either made their way home, or went to bed with a full stomach and exhausted after such a wonderfully busy and happy day.

7

On the cold and windy morning of the 6th of January, Tilly's heartbroken family waved her off from the Tilbury Docks. The disconsolate daughter and mother wept into her handkerchief, not knowing when she would see her loved ones again. She waved to her son and blew him kisses, calling out how much she loved and would miss him as the ship sailed from port…

CHAPTER NINETEEN

Adulterous Pleasure is Anarchy to Domestic Bliss

The dark and thunderous clouds welcoming Tilly on her arrival in Sydney on the 9th of February, matched her mood. She had misplaced her trust in her husband, but the fact that he had used her girls as bargaining chips and almost sent her broke, were betrayals she could not forgive.

When she arrived at Circular Quay, she set her trunks down on the edge of the kerb as she waited for a taxi.

"Where to madam?" The driver asked.

"335 Malabar Road, Maroubra, thank you, cabbie." Tilly politely answered.

"Good oh."

When she arrived at the house, Tilly noticed female clothing alongside Jim's on the clothesline. A suffocating feeling of dread overcame her. She handed the cabbie a ten-pound note after he placed her trunks near the front steps and told him to keep the change.

Generally, Tilly was impulsive, but this time it was her marriage at stake. Uneasily, she looked toward the front door. Then, taking a deep breath Tilly took a few steps toward the house, stopping when she thought she heard the sound of a woman's laughter. Closing her eyes and swallowing, she mounted the steps to her home, retrieved the front door key from her handbag and with a trembling hand, she inserted it into the lock.

Upon entering the living room, she was disgusted to find her normally orderly home defiled by discarded clothes, dirty dishes, glasses, empty bottles of alcohol and overfull ashtrays which were strewn everywhere. On her once highly polished Edwardian dining table, was residue of white powder and stains from spilt drinks.

Enraged, Tilly threw her handbag on the settee and stormed into her bedroom, only to find Jim involved in a sex act with a blonde woman. The look of astonishment on their faces would have made Tilly laugh in any other circumstances, but this was *her* home, *her* husband, and *her* bed.

"Get the fuck out orf 'ere, you fuckin' 'ore! Who the fuck do you think you are fuckin' my 'usband! I'll fuckin' run my blade right through your guts and cut out your fuckin' cunt!" Tilly roared before grabbing Anna by the hair and dragging her to the floor.

Anna was no match against a streetfighter like Tilly. Jim knew she would kill her and probably him if he didn't act quickly. Opening the drawer to his nightstand, he pulled out a pistol and pointed it at his wife. "Get the fuck away from her, you mad fuckin' bitch! Touch her again and I'll put a bullet through your thick skull!"

Tilly stopped and took a step back. Tears burned her eyes s hurt was she that her husband had taken the side of another woman over her. "You and this 'ore can get the fuck out of MY 'ouse before I shoot the fuckin' both orf you!"

"You lost this house as soon as you took off to fuckin' England!" Jim bellowed as he chased after Tilly threatening to fill her head with lead.

Jim jumped out of bed and grabbed his coat that was hung over the back of the chair at Tilly's dressing table and stormed toward his wife. Fearing fir her life, Tilly raced out of the bedroom, frantically screaming out for help. Upon hearing her terrified screams, her neighbour rang the police and was speaking to an officer as four shots rang out, echoing through the telephone. The policeman told the woman that they were on their way and to remain inside her house.

Tilly stumbled, breaking the left heel of her brand-new stilettos as escaped to the garage. Her heartbeat quickened when she heard Jim cursing after treading on the nearby bindies in their yard nearby.

For the first time in a long time, Tilly prayed to God that the police would get to her before a bullet from Jim's pistol did. Afraid of being cornered, she left by the door at the back of the garage. As she headed toward the house, she saw Anna with bag in hand, dressed in her underwear and petticoat, and jumping over the side fence. "Yeah, you'd better run, and keep on fuckin' runnin', you fuckin' 'ore!"

When she turned around, Tilly saw Jim barging through the garage door before two more shots rang out. One bullet was so close that it skimmed the edge of her hat. "You fuckin' stupid bastard, you could 'ave fuckin' killed me!" Tilly shrieked.

"I'll more than fuckin' kill you when I reload my fuckin' gun! You know I've gotten away with murder enough times and I will again! The cops will consider your death a fuckin' mercy killin!" Jim growled as he followed Tilly up the back stairs into the house in a murderous rage.

Four cars loaded with police arrived. Two officers tackled Jim, disarming him of the gun and a straight razor they found in his coat pocket. Two constables arrested him, then after manacling him, placed him in their car. The detectives that had arrived late to the scene, accompanied a shaken Tilly to the settee.

Tilly gave the detectives a statement about what had occurred. When one asked who the woman was, she replied, "I've never seen the fuckin' 'ore before, and she'd better 'ope that I never see 'er again!"

Twelve months of peace, relaxation, and unconditional love within her family environs was the antithesis of the austere and unpleasant atmosphere of the courtroom where Tilly found herself less than three hours after her return to Australian shores.

Dressed in a black dress, black hat and a stone-marten fur at her throat, Tilly's apparel matched her sombre mood. She sat behind the prosecution's table in the crowded gallery as Jim entered the courtroom alongside his solicitor, Mr. W. Sheahan. He cast a glance and a nervous half smile toward Tilly. She glowered at her him in return and turned away to face the bench.

Devine was surprised that his wife had dogged him to the police over a lover's tiff. He had let Anna go, and to Jim she was one of the best fucks he'd had since he first screwed Tilly in the laneway at the Strand. He had fallen in love with Anna, but she couldn't make him the money that Tilly could. Being good in bed is one thing but being good in bed and making money was more important to Jim, and Tilly was talented in both essentials.

The police prosecutor, Sergeant Napper approached his desk and smiled derisively toward Devine. He then looked back at Tilly to make sure she was still on the law's side this time. Her stern and determined nod was the only confirmation he required.

As Mr. Williams, S.M. made his way to the bench and cast an eye towards Devine as he took his seat, briefly shaking his head. After everyone was seated the magistrate asked for the hearing to proceed.

"It is alleged," Sergeant Napper the police prosecutor stated, "that at ten o'clock this morning, Mrs. Devine returned to her home, and found the defendant in her marital bed with another woman. Hot words passed, and a fight ensued. Several neighbours called the police after hearing a woman screaming for help and numerous shots fired. It is alleged Devine fired a military revolver at his wife. Later, when arrested, the pistol was removed from Devine as well as a straight razor that a constable found inside his coat pocket. He stands before you on the charge of attempted murder."

Kate Leigh who was in court on another matter, spotted the Devines in the courtroom and couldn't pass the opportunity of witnessing the courtroom drama. When Mr. Williams mentioned bail, Sergeant Napper said that it was a matter for the Bench but added that Mrs. Devine had informed him she was afraid her husband would shoot her. After the prosecutor made that statement, all eyes, including Leigh's, were upon Tilly. They too saw that she did indeed look afraid.

"We have a complete answer to the charge," Mr. W. Sheahan. "The facts are that Mrs. Devine only recently returned from England, and during her absence Devine employed a housekeeper. It was because of this woman's presence in the house that there was an altercation. We deny that Mr. Devine and the woman were in bed together and that any shots were fired deliberately at Mrs. Devine, and we undertake no attempt will be made to interfere with her. We say the whole trouble is due to her jealousy. The shot, if any, was fired into the air, and was done to pacify her."

Every now and then the judge would throw a stern frown toward Tilly whenever she scoffed or laughed throughout Mr. Sheahan's response to the charges. However, Mr. Williams had to admit to himself after reading the evidence, that Devine's defence was shifty and remanded him until the 16th of February on two hundred pounds bail.

When Jim sheepishly entered the Maroubra house that afternoon, he found Tilly on her hands and knees on the floor, scrubbing her Persian carpet.

"Tilly, I would never have fuckin' shot you." He claimed as he skulked into the living room.

"Bull fuckin' shit! You were after my blood. You took the side orf your fuckin' slut over me, your wife! I'll never forgive you for that! I 'ave stuck by you thick and thin James Devine. I turned the other fuckin' cheek when you fucked all those other 'ores because you always came 'ome to me! This time you brought the rubbish *into* my 'ome and into *my fuckin' bed*! You can fuckin' go and buy me a new bed and fuckin' mattress. I don't want to catch whatever that filthy bitch has got!"

"I was hiring her as a housekeeper, and she caught me in a weak moment. You know I'll never leave you!"

"A 'ousekeeper polishing your cock with 'er cunt! Do you think I'm fuckin' stupid!"

"I woke up and found her on fuckin' top of me. It just happened before you arrived. She put something in the snow! I was knocked out most of the night!"

"I don't believe a fuckin' word you say, and if you know what's good for you, you'd get the fuck out of this 'ouse so I can clean up after your fuckin' 'ousekeeper's mess!"

"Till, you can't have me charged. I'll do gaol time for this. I don't know what got into me. I had a lot of snow last night. You know I'd never shoot you! C'mere and let me make it up to you." Devine pleaded.

"You play with your fuckin' gun more than you do your cock. You won't be layin' your 'ands on me again!"

"Tilly, we've been married since you were sixteen. You know you don't want me to leave. It's just your green-eyed monster rearing its ugly head." Jim grovelled as he reached out to touch his wife.

Tilly pulled her cutthroat razor from her apron pocket. "You lay a fuckin' finger on me and you'll lose the fuckin' thing! You can fuck orf with your fancy lady for all I fuckin' care, but before you do, I want every fuckin' piece of jewellery you pawned and every fuckin' penny owed to me from my 'ouses returned! You thievin' fuckin' cunt! Now fuck orf!"

Jim's face went deathly white. He was unaware Tilly knew about the jewellery or the money. He surmised that she had been corresponding with her girls whilst she was in England to have knowledge of the information. Knowing her vicious temper, he made a hasty retreat to the Tradesman's Arms to work out how to get back into his wife's good graces.

The following afternoon, Sid McDonald arrived at the Maroubra house on the behest of Jim. He spread the jewellery and silver out on the polished dining table. While Tilly was sorting through her precious jewels, Sid grabbed a bottle of beer from the green Healing refrigerator and sat at the table, placing it in front of him.

"You've lived 'ere and know the fuckin' rules. Get the fuckin' bottle orf my table!"

"Sorry, Till. Listen, Jimbo's sorry for what he did, but that's none of my business, and I told him that I'm not gettin' involved in your marital problems. But have you thought about how this will affect you with the other gangs? You're as tough as nails, the toughest woman I've ever met, and I admit to being shit scared of you. Together you and Jim are strong, divided… who the fuck knows what the other gangs will do. That fuckin' Leigh bitch is already sprouting off that she'll soon be the queen of the underworld and she'll have you gone in weeks."

"That fuckin' flounder faced wench wouldn't want to start anything, or she'll end up in the back of a butcher's truck! You tell Jim to come over tomorrow morning. I'll talk to 'im then. Now get out orf 'ere, I've got things to do."

On the 16th of February, the charges against James Devine were discharged. Tilly refused to testify.

7

Upon inspecting her properties, Tilly was overwhelmed with disappointment to see how rundown the brothels had become since she left and the sorry state of the few remaining girls. Most of the women she'd employed since she first set up Palmer Street had left. A majority of those who had remained had previously only ever serviced punters in the laneway for a quickie.

As always, she was quick to put her money into action. Tilly brought in an army of unemployed builders, painters and cleaners who got straight into repairing each of the houses. She then went out on a shopping spree throughout various department stores for soft furnishings, linens, new beds, and furniture.

Before the brothels were ready to operate again, Tilly employed prostitutes of every age and background. Seasoned streetwalkers, tired of receiving consorting warnings, decided to work for Tilly instead of paying most of their earnings in fines and bribes.

Tilly had the reputation amongst the prostitutes as a benevolent madam. They knew if they did their job properly, she would protect and look after them. They had also heard that if they did her wrong, they would be lucky to survive her wrath.

Overwhelmed by the number of women seeking to work in her brothels, Tilly was able to pick and choose who she hired. Those who had children and were unsuccessful she gave them five pounds to help feed their family.

7

The feud between Tilly and Kate was reignited over a dog in February. Leigh had found a lost King Charles Spaniel and knew that well pedigreed dogs were worth good money. In a pretence of a truce, Kate telephoned Tilly and asked her if she would like to buy him, telling her that she had paid eight pounds for the champion dog. Tilly told her to send her driver over with the dog, and if he was good looking enough, she'd pay five pounds for him. Leigh agreed with the deal and gave her new lover, Jack Baker, the dog to ferry over to her arch nemesis.

Tilly immediately fell for the young dog and told Baker to wait at the door, returning a few minutes later with five pounds. Baker thanked her, and Tilly closed the door without uttering a word.

Two days later, after her newly purchased pedigreed dog, Herbert, rolled in horse manure and Tilly gave him a bath. To her surprise, the water suddenly became a milky colour and Herbert was almost all brown! "That fuckin' cunt of a bitch! She fuckin' painted 'erbert!"

Jim rushed into the bathroom thinking something was wrong and had to refrain from laughing.

"Look what that slut did! She painted white patches on 'erbert!" Tilly yelled while the poor dog cowered in fear.

"I'll take him back and get your money and then some." Jim offered.

"I'm not sending the poor sod back to that fuckin' callous bitch! 'e can stay 'ere with me." Tilly mewled as she kissed and cuddled Herbert.

The following weekend while Tilly was talking over the fence with Shirley, her neighbour, she learned that a six-year-old girl was looking for her lost King Charles Spaniel named Daney. Tilly wondered if Herbert was the lost dog. Not believing in coincidences, she asked Shirley the young girl's name and address, and once she received it, she went inside and told Jim about it.

When Tilly learned that the little girl attended primary school at Sacred Heart in Darlinghurst, she immediately knew that the dog came from a fine home that had a little girl who was missing him. She placed Daney in a box with a blanket, "Jim, take this sweet little boy over to that bitch's 'ouse and make sure she take's 'im back. I'll go over to little Ursula's 'ome and let her know I've found 'er missing puppy." Tilly directed.

Ursula was over the moon when Tilly told her that she knew the whereabouts of her Daney and hugged the surprised brothel madam in thanks. Ursula's mother told her that her daughter had barely slept and refused to go to school since Daney had disappeared.

Tilly looked down at the little girl and patted her on her head, "Lovey, 'ere, take this and buy a collar and lead for your Daney and some good meat from the butchers. Keep 'im inside and you tell old Tilly 'ere if 'e ever goes missing again."

"Look Mum, ten pounds! I've never had ten pounds before!" Ursula squealed as she showed her mother the money.

"Thank you, Mrs. Devine, for your kindness. Ursula is incredibly happy."

Ursula's mother drove her daughter to Leigh's Riley Street house and stood beside her daughter as she knocked on the door. When Leigh answered, the brave and determined six-year-old said: "You've got my dog! I want him back and sixpence or I'm going to the police!" Kate immediately scuttled off inside and returned with Daney, handing him to Ursula in the box with the blanket and ball Jim delivered him with, as well as a pound note.

Tilly was across the street sitting at the wheel of her new 1931 Ford Model A Sports Phaeton car and watched Ursula in action. She giggled to herself to see Leigh move so quickly and being afraid of a six-year-old child.

7

On the 19th of December, Tilly was in a rush to vote. Worried that Prime Minister Scullin would be voted out of power, she advised her girls to vote for him, as well as anyone she could stop in the streets.

"Get your arse movin' Jimmy. I want to get down to vote for the best prime minister there will ever be!" Tilly called from the back door to hurry her husband who was mowing the lawn.

"Settle down. The booths don't shut for fuckin' hours yet woman!" Jim impatiently replied.

Almost an hour later, Tilly and Jim were on their way to the polling booths at the Maroubra Soldiers Memorial Hall. As they made their way in, Tilly wished the local Labor representative luck, and told the others to "fuck orf" whenever they approached her to hand her a leaflet about their candidate.

Later that night, with a glass of champagne in hand, Tilly was mortified as she listened to the election results on the radio and learned that the incumbent Australian Labor Party were defeated in a landslide victory by the United Australia Party.

"Fuckin' turncoat Joseph Lyons got in! Scullin's the scapegoat because those fuckin' dumb arse Americans caused the Depression! 'ow stupid are Australians to fall for the bullshit from this bastard, Lyons! 'onest fuckin' Joe my arse!" Tilly grumbled as she downed her champagne in commiseration for Scullin.

7

On the 6th of February 1932, with her blood pulsing and heart racing, Tilly stormed into the *Truth* newspaper office battering the receptionist with a tsunami of words about Kate Leigh. She then unceremoniously demanded an appointment with the editor.

"I 'ave a complaint and 'e's the only person who can 'elp me."

"Excuse me, madam, but you need an appointment to see the editor, he is a very busy man," the receptionist explained.

"Lovey, 'e'll want to see me. Tell 'im Tilly Devine's 'ere!" Before the receptionist could leave her seat, Tilly bustled past her desk, past the typing pool and the messenger boys sitting along their bench, and headed straight into the editor's office, catching him mid sip of his cup of tea.

"I want to speak to you about that two-legged bitch, fuckin' Kate Leigh! 'Ave you 'eard what she's been saying in court about me? In court mind you. The fuckin' nerve orf 'er!" Tilly almost shrieked as the editor attempted to mop the spilt tea from his tie with his handkerchief. "She's appealing against her sentence for consorting. That bloody solicitor orf 'ers said in a packed courtroom, that a certain underworld woman… meaning *ME*, 'ad been given a chance to go to England after being convicted for consorting. Let me tell you as I am standing right 'ere in your office, I was never convicted of consorting!" Tilly robustly declared as she pulled her large black hat from her head, placed it on the desk and promptly plopped herself in a chair.

"Mrs. Devine, I'm not privy to the court records, nor to Mrs. Barry's testimony, let alone know who has been charged with consorting. Please excuse my ignorance but isn't it the solicitor's duty to bring up precedence of law?" The flailing editor stated.

"Not when that bloody law makes a lie out of what I did. I was never deported. I told the magistrate that I would return to England and come back. I went to my parents' 'ome, and I'm back 'ere now. I did what I promised. It's over twelve months ago that all this 'appended!" Tilly adamantly insisted. "Why for the love orf God bring it all up now!"

"I think it's just a simple case of her solicitor putting her case forward the best way he can to reach an agreeable solution other than imprisonment."

"Listen, I'm not like 'er. I'm not a bad woman. I'm not like Leigh, in any way. I might drink and swear and 'ave a run in with the police now and then, but I don't take dope, and no-one can say I 'ave ruined young girls. Leigh does all this and more. I'm a lady, I am." Tilly imperiously asserted. "I can talk with the best people in Sydney. You might be the Editor of *Truth*, but I 'ave as much education as you, probably more in the businesses I'm involved in. I certainly know more about the truth orf life than you and anyone who works at the *Truth* newspaper! I can tell you this, if someone throws rocks at me, fuck, I'll find a 'and grenade and throw it in return!"

The following day, the headlines read, 'K-K-Katey. You're the Only Girl That I Abhor!' TILLY DEVINE 'LEIGHS' DOWN THE LAW TO 'TRUTH'

CHAPTER TWENTY

Sustaining the Great Depression

Due to the continuing financial depression, Sydney suffered the highest number of unemployed and it wasn't long before the domino effect of retrenchments began. Evictions due to failure to pay rent or mortgages, forced penniless families to relocate to humpy towns. Fathers scavenged corrugated iron, timber, cardboard, and hessian flour bags to build makeshift shacks that lined the sand dunes of Happy Valley in La Perouse. The land was leased by the New South Wales Golf Club, who allowed the families to use the area for shelter.

To make their new 'homes' weatherproof, the humpy tenants painted the flourbags with a mixture of lime and fat boiled up in saltwater. They were used as walls, while the corrugated iron served as roofing and the sandy floor was covered with flour bags or cardboard.

Donations were left for the disenfranchised at the camp's 'trading post' where they were distributed amongst the families. Happy Valley was a well-organised and close-knit community. The residents had formed a committee to assist one another in constructing the humpies and fairly distributing the donated food and clothing. Local Chinese market gardeners, fishermen, and grocers donated leftover produce. The city Dairy Farmers Co-operative gave the camp sixteen gallons of milk each day.

Over the following months, humpy towns were also established on vacant crown lands at Brighton-le-Sands, Rockdale, and Long Bay.

Indigenous women suffered greatly throughout the Depression. Unlike white Australian mothers, they were ineligible for the New South Wales Government's child endowment, which was paid to mothers with children under the age of fourteen years of age. They also didn't qualify for the Australian Government's maternity allowance, due to being unrecognised as Australians due the racist 'White Australia' policy.

Happy Valley and Long Bay had a predominately high occupation of our Indigenous families. During the hard times, they were no different to the white families who had found themselves disenfranchised from their pre-depression lives. In fact, they were invaluable to their white counterparts in assisting them with living such a life where they were on the fringes of society and starving.

The Depression hadn't made much of a difference in Tilly's brothel earnings. She was still making good money, however, for the likes of Kate Leigh, the Depression had hit them hard, forcing the closure of many sly groggeries and illegal gambling dens. The falling economy also made cocaine affordable only to the wealthy, culling a large proportion of Sydney drug dealers.

Tilly felt guilty that she was still able to live a normal life, while many around her were struggling to feed their kids, let alone themselves. She was also aware that mothers were going without so their kids could eat what little food they could manage to buy.

Twice a week, she sent her men to buy fruit and vegetables from orchards and farm owners to distribute to local families. Every Monday and Friday, Tilly served soup to the endless lines of people that queued outside Circular Quay, waiting to collect the 'Susso'—dole payment and food coupons. On Thursdays and Sundays, she and several of her girls would leave crates of vegetables, milk and personal hygiene needs at the Happy Valley trading post.

7

The 19th of March 1932 was the grand opening of the Harbour Bridge. The construction of the magnificent span had been the saving grace for many families during the Great Depression, earning itself the nickname 'the Iron Lung'. At the time, the Sydney Harbour Bridge was the largest single span arch bridge in the world.

It was a spectacular and important event that for one day, the people of Sydney could forget about the Depression. Tilly was hoping to rub shoulders with the Honourable J.T. Lang, M.L.A., Premier of New South Wales, who would cut the ceremonial ribbon to officially open the Harbour Bridge.

An ardent Labor voter, Tilly was impressed by what Lang had achieved in the short amount of time he had been Premier. Although she fussed and gushed over the royal family, at her core, Tilly was a socialist. She and around seven hundred and fifty thousand people excitedly waited for Jack Lang to cut the long white ribbon that spanned across the width of the bridge.

With a pair of gold scissors in his extended right hand, the Premier approached the ribbon, when suddenly a man in military uniform charged toward him astraddle a chestnut thoroughbred horse. Bringing down his ceremonial sword, the interloper slashed the ribbon, proclaiming, "decent citizens of New South Wales, I declare this bridge open!" He then turned the horse around and faced the dozen police officers standing not more than twelve feet away and shouted: "I am a King's officer, stand back, don't interfere with me."

Enraged by the effrontery of the dissident soldier, Tilly along with all who witnessed the event, jeered and abused the horseman as police rushed toward the encroacher.

Superintendent William MacKay, officer in charge of the CIB, was the first to reach the rider. He grabbed hold of the man's waist and forcefully removed him from his horse while a uniformed officer held tightly onto the horse's reins. The dissenter fell onto the road before McKay aggressively pulled him up and hauled him away.

The ribbon was expeditiously re-joined and moments later, Premiere Jack Lang cut it in two, officially opening and naming the spanning arch of iron and metal, the Sydney Harbour Bridge. The crowd cheered and clapped as a twenty-one-gun salute and a RAAF flypast followed the momentous occasion. An armada of passenger ships, privately owned boats and yachts blew their horns, joining in on the festivities as they sailed below the newly opened bridge.

After the bridge opening, speeches were made by the Governor of New South Wales, Sir Philip Game and the Minister for Public Works, Lawrence Ennis which was followed by a possession of decorated floats. The public were then permitted to walk along the deck of the bridge which was an honour for all who had taken advantage of the opportunity.

The fascist subversive was later identified as Irish born Francis De Groot, a leader in the right-wing paramilitary group called the New

Guard. After his arrest, he was escorted to Callum Park for observation and evaluation. When he was proven to be sane, De Groot was re-arrested for offensive behaviour.

7

Early on the morning of the 5th of April, Tilly was at her hairdressers having her hair done so she would appear at the courthouse looking her best. Sally had opened the salon early for her special and generous client. However, Tilly's court attendance was an inconsequential detail to her. Her plan for being at the courthouse that day surrounded a certain nationalist insurgent who was also appearing at court that morning. She was hoping the newspaper cameramen would be covering the court hearing as she planned to put on a good show for them!

Whilst Sally was adding the final touch to her kiss curls, Tilly's mouth dropped open when she overheard an important newscast—Phar Lap had died from colic in America the day before. The radio announcer gravely stated that the vets tried hard to save the racing champion's life, but he succumbed to the illness. Her tears fell when the commentator revealed that upon the death of his beloved charge, his strapper, Tommy Woodcock threw his arms around Phar Lap's neck and needed to be dragged away from the horse.

"The fuckin' Yanks did it! They killed the best racing "orse in the world! Jealous bastards!" Tilly exclaimed.

7

On his way to court on the 5th of April, Francis De Groot, surrounded by throngs of people, had the misfortune to literally run into Tilly Devine. I'm sure the paramilitarian would have much preferred to face a pit full of venomous snakes instead of the rebellious and wrathful brothel queen. "Are you De Groot?" Tilly asked, and when he answered in the affirmative, she prodded him in the chest with her right index finger. "You ought to be denounced! You are from the New Guard Nationalist basher gang. You cut the ribbon so Lang couldn't! Wait until the Nationalists get back in, you'll starve then! You are too much of an elitist to give a dying man a feed! I wish your wife were 'ere, I'd give 'er a good go too!"

The quickly gathering crowd witnessing the discourse, cheered in agreement with Tilly. Included in the throng was a newspaper reporter from the daily Telegraph. The police waited until Tilly's tirade of abuse had finished before escorting the stunned De Groot into court.

Tilly attended her court appointment and was granted bail after she appealed against her six months gaol sentence for consorting. She thanked the court and then rushed to the courtroom where De Groot's matter was about to begin.

Appearing before Mr. Laidlaw on charges of maliciously damaging a ceremonial ribbon that was the property of the NSW government and causing damage of excess of two pounds and behaving in an offensive manner at the junction of Bradfield Highway and the Sydney Harbour Bridge. The police also added a further charge of using threatening words to Stuart R. London when stating, "I am a King's officer, stand back, don't you interfere with me". De Groot pleaded not guilty to all charges.

During the court proceedings, she listened as De Groot testified that he opposed Lang's leftist policies and was resentful that a member of the Royal Family had not been asked to officiate at the opening the bridge. He said that he was not a member of the regular army and he wore his uniform to blend in with the real cavalry. He was fined five pounds on a charge for offensive behaviour in a public place.

Tilly didn't have a chance to have another go at the xenophobic paramilitarian, his solicitor had paid a court clerk to clear the way for him to escape the courthouse via a back entrance.

After a successful appeal, De Groot's conviction was reversed. De Groot then instructed his Barrister, Mr. Charles Aubrey Hardwick to serve a writ upon the Commissioner of Police for wrongful arrest. The legal action was decided in De Groot's favour and he was awarded an undisclosed out of court settlement.

7

In August whilst Tilly was shopping in Glebe, Jim came upon an illegal SP betting business that was set up in a well-fortified garage. He was surprised that the cops hadn't raided the place with it not being as inconspicuous as he would have made it. At first, the doorman thought Jim was a detective due to his size, but when he told the man who he was, he was immediately granted entry.

Due to the unaffordability of cocaine, Jim was looking for another moneymaking scheme, and felt he'd happened upon one. He played close attention to the way the bookie was running the betting shop and decided that he'd establish one himself. Jim knew the top cops already on the take would ensure their police officers would turn a blind eye to his gambling shop.

He spoke to Tilly about establishing the business during the car trip home and asked if she could loan him the money to set up.

"I ain't lending you no money. You fuckin' pilfered enough from me when I was 'ome with our son. I'll go into partnership with you. But there's conditions, Jimmy."

"Jesus woman! How much do you fuckin' want?"

"You can lose the attitude, or I won't fuckin' 'elp you at all! Don't think because I let you back into my 'ouse and bed, that I've forgotten what you did!"

"Just what the fuck do you want?"

"Thirty percent orf the earnings, and you donate five percent orf it to St. Vincent De Paul. There's no negotiation with this, James."

Devine knew that when his wife called him James, she meant business and wouldn't waver no matter what he offered, unless it was a higher percentage, of course. "It's a deal," he sullenly replied.

The following Tuesday, Tilly purchased a fruit shop in Oxford Street and Jim set about establishing his SP business above the shop. Within the first week, four phones were connected to both the fruit shop and the flat upstairs. In the flat, six tables and chairs soon lined the living room. Each table was topped with a telephone and radio. Jim told the owner of the Tradesman's Arms hotel to discreetly advise the punters that drank at the pub that he would be operating the SP shop from the following Monday.

Tilly, aware that she had more clout with the police than Jim, set up a meeting with two of her pocket policemen. In a seedy and urine stinking alley, she told the cops to let the word out that police who placed bets through her betting shop would receive a two percent increase on any winnings. This offer insured the safety of the Devines' SP bookmaker business.

Knowing there were gamblers that visited her girls, told them to recommend Jim's bookmaking business to them. She then contacted her gang members and told them to also get the word out.

Tilly drew up a book for Jim to write the names and phone numbers of the shop's clients. This way he or one of his men could contact everyone with access to a telephone to place their bets. Tilly's henchmen were on call if the need arose for muscle to obtain money from losing punters. It also gave Jim the means to obtain information about on-course prices and to place a wager with other bookmakers to reduce his liability on certain races, or to cover his bets by bet-backing with the other bookmakers if he over committed.

The fruit shop below the SP business wasn't forgotten. Tilly paid several of her workers a pound a day to rotate shifts as salesgirls. Four of the women told Tilly if they could make a wage at the fruit shop, they would give up prostitution and work in the shop instead. It suited Tilly to hire them on as staff, bringing in new girls always meant more money in the brothel business. Having her girls in the fruit shop also furnished her with spies that could keep an eye on the comings and goings upstairs.

Within the first three months of operating, the betting shop had brought in over two thousand pounds. Punters who couldn't afford to pay a shilling tram fare to the track, found it more convenient to place the bets through the phone at their local pub or at the shop.

7

Kate Leigh was in her early fifties and due to the financial depression, she had been forced to shut down her brothels and two of her groggeries.

Tilly, on the other hand, was still making money and the SP betting shop was bringing in thousands of pounds. And with the Great Depression easing off, Tilly's brothel income started increasing. In fact, her finances were so healthy, that in late December 1933, Tilly purchased a further two properties which she set up as brothels. One house, she cheekily opened on the outskirts of Kate Leigh's turf. She wasn't concerned about any threat of retribution.

Due to the establishment of illegal off course betting shops, the attendance at the racecourses and on-course betting had more than halved. The illegal betting shops had also decimated the finances of the jockey clubs and the tax earnings for the New South Wales government. The phenomenal losses forced the Australian Jockey Club to apply pressure on the police and local political parties to rid the state of illegal SP betting shops. Their complaints brought about the formation of a special SP squad and almost four thousand arrests were made within the first two years of its inauguration. These arrests made history in the police annuls. Gambling offences outnumbered all other arrests for the first time in New South Wales' history.

The Devines' fruit shop/SP gambling establishment was never visited by the police, except those there for the purpose of placing bets.

7

In February 1934, Tilly and Jim decided to leave for a holiday to Melbourne. They left the SP business in the capable hands of Sid McDonald. The Devines had only been in Melbourne for less than seventy-two hours when trouble caught up with Jim. At loose ends, while Tilly was visiting a few of her former prostitutes, Jim decided to pay a visit to the Palestine Club, an illegal gaming house. During his game, a fight broke out when Jim accused one of the dealers of taking a card from the bottom of the deck. The dealer, taking umbrage to the accusation, reached across the table and punched Devine at the side of his head. Enraged, Jim grabbed him by the throat and punching the dealer hard that he knocked him unconscious. Suddenly experiencing a sharp pain at the back of his head, Jim spun around and was struck again by a cricket bat before falling to the floor alongside his victim. When he regained consciousness, Jim found himself lying in the gutter about fifty yards away from the club.

Tilly's stay wasn't without problems either. She was in Carlton visiting Dolly Quinn, they were discussing the upcoming royal visit of the Duke of Gloucester. Tilly had just finished saying that she had read in the newspaper that the Duke could be part of the centenary celebrations when the police broke their way through the front door. When one of the constables told Dolly that they were there to raid the brothel, Tilly shook her head and whispered to herself: "Orf all the fuckin' dumb luck for me to be in the wrong place at the wrong fuckin' time!" Ten minutes later, manacled alongside Dolly, Tilly was charged with administering a brothel.

When she appeared at the Carlton Courthouse, Tilly pleaded her innocence. She urged Judge Hauser to understand that the police had got it wrong. She explained that she was visiting from New South Wales and had no idea that the house was a brothel. Her eyes glistened with tears as she told the court that she had applied for a room to rent in the house and Dolly Quinn was the lovely landlady.

Hauser wasn't persuaded by Tilly's acting ability and sentenced her to twelve months gaol. Dolly received six months imprisonment after pleading guilty. Tilly requested bail so she could appeal against the sentence and was released on one hundred pounds bail.

Tilly had no intention of waiting in Melbourne for the appeal. She visited Dolly in prison, who was most apologetic for getting her in trouble. Always the prolific gift giver, Tilly gave her friend several blocks of chocolate, biscuits, perfume, and peppermints and told her to visit her one day in the 'Loo.

That afternoon the Devines scarpered back to Sydney.

7

The week before the arrival of the royal prince, Tilly was in a tizz of excitement. An avid royalist, she wanted to look her best in case she was close enough to meet the Duke of Gloucester. She spent the entire week shopping for outfits, shoes, and jewellery, sending both Jim and Sid McDonald crazy driving her from boutique to boutique looking for the perfect frock. The day before the prince was due to arrive in Sydney, Tilly attended her salon for a manicured and to have her hair styled.

Six hours later, happy with her hair and nails, Tilly paid Sally and left for her car to find Sid asleep in the driver's seat. She tapped him on the shoulder to wake him before heading back to her Maroubra home.

The morning of the royal visit, Tilly fussed and swore as she tried on frock after frock, finally selecting a blue dress that was a slightly lighter colour than her blue percher ostrich feather hat. Then after sliding rings on every finger and clasping her sapphire and diamond necklace, Tilly pulled on her powder blue gloves and made her way to her car.

As they headed into the city, Tilly asked Sid to drive her as close to Martin Place as he could. Once she was nearby, Tilly climbed out of the car and pushed her way through the crowds to be close enough to the Cenotaph to see the prince.

The royal possession made its way from Farm Cove where the prince had arrived aboard the *HMS Sussex* and continued their way to Martin Square. Tilly excitedly waved her British flag and called out a welcome to the prince as he strode along the pathway to the monument. "Did you see that? The prince nodded and smiled at me!" Tilly said as she nudged the woman standing to her right. She then continued cheering along with the crowd as the prince laid a wreath at the Cenotaph. He then walked over and spoke with widows, mothers, and orphans of fallen soldiers, thanking them for coming out to see him on such a hot day.

As Prince Henry and Premier, Bertram Stevens, made their way to their cars, Tilly hustled, bustled, and pushed her way through the crowds to meet Sid to drive her to the next stop. Upon her arrival at Macquarie Street, Tilly again elbowed her way through the crowds before pushing her way through to the barricades. It took a little while for the slow-moving royal cavalcade get there, but when it did, Tilly gushed and cheered as the car holding His Royal Highness slowly drove by on his way to Government House.

As soon as the gates to Government House closed, Tilly once again rushed to her car and told Sid to drive her home so she could change. After a little over ten minutes of procrastinating, she finally decided to wear her black silk and chiffon evening dress. She hoped the diamantés and crystal beading around the neckline would glisten in the sun and garner the prince's attention once more. She ruffled the ruched sleeves a little, stepped into her new black leather pumps, and then with a quick tidy up of her hair around her beautiful black velvet and tan mink hat she brought back with her from England, Tilly was ready to go.

Randwick was a sea of colour with ladies wearing fashionable colourful gowns and hats when she arrived. She realised that almost half of Sydney had the same idea as she had and arrived early to get a glimpse of the prince's arrival. Tilly had paid a premium price to sit in the VIP stands and felt like royalty herself when she took her seat. When she saw Sid walking along the grass at front of the stands, Tilly waved down to him. She watched as he showed the steward his ticket before being admitted and gladly accepted the glass of champagne, he had waited in line for such a long time to buy. After taking a few sips of her champagne, Tilly told Sid to put his beer down and go and place ten pounds bets on horses five, seven and two in the first, second and third races, and fifty pounds each on Peter Pan and Oro in the Duke of Gloucester Plate.

His Royal Highness arrived and was greeted by his host and the Randwick Race committee. After the obligatory waves and smiles to the crowds, the royal entourage made their way to the luncheon area which was only a stone's throw from where Tilly sat. This time the brothel madam was a lot more sedate. The last thing she wanted was to embarrass herself, her birthland and the prince, and be thrown out of the racecourse.

The horses were lining up ready to race in the Duke of Gloucester Plate. Tilly along with thousands of others, and the Prince Royal, waited with bated breath for the race to begin.

The starter pistol blasted, and the horses were off! The crowd cheered their horses on, Tilly watched the race intently, not knowing which of her chosen horses to cheer for. Six furlongs from the finish, she screamed out that a jockey was riding Peter Pan along the rails. Sid tapped her on the arm and made a sidelong glance toward the Prince, gently reminding his boss that they were in close proximity of royalty. Tilly nodded and sat back on her seat. Peter Pan was trapped by the rider on Magnitas. The brothel madam wanted to vent her rage but knew she must mind her manners. Other people surrounding her were also grumbling about the treatment of the favourite, some cursing, others demanding an inquiry.

The race continued and Oro was in the lead, speeding forth like a locomotive in fourth place. At the fourth furlong, he was hemmed in for a few seconds, but his jockey wrangled him out of the trap at an easy pace. With a furlong to go and the finish line in sight, Pratt gave Oro's his head. Magnitas still hadn't recovered from the check at the rails. Oro surged forward, responding to the whip and beat Mr. Kerry by a nose and running the mile and a half race in the course record time of 2.29, a half second faster than the previous record held by Clever Fox.

Tilly watched in awe as the prince spoke to Pratt, the jockey who rode Oro. The Prince Royal then presented the gold cup to the horse's owner, Mr. Hunter White, who, along with the trainer, J King and Pratt all held the cup in the air as a sign of victory.

While listening to the news on the radio later that night, Tilly heard that R. Carter, the rider of Magnitas was later suspended from racing for interference to Peter Pan during the Duke of Gloucester Plate. "The fuckin' bastard should orf been!"

CHAPTER TWENTY ONE

Battle of the Femme Fatale Bosses

Tilly and Kate Leigh had many things in common, they had both dragged themselves out of a life of poverty to become queens of Sydney's underworld. They had also spent time in prison, fronting court and operating illegal businesses. And they shared another interest, they doted on their precious Pomeranians.

Tilly owned a pack of four little pommies that Jim derisively called the 'powder puffs', often complaining that there wasn't enough room on the bed for him. Tilly frequently reminded him that there was always a spare bedroom he could use. Not having children to dote upon, Tilly turned her love to her dogs, treating them like royalty with the best cuts of meat and throwing them each a birthday party every year.

Leigh was also very fond of dogs. However, unlike Tilly, she wasn't averse to giving them a kick, a clip around the head, or a sharp tongue lashing whenever she was in a foul mood. Kate owned twelve dogs— eight Pomeranians, a Fox Terrier, and her favourites, three white French Poodles. Often, when appearing in the newspaper, Leigh refused to sit for a photograph unless she had a poodle on her lap. That was the only thing that Tilly lacked in comparison to Leigh—public relations puffery. Kate had a penchant for self-promotion.

Kate was one of the greats when it came to bullshitting. She was better than any man at the pub relating his fishing story. She also contacted newspaper to publicise her philanthropic endeavours, and that's exactly all they were—Public Relation stunts. There were many front-page stories showing Leigh meting out gifts to poor children with Santa in tow or a man dressed in a red suit standing beside her on her upstairs veranda.

Tilly, however, shot straight from the hip. She didn't care whether people liked what she said or not. The donations, parties, and assistance she administered were done without pomp and ceremony. She felt the disadvantaged were entitled to their privacy and she didn't feel the need to show off what she did for them, the hospitals, or the churches.

Upon learning about Tilly's champion stud dog, Leigh wanted him to serve her Pomeranian bitch. She paid one of her henchmen's wives, Coral, to approach Tilly and offer her five pounds to breed 'her' bitch to her stud. When the woman arrived at the Maroubra house, Tilly invited her inside and offered her a cup of tea. The 'plant' oohed and aahed over Tilly's King as she showed her photos of 'Princess'. Tilly was impressed with the style of the woman's dog and told her to let her know when she was next in heat. The fix was done.

"Oh, I think she's ready to breed now. She started her cycle four days ago and should be ready." Leigh's infiltrator was quite the actress and she had Tilly so convinced that she left that very afternoon with the brothel madam's beloved King in tow.

Two days later, there was a knock at the Maroubra house door and when Tilly opened the door, she found a box on her doorstep and caught a glimpse of the rear end of a black Studebaker speeding off down Long Bay road. Tilly cautiously picked up the box and felt something moving within. When she opened the box flap, she was surprised to find a Pomeranian looking up at her. Frowning, she picked the dog up and read the note attached to its collar: 'Thank you for the use of King'.

Suspicious, Tilly looked into the dog's eyes. A stabbing pain pierced her heart when she realised the woman had switched her beloved boy for an inferior mongrel. Livid, she stormed outside, put the dog on the front seat of her car and sped off to the woman she knew was behind the substandard exchange.

When she arrived outside 212 Devonshire Street, Tilly carefully picked up the dog and stormed to the front door and banged on it twice: "Get your fuckin' big ugly arse to the door you fuckin' thievin' bitch!" She bellowed.

Baker cautiously answered the door and told her that Kate wasn't home. Tilly wasn't having any of that, she handed the Pomeranian to

Kate's lover, pulled out her pistol and pointed it directly at him: "Stand in my fuckin' way and I'll shoot both your fuckin' arms orf! Fizgig to the cops and I'll cut your fuckin' throat!" She threatened before pushing past him and making her way upstairs.

She found Kate propped up in bed with a cup of tea in one hand and the newspaper in the other.

"What the fuck are you doin' here?" Leigh roared in her somewhat masculine voice.

"Give me my fuckin' dog back or I'll cut your guts out!"

"You're fuckin' mad. I don't know anything about your dog!"

However, upon hearing his mistress' voice, King began crying from the bathroom. Tilly rushed across to the room, pulled open the door and was met with her very appreciative Pomeranian. Kate reached under her pillow and pulled out a revolver and aimed it at Tilly.

"You've fuckin' got what you want, you fat bitch, now get the fuck out of here before I shoot you between the fuckin' eyes!"

"Touch my dog again, I'll fuckin' kill you and burn your fuckin' house to the ground."

7

Christmas was always a celebratory affair for Tilly. No matter what she was going through at the time, she always took the time to hand out gifts and cheer to the children in the local hospital. Each year, she also gave the new mothers in Crown Street Maternity five pounds each and brightened up the lives of the poverty-stricken Darlinghurst and Kings Cross families by delivering toys to the children and a food hamper with five pounds included for their parents. She would also visit St. Vincent's Hospital where she donated money to fill prescriptions for the poor. The Jesuits and the Salvation Army also received an annual one hundred pounds donation from the brothel madam.

Tilly often hosted parties at the Palmer Street house for the local children. She loved to sing nursery rhymes or music hall favourites from her younger days. She and Kate Leigh often competed to see who could throw the most lavish parties for the needy children and give the most gifts. The cost didn't affect the crime queens' cash balance, but it sure brought a lot of happiness to the kiddies.

This philanthropic side of Tilly was in stark contrast to the depiction portrayed of her by the police and newspapers. There were many police officers who were a party to her generosity, which fortunately for Tilly, kept her out of court and gaol more often than not.

7

Matilda Devine was no slouch during 1934 and 1935. She was arrested eleven times in New South Wales for consorting and using indecent language in the street, and five times for resisting arrest. Deciding to take a wee break from her trials and tribulations, Tilly talked Jim into visiting Kalgoorlie to look into opening a brothel in the mining town. They stayed at a property belonging to one of Jim's friends for a few weeks. While there, Tilly saw firsthand how tough life was in the outback. She witnessed a steer being slaughtered, watched as sheep were shorn, and was almost driven crazy by flies.

"You know what Jimmy. I'm fuckin' glad you didn't own a kangaroo farm! These bloody flies are unbearable!"

The Devine's said their farewells, leaving a gift of fifty pounds behind for their gracious hosts before making their way to Kalgoorlie.

On the 4th of July, whilst she was sitting in the lounge area of the Exchange Hotel, a local brothel owner recognised Tilly from when she had taken a trip to Sydney to investigate how the popular brothels operated before opening her own 'house of sin' in Kalgoorlie. She had worked as a prostitute in the Palmer Street brothel for three months, before returning to the mining town. She and the brothel madam had formed a friendship, being from her own area in London. Tilly had taught her a lot, and she operated her brothel in the same manner, except she took a higher cut for the house.

She walked over and sat at a table opposite Tilly who was drinking a shandy while Jim was at the bar buying himself another whiskey.

"Well, well, well… fancy seein' you 'ere and all." She remarked. "Australia's own famous brothel madam all the way up 'ere in Western Australia. 'onoured I'm sure."

"Bronwyn isn't it? You worked for me a few years ago in Palmer Street. Fancy seeing you 'ere!"

"I own a 'ouse 'ere, darlin'. Do you want to come up for a look?"

"That's nice of you. Wouldn't mind 'aving a look through."

Tilly was impressed with Bronwyn's brothel and told her such. As they sat down and chatted in the kitchen, Tilly mentioned that she was interested in starting a house of her own in Kalgoorlie. "There's plenty orf girls looking for work in Sydney. A bit orf new blood up 'ere wouldn't 'urt."

"I've got girls coming up e're every few months. They make their money, leave and a few days later another load arrives. I don't think you'll do as well as you do in Sydney e're, Tilly."

"Only one way to find out sweet'art."

Tilly spent most of the afternoon with Bronwyn, chatting with her girls, helping one of the new girls out who didn't know how to use a douche, and every now and then keeping the gentlemen company while they waited for a girl to become available. However, when she realised that it was almost four o'clock, she told Bronwyn that she had better get back to Jim.

As she walked past the brothel henchman at the door, he grabbed her by the arm and asked her for the money she had stolen.

"What the fuckin' 'ell are you talking about, you stupid bastard! I 'aven't touched any fuckin' money 'ere! Ask your fuckin' boss!"

"She's the one what said you stole it!"

The fracas was overheard by two passing detectives, Trait and Smith, who immediately attended the melee. When detective Trait grabbed hold of her left arm, Tilly turned around with a swinging right hook to the side of his head, knocking him to the ground. Detective Smith, with the assistance of the brothel henchman, apprehended the combatant Tilly, and held her against the front of the building.

"Did you take bloody boxing lessons?" The felled detective growled as he pulled Tilly's arms behind her back and manacled her.

"I must be slipping lovey. I meant to knock you out!"

Tilly was paraded through town as the detectives led her to the police station. Jim, who was standing outside the pub with the other onlookers, moved to the back of the crowd not wanting his wife to see him. That night he hightailed it back to Sydney.

Tilly was charged with being idle and disorderly. At the police station, she denied the charges, explaining that she was only standing up for herself after being accused of stealing money. "You can 'ave a policewoman come and strip-search me if you want. 'ere's my 'andbag! Look through it. You'll find no money, my 'usband has it all! That bitch Bronwyn. I should 'ave known she was up to something. She was being too bloody nice!"

"Where's your husband now, Mrs. Devine?" The young constable asked.

Tilly felt strange talking to the young constable. He looked like he was only sixteen years old and scarcely had any whiskers. "I don't know where 'e went. Typical bloody Jim, 'otfooting it whenever I need 'im!"

When she walked into the courtroom the following morning, a solicitor, Mr. F J O'Dea stopped her and told her he was there to appear on her behalf. He and Tilly sat at the rear of the court while she explained what had occurred the day before. O'Dea looked at his watch and told her that they had better go to their seats, telling her he had been warned that the magistrate was in a bad mood and would not allow any tardiness in his court.

Magistrate E. McGinn looked Tilly up and down when he entered the room. She had a funny feeling that things were not going to go well for her. Her solicitor explained the circumstances of her arrest: "I feel that the woman who ran the local house of ill repute has lied about the situation to force Mrs. Devine out of town."

"I don't care what happened. The woman is an undesirable person and a menace to society! She will be held in the local gaol for six months for vagrancy!"

Tilly let out a shocked scream when she heard her sentence. She was innocent this time of any crime. She sobbed as her solicitor pleaded on her behalf: "Your Honour, I beg the court's mercy. There was no money found in Mrs. Devine's possession. I feel she is being convicted solely on her record in New South Wales. I beg the court to change his ruling to a suspended sentence and my client has offered her assurance that she will leave town."

"The defendant is thirty-four years old. In that short lifetime, she has accrued sixty-six convictions. I will not pass my responsibility to another. With such a high number of convictions, she has exceeded the bounds of toleration. The sentence of six months stands! McGinn growled.

7

Released early upon a second successful appeal, Tilly returned to Sydney and found Jim asleep in bed. With one almighty shove, she pushed him onto the floor. "Leave me alone in fuckin Kalgoorlie you bastard! It took five fuckin' trains for me to get back 'ome! Coward in the fuckin' war—fuckin' coward still!"

"Shut your fuckin' mouth before I shut it for you!" Jim growled as he climbed out of bed and made his way to the toilet.

"Lay a 'and on me you fuckin' poor excuse for a 'usband and you'll lose what's left of your fuckin' balls!"

CHAPTER TWENTY TWO

Winds of Change

1936 heralded a new NSW Police Commissioner with the swearing in of William MacKay. The well-educated Scotsman told his police force that he would do whatever necessary to gain control of the Sydney underworld. He was just what New South Wales needed at the time.

MacKay had more experience than previous police commissioners after studying police methods in Britain two years beforehand. Whilst there he learned varying techniques which he planned to implement into his police department. 'I believe that it is true that Detectives are born and rarely made, but I also believe that the born Detective can be improved by tuition on his duties', he stated when he recommended that a specialised group of detectives needed to be trained to address different areas of crime, like prostitution, car theft and drugs.

The following year, to further study policing procedures, MacKay left on an eight-month tour of police stations throughout Europe and the United States. In America he was impressed on how J. Edgar Hoover operated the Federal Bureau of Investigation. He and Hoover spent hours discussing different investigative techniques, some of which he planned to initiate in New South Wales. But it was in Germany where he was mostly impressed by the proficiency and conduct of the German police and the well-disciplined community. He spoke at length with leaders about their labour youth battalions, expressing that they 'subordinate the individual to the welfare of the nation'. When he returned to Australia the following April, he established the first of the Police Boys' clubs and in 1938 he changed the name to the Federation of Police-Citizens Boys' Clubs.

When meeting with government minsters and senior police, the Police Commissioner austerely explained that it would be impossible to eradicate prostitution. He said that he would be trying a different approach to the problem and would seek assistance from those involved. Aware of the long-running matriarchal feud between Tilly Devine and Kate Leigh, MacKay decided they were the key to bringing peace to East Sydney, so he had the queens of crime brought into his office.

During the meeting, MacKay told the vice vixens that in the spirit of wanting to live within a peaceful community, he had ordered the police to turn a blind eye to their illicit enterprises.

"However, there are conditions that must be followed. Tilly, you are to operate your brothels quietly, cleanly and without violence. Kate, you are to run your grog shops quietly, without violence and stop selling cocaine. You are both to continue to inform police about the illegal activities of other criminals. Don't give me those shocked innocent faces. You both know you're snitches!"

He went on to tell the women that they would be arrested occasionally and would face conviction and a short gaol sentence for appearances' sake. "That should keep you both bloody honest!"

Tilly and Kate looked at one another and then MacKay, and begrudgingly shook hands in a show of acceptance of his proposal. The crime queens knew MacKay meant business and was a man of his word.

"If this agreement is breached by either of you in any way, let me make this clear, I will come down on the guilty party heavier than any cop has done before. I will parade you in front of the Darlinghurst police station in manacles for the reporters to photograph for the front page of their newspapers! Then I will ensure that you receive a lengthy gaol term."

He let his threat sink in for a moment.

"Tilly, you make sure that husband of yours toes the line! You tell him that I'll be watching him. I'll be watching your 'chauffeur', as well, Kate."

Jim refused to be brought to the Commissioner's heel and told Tilly that he hadn't been brought before the bastard before, so he didn't owe him any obedience.

Kate, not wanting to be held to any deal made with the cops, found more clandestine ways of dealing cocaine. Tilly wasn't concerned about the conditions MacKay had set out in regard to maintaining her brothels. She had always run clean establishments. Her girls were health checked regularly and the clients were made to wash themselves before transactions were initiated.

On the 4th of June 1936, Leigh, unaware she was being tailed by a plainclothes constable, made her way to McDowell's. She walked through the store browsing through books, before heading to the ladies' section. The policeman followed a few feet behind her and watched as she placed a garment under her coat. She was then arrested for shoplifting a cardigan valued at six shillings and sixpence.

Kate spent four weeks in gaol for the shoplifting offence. MacKay and his police officers were dumbfounded as to why a woman, one of the richest people in the state, would commit such a lowbrow crime. To Kate, it wasn't the need to have whatever she stole, shoplifting filled a void in her life and gave her a safe 'high' to get away with something in the midst of a crowded store. Other times it was a cat and mouse game, to see if she could outwit the store detectives, which more times than not, she easily did.

Tilly hadn't escaped her pact with MacKay. She was arrested and charged with consorting, twice within twelve months, serving a two-week stint in Long Bay Gaol each time.

7

Late 1938 brought a new policeman into Darlinghurst, a man who almost turned the crime world upside down. He didn't manage to free the area of crime, but he sure shook it up… a lot!

Francis Michael Farrell was born into a strict Catholic family. No matter how broke they were, the Farrells made sure there was always food on the table and their children received a good education. Frankie, as he preferred to be called, was educated at Ferncourt, and later attended Marist Brothers High School in Kogarah.

In 1937, Frank 'Bumper' Farrell enlisted at the New South Wales Police Department recruitment office in Surry Hills.

After passing an aptitude test, Frank was told that he wasn't tall enough to work as a policeman. The recruitment officer told him that at 5 feet 9½ inches tall, he was half an inch too short for the height requirement. Desolate, he returned home and found his father reading the newspaper at the kitchen table. He told him what had happened as he poured himself a cup of tea.

"Get that tea into you and I'll take you to the gym." His father announced.

"I don't want to work at the gym, Dad. I want to be a copper."

"Just wait and see."

Then, the story that follows goes like this…

When they arrived at the Darlinghurst gymnasium, Frank's father told him to wait as he went and spoke to the gym instructor. A few minutes later, he returned and told his son to go over to David, the instructor who was standing by a rack with weights. The following two weeks, Bumper laid outstretched on the contraption and David would stretch out his arms and legs and apply weights. On the Monday of the third week, Frank showed up at the police recruitment office, and lo and behold, he met the required height.

Bumper carried his code of honour of loyalty and to protect, defend and fight for those that he loved, into the police force. His recruitment posting began on the 5th of January with the NSW Police Department's border patrol based at Cobram on the Victorian border.

There were no police barracks for him to sleep in, so during the four months of his tenure, Frank's home was a gypsy-style corrugated iron hut on wheels that was parked in bushland along the Murray River.

In Victoria at the time, there was an outbreak of poliomyelitis. Frank was given the task of stopping cars on the Barooga Bridge and if any of the passengers looked sick, he was given the discretionary authorisation to refuse their entry into NSW. Not being medically minded, Frank didn't know whether he stopped sick people or not.

In May, when his four-month stretch in Cobram had ended, Frank was called back to Sydney. He returned to the labour force until he was officially accepted into the police department on the 5th of September 1938. From that day onward, the probationary constable was nominee Service No. 1918, of the NSW Police Service. Bumper was stationed at the Darlinghurst Police Station, District No. 3 in Forbes Street, an area where prostitution, illegal gambling and sly grog were rampant, as was gang violence.

Bumper laughed to himself when he received the placement. During his childhood, he and his friends had called the 1899 Edwardian style brick and sandstone building, 'The Castle', due to its pointed turreted roof.

Never did he imagine that one day he would be working in the "Castle" as a police officer. The morning of his swearing in, Frank followed the other newly appointed constables into the main office. There, Sergeant Turner handed each of the men their official warrant card and uniform. Then, after listening to the swearing in speech made by the Sergeant, the newly enlisted Constable Farrell, made his way home.

Darlinghurst police station was no place for the lily-livered. The police officers who worked there faced evil, death, and violence every day, and were paid a small wage in return for the risk to their lives and the long hours they worked. Each day they dealt with the most dangerous criminals in Australia. Bumper was a rough and tumble man who wasn't afraid to use brute force. He was exactly what East Sydney needed.

When he arrived home, Farrell's mother gushed and fussed over him before asking him to change into his uniform so they could see how smart he looked. When Frank walked out of his bedroom dressed in full police uniform, his father stood proud with a proud smile as wide as the Sydney Harbour Bridge on his face. "March around the room, son."

"You look so smart and handsome, my love. You remind me of your father when he was your age. But without the uniform." His mother remarked as proud tears rolled down her cheeks.

The following Tuesday when he reported for duty, Bumper was told that their station had jurisdiction over Darlinghurst, Woolloomooloo, Edgecliff, Kings Cross, Rushcutters Bay, Paddington, and Moore Park. The officer in charge warned him that most of the areas were dangerous and held their fair share of violence every day. He told Farrell to go in tough and take no shit from anyone. He also warned him about Matilda Devine and Kate Leigh. "They may be women, but they're tougher and cagier than any man I've met!"

"Man or woman, if they break the law, they'll be treated the same." Constable Farrell bluntly replied.

The weeks prior to starting his police duties, Bumper drove around the Eastern suburbs' high crime areas. Not being able to see much from the window of a car, he decided to flat foot it through the filthy lanes, dirty streets, and shifty pubs. It wasn't long before he learned who was who in the criminal world.

His first Saturday night on duty, the young constable sat across the street from the Hasty Tasty hamburger shop. He watched as a pickpocket he had seen targeting the rubes and geeks around the shop was at his illicit craft again. Dressed in plain clothes, Frank watched as the thief furtively picked wallets and train tickets from passers-by. When he saw him bend down to lift a woman's handbag while she was tending to her baby in a pram, he took the opportunity to apprehend the man. Locals jeered and jostled the pickpocket and cheered Bumper as he frogmarched the thief the thousand yards to the Darlinghurst Police Station, pleased that he was the cop who had finally arrested the habitual menace.

Wanting to find out information from those close to the ground, Bumper paid homeless men one pound for information. He concentrated on the Saturday night bare-knuckle fight venues, sending in a different homeless man each week to ascertain who was running the show. The informants proved to be invaluable sources of information. Through them he obtained knowledge about the cocaine cafés, haunts of SP bookies, the sly groggeries, and pickpocket lairs—information that would have taken him some time to discover if not for the indigent men.

It didn't take long for Constable Farrell to become the archenemy of the local criminals, drunks, and fighters. He had netted a healthy crop of informants amongst the criminals, gang members and prostitutes. With his up-front and bruiser style, on a busy night he would make a few arrests, but once it hit midnight, those who committed lighter crimes, he did what he loved to do—fight. Bumper preferred to use his fists than police batons. He'd knock the criminals around a bit before giving them a good kick in the guts, leaving them lying in agony or unconscious where they fell.

It was a hot December day when Bumper first met Matilda Devine. Tilly was in the middle of arguing with a client at her Palmer Street brothel, calling the man every curse name under the sun. Farrell told the man to leave and Tilly to get back inside the house.

"Fuck orf you and mind your own business, you nosy bastard!"

Bumper, not one to take abuse from anyone, especially someone who wore a frock and heels, grabbed hold of Tilly's arm, and shoved her into his Morris police car. Upon arriving at the Darlinghurst Police Station, he charged her with offensive behaviour and indecent language, earning Tilly a fine of two pounds.

This was the beginning of Bumpers vacillating relationship with the Darlinghurst queen of crime.

7

In April 1937, Phil 'The Jew' Jeffs, opened another club. Needing a little more money injected into establishing the 400 Club high-society sly groggery, he went into partnership with a well-heeled upper-class doctor. However, the following September, when the doctor didn't see eye to eye with Jeff's 'management techniques', an argument ensued, and in the true style of a standover man, Jeff's viciously assaulted his partner, before kicking him down the stairs, banning him from the premises and refusing to compensate him for his share of the business.

Devine was sitting at a table with a few of his poker mates playing a hand of '*Oh Hell*', oblivious to the violence occurring no more than six feet away.

7

Since returning home from England, Tilly noticed that Jim was spending more and more time away from home. He hardly spoke to her and whenever she received letters from their son, he never showed any interest in them. He'd also been stealing money from her purse. She knew he was upset about having to give up the cocaine business, but due to his cocaine addiction and drinking, he had also let the SP betting shop slip. He had left men in charge that didn't know how to keep the books, and most times, how to work out the odds to cover the bets. Tilly had kept the business afloat by injecting her own money in an attempt to keep it open. But that wasn't enough for Jim. He constantly asked her for money and when Tilly refused, she was bashed until she helplessly fell to the floor. Jim would then put the boot in until she gave in and gave him the funds.

One morning when Jim returned home looking pretty dishevelled, Tilly picked up the scent of perfume that she didn't use. She became suspicious that he was seeing another woman. When she questioned him about it, Jim, not in the mood for answering any of her questions, Tilly copped a backhand before he stormed out the door, returning home several days later as if nothing had happened.

7

At 9:15 on the 3rd of September 1939, Robert Gordon Menzies announced Australia, along with Britain and France, had declared war on Germany.

Due to not maintaining a significantly sized armed forces during peace time, Australia was caught unprepared for the war. The Prime Minister ordered the muster of a volunteer corps which was called the Second Australian Imperial Force. He then proceeded to work on a plan with parliament to gradually supply Australian military assistance to Britain.

Allegiant men and youths gallantly lined up to volunteer to fight alongside their British allies. Knowing they were needed to support those who enlisted in the military, countless patriotic women, many of whom had the sole responsibility of caring for their children and families, volunteered to help with the war effort.

With the male workforce all but depleted during World War II, wartime production that was crucial to the war effort fell to the women to play a significant role. For the first time in Australia, women were needed to undertake employment in roles that were previously dominated by men.

Women trained at shipyards to build ships, and motorcar factories where women only crews manufactured motorcars. At aircraft factories, women worked alongside men in assembling fighter planes. Other women became drivers of trains, trams, and fire engines, while others became fire and evacuation officers, or assisted the infirmed in their home and hospitals.

Tilly did her bit for the war effort. As soon as the war aid offices opened, she donated six hundred freshly minted pounds. Placed in each of her brothels were empty milo and powdered milk tins for the women and punters to donate to the war effort. Tilly also hosted monthly dinner parties where each guest was asked to donate ten pounds, which she then handed over to the war aid office the following day. She also helped local women and their children, whose husbands and fathers were away fighting in the war. Tilly often arrived on their doorsteps with clothing donated to her from women living in the richer suburbs, along with a crate of food and five pounds.

In her brothels, Tilly made sure any man in uniform was serviced by her girls for half price. However, some larrikin Australian men used uniforms their fathers or brothers had worn during the First World War. Tilly woke up to their con and began asking men for up-to-date service papers before offering the discount.

7

The ceasefire between Tilly and Kate didn't always remain peaceful. Old habits and hostilities die hard. The women weren't averse to a few little pokes and pushes every now and then whenever they crossed paths when down the street in Surry Hills, Darlinghurst, or Woolloomooloo. Tilly was almost forty years old and Kate had not long celebrated her sixtieth birthday. Long gone were the nubile and restorative bodies of their youth and after a violent stoush, they headed straight for the Bex and a long lie down when they returned home.

Times were changing, but Tilly and Kate still enjoyed the notoriety of their past and lived up to every ounce of their reputation. Though they were aging, their feistiness never abated. Both women were still as tough as nails, ruling their gangs and workers with iron fists.

Unfortunately, Tilly's home life wasn't faring as well as her businesses. In the second week of March 1940, her fears about Jim having an affair proved true. She had given him the best years of her life and had remained faithful to him even though she'd had numerous offers from men over the years. She had turned them down because to her, the wedding vows she made were important.

Tilly watched as Jim moved out of their Maroubra house and didn't attempt to stop him. She had decided that if he wanted to move into a flat with the whore, she was welcome to him. But what pleased Tilly the most, was that she could keep her earnings and not receive the unprovoked beatings every time Devine was drunk, under the influence of cocaine, or didn't get his way.

Hours later, while Tilly looked around the room at the photos of her and Jim together, it hit home that her marriage was over. She shook her head and refused to cry. Jim hadn't been the best of husbands… she wore the scars from his many beatings. Tilly sighed as she raised herself up and made her way to the bathroom. She turned on the taps, poured lavender bath salts into the tub and laid back in the soothing warm water…

Two months after Jim moved out, Tilly flew to London to visit her family. After decades of taking the long ocean passage of many weeks on steamships and ocean liners, she was impressed when she arrived at London's Heathrow Airport in thirteen days!

Tilly made the time with her family as special as she could. She was shocked at the sharp decline in both her parents' health since the last time she was there. She knew in her heart that it was probably be the last time she would ever see them.

When she learned that her Freddy was a soldier, her eyes glistened with tears as she thought of him somewhere out in the dirt or mud, fighting for his country.

One night when dining at the Savoy, she again thanked her parents for adopting her son and giving him such a wonderful life and education.

"Darling child, we wouldn't have been able to give our lad a quarter of what we have if not for you and the money you sent us. You were also an exceptionally good mother to your son, and he knows just what you did for him. Bless you sweetheart." Her mother gently said as she placed her frail hand over her daughter's.

The two weeks passed by quicker than Tilly expected. She ordered four taxis to drive her and her family to Heathrow, paying the drivers handsomely to wait while they were seeing her off and then to return them home.

The Twiss's farewell was an emotional one. They all knew that this was the last time they would probably see their Mattie. She told her mother and father that she would write to them every week, and if there was anything they ever needed, to let her know and if it were within her power, she would help.

When she arrived home, Tilly walked into an upturned house. Her settee and chairs were ripped open, as were the mattresses in all the bedrooms. Some of her good crockery and glassware was smashed and the contents of every drawer, wardrobe, and cupboard in the house was emptied onto the floor.

"Jim, you fuckin' bastard! You won't find any of my fuckin' money in my 'ome! Stay away you fuckin' no 'oper!" Tilly screamed down the phone when she rang her estranged husband. "You come near this 'ouse again, I swear, I'll shoot you fuckin' dead!"

Tilly was in the bedroom rehanging her clothes in the wardrobe when Devine stormed into the room. "You've gone too far this time you fuckin' bitch!" He roared before he proceeded to beat her. He assaulted her so grievously, that Tilly had to be hospitalised with broken ribs and a severe concussion. While she was in hospital, a long-time criminal friend of hers and Jim's, Donald 'Skinny' Kenney visited her.

"I heard you got banged up pretty badly, Tills. I thought I'd come to see how you're going seeing Jim's no longer on the scene."

"It's good to see you Skinny, it's been a while. Jim's gone and he'll fuckin' stay gone after this."

"Don't you worry Tilly. The bastard will pay."

Two weeks later while Tilly was laying on her settee reading the *Women's Weekly*, Donald showed up at her door. He was sporting a shiner on his left eye, his nose had been broken and his top lip was stitched, but he told Tilly that Jim had come off second best.

That day, Donald moved into Tilly's Maroubra home and they started living together, and 'Skinny Kenney' became her main stand-over man.

7

With WW2 came an influx of American Servicemen who had heard the legend of the great brothel madam, Tilly Devine, made a beeline to her brothels so they could say they had screwed a hooker who worked for the 'Razor Gang Queen'. The GIs compared the brothel madam to Al Capone and declared that she'd give any of the American mob bosses a run for their money.

One night, Bumper heard that Kate's gang had attacked several GIs who had overstepped the mark at one of her groggeries. Knowing Leigh had broken the agreement with the Commissioner, he made his way to her Riley Street address and pushed his way inside. On alert for trespassers, five of the groggery queen's gang members took the burly copper on, coming out of the melee battered, bruised, or knocked unconscious.

"Kate, tell the boys when they want to play in the big league, to make sure they know the strength of their mark first." Bumper boasted.

Farrell enjoyed being the adversary and antagonist of Tilly and Kate, but he also held a high regard for them, as they, even though they would never admit, did for him. The policeman continued to maintain the status quo and let Tilly and Kate run their illegal businesses, continuing to charge them with minor crimes every now and then.

Leigh was a significant snitch of Bumper's. She covered her informing by making a big song and dance about how much of a bastard and bully he was. Farrell often turned a blind eye to her fizgigging. Due to Leigh's information, he had notched up more arrests than any other police officer in the local districts.

Tilly also informed on fellow criminals, but mainly when her opposition was a threat to her business. Unbeknownst to the vice queens, whenever his snitches warned Bumper that a rival gang or an up-and-coming criminal aspired to take them down, he would pay them a visit, and in his own brutish way, encourage them leave the women alone.

With the high presence of American service personnel, Tilly's brothels were humping and bumping twenty-four hours a day. Money ran through the brothel madam's fingers like a conveyor belt at the mint. However, along with the honey came the sting of a bee when every now and then, drunken sailors arrived, and a brawl would ensue whenever they wanted to see either Nellie Cameron or Dulcie Markham. Knowing that the American soldiers preferred blondes, Tilly solved the problem by hiring more blondes to work in her brothels.

One particular night, two sailors fought over Lizzie, a recently hired girl in the Rozelle brothel. She had been the main attraction for most of the punters since starting two weeks before. Once the American sailors discovered the Rubenesque redhead, her 'dance card' was full day and night. A young GI who had arrived inebriated, demanded to see Lizzie, who was otherwise occupied. When Tilly told him she was booked out, he stormed off and started opening doors, searching for her.

Tilly tried to stop the enraged man when he finally reached her room, but he pushed his way past her and pulled the client out of the bed and told him to 'get the fuck out of the room'. A fight ensued between the men, quickly attracting a crowd outside the door egging them on.

Tilly pulled her pistol from her pocket and pointed it at the men: "Get the fuck out orf my 'ouse or I'll shoot both orf you!" The drunken encroacher swung around and slammed Tilly across her face, knocking her out cold before grabbing hold of the pistol, training it on the other man.

Fortunately for the brothel madam, Ada, one of her girls, had the foresight to ring Bumper. When he arrived, the men were wrestling in the hallway, and the pistol was laying on a settee. Upon seeing Tilly unconscious, he turned to the men and roared, "which one of you bastards hit the woman?" The brawling men stopped in mid-fight when they heard the thunderous boom of Bumper's voice. When they saw the hulking policeman standing in the doorway, the naked sailor reached for his pants, and the drunken GI told him that it was him who had hit the annoying broad. That's all it took for Bumper to punch the soldier in the mouth before giving him a good thrashing.

When Tilly regained consciousness, Bumper reached down and offered her his hand to help her up and laughed: "Good to see that even when knocked on your arse, you can take it like a man."

"Just get your big fat ugly fuckin' nose out orf my way and let me at that fuckin' Yankie bastard!"

"He's long gone, love. But if I were you, I'd be putting some cream on that fuckin' shiner of yours. Rawleighs will do."

"Ahhh, it's nothin'. It's good for business when I wear a fuckin' war wound every now and then. It makes the men think before bargin' into my place and startin' trouble."

CHAPTER TWENTY THREE

The Final Blow

Even though they had been separated for two years, Jim still expected his pound of flesh from Tilly in the form of pound notes. Tilly was no stranger to Jim's abuse. She had put up with beating after beating during their marriage.

"I can't keep giving you money to take 'ome and spend on the 'orse and dog races, or that fuckin' bitch you left me for! Get a fuckin' job!" Tilly's opposition was answered with a punch in the mouth and another to her face, knocking her to the floor. Jim then grabbed hold of her handbag and removed ten pounds from her purse.

"You're still my fuckin' wife. I'm entitled to the fuckin' money!" Jim roared before kicking her once more and storming out the door.

Tilly had thought with Jim living off another woman, she would no longer be his punching bag. But she learned the hard way that he was just as greedy and violent as he was when they were together.

Again, like so many times before, Tilly's girls cleaned her up. She was as tough as nails, but when it came to matters of the heart, Tilly was a sentimentalist and believed in her marriage vows of 'death til us part'. She just hoped that her death was not by her husband's hands.

When Donald walked into the Palmer Street brothel's kitchen and saw the state Tilly was in, he immediately flew into a rage. He didn't say a word. He turned around, climbed back into his car, and drove to Jim's flat in Surry Hills. When he knocked on the door, it was answered by Anna who told him that Jim wasn't home.

"I'll just wait for the bastard outside!"

Sitting in his 1937 Hudson, Donald chain smoked while keeping an eye on his rear vision mirror for Devine. He was hoping Devine wasn't at the pub and Anna hadn't warned him about his presence. Almost two hours later, he saw Jim walking down the street in front of him and started the car. The rage he felt when he saw Tilly earlier that afternoon, quickly returned. He waited until Devine was closer and slammed his foot on the accelerator and sped toward him.

Devine's scream broke through the quiet of the afternoon as he leapt over a neighbour's hedge to get out of the way of the speeding car. "What the fuck are you doing, you fuckin' stupid bastard!" Jim roared as Donald jumped from the car and stormed toward him. Kenney didn't utter a word, he walked straight up to Devine and delivered a blow to his jaw before landing an uppercut to his chin, lifting him off his feet and sending him sprawling to the ground.

"Lay a hand on Tilly again and I'll fuckin' kill you!" Donald threatened before returning to his car and driving off.

7

The relationship between Kenney and Tilly eventually came to an end. Tilly liked Donald. He was caring and their relationship was a passionate one, but her heart still belonged to Jim. She was honest with Donald and explained that she did have strong feelings for him, however, still loved her husband. She told him that she couldn't in good conscience continue their relationship where the love was one-sided.

"I wish he treated you like the queen you are Tills." Then in true gentleman style that belied his violent lifestyle, Donald kissed Tilly on the back of her hand and left to pack his belongings.

7

On the 12th of August 1942, in a final attempt of resurrecting her marriage, Tilly planned an extravagant Silver Anniversary party for her and Jim at her Maroubra home. She spared no expense on hiring caterers, decorators, entertainment, and grog. A beautiful three tier blue iced Anniversary cake was placed on a table that was surrounded by buffet tables. A large bar area was set up at the side of the backyard, leaving an area at the rear for the band and dancing.

Tilly was dressed in a stunning red satin, full-length dress embellished with scatters of sparkling rhinestones that caught the light whenever she moved. She wore a new pair of red suede peep shoes and topped her sensual look off with a Marcha designed red hat with feathers and netting. Her fingers, wrists, and neck as usual, were aglitter with diamonds and pearls.

The party was in full swing, but when the clock struck nine and Jim had not shown up, Tilly went into the living room and rang him. When his girlfriend answered the phone, Tilly saw red: "I don't want to speak to a fuckin' 'usband stealing 'ore!" She screamed into the phone before slamming the receiver down.

Tilly returned to the party and told her guests that she was unable to contact Jim and that he was probably on his way over. But it was Phil Jeffs who found Devine hours after the party had begun. When he went out to his car to get Tilly's gift, he spotted him sitting on the front doorstep in a sullen mood. He sat beside his old cocaine selling mate for about half an hour and finally convinced him to join the party.

When Devine walked through the gate into the backyard and saw Tilly dancing with Sid McDonald, in a jealous rage he marched over to where the pair were and pulled the two apart.

"What the fuck is wrong with you! I put this party on for our silver anniversary!" Tilly screamed. "And you come in 'ere this late and fuckin' drunk! Where the 'ell 'ave you been?"

"You have no right asking me where've I've been. Where do you think I've fuckin' been?" Jim drunkenly scoffed. "I've been with the woman I'm living with. My future wife!"

"You're a fuckin' bastard, James Devine." Tilly said, smarting and embarrassed by the statement he made in front of her guests. "Don't mention that 'ore in my 'ome!"

Enraged by Tilly's offence, Jim grabbed her by the hair and dragged her over to the cake table, pushed the Anniversary cake onto the grass and grabbed a bottle of beer and hit her over the head with it.

Tilly fought to free herself from Devine's grip, but he started hitting her hands with the broken bottle, cutting them deeply. "I should cut your fuckin fingers off! How will you wear your fuckin' wedding ring then!"

Phil, Sid and one of Tilly's henchmen, who had arrived just moments before, pulled Jim away from Tilly while her friend, Olive, and two of her girls, helped her into the house. She was bleeding profusely from where Jim had hit her with the bottle. Olive called an ambulance and upon its arrival, the attendants wrapped Tilly's head and hands in bandages and rushed her to St. Vincent's Hospital.

The doctor attended to Tilly immediately when he saw the blood-soaked bandages around her hands and her head. She started vomiting and was acting confused and slurred while she answered the doctor when he asked her what her name was. After almost thirty seconds, Tilly replied that her name was Matilda Twiss. The doctor checked her eyes and asked the nurse to clean up the fluid that was leaking from her nose. Olive asked the doctor if Tilly was going to be all right, and he told her that she had suffered a basilar skull fracture and required hospitalisation.

Tilly looked like a raccoon the following day when Olive and a few of her girls visited her. She was still a little vague and confused, but managed some conversation, albeit a little scattered.

Within two days of her hospitalisation, Tilly's room was filled with flowers. One of the nurses asked if she was royalty to receive so many. "I'm the Queen of the 'Loo darlin', or so they say."

Three weeks later after several courses of antibiotics and a lot of bedrest, Tilly was released from the hospital. But she wasn't the same Tilly who had thrown the party that left the hospital. She was nervous and cried easily. But she was resolute about one thing, she was going to divorce James Edward Devine.

7

On the 2nd of April 1943, Tilly attended Divorce Court for her divorce hearing. She was dressed as a woman of substance wearing a Christian Dior black silk dress, a thick mink coat, and a wide brimmed black hat decorated with peacock feathers. Her lips were painted with bright red lipstick, her hair styled in her earmark kiss curls and ringlets, and every finger glistened with diamonds. She gave her address as 193 Palmer Street and an Entertainment Co-ordinator as her profession. Tilly relayed the many years of abuse she had endured at her husband's hands. She spoke of the money he had stolen and how he had broken into her home several times and stole money from her dressing table drawer and purse.

"Last July, Judge, Jim asked me to sell tickets for the Navy, Army and Air Force Ball at David Jones's. I sold twelve tickets and I also bought one to be with the 'appy party orf friends that paid me for the tickets. I 'anded' 'im all the money but 'e never produced the tickets. So, I went around to 126 Flinders Street in Paddington to Jim's 'eadquarters and 'e wasn't there. I found 'im at the pub. I asked where the tickets were for the ball and 'e flattened me on the floor after punching me. Then 'e picked up a chair and made out that 'e was going to 'it me with it. My driver rescued me from the barroom floor and carried me out to the car. Just as we were about to drive out, Jim threw himself on the road in front orf the car and told us to run over 'im and then 'e could 'ave me up for murder."

"Are they the only occasions Mr. Devine has been violent toward you Mrs. Devine?"

"No, there were plenty. Once 'e clouted me over twenty-six pounds 'e knew I 'ad 'idden on the shelf. I told 'im that I'd used it and was broke. That's when 'e 'it me. I took orf because I didn't want another beating. Another time, I was up Oxford Street and Jim found me. The mongrel wanted money for the races. I 'anded him a few quid and 'e said it wasn't enough because 'e also 'ad debts to pay. When I told 'im that 'e already 'ad the twenty-six pounds 'e king 'it me and put the boot in everywhere."

"What do you mean by everywhere?" Mr. Justice Edwards asked.

"'e kicked me from all angles."

"You mean he kicked you in all parts of the body?" Mr. Munro, Tilly's solicitor asked.

"Yes,"

"On the chest and thighs and stomach?" Mr. Munro questioned.

"Yes, from all angles. I think I showed you the bruises one day, Mr. Munro,"

"I cannot tell the court about that." Mr. Munro hurriedly replied.

"Do you have any children from your marriage Mrs. Devine?" The judge asked.

"We 'ad two children. A daughter and a son. My daughter died." She replied with a wistful glance toward the ceiling. She then took in a deep breath and continued. "My son was adopted by my parents. My boy's name is Frederick James Twiss, 'e has my parents' surname now. Freddy's away fighting for the British Army in the Middle East. My mother said I was too young to bring a little baby to Australia."

"I'm sorry to hear about your daughter and the adoption of your son. It must have been exceedingly difficult for you," Mr. Justice Edwards said. "Do you have a copy of your marriage certificate Mrs. Devine?"

"Thank you, Your 'onour. That was kind of you to say. I don't 'ave the marriage certificate anymore. I brought it to Australia, but 'anded it in at Victoria Barracks in 1920 in connection with Jim's pension. I 'ave been to the barracks and they told me it was lost, or at least it couldn't be found."

Tilly's solicitor explained to the judge that in these abnormal times it was practically useless to write to Somerset House for a copy of the marriage certificate. "I dispatched a registered letter which was not answered after six months. There is the danger too of the loss of documents at sea as the result of enemy action."

Tilly had two witnesses to give evidence on her behalf, they each followed her into the witness box.

"Your name please, sir?" Mr. Munro asked the next witness.

"Dr. Henry Harold Crowe, medical practitioner."

"How do you know Mrs. Devine, Dr. Crowe?"

"I have attended Tilly on and off over a period of 12 years."

"What is her condition today compared with a couple of years ago?"

"Her nervous condition has degenerated appreciably due to nervous strain and battery."

Mrs. Olive Odman was called next. She gave her address as 13 Kings Cross Road, Kings Cross. She said she lived apart from her husband.

"How long have you known Mrs. Devine?" Mr. Munro asked.

"For about twenty years. I have seen her husband flip a table with an anniversary cake on it and attack Tilly with a beer bottle. I've been a witness to numerous other kicking's and punching's. I've cleaned her up after numerous beatings. I've seen his boot marks on her body. I've seen Tilly out to it on various occasions as a result of her husband's beatings." She then broke down in tears and collapsed on the stand.

After the emotional testimony from Tilly's friend, Mr. Justice Edwards adjourned the case until Tilly had a copy of her marriage certificate.

7

With the government not having the power to act under National Security Regulations to declare an establishment a 'Disorderly House', the police and the court took responsibility of the duty. On the 18th of June 1943, Inspector Courtney, chief of the Sydney Police Vice Squad, declared in an affidavit that premises occupied by Mrs. Tilly Devine at 191 Palmer Street, Sydney, where police had found reputed criminals on the premises and were likely to be found there again. He added that many soldiers had reported that they were robbed of their money at the premises.

Mr. Justice Street, upon receiving the affidavit from Inspector Courtney, declared the premises at 191 Palmer Street a disorderly house, making it the first brothel to be declared as such under the new Act.

Whilst appearing at the Police Court before Mr. Hardwick, S.M. for being the owner of a Disorderly House and consorting with criminals, the police prosecutor mentioned that Tilly had also been charged with maliciously wounding Ellen Grimson. A young policeman took the stand as a witness for the prosecution. He testified that he was at the Palmer Street premises, when he heard a woman screaming, 'Let me go, let me fuckin' go. Don't hold me while she cuts me up!' The constable stated that he then heard Tilly Devine say, 'I'll cut her fuckin' guts out, the slut. Put the 'bitch in there until I get my gat! I'll put a hole right through her!'

In further testimony, he said that when Tilly was arrested, Grimson was bleeding profusely from the face. He went on to say that the victim told the officers that Tilly's friends held her while Tilly cut her lip with a knife. He added that the wound had taken eleven stitches to seal. He said that Tilly had told him that she had turned on her employee because the bitch kept getting drunk and leaving all the lights on in the house. She said that's what started the fight. She stated that Grimson then hit her over the head with a vase and if we hadn't arrived when we did, she would have killed her. He testified that Tilly had denied using a knife or a razor but admitted that she had punched Grimson with her diamond studded fist.

The Magistrate found Tilly guilty of being the holder of a disorderly house in Palmer Street frequented by reputed thieves and a second charge for consorting. He sentenced her to two years imprisonment on both charges which were to be served wholly cumulatively. Mr. Hardwick S.M. also committed Tilly for trial on the maliciously wounding of Ellen Grimson for the 12th of October.

Upon receiving the two sentences, enraged, Tilly screamed at the magistrate from the dock, "Couldn't you give me any more time?" However, she was quickly silenced by her solicitor when he advised her that abusing the magistrate would not garner her bail.

In late July whilst out on bail, Tilly reappeared in the Divorce Court before Mr. Justice Edwards. She handed him a copy of her marriage certificate that her sister had sent from England. Tilly confirmed that the details were correct except her age. "I was sixteen when I got married, not twenty-one. The canon must 'ave made a mistake."

Unfortunately, even with the marriage document, Mr. Edwards was not prepared to grant a divorce. He told Tilly that he needed to hear further corroborating evidence that her husband had 'habitually and cruelly' beaten her.

Tilly tearfully dropped to the chair in disbelief and frustration. She wanted to scream out to the judge that she had been a victim to James Devine's violence since before she was married. She wanted to tell him that her daughter was dead because he had slept with so many unclean prostitutes and she was born deformed due to syphilis. She wanted to show him the scars all over her body from the beatings she had endured over the years. She wanted him to know that she had been tricked into coming to Australia by her husband and forced back into prostitution. But most of all, Tilly wanted Mr. Justice Edwards to know, that sitting there in his courtroom, she felt like he had kicked her in the guts and made her a victim of the court. But instead of shouting her realities to the judge, Tilly just sat there as two men made decisions over her life. She wanted to flee the courtroom and escape back to the domain where she called the shots, East Sydney, and her brothels.

Her solicitor tried to explain to the judge that it may be difficult to find witnesses to come forth and testify on his client's behalf. "Mr. Devine has a terrifying reputation and people would fear for their lives if they spoke out against him."

However, Mr. Edwards was unmoved. "Surely you don't suggest the stage has been reached in our society when persons can be intimidated against giving evidence in court?"

"There are many," Mr. Munro replied, "that would rather travel to the back of Bourke than go in the witness box and say one word against James Devine."

"I think, Mr. Munro, that you had better get corroboration. Marriages are not dissolved without complete proof of matrimonial offences having been committed when the evidence is such that corroboration is readily available."

Tilly whispered the name Mary Singer to her solicitor. Tilly must have paid Mary a tremendous sum of money because just a few hours later, Miss Singer, Tilly's neighbour, sat in the witness box and in a quivering voice, told Justice Edwards that she had seen Jim hit Tilly with a bottle at the anniversary party. She said she had also witnessed him blacken her eyes and try to kick the door down when she escaped from him at the Maroubra house. Mary said on many occasions she had harboured Tilly in her home when Jim acted like a wild beast when drunk or high on cocaine.

Mary's evidence satisfied Judge Edwards, and he granted Tilly her *decree nisi*, telling her that in six months' time her divorce would be final.

That night, Tilly, her friends, and girls partied around the pubs of Woolloomooloo, Surry Hills, Darlinghurst, and Paddington—her kingdom of crime. The soon to be divorced woman splashed her money around like she had wardrobes full of it… she did, but no-one knew where her stash was hidden.

On the 30th of January 1944, Tilly was granted her divorce from James Edward Joseph Devine, on the grounds of cruelty.

7

In the Quarter Sessions on the 12th of October, Tilly was relieved when she was acquitted of having assaulted Ellen Monica Grimson. In court, she testified that she had struck Grimson with a backhand blow in self-defence, and that the injuries must have been caused by the rings she was wearing. She denied having used a razor or a knife.

Tilly's victory was a short-lived one. Two days later, she lost her appeal against consorting and being the holder of a disorderly house. She was sent to Long Bay Women's Gaol to serve two concurrent six-month sentences.

Tilly's stay in prison was like a holiday home as always. She chose to work in the kitchen and was again given the role as head woman. She also had the freedom to make phone calls whenever she needed. Tilly's reputation had preceded her, and not one of the women in gaol challenged her about her abundance of privileges, not even the 'top dog'.

CHAPTER TWENTY FOUR

Twilight of a New Dawn

After spending only three months in gaol, Tilly earned an early release for good behaviour. When she arrived at the Palmer Street house, she was astonished to find her friends and working girls had put on a surprise welcome home party for her. The party was in deep swing when Tilly realised that they had run out of whiskey and rum. She and Olive walked across to the Tradesman's Arms for top ups and whilst waiting for their order, Tilly met forty-three-year-old Eric Parsons.

She was immediately attracted to the well-built and handsome barman and he was just as attracted to the striking blonde who exuded such polished confidence he had never seen in a woman before. Tilly invited him to her party, telling him she was at 191, just across the street. She found the barman's blush endearing when he realised which *house* she was referring to but agreed to go over when his shift had finished.

As the clock ticked over, Tilly kept an eye out for the barman and was pleased when she saw him walk through the back gate just after ten o'clock. She quickly poured a whiskey and made her way over to where he was standing like a puppy stuck in a puddle.

"Pleased to see you made it, 'ere's a drink for you. I'm Tilly, I own this place."

"Good to meet you, Tilly, I'm Eric Parsons. I'd never thought I'd be standing in this backyard." He nervously laughed.

That night, Tilly and Eric sat in the front room of the house which usually was full of scantily dressed women making provocative suggestions as they tried to reel in a punter for an hour or so. But that night, Tilly had given them the night off to party.

During their pleasant time together, Tilly had learned that Eric had been a seaman on the *HMAS Kuttabul* when it was torpedoed by one of the Japanese midget submarines in Sydney Harbour in 1941. He told her how the sub had fired on the *USS Chicago*, but it missed and detonated under the hull of the Kuttabul. He caught a sob when he told her about how the ferry was cut in two and immediately sank to the bottom of the harbour. He humbly revealed that he was one of the men who helped rescue many of the drowning men.

Captivated by his story, Tilly lost all track of time, and when they'd finished talking, it was almost four o'clock in the morning and most of the party guests had left.

After that night, Tilly and Eric were almost inseparable. In Eric, Tilly felt she had found someone who genuinely cared for her and her welfare. And she loved how his eyes expressed his feelings toward her.

Eric never asked Tilly for a penny, even though he knew she was good for it. Whenever she offered him money, or to pay for dinner when they dined out at a restaurant, Eric refused, saying that he worked for a living and wanted to spend his hard-earned pounds on the woman he loved.

So happy was Tilly that she had finally found a gentleman who was not involved in crime, drugs, or prostitution, she asked Eric to move into her Maroubra home. Eric agreed, and told his wife, Mary that he was leaving her.

Tilly was like a schoolgirl again. She had never felt so loved and secure with Jim nor had she been treated with such love and respect. She laughed at all of Eric's jokes as he helped her in the kitchen and his sly attempts at cheating when they played poker, but most of all, she enjoyed how he held her as she fell asleep, only to find herself still wrapped in his arms when she woke.

7

On the 7th of July 1944, Mrs. Mary Jane Parsons of Dowling Street, Moore Park, appeared in Sydney Divorce Court for her application to divorce Eric. She told Mr. Justice Herron that she wanted to divorce her husband because of his adultery. The judge asked her for the woman's name. Afraid of violent repercussions if she were to publicly name Matilda Devine, Mary told the judge that she didn't know the woman's name but described her as a blonde with plenty of cheek.

She told Justice Herron during her evidence, that one night she woke and found the blonde woman beside her bed. Her husband then left with her dressed in his pyjamas. One day she received a letter from her husband advising her to apply for a divorce. In the letter he had admitted to committing adultery with a woman he was living with. She said that after the divorce petition had been served on Eric, he came to see her one night at their home. She sobbed as she revealed that he broke her heart when he walked into the house with two girls, one on each arm.

When Mrs. Parsons' landlady, Mrs. Ellen Grace Webster was called to the witness stand, she said, "I recall that this fair woman came out to the flat where Mrs. Parsons was living with Mr. Parsons on a number of occasions. Mr. Parsons left with a woman in his pyjamas and dressing gown. Sometimes he would not come back for a few days."

"How would he be dressed when he came back?" Mr. Justice Herron asked.

"Still in his pyjamas and dressing gown." Mrs. Webster replied.

Mr. Justice Herron was satisfied that Mrs. Parsons was honest with her testimony which was substantiated by her landlady. He granted her *decree nisi*.

7

Tilly's newfound happiness nearly ended on the 19th of February when she found one of Jim's revolvers hidden under a heavy oak wardrobe in the spare bedroom. She had family arriving from England, so she was preparing the rooms for them to use whilst they were in Sydney. When she picked the pistol up, she didn't realise it was loaded and inadvertently shot Eric in his upper left thigh. Tilly almost fainted when she saw what she had done. Eric fell to the floor groaning in pain and bleeding heavily from the wound. Tilly raced to the bathroom and grabbed some towels and got Eric to hold one tightly on the wound while she rushed to the kitchen to get bandages and antiseptic.

Tilly apologised and apologised to Eric. He told her to calm down and jokingly told her: 'at least you didn't aim for the heart'. Tilly did all she could to stop the bleeding and retrieve the bullet, but she couldn't do much without pain relief for her lover.

"Listen, you get us both a drink of brandy, and when the pub shuts, drive me to the Arms and call the police and say that I've been shot," Eric proposed. "The last thing I want is to see you in gaol, my girl!"

Tilly was beside herself. She trembled as she poured the whiskey into two glasses from the decanter. Tears clouded her vision as she walked across to Eric. "You're bleeding still. You need to go to the 'ospital now."

"I'll be right girl, I'll be right." Eric assured her.

An hour later, Tilly rang the ambulance. Eric had become weaker and she was afraid of losing him. She drove him to the back of Tradesman's Arms and waited with him until the ambulance arrived, and then returned to the house to clean up the blood.

The police were notified about the shooting by the hospital and they waited until Eric had regained consciousness and questioned him. Detective-Sergeant Strettles asked if he knew who had shot him, and Eric told them that he hadn't seen the person. He said he was walking along the street and heard a bang, and then felt a pain in his leg, and when he looked down, he was bleeding.

"It's a bit hard to be shot in the leg when your trousers are unmarked. Shooters don't generally clean and dress a wound after shooting a person either. It seems like you were shot without any trousers on. You were in the vicinity of 191 Palmer Street, a known disorderly house. Were you shot there, Mr. Parsons?" Detective-Sergeant Harold Gilmour inquired.

Eric stood by his story and the police left, frustrated by his replies. The detectives then searched the Palmer Street house and found no signs of a shooting. They then they drove to Maroubra. Tilly answered their knock at her door and invited them in. Gilmour asked her if she knew Mr. Eric Parsons, and she told them that he was her de facto husband.

"Do you know how he came to be shot, Mrs. Devine?" Gilmore asked.

"Eric's been shot. 'Ow is 'e? Is 'e all right? Where is 'e?" Tilly asked with true and honest concern.

The constables had a look around the house and when Constable Strettles noticed drops of blood near the wall, he pulled the lino back and discovered a large pool of blood.

Tilly was arrested, and after being charged with shooting with the intent to murder, she appeared at the Central Court. Mr. Munro appeared for Tilly and told the court that his client was innocent of the crime. The Prosecutor countered that there appeared to have been an altercation at the premises and that a large amount of fresh blood was found under the linoleum in a back bedroom.

Tilly trembled throughout the hearing. She wasn't worried for herself, but for Eric and how he was after his surgery. She just wanted court over and done with so she could go and see him. Mr. Munro then told the magistrate that he had spoken personally to Mr. Parsons at the hospital and he had told both him, and the police that Mrs. Devine did not shoot him. On the information before the court, the magistrate had no other option than release Tilly on four hundred pounds bail and remanded her to appear again on the 6th of March. As soon as she left the courthouse, Tilly caught a taxi to the hospital.

For almost twenty-four hours every day for two weeks, Tilly remained by Eric's side while he recovered in hospital. She rang her family and asked them if they could postpone their visit as Eric had met with an unfortunate accident. They were understanding and wished Eric a quick recovery.

Tilly took good care Eric. The guilt was eating away at her. The nurses were too afraid to ask her to leave of a night. She refused to allow them to bathe Eric, she gave him a bed bath morning and night. Tilly also ensured that he received the absolute best of care and instead of eating hospital food, she brought him meals from the local cafés and restaurants.

When they returned home on the day Eric was released from the hospital, they were surprised to see that the house had been ransacked. Most of the furniture was missing and the new refrigerator she had purchased only a few weeks before going to gaol was gone too. She looked toward the sideboard that Jim hated, and almost all her good china and crystal was gone.

"Bloody Jim did this!" Tilly seethed. "The bastard is still looking for my money and jewellery!"

"Are you sure it was him?" Eric asked as Tilly helped him to the settee.

"See that mark up the wall in the 'allway… that's where 'e pissed! 'e would have pissed on our bed too!"

"Why would he do such a thing? Absolutely disgusting."

"Because 'e's a pig and thinks 'e's a tom marking its territory."

"Well, that will all stop once we are married," Eric said to the surprised Tilly as he patted the settee beside him.

"You want to marry me?" Tilly asked as her tears welled in her eyes.

"I'd get down on one knee, except you tried to shoot it out from under me."

Tilly slapped his arm before telling him that she would marry him, and the sooner the better.

On the 29th of March, in between all the wedding arrangements, and running her brothels, Tilly appeared before Mr. Kelly, S.M., at the Central Police Court with having shot at Eric Parsons on the 19th of February with intent to murder him.

When Eric's name was called as a witness, he didn't make an appearance.

Detective-Sergeant Gilmour took the stand and testified that he and Detective Sergeant Strettles had received a telephone call from a nurse at St. Vincent's Hospital stating a patient had been brought in with a bullet wound. "Detective Sergeant Strettles and I visited Eric Parsons at the hospital and found that he had been shot in one leg. He told us that Matilda Devine had not shot him." Gilmour then testified that he, Strettles and two constables went to Mrs. Devine's Maroubra House. "She denied shooting Parsons, but when I pulled up some linoleum in a back bedroom, I discovered a great deal of blood. The walls and linoleum also smelled like they had recently been cleaned. We questioned Mrs. Devine and she denied knowing where the blood came from."

When the detective left the witness box, Mr. Munro stood: "On the evidence presented, there is no *prima facie* case for Mrs. Devine to answer. All charges against her should be discharged." The magistrate agreed and Tilly was allowed to return home.

With her Maroubra house on the market, Tilly moved her expensive polished furniture, fine art, crystal, and imported dinner sets into her 193 Palmer Street home. She then hired the best decorators to prepare her home for the wedding

On the 19th of May 1945, surrounded by over seventy friends, Tilly's beloved Pomeranians, and with a large crowd of spectators and neighbours watching on, Tilly was set to marry her Presbyterian fiancé in a private ceremony. The wedding was officiated by Reverend J. Faulkner as the interim moderator, and Mr. W.J. Spence from the Palmer Street Presbyterian Church. Mr. Spence had known Tilly since she was a child living in Camberwell.

Tilly looked every inch the beautiful bride dressed in a plain powder blue frock and blue mesh pumps. A blue ribbon was braided through her Edwardian-style plaited hair and several curls lined her forehead. To finish off her bridal elegance, Tilly clipped on a pair of diamond earrings, her favourite, brooch, a diamond and sapphire necklace, and then slipped eleven rings on her fingers.

Standing in the living room holding a bouquet of crimson sweet peas and carnations, Tilly impatiently awaited the wedding music to start. Her Matron of Honour, Olive Odman, tried to keep her calm.

Eric looked resplendent with his blonde wavy hair Brylcreemed slicked back, wearing a dark grey pencil double-breasted dinner suit and a blue bow tie. His black Oxford shoes were so shiny not even a General could complain. He and his best man, Bert Connolly, wore a white carnation in their buttonhole.

The hired band began to play the couple's wedding song, "I Love You for Sentimental Reasons", by The King Cole Trio, Tilly made her way to the floral arbour in the backyard and into the arms of her adoring fiancé.

As they exchanged vows, several of Tilly's girls openly wept in happiness for their madam. Many had witnessed the violent and torturous life she had led with Jim and were overjoyed that she had at last found a decent man and happiness.

After they were officially wed, Eric presented his not so blushing bride with an expensive pendant of diamonds, pearls, and rubies for honouring him by becoming his wife.

Along a table draped in a white silk tablecloth, wedding gifts valued more than one thousand pounds waited to be unwrapped. Amid the beautifully decorated tables, was a smaller table bearing the Parson's four-tier wedding cake enhanced with white roses, ribbons, and a powder blue horseshoe with the tribute, 'Good Luck' embroidered along the bottom.

Before leaving, the clergymen toasted the newlyweds with a lemon squash and the caterers began carrying the duck, chickens, meats, savouries, cakes, sandwiches, salads, and gorgonzola cheese out to the tables. A bar, tended by two of Eric's barmen mates from the Tradesman's Arms, was to the left of the tables, where eighteen crates of champagne, sparkling burgundy, beer, and German hock awaited the guests.

After the toasts were made to the Bride and Groom, an intriguing young man dressed in a black frock, veiled black hat, furs and wearing bright red lipstick announced: "For Tilly and Eric, I will sing, 'Because'." And he sung it beautifully, much to the appreciation of the newlyweds and their guests. An elderly gentleman asked the man if he could sing

'Sympathy' for him, which the impromptu singer obliged. When he had finished, there was barely a dry eye among the guests.

After the dancing concluded, Tilly and Eric opened their home up for the neighbours and spectators outside. She also contacted a few of the people she'd had words with over the past years, inviting them to have a drink and to forget about past quarrels.

Tilly had even contacted Kate Leigh to bury the hatchet. Unfortunately, Kate was out of town and the person who answered the phone said she wouldn't return for at least a week.

Their celebration also attracted an uninvited guest… Jim Devine. He had parked his car alongside the Tradesman's Arms hotel and remained there throughout the night until mid-morning the following day. He and his new squeeze had broken up the month before because Helen, his girlfriend, like Anna, believed he was still in love with his former wife.

Jim hadn't slept in days due to his jealousy over Tilly's marriage. He had made a mistake and was too much of a coward to admit it. Now it was too late. He had lost her for good. But he wasn't going to let Tilly and Parsons get away with it. He was going to make their life a living hell.

Tilly and Eric were like young lovers throughout the entire reception, each hardly leaving the other's side, laughing, dancing, and sneaking kisses from one another every now and then. Later in the night, Tilly broke out in songs of sentimentality and patriotism and was joined in by those who were inclined to take time from their eating and drinking to sing.

It wasn't until after midnight that the newlyweds finally crawled into bed. Guests fell asleep where they had dropped in a drunken stupor or made themselves a bed in the living room and spare bedrooms. Tilly's beautifully furnished home resembled a slum house when she finally woke up the following afternoon. There was no way she was going to be left to clean up such a mess. She woke everyone up, fed them sausages, bacon and eggs and pots of coffee, then demanded they help her clean the house.

Shortly before noon on the 22nd of May, Tilly, wearing peach coloured Chinese silk pyjamas, opened the door to an army of firemen who had arrived at the house in five fire trucks. They had received a phone call reporting that her house was on fire.

Shaking her head, Tilly assured the fire crews that she and her house were safe and apologised that a troublemaker had wasted their time.

Mid-afternoon, no sooner had they sat down to the tea and scones that Eric had prepared, when there was another knock on the door which the man of the house answered. This time it was an undertaker who said he had been summoned to the house to arrange the funeral for 'Mrs. Devine's mother'. "There must be some mistake, Tilly's mother is alive in England." Eric replied.

The Undertaker said that the woman who he had spoken with on the telephone had a cultured voice.

"It was that fuckin' Kate Leigh!" Tilly fumed, "Putting on 'er airs and graces! She'll get 'er comeuppance if it was!"

Later that afternoon, after receiving an anonymous call from a gruff-sounding male, a reporter from the *Sun* newspaper called and asked Tilly if she knew who was behind the hoax calls to her address. Enraged that someone had gone to the papers, she tersely replied 'that ever since 'er wedding on Saturday, she had been answering anonymous telephone calls and putting up with firemen, undertakers and real estate agents knocking on 'er door'.

Unbeknownst to the Parsons, Jim was parked across the street was watching the events after each of the phone calls he and his paid streetwalking accomplice had made to harass and harangue the newly-weds. After the last prank of the day, he ran to his car in fear when Tilly chased him off with a pistol in her hand.

As he climbed into his car, Jim looked back at Tilly and yelled, "You will always be Mrs. Matilda Devine!"

7

On the 4th of November, Tilly received a surprise visit from her friend Olive who appeared to be terribly upset. "Till, Phil Jeffs died yesterday."

"The Jew is dead? I can't believe it!" Tilly shrieked in surprise as tears welled in her eyes. "Phil was just 'ere last week. 'e said 'e was feeling poorly. But dead? Just when 'e got where 'e wanted in life."

"They're saying he died from septicaemia caused from when he got shot in the Blood Alley brawl. The bullet had corroded and caused an infection. He didn't even make it to his fiftieth birthday."

Tilly attended the extravagant Jewish Funeral when Phil was buried under the alias he used after retiring from crime, Phillip Davies. As a Rabbi read a Jewish prayer, Phil's orchid covered casket was lowered into the ground.

Phil had bequeathed his lovers and friends substantial gifts of money, property, furniture, and jewellery. Tilly was left two thousand pounds, a gold watch, and several pieces of art.

On Sunday the 21st of April 1946, Tilly was woken by the police at two o'clock in the morning. They informed her that the furniture in four of her rental houses in East Sydney had been set alight.

Tilly shook her head in disbelief. She hadn't caused any problems with anybody and she wasn't at war with any of the gangs. Since marrying Eric, she had become somewhat sedate, except for the time she knocked out a Fijian sailor that was twice her size after he had assaulted one of her girls. But he had long sailed out of port. She told the police that she had no idea who could have started the fires, or why, adding that since her marriage to Eric, a lot of strange things had been happening.

That night, Jim Devine threw several empty Shell gasoline cans into the Hawkesbury River.

7

In early August 1948, after hearing from her sister that their father was gravely ill, Tilly booked passage to London to see her eighty-three-year-old father for one last time. She called a press conference and told the reporters who attended, that she was visiting her seriously ill father and then would visit Ireland for a bite of food, before travelling to Germany and many other European countries. Tilly may have been an aging 'Queen of the Loo', but she still made news and when she called, the reporters came running.

Using her cunning, Tilly told the reporters that she would be boarding the *Orontes* in Adelaide, as she would be arrested for skipping bail if she were to board the ship in Melbourne. The brothel madam kept reporters—whether they loathed or loved her, amused with her shenanigans.

Tilly, having suffering with severe bronchitis for several years, took the opportunity of revealing to the reporters during her interview, that she felt that this trip to her homeland would be the last: "My newspaper friends, I am saddened to announce that my health is in such a decline, that I feel that this journey home to Mother England, may well be my last. You can rest assured that I will be making the most of whatever time I have left."

7

Tilly had one last visit to make before leaving, two days before she was to leave for Adelaide, Tilly had her chauffeur drive her to Long Bay Gaol where she visited one of her former prostitutes, Stella Croke. She was in prison for the long haul, a life sentence after her husband had beaten Ernest Hoffman, a chef from the Royal Sydney Golf Club, to death after a ginger job went horribly wrong.

Tilly stopped at a store on her way and bought tins of tuna, a chicken, fresh fruit and vegetables, and some sweets. However, when she arrived, one of the warders made a derogatory remark about her weight and asked her how much money she would make laying on her back now. Tilly being Tilly wasn't going to take that insult laying down! She abused the man and told him what she thought of his ears and how she felt sorry for his wife for having a 'usband who's a bigger dick than the size of 'is cock'. In an act of revenge, the warder refused to accept the food for Croke.

Tilly then yelled out at the top of her lungs for all and sundry to hear: "I was taking this stuff for poor Stella, she's serving life for murder, you know. The screws wouldn't let 'er 'ave it. Fancy not allowing a person to 'ave a paltry cauliflower. I took in a chook, too, but they said she couldn't 'ave that either. I've been bringing out chooks for the poor woman once a month and this is the first time, she 'asn't been allowed to 'ave one! I was so mad that I threw the chook at the screw!"

<h1 style="text-align:center">7</h1>

After hearing from one of her men that Kate Leigh was being threatened by some of the gangsters that had set up business in Surry Hills in an attempt to topple her reign, Tilly decided it was time to let bygones be bygones. She also remembered the editorial in the *Truth* newspaper where Leigh had impugned her reputation during her previous trip to London, Tilly hatched a plan to prevent a repeat performance.

She contacted Kate, who was also tired of their rivalry and agreed to sit with Tilly in a show of comradeship. Times were changing and new up and coming gangsters had arrived in town. Tilly had almost conceded that her days of being the Queen Pin of East Sydney were drawing to a close, but she wasn't ready to be forgotten yet. She and Kate had settled down in what could only be considered as an unspoken tenuous truce.

With Kate's blessing, Tilly contacted the *Truth* newspaper and spoke with the editor: "You know that Kate and I haven't had blue for some time, so she I was thinking that it would be a good news story for your paper to snap a shot of us together in a 'live and let live' pose. What do you think?"

As planned, Tilly arrived at Kate's Lansdowne Street home with a bunch of fresh flowers from the local florist. Kate greeted her former nemesis like a long-lost friend when she opened the door and thanked Tilly for the beautiful flowers. The heavily bejewelled crime Queens embraced and kissed each other on the cheek before Kate invited Tilly into her home. The photographer took a few snaps as he followed Tilly and Kate through to the living room.

Leigh, ever the amiable hostess, invited Tilly to sit on the settee and the photographer stood by the warmth of the fireplace. For March, it was unseasonably cool weather forcing people to rug up to stay warm. After wishing Tilly safe travels for her upcoming voyage, Kate handed her a gift-wrapped box with a good luck charm, a plaster icon of St. Therese and a box of Winning chocolates.

Overcome by emotion, Tilly hugged Kate and thanked her for her kind and thoughtful gesture.

Sixty-eight-year-old Kate was grinning from ear to ear as she sat on a lounge chair opposite Tilly. Both women were dressed to the nines, donning black frocks and furs, with Tilly wearing her signature array of diamond rings on each of her fingers. They sat sharing stories as they sipped from Colclough China cups while the photographer snapped away with his camera. Before leaving, the photographer asked for a photo of them in embrace, which Tilly and Kate were happy to pose for.

Left alone, Tilly, still a little wary that Kate may have one of her henchmen hidden in a bedroom, accepted a plate of sandwiches she brought in from the kitchen. Decades of hatred, razor slashing, arguments, threats, and animosity were soon washed away like blood from a chalice, when the women revealed their innermost secrets to one another.

"While we're being honest and all with each other, Tilly, I want you to know that it wasn't me who sent the fire trucks and undertaker to your house after you got married. It was a bloody low thing for anyone to do." Katie stated.

"I know. It was Jim…"

When the new friends parted, they wished each other well and Tilly drove home to Maroubra to prepare for her farewell party.

7

From the moment the taxi picked up Eric and Tilly, who was dressed in her full-length mink coat, from their Maroubra home on Friday the 13th of August, to take them to the Mascot Airport Terminal, they were followed by reporters and cameramen.

"They just never know when to leave a person alone." Tilly apologised to the driver as he swerved away from other cars to get away from the reporters who had given chase.

When their plane landed at Perth Airport, the media pursuit was on again. As usual, forty-eight-year-old Tilly was way ahead of the press. She had placed a trunk call to a steward on the *Orontes* she had met during her last return passage. He then contacted a co-worker who was stewarding that voyage, who then contacted the *Mirror* and told them that Tilly would be stopping at Boans department store and then at a beauty salon.

The cabbie, under Tilly's instructions, sent the *Mirror* reporters waiting outside the airport on a wild goose chase, driving up Mount's Bay Road, then Mill Street, through the subway, over Horseshoe Bridge and into Wellington Street. When the taxi finally pulled to a stop outside Boans, Tilly and Eric met the contact in the store, who advised them that he had a friend who was a delivery driver waiting outside in the loading dock. The Parsons made their way through the store to the dock and were whisked away in the delivery truck to Victoria Quay.

However, a *Mirror* journalist was just as cagey as Tilly and had paid one of the stewards to allow a second lot of reporters into her first-class state room. Unfortunately for the press, Tilly had seen them go aboard. She, and Eric, who was enjoying the cat and mouse game immensely, then boarded the ship and remained hidden in the stewards' room until the reporters and cameraman had left in preparation for the gangway to be removed.

When the coast was clear, the Parsons made their way to the upper deck and waved down to the outsmarted press. Conceding they had been outfoxed by the Queen of the 'Loo, the reporters laughed and took their hats off to hail the victor.

"Where did you get to in Perth, Tilly?" A reporter called out from the dock.

"It's a secret. I was too good for you! Heilo-ah! Goodbye now." Tilly gleefully gloated.

"Where are you going?" Another reporter asked.

"England. I'm doing the Continent and I'm going to Ireland for a feed!"

"You're taking a risk sailing off on Friday the thirteenth. It's always unlucky!" A Photographer shouted.

"It's always lucky for good people!"

She told the press that she was definitely coming back to Australia. "I want to show my wonderful husband off." She boasted. The press asked her to stand on the gangway for a few photos of her and her husband, but Tilly declined lest the police were nearby.

The passenger ship moved into mid-harbour and Tilly waved goodbye from her diamond ring laden left hand, as she threw colourful streamer down to the wharf with the other.

"Au revoir now, boys! It's time for us to go. Give my love to Mr. Jack Doyle. I'll never forgive you if you don't!" She called out, waving her heavily bejewelled right hand as the *Orontes* sailed out of Victoria Quay.

CHAPTER TWENTY FIVE

Home Fires Burning

The voyage to pay her final visit to see her octogenarian parents was a heartbreaking one for Tilly. The only people she had confided in about her sorrow was Eric, and surprisingly, Kate Leigh. She was pleased to be returning home again, especially after thinking the previous trip she made was the last time she would see her family.

Her own health was causing her concern. The doctor had told Tilly that her intermittent cough and sore throat was caused by bronchitis, and for her to be careful of the cold weather whilst in England.

Eric tried to take Tilly's mind of the ostensible sorrow that would greet her on her arrival at her family home. He took her out of a night to dance or down to play games on deck, anything to see her smile. One morning the Parsons were surprised when a steward knocked on their state room's door and handed Eric an envelope sealed with red wax.

"What's that?" Tilly asked.

"Give me a moment to open it, love."

The envelope contained an invitation from the ship's Captain, which excited both Eric and Tilly.

"I'll spend all day deciding what to wear!" Tilly exclaimed!

"Just my blue suit and tie for me, darling."

"It's not so easy for women. We 'ave to dress like a peacock to impress. I'll wear my diamond and ruby necklace and the diamond bracelets you bought me for my birthday and Christmas," Tilly said as she sorted through the wardrobe full of frocks and furs.

That night they dined on ham soup, broiled chicken, steamed potatoes, broccoli, and finished the meal with rhubarb and apple tart. The conversation around the Captain's table remained light, with the Captain entertaining his guests with hysterical stories about passengers he had sailed with in the past. Each person at the table briefly discussed their life as well as whatever business they were involved in. When it came to Tilly's turn, a look of sheer terror passed across the Captain's face.

Tilly slyly winked at him and said that she was a boutique owner specialising in upmarket women's clothing. A bottle of champagne compliments of the Captain awaited the Parsons' in their state room after dinner, with a note that simply said, 'Thank you Tilly'.

The rest of the voyage remained uneventful. Tilly spent a lot of time on the deck listening to the radio while poor Eric spent a majority of the time in their state room suffering with sea sickness. Not having any interest in listening to her fellow first-class passengers bragging about their riches and lifestyle, Tilly spent more time with second-class passengers, enjoying games of poker and playing deck games during the final days of the voyage.

Tilly's brother, Richard, who had caught a bus to the port to greet his sister, was waiting when they disembarked in Southampton.

"Good to see you again, darling. Is dad all right?" Tilly asked after kissing her brother hello.

"He's a lot better now. These antibiotics they have now seem to be working and the district nurses have kept a good eye on him over the past weeks. Pleased to meet you at last Eric. Mattie has told us a lot about you." Richard smiled as he shook Eric's hand.

The family reunion was interrupted by a bevy of Fleet Street newspaper reporters throwing questions at Tilly left right and centre. She smiled and turned on her charm. One of the journalists asked her if she owned more jewellery than any other woman in Australia. She agreed that she did and was proud of her collection. "I own more jewellery than the Queen!"

Another reporter asked if she enjoyed her life as an underworld brothel madam. Tilly gave the man one of her well-known death stares, and told him unequivocally, that she had no association with the Sydney underworld.

Not wanting to talk about her life in Sydney, Tilly regaled the journalists with a song and threw in a lively buck and a wing before telling them she had to leave as she had family waiting for her.

Tilly had arranged to have a chauffeured vehicle to meet her before leaving Australia. On arrival, the limo was waiting outside the Port of Southampton. Tilly waited by the Daimler while Eric and Richard set the trunks at the rear of the car. After storing the luggage in the boot, the chauffeur opened the doors for his passengers, before heading to Camberwell through war-torn London.

When they arrived at her family home, Tilly was both shocked and disappointed in how dilapidated it had become. She was aware that the newly initiated National Health service gave free medication and healthcare, so she wondered what happened to the money she had been sending to her parents every three months.

"What the fuck 'appened 'ere Richie? The place is a fuckin' dump! What 'appened to Mum's beautiful gardens?" Tilly growled, embarrassed that her husband was seeing such a dismal sight.

"I can't look after both Mum and Dad as well as keep the house. None of the others come over to help! They take the money you send, buy food, pay the bills, and give us a pittance. Their homes look good… ours… looks like this!" He sullenly complained.

"You should 'ave told me! We'll see what we can do while we're 'ere. Eric is good with 'is 'ands. I'm sure we can get it tidied up a bit before we leave for 'ome. Don't you worry."

A bigger shock awaited Tilly when they entered the house. Her parents were sitting in their armchairs watching television, her mother looked far sicker Tilly had expected. Her father greeted her with a smile, beckoning her over for a hug, which she lovingly obliged him. However, when she bent down beside her mother, she looked at her as if she didn't know who she was. Tilly looked up to her brother with a look of concerned bewilderment upon her face.

"Mum has something wrong with her brain. The doctors said that it's dementia. Her memory comes and goes. I have to keep a close eye on her because she wanders off. Many times, the neighbours and I have searched for her throughout the night, or the police bring her back home after finding her roaming the streets looking lost."

"And no-one thought to let me know about this? What 'elp does she need?" Tilly asked, upset that she had not been appraised about her mother's health problems.

Eric left for the kitchen, which he also found in a dirty state. He wiped down the kettle and rinsed it out before filling it with water and placing it on the stove to boil. Knowing that Tilly would probably have a coronary if she saw the state of the kitchen, he began cleaning.

He had never seen so many dirty dishes in a home before, except after one of Tilly's famous parties. He was disgusted in the way the Twisses were living. He was even more disgusted that Tilly's siblings had forced their parents to live in such a slovenly way, and for taking advantage of their sister's generosity by keeping the money meant for their parents.

Wondering what was taking her husband so long, Tilly walked into the kitchen and was immediately impressed when she saw what he was up to.

"Only one thing for this," she said as she rolled up her sleeves, "This is a two-man job." She smiled and kissed her husband on his cheek.

After a couple of hours of heavy-duty elbow grease and polishing, the kitchen and dining room were spic and span and clean enough that you could eat off the floor. "Now we need to go to the store and stock up on food. We'll leave the cold food until we go to the department store and buy them a better fridge."

"They need a whole new house, love." Eric sighed.

"If they were twenty years younger, I would buy them one. Getting this place cleaned up is all we can do for now. Before we go back 'ome, I'll pay one of the local women to clean the 'ouse a few times a week."

The next day, Nellie, Tilly's sister rang and when Richard answered, she demanded to speak to Mattie. He told Tilly that the call was for her and warned that their sister sounded extremely upset. Not at all bothered, Tilly took the receiver from her brother, and politely answered, "Hello Nellie, it's nice to hear from you after so long…"

From there, the phone call turned into a venomous interchange of accusations, name-calling, and threats. Her sister was angered by the headlines in the afternoon papers, especially the one that read: 'The self-confessed Queen of Sydney's Underworld, a tough, dumpy blonde who owns the most glittering collection of jewellery in Australia'.

Tilly barked down the phone that she couldn't control what bullshit the trashy London press write in their papers: "I told the bastards that I'm not involved in the underworld. You 'ave a fuckin' cheek raging on me when you live 'igh on the 'og while Mum, Dad and Richard live in filth and squalor. You don't even come over to 'elp our Richard! You're a bloody 'ipocrite, that's what you are!" Nellie ended the call.

Over the following weeks, in between speaking with doctors and nurses about her parents' health, cleaning the house while Eric and Richard cleaned up the yard and planted flowers, Tilly bought a fridge, crockery, new furniture, linen, and bath towels. She was impressed with what they were able to achieve in only a few weeks. None of her sisters or brothers visited the house while she was there. "Too fuckin' ashamed to face me the bloody cowards." Tilly spat.

The news about her mother wasn't at all positive. Tilly asked the doctor if it would be better for her mother if she took her back to Australia. He told her it was a nice gesture, but it would be too unsettling for her. He explained about the illness and told her that patients who suffer with this disease of the mind were better to remain where they are familiar. He said that he was concerned about how the changes she had made to the house were going to affect her.

"Well doctor, I wasn't going to let my parents live in a 'ovel! The 'ouse was in a disgusting mess when we arrived. They deserve better!"

"I understand. I was disappointed myself when I saw the lack of help your brother was receiving. But I must say this, he has been doing a marvellous job on his own and should be commended."

"Yes, I have treated 'im to some new clothes and shoes to thank 'im for all that 'e does for our parents." Tilly replied. "Eric and I 'ave also extended our trip."

"Has he told you that your parent's home will soon be pulled to the ground for a new council estate?"

"No, when the 'ell is this 'appening?" Tilly asked both surprised and angered.

"I don't know, but it's in the works."

Two weeks before she and Eric were due to return to Australia, Tilly's mother passed away. She never remembered who Tilly was, which broke her heart. However, the last months of her mother's life was lived in a clean home, in new clothes and spent with those who loved her.

On a wet and miserable September morning, the Twiss family sat in church to farewell their beloved wife and mother. A slight ray of light shone through the windows of the Sacred Heart Church, adding to the solemnity of the occasion. Tilly looked toward the altar, the last time she was in the church, she was standing before a priest with Jim beside her, saying their marriage vows. Now, her mother's coffin topped with her favourite pink roses, stood pride of place at the centre of the altar.

Tilly's father sat to her right and Eric and Richard to her left, her siblings and close family friends were seated in the pews behind them.

Freddy and his family sat three pews away. Tilly wanted to go and console her son. She could see how heartbroken he was, but she was afraid of his reaction. Her mother's funeral was not a place for any family drama.

After the church service had finished, her father, Freddy, Eric and her brothers acted as pall bearers and carried Alice's coffin to the waiting Hearse. The funeral cortège followed, slowly making its way toward the Camberwell Cemetery.

After the priest finalised the graveside service, Alice's coffin was slowly lowered into the ground. Tilly, her husband, and family remained by her grave, each not wanting to be the first to leave their wife, mother, and mother-in-law. Tilly placed her wet and tearstained handkerchief in her handbag, straightened herself up and linked her arm within her father's and led him to their hired limousine. It was too wet for him to remain outside too long. He offered little resistance and sobbed each step he took away from his beloved wife, such was his grief.

7

Tilly attempted to talk her father into moving to Australia to live with her and Eric, but he told her he was too old to set off on such an adventure. "I'm too set in my ways here. I'll die in my home before those council bastards take it."

The pain in her throat and chest from her constant coughing, was becoming almost impossible for Tilly to bear. She knew she would need to return home to the warmer weather before her health worsened. Tilly tried once more to convince her father to return with them, but he was determined to live his life out in Britain.

One morning, Tilly received two letters, one had urgent written in red pen across the top of the envelope. It was from Mavis, one of her girls advising her that she was needed back at the Palmer Street house as soon as possible as they had been having problems with a few men. She said that one of the drunken men had driven their car through the front of the house and they currently had a canvas cover over it provided by one of her brothers.

The second letter was from Hazel, a girl she had set up in one of her Bondi flats. She was concerned about the woman in the flat below her. She said that she was bringing men home at all hours of a night, mostly drunk, and the tenants in neighbouring flats were threatening to contact the police…

Not being able to return home until she finished helping her father and brother. Eric flew back to arrange the repairs to the house and evict the tenant from the Bondi flat. Tilly asked him to watch over her ladies until she returned.

Tilly remained hopeful that she would meet up with her son who had made a career of singing at parties around London. However, after the passing of so many years, he wasn't interested in resuming a relationship with his mother.

Four weeks later, Tilly bid her tearful farewells to her father and brother before she melancholily boarded the *Orontes* for her return voyage to Sydney.

Again, even though she had booked first-class passage, Tilly spent her time with the tourist-class passengers, dining, laughing, drinking, and enjoying their life stories. One woman, Margaret Campbell-Bone, recognised Tilly as the notorious brothel madam she had read about in the Sydney newspapers. Tilly was sitting at a large table with around a dozen women, enjoying themselves drinking cocktails and champagne.

When Tilly noticed Margaret sitting alone, she invited her over to the table. She accepted the invitation and sat alongside Tilly, intrigued by the woman she had read and heard so much about. She saw that she was no longer the blonde-haired beauty depicted in the newspapers of her childhood. She did see that the brothel madam still was made of tough stuff, even though, at times, she was struck by a terrible chesty cough.

Tilly kept refilling Margaret's glass with champagne and asked her questions about her life, where she was from and what she did for a living. Margaret was a little concerned that Tilly was appraising her for a job in her brothel. At first, she was cautious with her answers to her questions, but as the night wore on and the glasses of champagne affected her prudence, Margaret laid her life out in the open for all and sundry to hear.

The ladies enjoyed their gossip and a wide variety of cocktails, with many of them letting their hair down and accepting requests to join gentlemen on the dancefloor. At the end of the night, Tilly ensured that her inebriated guests were escorted safely to their cabins by the ship's crew.

As the ship sailed closer to Sydney, Margaret, suffering with a hangover from the night before, sat beside Tilly on the deck. "I must apologise to you Tilly. When you first started talking to me, I thought you were trying to procure me to work in one of your brothels. But I found you to be delightful, entertaining, and amusing company. I know who you are and probably only a quarter of what you have actually done. But I want you to know what a pleasure it was for me to meet you."

"Loveys believe 'alf of what you 'ear and quarter of what you read. I'm too old for all those shenanigans now. I'm 'appily married to the most wonderful man and my life couldn't be better. You find yourself someone to love, or find something that makes you 'appy, and if you ever need 'elp, you come to Tilly. I'm easy to find."

On her arrival in Sydney, Tilly was overjoyed to see her husband again. She held him tightly as she wept into his shoulder, still grieving over the death of her mother.

"Is your father coming over, my love?" Eric asked as he comforted his wife.

"No, the stubborn bugger won't budge from the 'ouse. He reckons 'e's going to die there either naturally or when they bulldoze the place down. Richard's considering coming over when Dad dies. At least I'll have some family 'ere."

"And… your son? Any progress there?" Eric cautiously inquired.

"No, Freddy doesn't want to talk to me. Dad said, 'e's changed since the war."

Eric stopped at a barrow that had fresh flowers for sale, and bought Tilly a bunch of peonies, hoping to gladden her heart a little. He had greatly missed her while she was away and learned to appreciate her a lot more after discovering that managing the brothels was no easy task.

"'ow did the repairs go?"

"Very well. Mavis' cousins are builders and completed the job for half price."

"I'll 'ave to buy 'er a gift to show my appreciation."

"Already done! I gave her a bottle of Devon Violets perfume." Eric proudly stated.

"Your blood's worth bottling! I don't know what I'd do without you, love."

When they arrived home, Tilly was surprised to see her dining table set with fresh flowers, china teacups, a full teapot, decorated cakes, and biscuits, and several of her girls seated around the table.

"Thank you! What a lovely welcome 'ome! I missed you all!"

CHAPTER TWENTY SIX

You Can Never
Outrun the Bloody Law

Most of Eric's family had disowned him when he left Mary. Families are rarely privy to the happenings in their loved ones' private lives. His younger brother George always knew Eric had always been a bit of a scallywag and liked living on the edge. He also knew he had been arrested once for receiving stolen items in his twenties. Eric always joked that it was the only time he was actually innocent of a crime.

Eric was the perfect partner for Tilly—he was tough, strong and knew how to use his hands and fists. He was very protective of his new wife, not that she needed protection, but Eric's devotion made her feel loved by a man for the first time in her life.

To Eric, Tilly was like a ship in full sail. She was funny, straightforward, braver than any woman he had ever met before, but most of all, she knew her mind and what she was about. He loved how she wore rings on her fingers and on her toes. She told him that no-one had ever taught her how to dress and he admired how she went for the overstatement, 'This is me. I'm important. Take notice.' He often told Tilly she was like an old Victorian house, so stuffed with furniture that the clutter becomes interesting.

Tilly was also loving to Eric's nieces and nephews, spoiling them all rotten. They knew they could always go to her no matter what. She was their aunty, their confidante, and their friend. If their parents couldn't afford to buy them something, Tilly would slip a few pounds in the kids' pockets, so they didn't go without. She also had a bit of a soft spot for the younger of her mother-in-law's sons. Time after time George rang Tilly asking for help as he was in a 'bit of trouble'. She would always tell him not to worry, she would fix it. Which she always did.

George had a devil-may-care attitude with money, which Tilly was aware of. Whenever she visited their home, she would slip five or ten pounds in the sugar bowl, or give it to the younger George, her nephew, to give to his mother. She remembered how hard it was as a child living in poverty, and she did all she could to make sure no-one she loved or cared for would go without.

At first, Eric's mother refused to have Tilly in her home, let alone acknowledge the crime queen. But over time, she became quite fond of her, especially when she learned how affectionate she was towards her son, their families, and her grandchildren.

When young George first visited Tilly's house, she was hosting a dinner party with several of her girls. He naïvely asked his Aunty Tilly if the ladies were her daughters. Tilly hugged him and laughed, "Never you mind sweet'art, you're too young to be looking at or talking about ladies." His question endeared him to the girls who spoilt him rotten from then on, also becoming his 'aunts'.

When the bodyguards turned up, George found it exciting, it usually meant something big had happened, or was about to. He never witnessed any violence, but the thought of it appealed to him.

One particular bodyguard George got to know was James 'Skinny Jones' Harris, who always wore a gun in a shoulder holster. When he first saw the pistol, George asked Skinny if he could play with it, which he refused. But Tilly told him to remove the bullets from the .38 and to let him play with it. Much to his mother's chagrin. Skinny did as he was told, and the happy boy spent twenty or so minutes running around the house shooting the 'bad men'. Tilly laughed as her nephew played, but later told him that he'd had enough fun and to give the gun back to Skinny.

When he was older, George came to understand what his Aunt Tilly's life was about, and what the girls were. He also became aware of the danger that surrounded her life, but never felt unsafe while he was with her.

7

Jim Devine finally accepted that he was out of Tilly's life. He resumed his relationship with Anna after they had separated three years before. They moved to Melbourne. Anna did not want to risk Jim being too close to Tilly in fear of losing him. She was aware that he still loved his former wife. Devine was a shadow of his former self. Gone was the rough, tough, standover man, killer, and extortionist. Life was unkind to him, turning him into a much older and fragile man than the burly tough man of his youth. No longer able to live high on Tilly's money, Jim had found employment as a storeman in a local factory.

7

One afternoon, a loud knocking on her door interrupted Tilly's phone chat. She ended the call thinking it was the police, temporarily faltering in her step when she saw that it was Abe Saffron. She had met the arrogant small-time criminal a few times at The Roosevelt Club, which was owned by fellow criminal, Sammy Lee.

"Good afternoon Abe, what the 'ell are you doing 'ere?"

"I have a proposition for you, Mrs. Parsons."

Tilly admitted him, intrigued by what the young and arrogant petty criminal was about to put forth. She offered him a chair at the dining table and asked him if he wanted a whiskey.

"Yes, thank you, darlin."

"Mrs. Parsons to you…" Tilly snipped as she handed Saffron his whiskey.

Abe studied the whiskey in the glass for a moment. "We have a mutual friend. I don't need to say his name, but he tells me you have a few problems with the tax department. He is willing to help you for twenty five percent of your profits."

Tilly was surprised. She had spoken to only one person about her troubles with the taxation department. She knew exactly who the charismatic bagman was talking about.

"Rob's not in power yet. 'e doesn't 'ave the resources to 'elp me with the problems I 'ave with the government, except maybe the cops 'e's flirting with to line his pocket when and 'if' 'e becomes premier. And 'e's not long become a member of the legislative assembly, so there's a long road before he amounts to anything."

"Get in at the beginning, Mrs. Parsons, and reap the rewards later. Rob's a determined man and has big plans that he will see come to pass."

"Abe, I've only ever 'ad one man as a partner in business, and 'e almost fuckin' bled me dry. I'm not interested in any deals with anyone until they prove they can back up what they're selling. Until then, I'll bide my time."

"Don't get too comfortable, Mrs. Parsons, Kate refused us as well, and look where she is now."

"You just keep selling your black-market grog and cigarettes, lovey, and leave the brothel running to me."

7

The 1950s birthed a new era in Australia and the underworld. Newcomers brought about the demise to many of the old-school 1920s gangsters, and the evolving temperament of youth was changing the bygone ways of their parents and grandparents.

Australia became engaged in the Korean War, the wonder of television was introduced to the country, public school and university education was free. The creation of the Union of Australian Women in 1950, fought to safeguard the rights of women and children, as well as the problems Aboriginal women encountered. They also continued Jessie Street's fight for women to receive equal pay to their male counterparts and assisted childcare services for working mothers.

7

Tilly was turning fifty and planned a huge celebratory birthday party at her Maroubra home. Feeling sorry for Kate Leigh, she called and asked if she had recovered enough after her recent fall to attend the birthday bash.

"I'm still laid up with a crook leg, love. I wish you a good day and make sure you drop by for a cuppa when you're sobered up!" Kate replied.

In the days preceding the shindig, crates of champagne, wine, whiskey, gin, and beer were delivered and stored in the spare room. On the morning of the party, decorators hung bunting, balloons, and streamers around the backyard fences and clothesline.

On the big day, in between cooking his favourite dishes for the guests, Eric helped Tilly's bodyguards prepare a bar area to the left of the yard where the neighbours would remain undisturbed by rowdy drunkards. George arrived later in the morning and with the help of a few of his mates, began setting up the tables and chairs in the centre of the yard before taking Tilly to the hairdresser.

Later that afternoon, dazzlingly adorned with over two thousand pounds worth of diamonds, sapphires, rubies and pearls, Tilly looked the epitome of a queen when she walked into the living room. Eric wolf whistled and said he wasn't going to leave her side all night, lest some man came and whisked her away. Dressed in her new lemon and black gown and black court shoes, Tilly did an awkward pirouette to show off her new look. Eric jumped from the settee and grabbed her hand as she went over the side of her heels. Tilly laughed as she recovered from the faux pas without his assistance. "Just one more thing and then we'll go and greet everybody."

"You look perfect, sweetheart. Nothing can make you look any more beautiful." Eric whispered in her ear as he held her close.

"Get orf with you. Go sit down and wait."

Standing in front of the living room mirror, Tilly placed her English rhinestone tiara on her head, carefully weaving her fringe through the front and side of the coronet before spraying it with hair lacquer to keep it in place.

"I think I'm ready now, my darling." Tilly said with a smile as she tucked an unruly curl back into her tiara.

"Oh, bless. Look at you my love. You add more sparkle to my life than the stars in heaven."

"And you dazzle my world every moment orf the day, sweet'art."

"Are you ready to greet your guests, beautiful?" Eric asked as he took hold of his wife's hand.

"I sure am. It's time to get this party up on its legs!"

"The caterers 'ave done a bloody amazing job!" Tilly looked over a table laden with hams, geese, chickens, suckling pigs, turkeys, lobsters, prawns, and oysters. She walked over to the second table and inspected the salads, vegetables, and savouries, picking up one of the hors d'oeuvres and tasting it. "Delicious!"

The head caterer supervised the staff as they placed the sweets on the third table, and thanked Tilly for the compliment. "Happy birthday, Mrs. Parsons."

Standing by the gate, Tilly gleefully greeted each of her guests as they arrived. Over three hundred people—tipsters, jockeys, dogmen, her bank manager, as well as her interior decorator, solicitors, horse owners, friends, and employees, arrived to celebrate the crime queen hitting the half century.

An hour after her guest's arrival, Tilly mounted the back steps and stood on the small patio before asking for everyone's attention. "Now, the rules for this party are that everyone is to 'ave a good time. There'll be dancing and singing all night. There's plenty to drink and eat, thanks to my wonderful 'usband and caterers. But don't any orf yous put on a blue or rort out my 'ome. If anyone wants to be a galah, they'd better fly away now while they've still got the feathers to fly with!" Tilly winked toward the reporter she had invited from the *Smith's Weekly* as she emphasised the final rule.

The party was well into the celebrations when Tilly made her way to where Eric and George were slicing meat, she took hold of a carving knife and forcefully plunged it into a roasted pig. She smirked as she looked toward her guests and shouted: "Fair dinkum. I wish to God this 'ere suckling pig was Bumper Farrell!"

Everyone laughed and cheered.

After the multitude of birthday toasts were made, the guests all gathered around a table full of brightly wrapped presents. George tied a blindfold around his auntie's eyes, pulling it as tight as possible before he zigzaggedly manoeuvred her to the table as the guests playfully joked for her to be careful of her next step and not to go left, right, or straight ahead. When they stopped, Tilly felt around in front of her trying to gauge where she was.

"C'mon Till, feel your way over and open your gifts." Olive said with a laugh.

"I can't bloody see where I'm going with George at the wheel, let alone open the gifts."

When George finally removed the blindfold, Eric was standing in front of Tilly holding a small box wrapped in bright blue paper in his hand. When she unwrapped the gift and saw the glittering diamond pendant enclosed within, she gasped. "Oh, my darling 'usband, thank you! This is just beautiful! You spoil me so." Tilly wept as she kissed Eric. Their guests clapped them both before raising their glasses with a cheer.

"I'm going to need a 'ole new room added to the 'ouse to fit all these presents in!" She cheerfully shouted," Thank you everyone for the wonderful birthday gifts."

With the help of Olive, Grace and Maisy, Tilly began opening the presents and personally thanked the donor after each one. Almost half an hour passed before she opened the final gift. Then, with glistening eyes, she stood back and appreciatively looked over the jewellery, orchids, perfume, crystal, furs, lingerie, napery, and silverware from her friends and guests.

As they made their way toward the birthday cake, the guests made way for the birthday girl and Eric. With her bronchitis playing up, Tilly asked Eric to help her to blow out the candles. After a round of 'Happy Birthday' was sung, one of Tilly's associates, Archibald St Claire, better known as 'Tools Carpenter', toasted her. "It gets my goat up when I see the newspapers giving the coppers the big wrap-up. All they do for Tilly is get her scone hot! No-one can compare a good girl like Tilly with a mob of droobs and flat feet!"

Tilly thanked Archie for his kind words before turning to her guests. "Now you can all get stuck into the suckling pigs and scran!"

Eric was the first to pike out at around two o'clock in the morning when he started shouting that he was 'the best bloody cook in Australia!' Tilly laughed and hugged her inebriated husband before asking Neville and John, two of her henchmen, to put him to bed.

After returning from settling Eric, the journalist from the *Smith's Weekly* approached Tilly explaining that he would like an interview before heading home. He had recorded many of the night's events but wanted more information. They discussed the gifts, the food and Tilly's fabulous jewellery, but then he committed the cardinal sin and asked her for the names of her guests…

"Are you fuckin 'daft? I don't give out names. I'm no snitch! I only put these parties on to please my friends and Eric's relations. I make them extra grouse so I can nark old Kate Leigh, in a friendly way, mind you. We are the best of friends now. Poor Katie 'ad a fall and damaged 'er leg, else ways, she'd be 'ere beside me 'aving a go at you as well. Kate's parties were always drab, not as cheerful as mine. The names orf the people 'ere don't matter to you or anyone else. Just print in the paper that my solicitors, interior decorator, jockeys, and barmaids, 'orse and dog trainers and owners, gay girls, tip slingers, as well as family and friends had a grouse time. Actually, say this: "*Everybody* was at Tilly's menagerie except coppers, tip orfs, fizgigs and other mugs!"

"There's no-one here that would like an interview with me. I'm sure there are many who would like to brag about attending your wonderful birthday soiree…"

"Listen 'ere, see that bloke over there? Well, 'e's my bank manager. People like 'im don't want everyone knowing their business. You write what I told you and we'll remain good friends." Tilly gave him a bottle of whiskey, thanked him for attending her party and wished him a good night.

When the reporter left, Tilly then made her way to the makeshift stage and began singing. Three hundred family and friends joined in when she sang *If I had my life to live over*. She was surprised when Eric joined her onstage and they crooned *I'll be your sweetheart*, followed by her most favoured song that took her back to the music halls in Camberwell, "*Why don't we do this more often…*"

Around five in the morning, those partiers who weren't overly inebriated drove themselves home, others slept where they fell in the backyard. Those who were a tad more sober, made their way into the house and made their bed wherever they could find a vacant spot. After seeing several of her guests off with a sprightly rendition of *Knees up mother brown* on the footpath, Tilly stepped over the sleeping bodies and made her way to bed.

The telephone ringing woke Tilly and most of the hungover stragglers later that morning. It was a newspaper journalist calling to ask her if any police or criminals had attended her party. She caustically replied: "You weren't invited to my party because you're a fuckin' mug. Now piss orf!" before slamming the handset down.

7

In late October, a phone call from a well-respected journalist surprised Tilly one morning. Arthur Helliwell, a big shot columnist in the newspaper world who scribed for British Sunday tabloid, *People*. He was on an Australian stopover on the last leg of an international jaunt and rang to invite Tilly for a drink and a chat at a Sydney hotel.

She politely accepted the invitation as she fought to keep her excitement from her voice. Tilly didn't trust reporters. She understood that journalists needed to make money, which they usually made by stretching the truth, fabricating statements, and generally assassinating innocent peoples' characters. However, she felt an interview for *People*, no matter what crass and untrue statements Helliwell wrote about her, would be a feather in her cap.

Dressed to the nines and dripping with diamonds, Tilly strolled through the Long Bar in the Australia Hotel, like she didn't have a care in the world. She looked around the room and spotted a rotund man with a pencil moustache and wearing a tattered Homburg that had seen much better days, sipping on a scotch. He nodded his head when he saw her and waved her over.

"Mrs. Devine, I presume."

"Pleased to meet you, Arthur. Now, what are we going to talk about today?" Tilly asked, getting straight to the point.

"You, Mrs. Devine, and everything about you." Helliwell smiled dubiously. "But first, if it's okay by you, can my photographer take a photo of us together?"

"It's Mrs. Parsons now." Tilly corrected before turning to smile at the camera. The photographer took several shots of the two together, and then when she thought he had finished, Tilly took a deep draw of her cigarette, and the photographer snapped another photo.

"What did you fuckin' do that for? I wasn't ready for another picture to be taken!"

"They're the best kind." The photographer replied before hastily leaving the bar.

Helliwell began his interview which left Tilly unimpressed with the way the questions were going and told the columnist so.

"Let me tell you what I want you to know, and as usual Mr. 'elliwell, you'll make orf it what you will."

Tilly finished her narrative, then stood and tossed a shilling into a nearby chandelier and turned to leave.

"Mrs. Devine, I mean, Parsons, is the interview over?" Helliwell asked perplexed. "And why did you throw a coin into the chandelier?"

"I've spent enough time in your arrogant fuckin 'company listening to fuckin' sarcastic remarks about Australia and calling Australians fuckin' uneducated colonists. You're nothing but a priggish nobody who makes a name for 'imself by running down others. My work is much more 'onest than yours will ever be! As for throwing a coin into the chandelier, it's an age-old tradition 'ere. The money is collected and 'anded over to charity. Now good day to you and don't fuckin' call me again!"

Needless to say, Helliwell's editorial went ahead and was more flattering than Tilly had expected it to be. His headline read: 'This City Gave Me Such a Shock', above the photo of Tilly smoking with her diamond ring laden fingers holding the cigarette and him sipping from a glass of whiskey.

'The typical Sydney "sport" glosses over a marked inferiority complex with an irritating and aggressive rudeness. He laces his conversation with the army's favourite adjective to the point of monotony, insult strangers as a matter of course and generally goes around looking for trouble.'

Sydney, he reported, 'was a rough, tough, money-mad, good time city, where uncouth swearing, "sports", racetracks and two-up gambling schools were the main attractions. He also reported that most Australians acted like wild ignorant convicts.

He mentioned Sammy Lee's nightclub and Joe Taylor's Celebrity Club, and compared the food, the music and floor shows with Mayfair's best. But he neglected to mention the thousand pounds he was paid to write such a glowing report, or the lovely ladies who kept him company to garner his favouritism. He also paid homage to Thommo's Two Up School where he had indulged in a few lessons and hours of gambling.

'Sydney has an underworld that puts anything I have seen in London, New York, Paris or even Marseilles in the shade. Its sordid, lawless East End terrorised by a riffraff of thugs, hoodlums, gunmen and larrikins, who would make the spivs of Soho's naughty square mile look like characters from a charm school, is more dangerous than the jungle after dark.'

Tilly then read the part about her:

'Boss of the district and certainly Sydney's most colourful character, is the fabulous "Diamond Tilly" Devine, a peroxide blonde from Camberwell Green, who owns the most glittering collection of jewellery in Australia. Tilly, the self-confessed Queen of the Underworld, was decked out in thirteen expensive rings, two diamond necklaces, a ruby and sapphire necklace, two bracelets and a magnificent, jewelled wristwatch when I met her.

"Just a few little trinkets love," she said. "I don't feel dressed without 'em."

Tilly, who thinks nothing of donating £1000 to charity, or spending £500 on children's parties, is probably one of Sydney's wealthiest citizens.'

Chapter Twenty Seven

A Year of Wins and Losses

A very wet New Year's Eve for 1951 found Tilly once again bedecked herself in jewels, one of her best frocks, and wrapped in her French lapin fur coat to attend a party in Bondi. Eric tried to talk her out of going due to the heavy rain, but Tilly, always the party girl, insisted on attending.

Arriving fashionably late just after nine o'clock, the Parsons quickly blended into the crowd of revellers. It wasn't long before Tilly spotted several former associates, so she and Eric joined them. As they sat under a canvas shelter, the group reminisced about the past, shocking Eric into speechlessness several times. Tilly was surprised to learn, that like her, the men were leading somewhat normal lives, but all mentioned they were missing the hey days of the 1920s and 30s.

As the alcohol flowed and the night wore on, several of the guests became a little frisky. One woman stripped off her frock and danced amongst the party goers in her French silk underwear. Another removed all her clothing and turned cartwheels until Roger, the host of the party threw a blanket over her and his wife guided her inside. But on the whole, most of the guests were well behaved as they sang, danced in the rain, or chatted in little cliques, waiting for the countdown to midnight.

While Tilly was laughing and pointing at a drunken man wearing a brown paper boat hat, holding a bottle of beer in one hand, a bible in the other and citing bible verses, she felt a tap on her shoulder. When she turned around, she was face-to-face with James Devine.

"What the fuck are you doing 'ere!" Tilly blurted out in shock.

"Same thing you are, celebrating the coming of the new fuckin' year. I see you brought your war hero with you."

"You're jealous because 'e was more of a soldier than you were."

Still quick tempered, Jim punched Tilly in her mouth, knocking her to the ground and dislocating her jaw. He finished his assault with two kicks to her stomach. Several men rushed to Tilly's aid, a further two struggled to hold Devine back from continuing his attack.

One partygoer rushed to Roger, the host of the party, and told him to call an ambulance, it was an emergency. Two women helped Tilly into the house and sat her on the bed in the master bedroom. Tilly held her jaw in place as the voices of Eric and Jim arguing outside, sounded above the din of the party. Raising herself from the bed, she looked out the window just in time to see Eric punch Devine so hard he sent him sprawling to the ground. When the police arrived, it took two constables to pull Eric off Devine.

When he walked into the bedroom, Sergeant Ware was visually appalled by the injuries Tilly had sustained. It was his first meeting with the infamous brothel madam. Ware had been raised on stories of her antics and crimes by his father who was a sergeant at Darlinghurst Police Station for thirty-five years.

The bloodied and aged woman sitting before him didn't resemble the tough and robust Queen of the 'Loo he had envisaged. Roger led the ambulance attendants through to Tilly, and whilst they were treating her wounds, Ware returned and told her he had arrested her former husband and he would be taken to the cells at Bondi police station. Not even a broken jaw could keep Tilly down, she jumped to her feet and abused the sergeant and demanded that he leave Jim Devine alone. She screamed at him that Jim was drunk and didn't know what he was doing. Ware replied that his assault on her was a police matter and it was his job to protect the public from such a violent man.

"What kind orf a mug lair are you comin in 'ere with a 'ead like a boarding 'ouse cup of tea, mouthin orf! Just leave 'im alone you fuckin' prick! I won't press any charges against the bastard if you take 'im to court. All I want is for 'im to get out orf my life for good!"

Leaving Tilly with the ambulance attendants, Ware made his way to the backyard and found his constables had handcuffed both Eric and Devine. "Release Parsons. Take Devine to the station."

The following morning, Jim was released on bail and told not to leave Sydney until after his court appearance. True to form, Devine immediately broke his bail conditions and returned to Melbourne.

Eric told Tilly, who was still infirmed at St. Vincent's Hospital, that she'd been charged and fined three pounds in absentia for using indecent language to a police officer.

"I'll show him indecent fuckin' language!"

"Now, now, petal, I've paid the fine and all you have to worry about is getting home and back into my arms where I can look after you."

7

On the 17th of January at around eight o'clock in the evening, Eric answered a knock at the door. Tilly was relaxing in a cool bath suffering from being sunburnt after spending the day at Bondi beach. When he answered the door, there were two men standing there. "Can I…" Eric had not even finished his sentence when the man standing to his right, thrust a knife at him. Eric jumped back but was stabbed in his left cheek. The men then ran to a blue car that was parked across the road and sped off.

Tilly was relaxing as she lay back in the cool bath water when she heard Eric stumble into the bathroom. "What the fuck 'appened to you?!"

"Some mug just stabbed me at the front door!"

"Did you recognise them?" Tilly said as quickly climbed out of the bath. "God fuckin' 'elp them if I get 'old of the bastards!" She growled as she held a towel against her husband's bloody cheek.

"Never saw them before in my life. And you just leave it be. I don't want you getting into any trouble because of me!"

"I'll get some clothes on and drive you to the 'ospital. They will pay my love, no matter what you say"

"It's just a scratch love. It's not worth you going to gaol over."

But Tilly would not hear of it. She quickly dressed in a summer frock, stepped into her pink fluffy slippers, slid her rings on her fingers, and then drove Eric to St. Vincent's Hospital.

A nurse placed Eric onto a bed in a casualty room and went for the doctor, stopping by the nurses' station to call the police first. The hospital staff were well aware of who Matilda Parsons was and with her husband presenting at the hospital stabbed and bloodied, the nurse in charge was concerned that she had razor slashed her husband.

Mr. Parsons, what have you done to yourself?" Dr. Richards asked with a smile.

"Answered the front door." Eric joked in reply.

"You're a very lucky man, an inch higher and you would have lost your eye." The doctor said as he prepared to stitch Eric's wound.

"If I find out who did this…they'll lose more than an eye!" Tilly fumed.

"Don't bother your beautiful self about it. It could have been much worse, my darling."

As Tilly sat by her husband's hospital bed, two C.I.B. consorting squad detectives walked in.

"We're here to speak with you about your stabbing attack, Mr. Parsons." Detective Olsen stated.

"I'm sorry that you've made the trip down here for nothing Detectives, but I do not seek police action. It's probably a case of mistaken identity as I don't have any enemies." Eric replied.

"Was it James Devine, your wife's former husband who did this to you?" The second detective asked.

"Leave him out orf this! That mongrel's in Melbourne. A quick phone call will prove that. Jim's living 'appily with another woman and 'as no cause to attack Eric." Tilly almost spat. "Before you leave, can you please tell those reporters in the waiting room to go. We're not interested in an interview!"

7

"I feel like going to the Melbourne Cup this year," Tilly mentioned over breakfast one morning.

"There's nothing stopping us from going, is there?" Eric asked as he buttered his toast.

"Yeah, but there may be a problem with the Melbourne police. I skipped out on them years ago. I'm too old to go to gaol now."

"Change your name for the flight. No-one will know who you are then. That's if you behave yourself."

"Wherever I go, trouble follows me."

"The only trouble that will be following you my love, is me!"

That afternoon, Eric drove down to Mascot Airport and booked two seats on an Australian National Airways flight to Melbourne for the 5th of November. He registered Tilly's ticket in the name of Mrs. Mary

Davis. While he was away, Tilly rang the Menzies Hotel in Melbourne and booked a suite for four nights and asked them to arrange a chauffeur driven car for the duration of their stay.

The weeks before the Melbourne jaunt, Tilly visited her favourite city boutiques and purchased several outfits. She then went to Zink & Sons Tailors and picked up the suits and shirts she had ordered for Eric several months prior. When she arrived at the tailor's store that morning, she pushed through the line-up of men waiting to be measured, excusing herself as she told them that she had an order to pick up. Tilly always minded her manners at Zinks. She had a soft spot for the owners who always treated her like a proper lady whenever she was in their store.

The visit that day was one with sad tidings. Thomas Zink the store owner's son told her that his father had sold the store and it would soon be under new ownership. Tilly hugged the young man who she had seen grow up over the decades, and told him that times change, and she should know, she had survived two world wars and the changes that occurred after them.

After picking up the suits, Tilly stopped by Buckingham Palace Emporium, Reuben Brasch's and Winn's to buy new stockings and perfume, then the butcher's for lamb chops and sausages. Feeling a little peckish, she stopped at the delicatessen and picked up two corned beef and pickles horseshoe rolls before returning to her car.

As she drove up the street, Tilly smiled as she passed Thommo's, an upstairs illegal two-up business that was one of Jim's favourite haunts. He often arrived home with a headache from Thommo's pet cockatoo that squawked all night long. She waved at Jack Gibson, a third-grade rugby league player with St George, who was working as a bouncer at the entrance. Tilly had a soft spot for Jack, she found him a mischievous larrikin who always took time out for a chat.

Eric was sitting on the settee reading *The Mirror* when Tilly arrived home. She told him to close his eyes and then placed the suits wrapped in brown paper on the seat beside him and placed one of the horseshoe rolls on top. "Open!" Eric's face lit up with a smile when he saw the horseshoe roll.

"I was just thinking about making myself a sandwich. You read my mind, my darling girl. And what else do we have here… "He asked as he looked at the parcel.

"Open them and find out!"

"Oh, thank you, sweetheart," Eric exclaimed as he unwrapped his new suits and shirts. "You spoil me too much."

7

Before leaving for Melbourne, Tilly visited the Collaroy Crippled Children's Hospital. She had a few favourite kiddies there and wanted to give them each a toy to play with and a kiss goodbye. When she arrived, she was told that one of her favourite boys, Dennis, had died two days before. Tilly collapsed against the wall in shock and grief upon hearing the devastating news. The nurses helped her to a nearby chair and Tilly wept her heart out on the shoulder of Sister Caroline, whom she shared a close bond with. "Take this. You buy my Denny the best coffin in the funeral parlour and place a blue teddy with a bright blue ribbon beside 'im. Denny will think it's 'is Tilly keeping 'im warm in the cold ground." Tilly said as she handed the Sister fifty pounds.

7

The flight to Melbourne was a bumpy one. Tilly blessed herself and whispered a few Hail Marys thinking she was going to die. However, one rather bad patch of turbulence had her screaming, "Jesus, Mary and fuckin' Joseph!" at the top of her lungs as other terrified passengers let out screams or curses of their own.

Upon arriving at the Menzies Hotel, Tilly unpacked their bags. "I'm going to 'ave a shower and wash all this fuckin' cigarette and cigar smell out of my 'air!" Tilly grumbled as she stripped off her clothes and headed for the shower.

The following day she and Eric took in the views of Melbourne as their driver, Charlie, drove them around local points of interest. Eric asked the driver to wait outside the National Museum where he and Tilly spent over an hour viewing the mounted stuffed animals and skeletons. Next, Tilly asked Charlie to drive her to the Foy & Gibson department store and to wait outside. Whilst shopping, she thought she saw Jim and Anna. Her heart skipped a few beats. No matter what he had put her through, Jim still held a place in her heart. He was, after all, her first love.

Their next stop was the exclusive boutique, Georges of Collins Street. Tilly had read about the swanky boutique in several women's magazines and had always wanted to purchase one of their exquisite outfits. When she entered the store bedecked in her diamonds and pearls, the staff were quick to attend. She was offered a cup of tea and sponge cake as the models came out to show off the new season's fashions. Tilly bought up big, purchasing a pair of Gucci peep toe shoes which had their gold knight medallion insignia on the upper part of the shoe. She also purchased a 'Monarch' Hermes scarf, and a navy lace Dior dress.

By the time the Parsons returned to their suite, exhausted, they both fell asleep, only to be woken at six o'clock by room service delivering their dinner.

On Melbourne Cup morning, Eric was showered and dressed by eight o'clock. Tilly, however, was in a bother over which outfit to wear to Flemington. Eric advised her to wear the Dior dress, but she told him the hat she brought down didn't match it. So, in true Tilly style, she closed her eyes and whispered, "inky pinky ponky…" touching each of the outfits as she recited the childhood ditty, finally stopping on the one she'd wear.

Dressed in a purple, mint green and brown two-piece skirt set with a matching bolero jacket, Tilly stood at the mirror to make sure the shoulder pads sat snugly. Happy with her appearance, she slipped her feet into her lace mesh suede shoes, positioned her brown wide brimmed hat on her head before sliding thirteen sparkling diamonds rings on her fingers and clasping the sapphire necklace Eric had given her the previous Christmas, around her neck.

"You look absolutely beautiful my sweet!" Eric said as he admired his wife. "Here, this fur coat is just what you need to finish off your million pounds look."

"You look more handsome today than the day I married you, love." Tilly purred, returning the compliment as Eric helped her on with the coat before leaving their suite arm in arm to the limousine.

"Flemington Racecourse please Charlie." Eric almost sung as he directed the driver.

Both Tilly and Eric were big winners with the horses they backed in the races before the cup feature. Eric won over two hundred pounds on one horse after almost jumping the fence to chase it to the finish line.

However, for Tilly, the Melbourne Cup was the one she intended to splurge on. She read the form guide the hour before the race and noticed "Great World", one of the horses she was going to place a win and place on, had been scratched. "At least Double Blank, Akbar, Prince o' Fairies, Grey Boots, and Delta are still in the race." Tilly sighed as she ran her red polished fingernail down the form page.

Tilly placed all her winnings from the previous races on each of the horses, but added an extra fifty pounds on Akbar, Delta, and Double Blank. Ten minutes before the siren was about to ring, Tilly spotted Morse Code, the favourite to win, and was so impressed by him that she gave Eric twenty pounds to put a win and place bet on him.

She and Eric then watched and cheered along with the crowd when the twenty-eight horses took to the field. The spectators cheered louder as the horses headed toward the starting point. The clock ticked down for start off time and as soon as the starter pistol cracked in the air, the horses were off. Tilly was cheering for so many horses that at times, she confused their names, causing Eric and several people around her to laugh, especially when she called out 'Grey Fairy Boots!'.

Tilly and Eric, along with the other spectators watched in trepidation when the horses started running in a tight pack. Morse Code was the fourth from the lead, when his rider, Jack Thompson, made a dash around Blue Vest, he clipped the horse's heels, causing him to roll over. The crowd went deathly silent as they watched the mishap play out in front of them. A tremendous cheer then emanated from the stands when both the horse and Billy Cook, the jockey, miraculously escaped the fray, unscathed.

However, Morse Code's rider was forced to jump over Billy Cook, which cost him his winning position. Akbar's rider, Larry Wiggins, managed to get his horse to the front furlong and it looked like he was going to win the race, but Delta's rider, Neville Sellwood, spurred the stallion on and wore Akbar down, to take the lead and win the race by three quarters of a length.

Tilly was on a roll, picking the first three horses of the Melbourne Cup. She earned herself over four thousand pounds through her Sydney bookmakers and almost two thousand pounds from the Melbourne oncourse bookies. Eric made himself a cool nine hundred pounds.

After Eric picked up their winnings, they left to celebrate their good luck at the restaurant in the Menzies' Hotel. However, as Tilly was about to climb into the back of the limousine, she was arrested by Melbourne C.I.B.

"What the 'ell are you arresting me for?" Tilly screamed, "I've been 'ere enjoying the Melbourne Cup and I get accosted by the cops!"

"Mrs. Devine, we're here to arrest you on the consorting charge that was brought against you in 1934. We've been waiting seven years to nab you."

"Mrs. Devine? You've mixed me up with someone else. My name is Mrs. Mary Davis!"

"No, you are Mrs. Matilda Parsons, formally Mrs. Matilda Devine." A detective snarled as he shoved a police photograph in front of her that was taken at her arrest in 1934. "You're a lot older, but you are indeed the woman in this picture."

"I thought you buggers would 'ave forgotten me by now! Can't you give me a break? Please don't put me in gaol. I am much older now, as you say…"

"No, straight to gaol for you Mrs. Devine! You should be careful about how many enemies you make. One of them snitched."

Tilly didn't say another word to the police but asked Eric to take her handbag and find her a good solicitor. She realised at that moment it *was* Jim she'd seen at the department store, and he obviously saw her, too. No-one, not even her bodyguards, knew she was on her way to Melbourne.

When she appeared at the Melbourne City Court, Tilly was found guilty of escaping bail on the charge of consorting with known criminals in 1934 and was sentenced to twelve months in Pentridge Prison.

Eric was beside himself. He knew his wife was too unwell to spend so long in prison and pleaded for the court to take mercy upon her. But the magistrate said that he would not pass on his responsibility of protecting society from a woman who had excess of one hundred and eighty convictions on the sheets. He further stated that she had exceeded the court's limits of forbearance. Eric watched on helplessly as Tilly was led from the court sobbing.

The following morning, Tilly's friend, Dolly Quinn, whose house she was visiting in 1934 when she was arrested, arrived at the watch house with a cooked chicken, fruit, chocolates, and vegetables. Dolly wanted to make sure that her friend had good food to eat so her health didn't suffer any further.

Fortunately for Tilly, on Friday, the 6th of December, after only serving five weeks of her twelve months sentence, she was released by the Victorian Attorney-General. She had been coughing up blood whilst in the cold prison cell and spent most of her time in the infirmary. The doctor advised the Attorney-General that Tilly was not a well woman and would probably die in prison before serving the full sentence.

When she arrived at Mascot Airport, reporters, who were tipped off by Melbourne C.I.B, awaited her arrival. But Eric had Tilly's protection covered. He had called her trusted bodyguards to protect her from the frenzied press. The photographers were unable to snap a single photo of Tilly as Eric and her protectors rushed her to the car.

When a reporter from the *Truth* rang her and requested an interview, Tilly told him that she was still recovering from her ordeal in Pentridge but would allow an interview over the phone. She told him that the prison food was disgusting and inedible. She also said that she much preferred the food served in Long Bay. Tilly complained that the prison bedding was only changed once a fortnight as was their prison clothing. But her biggest complaint was about being 'strip searched down to the skin she was born in' for drugs and guns. Tilly then asked the reporter to thank everyone for the telegrams and letters she received from strangers whilst in prison, and the Christmas cards and letters that were awaiting her on her return home.

"My neighbours, who are on the square, came and shook hands with me when I got 'ome. All this kindness 'as made me vow never to get into trouble again. As a matter orf fact, I 'aven't been in trouble since I married Eric Parsons. No-one gives me credit for that."

7

As she had every year on the 23rd of December, Tilly delivered Christmas presents to the kiddies who were lamenting yuletide alone in hospital. Dressed in a Santa suit and sporting a fluffy long white beard, Eric carried two bright red bags filled with toys. When they had finished with the children at St. Vincent's hospital, the Parsons returned home to restuff the bags for the children at the Collaroy Crippled Children's Hospital.

The staff were accustomed to Tilly showing up to spoil the children. They knew who she was, and of her reputation, but they didn't care. The love the brothel madam showed the children, and the respect she gave the staff was all that mattered to them.

The last leg of their Christmas giving was made to the Maroubra house where they filled the bags with soap and baby gifts before leaving for the mothers and newborns at the Crown Street Women's Hospital.

Tilly's Christmas Eve party for the Palmer Street neighbourhood children and their parents was the highlight of the neighbourhood. Eric again donned his Santa suit and beard and walked around handing out toys wrapped in blue for boys and pink for girls. Each mother received a cake of scented soap and a duck or a chicken to roast for Christmas Day. The fathers received a bottle of beer.

At their Maroubra home, Christmas Day was filled with fun for kids of all ages, even adults with backyard cricket, chasing each other with the garden hose, hide and seek, and annoying the drunks who fell asleep in the backyard. This was Tilly's most favourite day when the family came together and shared presents, jokes, laughter, and love!

Tilly finally took time out on Boxing Day to go through the box of letters Eric had hidden away until she was in a relaxed mood. He chose his time well. After they had enjoyed a lovely meal of leftovers from Christmas Day and Tilly had imbibed several glasses of wine, he handed her the box while she was relaxing on the settee. Tilly opened the letter that was on the top of the pile, which was from her sister, Katherine, who had sent her the full page editorial Helliwell had written.

Tilly read Helliwell's description of her and was still surprised that it wasn't nasty after the words she'd had with him. "Fuckin snivelling coward didn't even 'ave the guts to say 'e almost pissed 'is pants in the Australia 'otel bar when I stood up to 'im! If 'e thinks we're going to be upset about his opinion of Sydney, the bastard's wrong. All 'e's done is told the world that we're tough down 'ere in Australia!"

"Sweetheart, there's more letters, many more," Eric almost whispered. He left the room as Tilly opened a letter from her brother, Peter and was stunned when hundreds of letters addressed to her from Britain spilled out from a satin pillowcase Eric emptied on the settee beside her.

"Why 'ave all these strangers written to me?"

"I haven't opened them. They're addressed to you, love."

After opening around two dozen or more letters, Tilly was ready to wring Helliwell's neck. Every single one of those letters were from people begging her to send them money before their children starved to death. Others needed money to be able rent a home, several mothers asked for money to put on a birthday party for their child, while most requested money to pay their bills.

"They're biting me for everything from thousands orf pounds to pay rent on six-roomed 'ouses and buying them washing machines. Several men even proposed marriage!" Tilly bewailed.

"Give them to me, love. I'll throw them on the fire."

"Next time I'm in London, I'm going to find that bastard 'elliwell and punch 'im on his bloody nose!"

7

With Darlinghurst police reinstating arrests under the *Disorderly House Act*, Tilly, ever the shrewd businesswoman, began setting her girls up in her blocks of flats in Kings Cross, Darlinghurst, and Bondi. The women paid her low rent and the normal share of their earnings, in return for a furnished flat, protection and their medical bills paid. 191 Palmer Street remained close to her heart, and Tilly couldn't bear to shut it down completely, so she allowed Mary, Maisie, and Hazel, her most long-standing working girls, to remain working from the premises.

The first week of March, Tilly received a phone call from Kate asking if she could come over as she needed to speak with her about something urgent. Concerned, Tilly told Eric that she thinks that there may be something wrong with Kate and was going over to check on her. "I won't be gone long." She said as she kissed her husband goodbye.

When she arrived, Kate was furtively looking around outside, then quickly closed the door.

"What's up, Katie? You're worrying me."

"I'm fucked, Tilly. The fuckin' tax man is chewing the fat off my arse! I'm going to be bankrupt!"

"When did all this 'appen? Are you okay? 'ave you got food? 'ave you got money 'idden?" Tilly asked concerned for her former nemesis.

"I have a bit hidden away that may keep the bastards from my door for a year or so, but unless I can get my old bones into something that will make me money like the old days, I'm done, bankrupt and headed to a paupers grave."

"Fuck. I'll 'elp you where I can," Tilly promised.

"They're after you too, Tilly. They'll be knocking down your door soon. They're bastards, not like our coppers at all. They won't turn a blind eye. Get rid of what you can, hide the rest or you're done for too."

Tilly remained at Kate's for a couple of hours as they pondered ways to get her out of her pickle. "I'm going to be poorer than those I've helped all these years."

Again, promising to help Kate, Tilly told her that she would talk to Eric and see if they could come up with any ideas between them. She hugged her worried friend before leaving and told her to call if she needed anything. As she made her way to her car, Tilly furtively looked up and down the street for any official looking men sitting in a car.

CHAPTER TWENTY EIGHT

Time Heals Old Wounds, the Present Brings New Scars

Tilly fell onto the settee in disbelief upon hearing that King George VI had died in his sleep.

"This is the most 'eartbreaking news, Eric!" Tilly sobbed into her handkerchief as her husband attempted to console her. "The King was such a good man. 'e did so much for us during the war. God bless 'im."

"I think what you need to cheer you up is another holiday, my love. Why don't we take a trip back to England for the Queen's coronation when it's announced?"

"Yes, that's exactly what I need. You think of everything, darling. It will be good to see my family again."

7

True to her word, once a week, Tilly turned up to Kate's place with a pot of chicken or rabbit stew, beef cuts, and personal toiletries. She was saddened by the fall of her friend and regretted the years they had fought as enemies, instead of two strong women working in a partnership that could have seen them rich enough for two lifetimes.

To help her friend out, Tilly allowed Kate to sell illegal alcohol through her brothels, so she could retain some pride by earning her own money. This enterprise made Kate around thirty to forty pounds most weeks, which was a great help to her. However, she didn't know it was Tilly who was buying most of the grog. The majority of the brothel clients preferred to buy from bootleggers selling stolen quality whiskey.

7

Tilly found herself in court again on the 19th of July 1952, when she was brought up on charges of running a disorderly house at 191 Palmer Street, which effectively closed the premises down. She received a five pounds fine and left the court cursing that Australia's legal system was filled with puritanical and moralistic hypocritical prudes, especially seeing the Supreme Court judge was once a regular client at her Rose Bay brothel.

Not to be outsmarted, the brothel madam moved all her girls into her units, intending to re-open Palmer Street when she returned home from England.

7

The Queen's Coronation was set for the 2nd of June, so Tilly, wanting to arrive in London with their suitcases filled with up-to-date fashions, took her husband out on a shopping spree in the Sydney up-market boutiques and menswear stores. A few good-natured tiffs broke out between the couple when she wanted to buy Eric a mustard and white long sleeve shirt and a tie with yellow, crimson, blue, and white triangle patterning. Eric won that battle, but Tilly won the war when she went ahead and purchased him a pair of dark blue gabardine trousers and a long sleeve shirt patterned with crimson coloured diamond shapes.

"Till, my darling, I know diamonds are a passion of yours, but must I wear them on a shirt?" Eric joked as he conceded defeat and took hold of the bag of his newly acquired clothing.

As usual, Tilly wasn't shy about flashing around her wads of pound notes. Within moments of stepping into Chelsea's Boutique, she amassed an armful of dresses and made her way into a changing room. By the time they left the shop, she had purchased five new hats, six pairs of shoes, eight dresses, three cardigans, two woollen coats, and two dozen pairs of stockings.

Plans for a swanky bon voyage dinner was afoot, which the Parsons' decided to host at the Grand Central Hotel. Tilly told reporters who crowded outside her home a few days before the dinner, that she 'Extends an open invitation to everyone who has a kind thought for a sinner like me. I don't particularly want screws or wallopers, but if they turn up, I'll do the decent thing by them.'

On the 4th of January, Tilly told her guests during the farewell party, that she had already packed three travelling trunks with her best furs, frocks, and footwear, as well as a dozen expensive evening gowns. "I've been dreaming about this day since the death of our beloved king. May 'e rest in peace! Unless I'm six feet under the ground, I'll be there waving to our new queen from a good vantage point!"

"Did you have any room for Eric's clothes?" Shifty Steve, a friend of Eric's from the Navy, jokingly asked her.

"Eric will 'ave all the ladies chasing 'im with the dapper suits 'e'll be wearing. 'e's going to look more 'andsome than the Duke! We 'ave the best clothes money can buy!"

When Tilly and Eric arrived at Circular Quay to board the SS *Himalaya*, they were besieged by local reporters. Eric had to push a path for them to get to the gangway. Tilly smiled for the cameras and answered the volley of questions that were thrown at her as Eric guardedly escorted her up the gangboard.

"Tilly, I love your hair!" A young reporter cried out.

Lightly touching her blonde curls, Tilly smiled and replied: "Thanks, lovey. One knob made a crack about my 'air being a wig. I told the old tart what she could do with 'erself! Just because a woman takes care orf her coiffure, that's the kind orf thing she gets!"

"How are you paying for the trip, Till?" Another journalist shouted out.

"We backed Dalray in the Melbourne Cup!" She replied with a laugh.

"Tilly, are you glad to be travelling first class?" A member of the press she hadn't seen before asked.

"I'd rather travel tourist love, but my bronchitis is playing up and a bit orf swank is good for the soul every now and then."

"Did you pack your diamonds?" Another reporter asked.

"Sweet'art, I am a lucky, lucky girl. I 'ave more diamonds than the Queen of England's stowaways - and better ones too!"

Reporters continued shouting out questions as the Parsons' stood among the other passengers as they waved goodbye to friends and loved ones. Tilly blew kisses as she threw colourful streamers from the deck as they waved farewell.

Tilly and Eric hugged one another near the railing as Tilly called down to everyone below: "ooroo, we'll be back when the money runs out!"

The *SS Himalaya* sailed out of Circular Quay while tugboats on either side of the ship tooted as they made their way to a stranded ship. Tilly and Eric offered one final wave before making their way to their luxury cabin.

Midway in their voyage the seas became quite rough. The choppy water caused the ship to roll and lurch from side to side and front to back, inducing a bout of seasickness for Tilly, a malady she had never experienced before.

"Oh, Eric love, my 'ead is swirling, even when I lay down and close my eyes, it won't go away. The walls and floor feel like they're moving. I feel like I'm going to die." Tilly complained before rushing to the toilet in the cabin to be sick.

"I'll just go to the ship's doctor and see what I can get to help you, sweetheart." Eric whispered as he lovingly brushed his wife's hair away from her face.

Eric returned to the cabin with a small box of Epsom salts and after adding several teaspoons of the powder to a glass of water, he handed it to Tilly.

"This tastes like fuckin' poison." Tilly complained with her face screwed up in disgust at its taste.

"It's all the doctor has for seasickness, love."

When the seas calmed, Tilly threw herself into getting to know the other passengers, dining and drinking bottles of champagne almost every night at a different table. She was the belle of the ball most nights, with everyone enjoying her lively personality and often, her bawdy stories.

On the 5th of February, Eric, and Tilly, dressed in her thick mink coat, disembarked the luxury liner at Tilbury. When she stepped off the gangway, she was immediately surrounded by the Fleet Street journalists. The newspapermen couldn't wait to interview the notorious and interesting brothel madam from Down Under and started shouting out questions.

When asked why she was in London, Tilly told them that she was there on a Coronation holiday. She added that she had travelled first class and it was her second time there with her husband, Eric. After writing down and rehearsing her speech for the newspapermen during her voyage, Tilly kept to script and told them that she did very well in Australia since arriving there as a nineteen-year-old girl in 1920.

"Are you still the queen of the Sydney underworld?"

"Contrary to what 'as been previously reported in the British newspapers, I 'ave been lucky on the racetrack and 'ave bought and sold properties to make my money, dear. It's been eighteen years since I was last in trouble. I am not a member orf the underworld. I mix only with nice people."

"Are you going to open a business, say… around the Soho area and engage in the night life?"

"If I did, I'm sure I'd see you there every night… but lovey, the English climate is bad for my bronchitis."

"How much did you bring for the Coronation?" Asked a large reporter at the front who had dribbled his latest meal down the front of his coat.

"Enough to keep my Chinese laundry bills paid. But I might need to go back 'ome in steerage!" Tilly said as she walked toward the hired limousine.

"Where are you going now?"

"To visit family."

"How many rings are you wearing Mrs. Parsons?" A reporter called out as he chased Tilly to her waiting car.

Tilly held both her hands up in the air and wriggled her fingers. "Let's just say I own more diamonds than the new queen!"

After the limousine driver skilfully lost the ensuing reporters and cameramen, Tilly and Eric arrived at her fifty-one-year-old sister's home. It had been many years since she had seen her younger sister and her husband, Frank, and they greeted each other warmly. Eric shook Frank's hand and thanked him for welcoming them to their home.

When everyone was seated, Frank left for the kitchen and five minutes later returned carrying a tray with a pot of tea, cups, and a cake. Lilly poured a cup of tea for them all and placed the cake and side plates on the coffee table for everyone to help themselves. Tilly was thrilled when she saw the cake. It had been some years since she had eaten an Eccles cake—her favourite treat as a child.

"Oh, Lilly, thank you. The Eccles are a lovely surprise! I've not 'ad one since leaving England! We eat a lot of sponge cakes, lamingtons, and scones in Australia."

"I thought as much. Eat as many as you like. I have some in a biscuit tin for you to take with you."

"Where are you staying?" Frank asked.

"I booked a suite at the Savoy until we find a temporary flat to rent during our stay."

"You can stay here with us if you wish. We have spare rooms now the children have married." Frank offered.

"It would be lovely if you could stay, Mattie. It's been ever so long since we spent time together."

"If it's not too much orf a bother, we'd love to." Tilly smiled. Feeling loved by family was something she rarely experienced.

Throughout their stay, Tilly spent a little time with Freddy, his wife Maude, and her grandsons, Richard and David. Unfortunately, her son was still cold and distant. He was more amicable with Eric, who he took to the local pub several times, leaving his mother at home with his family.

Tilly also visited her other siblings, including her sister, Nellie, who apologised for her rudeness when their mother was sick. United again with her siblings as well as her nieces and nephews, Tilly's heart was at peace.

The 2nd of June, the day of the coronation, Tilly looked out the window from her bed and saw that it was miserable and rainy. Not allowing the weather to ruin her day, she rifled through her wardrobe selecting warmer clothes and her best mink coat.

After months of anticipation, the Parsons joined the thousands of people who braved the pouring rain to await the arrival of the princess. The wet weather couldn't dampen Tilly's spirit, she was all geared up with British and Australian flags and an official souvenir coronation program.

The Parsons' made themselves comfortable along with numerous others in their pre-paid seats in the Mall. They were two rows from the street and could see the roadway quite clearly. Tilly looked around the area that once was familiar to her… she had once sold herself on the street not more than five hundred yards away. It was also where she had met Jim for the first time, almost thirty-eight years before.

Shivering in the freezing rain, Eric passed around a couple of small bottles of brandy he had in his coat pockets in preparation for the inclement weather. The cold and wet spectators thanked him as they eagerly sipped the body-warming liquid. One lady complimented Tilly on her beautiful hairdo, and she proudly replied that she'd had it styled by a French hairdresser the day before. While they were talking, the crowd burst into laughter when a band began playing *It ain't gonna rain no more.*

Tilly's party didn't have to wait long for Her Royal Highness to appear. The cheering crowd alerted them to her arrival. Tilly, Eric, and those around them waved their Union Jack flags in front of them. Tilly cheered loudly as the ornate gold state coach, pulled by eight Windsor Grey horses, passed them with the princess raising her hand in her stinted royal wave to the cheers from her subjects and tourists, along the way.

Just after half past twelve, cannons in Hyde Park and the Tower of London boomed as Big Ben chimed, proclaiming that Queen Elizabeth had been crowned. The crowds cheered and many within the crowd sang *God save the Queen* in unison.

Following the coronation ceremony, Tilly, along with millions of other royalists, witnessed the pomp and pageantry of the royal parade. The newly crowned Queen, her husband, Prince Philip, and representatives from more than forty Commonwealth states, waved as they passed the rejoicing well-wishers. Tilly had saved her loudest hurrahs and vigorously waved her Australian flag for when the Australian police and soldiers, who looked resplendent in their uniforms and wide-brimmed hats, marched by. Her cheering continued as the carriage conveying Robert Menzies and his wife Patty made their way past. She was thrilled when Menzies nodded toward her and smiled and waved.

Wanting to watch the rest of the procession in the comfort of somewhere dry, Tilly and Eric made their way to a crowded pub. Not being able to find a single chair, they stood alongside other patrons and watched the telecast of the remainder of the parade.

Seeing Queen Elizabeth together with her family on the Buckingham Palace balcony brought a tear to the sentimental brothel madam's eye. The proud and dignified look on the monarch's face touched her deeply. With a sea of people surrounding her, the Queen remained composed, but Tilly reckoned she would be greatly relieved that the coronation was finally over.

As Tilly and Eric left the pub, the booming sound of jet planes thundered through the air. They looked skyward and watched as the Royal Air Force flew across the sky in a tight aerial formation until they disappeared into the horizon.

Wanting to leave before hordes of people converged on the roads, Tilly stopped by a newsstand and purchased postcards to send to friends back home, and to also give her family in England.

She had not felt so excited and satisfied in her life. Tilly had seen the Queen. She had witnessed the coronation wearing more jewellery than the Her Majesty herself. "What a long way a lowly-born girl from the slums of England, 'as come. No matter 'ow, I am 'ere. I 'ave now fulfilled a dream. I can die 'appy!" Tilly whispered to herself.

7

Toward the end of their holiday, Eric woke up one morning with his left eye red and watery and complaining that the area was sore. Thinking something had flown into it, Tilly rinsed his eye with water. However, over the subsequent week, the irritation worsened, so Frank drove Eric to their local doctor.

Concerned by what he saw, the doctor immediately sent Eric to the hospital. The following morning his cancerous eye was removed. Tilly was beside herself with worry and blamed the cold English weather for her husband's illness.

Tilly remained by Eric's side, refusing to leave the hospital except to bathe and change her clothing and buy non-hospital food for them to eat. Eric's illness forced Tilly for think for the first time since their marriage, about losing her husband, which broke her heart. He had shown her what true love and devotion was. He had stood by her no matter what, never raised a hand to her or even yelled at her, even though she had given him good cause on numerous occasions. Eric worshipped and loved her, heart and soul and Tilly wasn't ready to say goodbye.

After Eric was released from Hospital, Tilly arranged their return home. She wanted her husband to be cared for by Australian specialists. She also wanted him home where he would be more comfortable than being thousands of miles away from his homeland. Tilly contacted the shipping office and asked for her ticket to be changed to an earlier date. When the clerk told her that he was unable to alter the ticket, she immediately purchased two first class tickets to Australia.

On their return voyage, Eric's health worsened. He experienced difficulties walking, suffered with persistent headaches, and blurred vision. The ship's doctor was concerned about Eric's symptoms and explained that he could only help with pain relief until they arrived in Sydney. He said that he would phone ship to shore and arrange for an ambulance to meet them to transfer Eric to the hospital when they dock in Sydney.

7

After several days of tests and x-rays, Eric and Tilly waited in the private hospital room for the prognosis. Tilly sat beside her husband, holding his hand tightly, every now and then lifting it to her lips, gently kissing it. But when she saw the expression on Dr Stewart's face when he entered the room, she knew then, the news was not going to be good.

"I'm sorry, Eric, but I have very grave news for you. The tests have revealed that you have an inoperable brain tumour."

Tilly let out a scream and promptly fainted. Eric was his usual unflappable self and was more concerned about his wife. He cradled Tilly in his arms and waited for her to come around as the doctor placed smelling salts under her nose.

When they were alone, Eric placed his arm around Tilly's shoulders and kissed her gently. "My love, I'll stay with you as long as I can. Your love will keep this old heart beating."

"You'll live forever then, my sweet'art. I love you more than life itself."

7

In October, Tilly was approached by her neighbour, Beryl. She was surprised to see that she was pregnant again. Beryl already had a four-year-old daughter and had given birth to a second daughter the previous year. She had tried to procure an abortion, but each doctor she visited had refused. She'd heard so many stories about backyard abortionists and didn't want to take the risk of dying or becoming sterile, so she placed the infant up for adoption. Beryl told Tilly that she was eight months pregnant and asked her if she would like to adopt her baby.

Tilly discussed the adoption with Eric, and he told her that they would be wise to seek the advice of a solicitor before deciding. Beryl, Tilly, and Eric met with Tilly's solicitor and one of his associates who had a greater understanding of family law. After a lengthy discussion and answering questions from the trio, he told them that he would draw up papers for a private adoption. He told Beryl that all she was required to do was to sign the consent for the adoption. Beryl was pleased that the process was easier than what she had endured after the birth of her daughter. She told the solicitor that as soon as the baby was born, she would be at his office to sign the required documents.

Eric knew that he wouldn't live to see his infant grow into an adult, but he couldn't bear the thought of Tilly being alone after he was gone. He was also aware of how much she regretted leaving her son with her parents all those years ago, and this was a way for him to make up for her not being able to be a mother.

The following month, Beryl gave birth to a healthy boy. Tilly was present for the birth and spent every day at the hospital taking care of the infant until Beryl was discharged. The proud new parents named him John Eric Parsons.

The solicitor arrived at the Malabar Road home when John was four weeks old. He wanted to give Beryl the chance to change her mind, but she told him having one child as an unwed mother was enough. She signed the legal adoption documents without a second thought. Tilly then handed the solicitor five hundred pounds for the legal fees and costs, and John was officially theirs.

Eric and Tilly doted on their John. He was loved by everyone and had plenty of 'aunts and uncles' who spoilt him just as much as his parents. During the first few months, Tilly barely left the side of his crib. She had set hours that people could visit and took on the role of a mother as if she'd given birth to John herself. Eric also doted on his new son, whenever he could get him out of Tilly's arms.

7

The *Liquor Amendment Act 1954* was implemented on the 1st of February 1955, extending the closing time for hotels to 10:00 pm. This change killed Kate's illicit liquor trade. To bring in an income, she started hiring out handcarts to fruit and vegetable vendors for two shillings and sixpence a day. She also received help from Tilly, who out of all her friends, next to her nephew, was the only one who stood by during her darkest years.

7

In August 1955, Maude contacted Tilly and told her that Freddy would like them to migrate to Australia. Tilly wouldn't hear of them emigrating as '*Ten Pound Poms*', so she paid for their passage. Teddy recorded his mother as his closest relative to assist his passage to Australia. They arrived at Fremantle on the *SS Strathaird* on the 20th of August and flew from Perth to Sydney's Mascot airport.

Even though their relationship was still strained, Tilly wanted to help her son and his family. She told Eric she was going to give them one of her three-bedroom units to live in rent-free. The month before their arrival, Tilly and Eric went shopping at Anthony Hordern & Sons and brought every item of furniture, modern electrical appliance, and household affects her family could possibly need. She then arranged to have the purchases delivered to a first-floor unit in a block of flats she owned in Coogee. On their way to the unit, they stopped by Buckingham's Department store and purchased linen.

For an entire week, Tilly and two of her retired girls cleaned and set the unit up so it was ready for her family. The excited mother and grandmother knew her son and daughter-in-law would be impressed with their new home. Tilly also arranged for telephones to be installed in the living room and main bedroom, which was completed the day before her family's arrival.

Two days after her family arrived, Tilly received a call from Maude thanking her for her kindness: "I was wondering, if we could meet her in the shelter of the Bondi Surf Pavilion so you can spend time with Richard and David?" Tilly jumped at the offer, weeping tears of gratitude when she thanked her daughter-in-law.

It was a windy afternoon, so Tilly decided to leave John at home with Eric bundled up in front of the fireplace. Before leaving, she and Eric loaded the car with toys for the boys, perfume and soap for Maude, and aftershave and an electric shaver for Freddy. When she entered the pavilion, the usual headfirst and gutsy Tilly had disappeared, and a sedate and somewhat timorous woman had taken her place. She stood at the entrance unsure of how she would proceed as a roller coaster of emotions overwhelmed her.

"Look boys, there's your granny," she heard Maude excitedly say. "Go over and say hello."

Moments later, Richard and David had their arms around Tilly's waist saying hello and calling her 'granny'. Tears moistened her eyes as she took her grandsons by the hand and walked with them over to where their mother was sitting. The women talked about London, the children, and how they were settling into Australia. Maude carefully broached the subject about Freddy and how he still harboured hurt and resentment over her leaving him behind.

"He was also bullied when the newspapers printed stories about your lifestyle, the jewellery you wore and the crimes you and his father committed." Maude whispered so her sons couldn't overhear.

"Those days are long gone. I still 'ave a couple orf my businesses. But now I am married to a lovely man who is nothing like Jim. We live a quiet life."

"But you still have illegal businesses and Fred is concerned that we, and especially our children, may get caught up in your violent world and get hurt."

"I'm not involved in that world anymore. I'm too old for all that nonsense. I visit the kids' in the 'ospitals or stay 'ome with our little John and watch television with Eric. Some orf those programs are addictive." Tilly said, trying to lighten the conversation.

"It will take time. Be patient with him." Maude smiled as she patted Tilly's hand.

"Does 'e know you're 'ere with the boys?"

"Yes, he does. He's not ready to have you in our home yet. He's also upset about the adoption. He feels that John is living the life that he should have had."

"I can't change the past. I did as much as I could for my Freddy. If I could 'ave brought 'im 'ere, I would 'ave. I can't say sorry anymore. Freddy needs to settle 'is own mind and remember the good times we 'ad when I visited. Enough orf that now. I 'ave some toys in the car for Richard and David, and a few little things for you and Freddy. Is it okay if I drive you 'ome to save putting them all in a cab?" She asked.

"I'm sure that will be fine. But please, don't spoil us so much. Freddy thinks you are trying to buy our affection."

"No, love, I'm trying to make up for years orf not being there for Freddy, you, and my grandsons. You can't buy love, I 'ave to earn that. But I can make life easier for you while I can."

Maude called her boys over and they each held one of Tilly's hands as they walked across to their grandmother's yellow FJ Holden. Maude helped Tilly transfer the family's gifts into the boot and back seat, leaving just enough room for Richard and David to sit. On their way to the

Coogee flat, Tilly stopped at the supermarket and purchased food and fresh meat and vegetables.

7

In November 1955, Saffron dropped by Tilly's Maroubra house unannounced with offers to buy her Darlinghurst properties. He wanted in on the world of prostitution and what better businesses to own than whorehouses that had operated for decades and owned by Sydney's most famous Madam. Tilly refused. Her hands were itching for the money and she *was* getting older, but she would never send her girls into a snake pit owned by the likes of Saffron.

7

In 1956, Barbara Surridge, aka Stella Croke, was released from prison. Tilly had done her utmost to care for her whilst she was in gaol. She had been arrested for the murder of a chef named Ernest Hoffman. Barbara had not been physically involved in his death, but she had lured Hoffman into the Langley Street house in Darlinghurst where she and fellow prostitute Edna Harris offered him sex.

For some reason, her co-worker was found not guilty. Her husband, James 'Skinny Jones' Harris and Barbara's husband, William, had pummelled the chef to death, and were found guilty. Barbara was also unexpectedly found guilty. The trio were sentenced to death, but their sentence was commuted on the 14th of December when the State Cabinet overturned the death sentence, sentencing them to penal servitude for life.

Tilly drove to Long Bay Gaol and waited at the gate with a freshly made corned beef and tomato sandwich and a thermos of tea to hand to Barbara the moment she walked into freedom. She watched the gate and was shocked when she first saw her friend approaching the prison gates, barely recognising her. Gone was the overweight woman, a haggard looking, emaciated woman had taken her place.

"Tilly! It's great to see you again, old girl!" Barbara squealed as she ran towards the gates.

"Enough with the old bit, thanks."

The two old friends hugged each other before walking arm-in-arm to the car. "I made you a fresh sandwich. We need to get some meat back on those bones!"

"Yeah, the gaol food is fuckin' shit and as the years passed, less and less people brought me in food. The only real food I got was from you, Maisy and Betty whenever the screws would let you in."

"Well, love, there's plenty orf food at 'ome!" Tilly smiled. "Ave you got somewhere to live?"

"I'm moving in with my sister until I get back on my feet."

"I'll give you a few pounds to tide you over until you get sorted."

"Thanks Tills, I'll pay you back."

"No need to, love. Just get back to living and that's all the payment I need."

"Maybe I can work for you again?"

"I 'ave to say no, Barbara. I can't risk being arrested for consorting with you if you're seen in one orf my flats. The cops will be keeping a close watch on you for the next few months."

When they arrived at the Maroubra house, all was quiet until Tilly opened the front door and she and Barbara walked in. Suddenly, people emerged from everywhere cheering and offering Barbara a beer or handing her gifts. Overwhelmed, she fell to the floor in tears.

Eric started herding the guests outside where he had been cooking steak and sausages on the barbecue. Tilly took Barbara through to the spare bedroom and told her to have a shower and get changed. "The party will be waiting for you, don't you worry, love."

After she had freshened up, Barbara found Tilly sitting at the dining table. "Come with me, lovey." She said and led Barbara outside to where tables laden with food and an iced welcome home cake awaited.

"Tills, I don't know what to say. This is such a surprise!"

"You just go eat as much food as you want and talk to your friends. Your sister is 'ere too. Go 'ave some fun!"

The party was in full swing with music, dancing, merriment, and laughter. However, later in the night, one of Barbara's former streetwalking colleagues asked her if she had the money she had borrowed fourteen years before and an argument ensued. The woman then shot Barbara in the buttocks, thereby ending the party. Angered by the shooting, Eric ordered everyone to leave. "I don't want this bullshit in my home. Tilly and I live respectfully, and we have a child. It was made clear that no weapons were permitted!"

Tilly rushed Barbara to the hospital and told the nurse she had been accidentally shot when a revolver was being cleaned. When Barbara was placed in a ward, the police arrived to question her. Their inquiries were thwarted when she refused to identify who had shot her and where the 'accident' had occurred…

7

In July 1957, Saffron popped in to visit Tilly again. Thinking the aging brothel madam was older and none the wiser, he told her that the Palmer Street property had fallen into such disrepair that the house would need bulldozing and offered her a quarter of its value. Age hadn't wearied Tilly, nor had sickness, she was as still as sharp as a tack. She kept up to date by reading newspapers and watching the news and current affairs programs. She was aware the protégé of the early century crime bosses, like herself, was no longer a shoe polishing black marketeer and had risen in the ranks to become the kingpin of the red light and business district of Kings Cross.

"You want Palmer Street, Abe, you'll need to quadruple your price and pay each of my girls five thousand dollars and give them the option to leave if they wish."

"Tilly darlin', your days are all but over. It's time to hang your hooker frocks in the closet and put those tired old feet up and let the men get on with the job."

"Prostitution is a woman's world, Abe. The only reason men are needed is to pay to get fuckin' laid! You men will be the ruination orf the industry. Until you can lay on your back for eight or more clients a day, put on an orgasm for each and every one orf them, then go 'ome and look after your family, you don't deserve to be in the fuckin' business. You'll never earn your fuckin' hooker stripes. Bludgers like you buy and pilfer your way into this business and it's the women who suffer!"

Chapter Twenty Nine

Death and Taxes

The doorbell rang just as Eric started listening to his morning serials. He turned the radio volume down and pulled himself up on his walking stick to answer the door. "Darling, there's a couple of detectives at the door!" He called out when he saw two official looking men standing on the veranda.

"No sir, we're not the police, we're from the Taxation Department. We'd like to speak to Mrs. Matilda Parsons, formally, Devine."

"Well, you better come in and sit down then. Tilly's just in getting dressed to go out for lunch. I expect those plans will be cancelled now." Eric said as he nervously ran his hand over his balding head. "Excuse me while I go and let her know you're here."

Tilly almost fainted when she heard Eric's news. Trembling, she sat on the bed. "The bastards are going to bankrupt me just like they did Katie! She warned me this would 'appen! Go tell them I'm not 'ome!"

"Darling, they know you're here. You can't run from the tax people. They'll get you sooner or later. Best to face it now. Pay the money you owe them and get it over and done with. Come on, you've faced tougher adversaries before, sweetheart."

Putting on a brave face, Tilly walked into her living room exuding all the confidence and arrogance of a queen. "My 'usband tells me you're from the tax department. I'm not being rude, but I've learned not to take people on their word. Do you 'ave any identification that proves who you are?" Tilly probed, taking command of the situation.

The men each showed her their identification before the taller man of the two sat back on the settee, placed a briefcase on his lap, opened it and pulled out a pile of papers. It took all Tilly's might to not collapse on the spot when she saw how thick her file was.

"Mrs. Parsons, we don't need to tell you what an extensive real estate property portfolio you have. We've seen enough photos of your jewellery and furs in the newspapers to estimate their value. With all this in mind, we've only been able to calculate your income due the understated income returns you provided to our office. We're being more than charitable with an estimation of twenty thousand pounds being owed by you to the department." The officer declared.

"Tell me, where the 'ell am I going to get twenty thousand pounds? I'm an extremely sick woman. I can't pay this much dough before I die!" Tilly lamented, her face turning paler as the truth of her predicament sank in.

"You could sell some of your properties, jewellery, and maybe some of those expensive fur." The taxation officer who had been sitting silently offhandedly mentioned. "It's not like you live the life of a pauper."

"I've battled all my life and worked bloody 'ard for what I've got, whether you like what I do or not. Now you slug me with this lot. You government lot and the politicians with your soft-arsed jobs would run at the first mention of rolling up your sleeves and getting stuck into 'ard labour! This money will 'ave me beat! Now get out orf my 'ouse!"

The men fled in fear of Tilly chasing them with a straight razor or a revolver. They knew her reputation and the shooting deaths that had occurred at the Malabar Road address in the past and ensured that there were two policemen parked nearby in the event they were needed.

"Sweetheart, did you receive any letters from the taxation mob warning you about the money you owed?"

"Someone rang. But you know what my 'earing's like! I'm in a ton of trouble and will 'ave to ask the mongrels for time to pay. The bastards gave us clearances before we went to England, so why didn't they say something then?"

As Kate had just two years before her, Tilly sold most of her properties, including the Brougham Street house and the brothel in Ian Street, Rosebay, where she had the most wonderful Harbour View. However, she weathered the tax storm enough to maintain ownership of her beloved Maroubra house which Eric had convinced her not to sell after they married, as well as 191 and 193 Palmer Street, and the Coogee block of flats.

7

On the 3rd of October 1957, Tilly received a phone call from a woman who had worked with Barbara Surridge in a Surry Hills brothel. She told her that Barbara had died that morning from septicaemia after a cut on her thumb became infected. She also mentioned that there was no-one to claim her body.

Tilly thanked her for calling before returning to the settee where she wept for her friend. She hadn't seen much of Barbara since the party. Tilly knew she had been working in Kings Cross in one of the brothels owned by Abe Saffron, Lenny McPherson or one of the other up-and-coming crime lords. She didn't go in search of her because she didn't want anything to do with the new age kingpins, whose despicable crimes and operational practices made Tilly look like a divine nun.

Tilly took a deep breath and phoned the Thomas Dixon Funeral and Embalming Service and arranged for them to pick the body up from the morgue the following morning. She and Eric then drove to the hospital and identified Barbara's body. Tilly told the morgue attendant that the family had disowned Mrs. Surridge and that she would take care of the funeral costs. The attendant passed Tilly several forms. When filling them in, she wrote her residence as Barbara's home address, signed her name, and took responsibility of her friend's body.

After the service in the city chapel on the 5th of October, the small funeral cortege made their way to the Catholic section of the Botany Cemetery, where Barbara was interred.

7

In August 1958, Tilly pushed an ailing Eric in a wheelchair through the gates of St Joachim's Catholic Primary School at Rookwood. They were there to enrol their son for the following year.

They knew Eric wouldn't be alive to see John start school, so Tilly had him smartly dressed in his uniform. On John's back was a brown leather satchel which held sandwiches for a picnic after the enrolment.

408

John was eagerly anticipating starting school, but Tilly was overwhelmed by emotion and kept dabbing at her eyes with a handkerchief as she filled in the enrolment forms. Sister Mary Saviour, who helped with the enrolment, asked Tilly why her son was dressed in full school uniform. When she heard the reason, the nun blessed the Parsons family and told them that she would keep them in her prayers.

After completing the enrolment process, Tilly, Eric, and John stopped at a nearby park where John played as his parents watched on before eating their picnic sandwiches. The morning had taken its toll on Eric, and after an hour in the park, Tilly called John off the slippery dip and told him that it was time to go.

After settling Eric in his chair, Tilly made a pot of tea and a cup of milo before they sat in the living room and chatted about the school. John was excitedly talking about becoming an astronaut. "You'll have to study hard for that Johnny," Eric weakly rasped, "but I'm sure you'll do it."

Tilly could see her husband's health steadily declining. She did all she could to make him comfortable, but she knew in her soul that her beloved Eric wouldn't be with her much longer. Eric's memory was fading, and he could barely hold anything in his hands for too long. He was too weak to walk, so a wheelchair was his only means of mobility. Tilly wished there were something more the doctors could do, but knew his cancer was incurable.

Eric held on to life for as long as he could. During the agonising final months, Tilly refused to admit him to hospital. She cared for her husband day and night, as well as paid off-duty nurses from Crown Street Women's Hospital to help. The nurses, understanding the pain Eric was in, brought vials of morphine to help ease the agony. By October, Eric could no longer see and did not know who Tilly was, nor who he was.

Tilly was broken. The wonderful kind man that took almost all her life to find, was gone. She talked to the nurses about what was the best thing she could to do for him. Her husband's illness and pain management needed more care and medication than she could provide at home.

She reluctantly admitted Eric into St. Vincent's hospital and remained with him day and night. Tilly watched over him as his drips were changed and given needle upon needle to ease the agonising pain. On the 22nd of November, within minutes of being administered a dose of morphine, Eric peacefully passed away.

Tearfully, Tilly kissed her husband on his lips and sat back down beside him. She prayed to God to take care of the soul of her beloved husband. She told God that he was a good man, a hero who had saved lives, including her own, several times. When the nurse came in ten minutes later, Tilly told her that Eric had left to be in the arms of the Lord. The nurse patted Tilly's hand, knowing how much she loved her husband and told her she could stay with him as long as she wanted.

Three days later, surrounded by their family and friends, the grieving wife and son buried their beloved husband and father at Botany Cemetery. Tilly was an absolute forlorn figure dressed in black. Kate Leigh kept her on her feet in her strong embrace.

Losing Eric had winded Tilly. Gone from her eyes was the spark of life. Her face was drawn and clouded, and underneath her grief was the knowledge of a tectonic shift in her universe… she would be living the rest of her life without Eric, who loved her more than life itself and the man she shared the same adulation.

7

Christmas that year was subdued, but Tilly tried to make it as festive as possible for John. The Christmas tree sparkled with lights, and the living room was decorated in tinsel, but the empty chair at the dining table for Christmas lunch saddened them both.

Maude arrived on Christmas afternoon with Richard and David. Freddy was still ignoring his mother, only speaking to her by phone when it was necessary. He had a job singing at the Coogee Surf Life Saving Club, as well as bookings at surrounding venues.

The three boys excitedly unwrapped their presents, each showing off what they'd received before racing to the backyard to play. Tilly spent time with her grandsons during the holidays. She took the three boys on days out to the beach, carnivals, and the cinema.

The morning of John's first day at school, it was Tilly who was dragging her feet. John had gotten himself out of bed and attempted to make his own breakfast before she had even opened her eyes. As soon as he was in his uniform, John tied the laces on his shining new black school shoes, combed his hair and was sitting in the passenger seat impatiently waiting for his mother. Tilly was still brewing her morning pot of tea.

Parking the car outside St Joachim's, Tilly waited a few seconds while she thought back to the last time she was there. They were a complete family then. She sighed as she wiped away the tears and made her way to the school gate where John was already waiting.

The classroom was a hive of activity as Sister Brigid spoke with the new parents as Sister Mary Ruth showed the children to their allotted desks. John kissed his mother goodbye and Tilly wiped her red lipstick off his cheek before he almost ran off to his desk. Sister Brigid then asked the parents to leave so they could start their scheduled morning lessons.

Returning home, Tilly went straight to John's bedroom to tidy it up. She picked up toys and his pyjamas from the floor, books from under the bed and made his bed. As she folded John's train patterned pyjamas, she held them close to her chest, wondering what he was doing at that moment.

CHAPTER THIRTY

New Boys on the Block

During the 1960s, a new breed of criminal had taken a solid foothold in Darlinghurst and Kings Cross. They ventured into criminal and prostitutional enterprises that Tilly and Kate would never have dreamed off. They were men and to them, women were created to feed them, bed them… or to utilise to make as much money from as possible.

Prostitution was a whole new racket. Asian women had become a saleable commodity and were purchased from Oriental sex traffickers to work in 'massage parlours' where they performed whatever sexual acts their clients desired, mostly without a using a condom.

Kings Cross became 'The Cross' and was the go-to place for the less salubrious of people. It was the place to visit one of the many strip clubs, hire a prostitute, male or female, or just to walk down Darlinghurst Road checking out the weird and wonderful clothing stores. It wasn't unusual to see people sitting in cars ogling transvestites with their made-up faces, over the top wigs and glittering gowns, or the myriad of other interesting and bizarre folks that called The Cross home.

The new kingpins were making their millions from the foundations built by Tilly Devine and Kate Leigh. They walked the turf that had cost both women, blood, sweat, and tears without knowing or caring about the sacrifices paving the crooked path for them to become the crime bosses they were.

It was Tilly and Kate who instigated bribery and corruption in the police department, allowing the newcomers their freedom to run illicit businesses. It was the bohemian lifestyle of varied criminals, artists, closet gays, and lesbians that turned The Cross into a fantasyland, and it was Tilly, Kate, and the early 1900s gangsters that propagated the area into a garden of criminality, exploitation, and opportunity.

Samuel Lee

Born in Winnipeg, Manitoba, Canada in 1912, 'Sammy Lee" toured Australia as a drummer in 1937 with the Americanadians band. He fell in love with the country and settled in Potts Point.

Sammy used his astute business acumen to stretch the limits of decency when he opened the Roosevelt nightclub at Potts Point in 1939, introducing topless waitresses. He sold the Roosevelt in 1946. The following year, he opened Sammy Lee's Theatre Restaurant in Oxford Street, partnered by the Maltese gambler and illegal casino owner, Perce Galea.

The sixties was still a quasi-conservative era in Australia, but Sammy didn't care. He was a large man who sported a thin moustache, smoked Cuban cigars, and wore flashy, flamboyant clothes. He often turned heads when wearing colourful jackets over a semi unbuttoned black shirt and white trousers.

In 1963, he was a partner in establishing a whole new world of entertainment to the non-gentrified lovers of The Cross. Along with Lee Gordon, and Reg Boom, who owned 'Andres' nightclub in Castlereagh Street, the trio opened the risqué nightclub, 'The Carousel' to host *Les Girls* with money borrowed from Abe Saffron.

Les Girls pushed the envelope and further tested the perceived moral decency of the day when they opened the "Drag Queen" show. A titillating all male revue with the performers dressed in flamboyant attire as showgirls miming to female singing stars as they danced. The transvestite revue was opened to attract and thrill the curious within the "straight" market, which it did!

Les Girls opened the stage to pioneering drag performers such as Rose Jackson, Lea Sonia, Ken 'Kandy' Johnson, Ayesha, Carmen, and the ever dazzling and superlative Les Girls Queen, Carlotta. However, one "girl" was quite special to Matilda Devine. Thirty-seven-year-old 'Shiraz' shone brightly as a female impersonator. She was the crossdresser who had sung at Tilly and Eric's wedding reception. During one of McPherson's occasional visits, Tilly had mentioned her to him. Lenny was so impressed by her feminine figure and looks, he hired her.

Sammy was a generous, fastidious, mercurial, and aggressive businessman. He had cut his teeth on the Roosevelt Club when he dipped his toe into the illegal world of buying and selling black market liquor. In 1952, he gave evidence before the royal commission into the liquor laws and was questioned over the amount of alcohol purchases and sales he had made. After not having proof of receipts or invoices, Mr. Justice Maxwell found that there was a reasonable amount of evidence proving Lee had sold black-market liquor. He was indicted for perjury which he was acquitted of in 1954.

On the 28th of May 1967, Raymond Patrick 'Ducky' O'Connor, a violent and psychotic underworld enforcer, was shot in the head and killed by crime boss, Lenny McPherson, at Lee's Latin Quarter nightclub. The shooting caused a downturn in business, forcing Lee to change the look of his club. He turned the discotheque into an American style nightclub and named it the 'Cheetah Room'. The club's prized band was Southern Comfort and they attracted hordes of cashed up American servicemen who were flown to Sydney for rest and relaxation during the Vietnam war. The GIs were enticed by the rhythm and blues music and the long opening hours and spent up big.

The discotheque became a haven for Sydney crime lords to carry out clandestine illicit deals in semi-darkness privacy. Crooked police and corrupt politicians were often seen entering the club to host covert meetings, pick up their bribe money or pay blackmail money and collect damaging photos of them with local prostitutes and gay men.

Unfortunately, Sammy Lee, who was once known as 'the King of the Cross' lost touch with the entertainment needs of an ever-evolving society, and slowly faded into obscurity. He died in Vaucluse hospital from myocardial infarction on the 21st of July 1975 and was buried in the Jewish section of Rookwood cemetery.

7

Abraham Gilbert Saffron

Born on the 6th of October 1919, Saffron became one of the most powerful and successful crime bosses to rule Sydney. Driven by greed, sexual addiction, and a never-ending thirst for power, he was well suited to a life of crime. Saffron was a masterful manipulator, but he had an ego that demanded recognition as a loving and devoted family man and a law-abiding businessman.

Saffron's business and criminal acumen was learned from his father's stories about his wartime activities. Suffering from the economic depression caused by the World War One, Sam Saffron's turned to operating a black-market business selling nylons and other items that were hard to buy during the war.

Abe began his education in illegal activity at the tender age of eight, when he sold cigarettes and sweets stolen from local shops to his fellow pupils at school. Another of his rorts was buying textbooks from boys who no longer needed them and reselling them to new students the following year.

In 1937, Saffron began a jaunt in illegal bookmaking, earning him a conviction for operating an illegal premise and a sentence of six months hard labour at Long Bay Gaol or a five pound fine. He opted to pay the fine.

At twenty-one, Saffron was caught with a stolen car radio valued at twenty pounds and sentenced to six months gaol. The magistrate suspended the sentence and placed Saffron on a two-year good behaviour bond and a promise to join the armed forces.

On the 5th of August 1944, Saffron finally acted on his promise and enlisted in the army, fleetingly serving in the New South Wales Headquarters. He was discharged in 1945, without seeing active duty. Saffron then spent six months in the Merchant Navy carrying out administrative duties. Whilst engaged in these new responsibilities, he met Hilton Kincaid, a black marketeer who operated an illegal business selling alcohol and cigarettes.

Resigning from the Merchant Navy, Saffron used connections made through Kincaid and began selling stolen liquor, cigarettes, and whatever else that "fell off the back of the truck". Saffron started knocking on the doors of the King Cross nightclubs to sell his liquor and cigarettes and was fortunate enough to meet Sammy Lee. The uniformed doormen and a maître d' escorting guests to their tables, was where Saffron's inspiration of owning a club began.

The money he made in his early illicit ventures, Saffron was canny enough to invest in buildings and clubs during the late 1940s. Throughout the initial years, a majority of his profits were spent in bribing judges, politicians, and top cops so he could keep his illegal operations open. He was also the second criminal to grease the palm of the supposedly incorruptible Bumper Farrell. Tilly was the first. Bumper spent many nights at Saffron's establishments. Knowing that Saffron had a lot of dirt on him, he became his main protector.

With his predilection for deviant sex and paying a small fortune to working girls for their services, it wasn't long until Saffron ventured into the business of running prostitutes. It was in this enterprise that he found a new currency for inducements, often using his girls as payment for the police to turn a blind eye to his enterprises, and politicians to vote against legislation that was abhorrent to his activities.

To add a bit of flavour to his vast entrepreneurial pursuits, Saffron started selling pornography as well as providing blue movies to cinemas, boys film nights and girls to entertain at private smokos. Over the following years, the now undisputed crime lord owned or had financial interests in over one hundred brothels, massage parlours and nightclubs around the country.

In 1960, Saffron opened Australia's first strip club, the Staccato, in Kings Cross. The legendary Pink Pussy Cat strip club and several others quickly ensued. Not content with what he had, the cagey entrepreneur called in his loan on Les Girls, and with the partners not being able to pay the outstanding loan, he took over the business. When he saw how popular the nightclub was, he discovered a new money-making enterprise and subsidised several gay clubs.

In the early 1970s, the Darlinghurst Road kerbs where Tilly and other streetwalkers once plied their trade, where Kate Leigh sold her sly grog, and where the bloody Kellett brawl occurred, became known as the 'Golden Mile'. It was a strip where red lights blazoned, advertising the delights that could be bought within. Where bars and clubs such as the Pink Pussycat, the Pink Panther, Les Girls, the Kit Kat club, the Venus Room, the Fox Hole, and many others, filled the desires and fantasies of all those who were drawn to the decadent and perverted lifestyle The Cross offered.

For over forty years, almost the same amount of time Tilly Devine had reigned in the area, Saffron was the king of crime who was involved in everything from extortion, arson, race fixing, bribery, corruption, murder, the death of Juanita Nielson, and insurance fraud, as well as sex and drug trafficking. His power and criminal endeavours were protected by the likes of Liberal premier Bob Askin, federal attorney, Lionel Murphy—who had accepted bribes and inducements including sex with under-aged girls, Bumper Farrell, Ray Kelly, and other high ranking police officers, including Police Commissioner, Norman Allen.

The 'King of Kings Cross', 'Mr Sin', 'The Boss of the Cross' or whatever pseudonym you want to call him, Abraham Gilbert Saffron died on the 15th of September 2006 at St. Vincent's Hospital, aged eighty-six. He is buried beside his second wife, Doreen at Rookwood Cemetery.

In his will, worth more than twenty million dollars, Saffron bequeathed considerable amounts of money to his grandchildren, his mistress, Rita Hagenfeld, and their illegitimate daughter, but to his only son, Alan, he left a pittance.

7

Leonard Arthur McPherson

Born in Balmain on the 19th of May 1921 to William and Nellie McPherson. He grew up to become one of Australia's most notorious and powerful crime bosses. He ruled Sydney's underworld through murder, violence, and fear for over two decades. His criminal roots started from petty thievery, car theft, breaking and entering, and fare evasion. McPherson's rise to power came as a surprise to some, but not to others.

Lenny's depravity knew no barriers. When his mother, Nellie McPherson, turned seventy years old, her family held a party for her at the local sports club. After driving Nellie home, her grandson left after seeing his grandmother safely indoors. Moments after he left, Nellie heard someone knocking on her door, and was surprised to see her youngest son standing on the doorstep holding a young white rabbit. She asked Lenny if the rabbit was a birthday gift as she had nowhere to put it in her pensioner flat.

"No, Mum, I came around to wish you a happy birthday. Did you have a nice party at the sports club?" Lenny spitefully asked.

"Yes, it was a very nice day, what with all the family and my friends getting together." Nellie replied.

"Not quite all the family. I wasn't invited!" Lenny angrily retorted.

"Well, you know how it is, son. With the criminal stuff and all the murders…" She never got to finish her sentence as she watched in horror when Lenny put his enormous hand around the throat of the baby rabbit and twisted its neck, before wrenching the poor animal's head from its neck. His mother let out a scream as blood splattered over her yellow floral dress, before slamming the door closed at the sight of the poor rabbit's body twitching on her welcome mat.

That was the last time the vicious and psychopathic murderer saw his mother alive.

7

Known as the 'Godfather of Crime", "Mr Big" and "Mr Ten Percent", McPherson was convicted of numerous petty crimes as a teenager. After committing one crime too many, he appeared at the children's court in 1934. His mother, as always, was there to beg for leniency. However, the wayward teenager was given no quarter after again breaking his probation and was sent to The Farm Home for Boys in Gosford. (Now known as Mount Penang Training School).

From the criminal "tutoring" he received whilst at 'the farm', McPherson opted to continue his life of crime, cutting his teeth working for Fred "Paddles" Anderson, so named due to his extremely large feet. Anderson was known as the true Godfather of crime. He's influence reached every nook and cranny of Australia.

McPherson was wise to join Anderson's mob. The crime boss was smart, connected, and refined enough to mix in the most elite of cliques. Anderson was the *capo dei capi*—the overboss of all overbosses. With just one phone call, every criminal to his heel when called, including petty crook, Lenny McPherson.

Finally feeling that he had the nous and followers to dip his toes in the murky waters of the criminal underworld, Lenny became a police informer. Trading information about his opponents, he received protection for himself and his close associates. He also open-walleted several corrupt cops, Detective Ray Kelly, Detective Fred Krahe, Detective Sergeant Roger Rogerson, and Detective Chief Superintendent Don Fergusson.

Lenny's "friendships" also extended to high political circles… Ray Kelly introduced him to his good friend, Robert Askin, who became "Premier Robert Askin", Liberal leader of New South Wales.

After building up a bank of trust, McPherson became Police Commissioner Fred Hanson and Ray Kelly's personal debt collector chasing up debtors of their illegal casino on the NSW Central Coast. McPherson swapped favours upon favours with those in power. One notable "good grace" was when Kelly used his friendship with Labor's State Attorney-General and Minister of Justice, Mr. Reg Downing to dismiss the Joseph Hackett murder charge against McPherson in 1959.

The next favour Detective Kelly mediated for Lenny, was with his wife Joy in 1960 after he arrived home drunk and became pissed off with her for not having his Monday roast on the table. He pistol-whipped Joy and threatened to kill her, before shooting a pot that was boiling on the stove. Joy complained to the police, wanting to have her husband charged with attempted murder. However, after a chat with Ray Kelly, she withdrew the complaint and immediately left Sydney and filed for divorce.

No longer shackled to Joy gave Lenny the license to marry his mistress, twenty-two-year-old Marlene Gilligan on the 9th of July 1963. The Balmain wedding reception wasn't without its shadow of criminality… During the evening, Lenny's minder and enforcer, Stan 'The Man' Smith received a phone call. Moments later, after whispering an excuse in his new wife's ear, McPherson and Smith left the reception.

After stealing a car, the dastardly duo made their way to exact revenge on the man who had shot and wounded Smith several months before. Armed with an Owen submachine gun, they set out to kill Robert James 'Pretty Boy' Walker, who after shooting Smith, bragged he was the 'toughest man in Sydney', further aggravating McPherson.

When he spotted Walker, McPherson gave Smith the signal and he slowly accelerated from the kerb. Lenny reached over to the back seat and retrieved an Owen sub-machine gun and steadied it on the half wound-down window. As the car drew up beside Walker, he placed his finger on the trigger and opened fire, spraying the unsuspecting man in a hail of 9mm calibre copper-jacketed bullets. The force of the volley of the bullets was so great that it spun Walker around and tore open his body as he fell to the footpath in a pool of blood.

Detective Kelly oversaw Walker's murder investigation and led fellow detectives into believing that McPherson's enemy, hitman Raymond O'Connor had carried out the shooting to get at him. In payment for his kind deed, in 1966 McPherson advised Kelly of the whereabouts of escaped prisoner, Ronald Ryan, who had killed a warder during his escape. Ryan had approached Lenny for help with fake passports to be able to leave Australia. McPherson told Kelly where Ryan was staying. The escapee was arrested the following day by the Victorian police. Ryan was hanged at 8:00 am on the 3rd of February 1967 in Pentridge gaol. He was the last person in Australia to be executed.

During 1971 and 1972, the Toecutter Gang, a violent Victorian mob tried to take over Sydney casino protection rackets. McPherson and his henchmen became embroiled in an ongoing violent and bloody battle to maintain control. Bodies began piling up, most of which were members of the Toecutter gang. With their membership decimated and surviving gang members refusing to continue the battle, the gang retreated to Melbourne.

McPherson's name was bandied around police headquarters as the man who had ordered the killings, but nothing ever came of it.

The popularity of poker machines during the 1970s opened another lucrative cash flow door for McPherson. He began purchasing poker machines and strongarmed the managers of registered clubs and owners of illegal clubs to install his poker machines. Those who were unable to place the machines in their clubs, were forced to pay a percentage of their takings. To them, paying the fee was a better alternative than being found floating in the harbour...

In 1983, McPherson was subpoenaed to give evidence at the Juanita Nielsen inquest. When questioned about the statement that he had made to a Federal police officer that detective Fred Krahe had killed Miss Nielsen, he denied ever making the statement.

After years of getting away with murder, assaults, robberies, brothel owning, human and drug trafficking, collecting, and executing debtors for illegal casino owners, in 1994, McPherson was finally imprisoned with the assistance of the National Crime Authority. The NCA had used phone taps to eavesdrop on Lenny for information about his crimes that would lead to a conviction or more. McPherson was finally tripped up when he was taped boasting about an assault he had ordered upon his previous partner, Darren Burt: "The boys just done a job for me, a fucking good job... they got this fucking bloke and broke his fucking arm and bashed his head in."

ordered on his previous liquor importing partner, Darren Burt. They were in possession of over one hundred hours of incriminating recordings.

Found guilty at his subsequent trial, Judge Roger Court sentenced McPherson to a maximum four years' imprisonment. He was eligible for parole in thirty months. Lenny was then taken to the Cessnock Correctional Centre in the Hunter Valley.

On the 28th of August 1996, Lenny rang his wife on the prison telephone. During the call he revealed he was feeling unwell and that he wouldn't live to see parole. Marlene tried to cheer him up, but to no avail. Lenny said goodbye to his wife and told her that he loved her before replacing the receiver in its cradle. Whilst returning to his cell, McPherson grasped his chest and let out a groan before falling to the corridor floor, dead.

At the age of seventy-five, Lenny 'Mr. Big' McPherson had suffered a massive heart attack.

Over four hundred mourners arrived to bid farewell to the kingpin of crime. The funeral guests rubbed shoulders with both the good and the bad. Family, friends, media representatives, sightseers, priests, and nuns, mingled with criminals such as Sam and John Ibrahim, Con Karageorges, Stan 'the Man' Smith, 'Big fella' McMillan, William 'Snowy' Rayner, and many others.

7

And the NSW police department considered Matilda Devine and Kate Leigh the worse kind of criminals in Australia…

CHAPTER THIRTY ONE

Fall of the Queen of the 'Loo

The ringing of the telephone disturbed Tilly while she was watching an episode of *Homicide*. "Sorry Inspector Connolly, phone calls this late means somethin's up," Tilly sighed at the television screen before switching it off.

Seconds into the telephone conversation, Tilly dropped to the chair beside the phone table. "Oh my God, not Katie!" She gasped, "I'll be right there."

With a trembling finger, Tilly phoned Olive and asked her if she could come over and watch John, explaining where she was going so late at night. While waiting for her friend to arrive, she attempted to make herself up to be the Tilly that Katie would remember.

Curling her hair with heated rollers, Tilly donned her best floral frock, black shoes, and fur coat, before sliding twelve diamond rings on her fingers. Olive arrived and sat in front of the television to watch the final minutes of Homicide. After one final look in the mirror, satisfied, Tilly thanked Olive and then drove to St. Vincent's Hospital.

As she walked through the corridors to Katie's room, Tilly felt the ghosts of the many friends and enemies that had passed through those same passageways. Some survived to live to a great age and die naturally, others died from their wounds long before their time.

Stopping at Kate's door, Tilly's legs became unsteady. She braced herself against the door frame as she blinked away the tears. To see Kate,

422

who was once such a strong and robust woman, laying in a bed with hair as white as snow, wearing an oxygen mask and tubes attached to her arms that were connected to strange beeping devices on tables beside her bed, shook Tilly to the core.

"What 'ave the doctor's said?" Tilly asked Kate's nephew.

"They say she has hours to live. Thank you for coming Mrs. Parsons."

"She's a tough old nut, mate. Katie won't leave us until she's good and ready!" Tilly clucked as she placed her hand on William's shoulder.

"When did she 'ave the stroke?" She asked as she sat beside Kate and took hold of her hand.

"She was talking to me and then the left side of her face dropped, and she began slurring her words like she was drunk… then she just went blank. I called an ambulance and they said she'd suffered a stroke." William stopped for a few seconds when he saw his aunt's eyes flicker. "The doctors said it was a massive haemorrhagic stroke and her brain is dead."

"But she's still breathing. She 'as a strong 'eart."

"The doctor said the heart is the last organ to stop."

With her nephew, William, sitting to the right of her, and Tilly to the left holding her hand, Kathleen Mary Josephine Ryan drew her last breath on the 4th of February 1964. Three days later, Kate's funeral was held at St. Peter's Catholic Church and was attended by over seven hundred mourners. Several of her family members attended, as did Tilly, the former NSW Deputy Police Commissioner, police officers, surviving gang members and underworld associates.

She was buried in Botany Cemetery. Tilly waited for everyone to leave before placing a wreath at the foot of her unfilled grave, "God rest your soul you old bitch. I'll be seein' you soon." She then picked up a handful of dirt and threw it over her coffin, "Rest in Peace, Katie. I'll miss you."

7

Losing Eric weighed heavily upon Tilly. Until she met him, she thought she had lost the will to love and trust any man again. She had loved Eric almost as much as she had loved Jim when they first met. Eric treated 'his Till' like a queen and she treated him as her king. The light in her heart had extinguished for several months after his death and she had spent her the first few weeks with only John after his funeral. However,

423

not accustomed to being a reclusive person, Tilly reached out to her old friend, Dulcie Markham.

Tilly was shocked when she opened her door to Dulcie. If it weren't for the slight scar on her right cheek, she wouldn't have recognised her. But Tilly knew that she also wasn't the woman that Dulcie once knew. Time marches to its own tune, and its melody had become off key to both women. After placing a tray with tea and scones on the coffee table, the women discussed where life had taken them since they last met. When Dulcie mentioned Frank Green, Tilly's pursed-corrugated-lips that Dulcie knew well, made her quickly change the subject.

Dulcie continued visiting Tilly whenever she had spare money to catch a taxi. Since retiring from prostitution, times were tough. During their visits they would often reminisce about old times, however, the nostalgia often bringing tears to their eyes. When not taking a trip down memory lane, Tilly and Dulcie would spend the afternoon in front of the tv, drinking tea and eating cake or scones while watching soap operas.

Another surprise visitor to her door one day, was Abe Saffron himself. Tilly had to hold on tight to the doorknob lest she fell, such was her shock. She looked past him and made sure he was alone, before inviting Saffron into her home.

"I s'pose you're 'ere for Palmer Street Abe?" Tilly said, getting straight down to business.

"Can't put nothing past you, old girl, can I!" Abe jokingly replied.

"As I said to McPherson—I'm not interested in selling my brothel to any men! You 'ave no idea how to run a brothel properly. You haven't done the 'ard yards or laid on your back twelve to fifteen 'ours, seven days a week. You pricks just burn the women out, buy more Asian girls and lock them up in a massage parlour, spread the pox and get rid orf them when they're too sick to work anymore! I'd rather shut the place down and walk away than see one orf your bastards' names on the titles!"

"Fuck Tilly! Old age hasn't settled that pit of vipers in your belly, has it! Still fighting to hold off the inevitable."

"Mrs. Parsons to you. What 'appens to Palmer Street after I'm dead will not bother me. But while I live and breathe, you and the other vermin of The Cross, won't 'ave a ghost orf a chance to own the place!"

7

Tilly often thought about her life. She had given so much of herself to Darlinghurst and Woolloomooloo but knew she received so much more in return. She was the one who had set several crime and legal precedence's in New South Wales. It was her blueprint of buying houses and setting them up for prostitution that many brothel madams and lords Australia wide would later follow. It was Tilly who made it a rule for her girls to be regularly checked for venereal diseases that brought about the many health services now available for sex workers.

It was Matilda Mary Devine who proved that you didn't need to have a set of testicles to be a long-term boss in the underworld.

Tilly's moral compass may not have always pointed north, but she survived two world wars, the Great Depression, changing laws, the police, gaol, a violent and abusive husband, and numerous battles with enemies armed with guns and razors, almost unscathed.

Now, living on an aged pension and bringing in a small income from her brothel, Tilly could only reminisce about the good life about which she often wrote about in letters to Maureen Cocks, her niece in England. At times she often giggled to herself about the irony of having a niece with the surname of 'Cocks', when she had made a fortune from that very thing…

7

After decades of suffering a constant cough and hoarse voice, which her doctor had told her was bronchitis, Tilly became emaciated, gaunt, and haggard looking. Her large black framed reading glasses made her face look shrunken and small. No longer was she the buxom strong woman who put the fear of god in you with just a glance.

Worried about her sickly appearance, Olive urged her to see a doctor and told her that she would drive her to the appointment. Two days later, Tilly attended a local doctor who referred her to a throat specialist. Dr. McDougall carried out a series of tests, one of which required two days hospitalisation to obtain several tissue samples. The following week, Dr. McDougall's receptionist rang Tilly and told her that the doctor wanted to see her at nine o'clock the following morning.

Tilly kept herself busy that day baking cakes and biscuits for John and making his favourite meal of beef stew with potatoes for dinner. After picking her son up from school, Tilly remained composed, ensuring not to show any signs of nervousness as she helped him with homework and later playing a game of monopoly together.

Whilst sitting in the reception area at the doctor surgery, Tilly checked her watch, "two minutes to go." She whispered to herself. Almost as soon as she finished muttering the words, the receptionist rose from her chair and carried a box of tissues into the doctor's room.

"Mrs. Parsons, Dr. McDougall will see you now." The receptionist said when she returned to her desk. She smiled when Tilly thanked her, but Tilly could see a touch of sadness in her eyes.

Dr. McDougall greeted Tilly with a warm hello when she entered the room and ushered her to a seat at the opposite side of his desk. "Don't soften the news for me, Doctor and I certainly don't need those fuckin' tissues."

"As you wish, Mrs. Parsons. I'm afraid the news is not good. Unfortunately, we found several cancer clusters in your throat tissue samples…"

"Well, am I goin' to die, or can you operate?" Tilly asked cutting the doctor off mid-sentence.

"I'm afraid there is nothing we can do. Your cancer has advanced into your lymph nodes at the back of your throat and into your lungs. If we had caught this a few years ago, we could have prevented the spread."

"Oh well, I'm nearing seventy. The cutthroat razors and bullets didn't fuckin' kill me, something 'ad to. But I'm a tough old fuckin' chook. I could live to be a 'undred!"

Angry at her previous doctor for not diagnosing her condition earlier, Tilly felt she would have recovered if 'e 'ad picked it up. "Going deaf in one ear is a symptom, the other an ongoing sore throat and cough… fuckin' quack!" Tilly would often complain.

It had taken years before the cancer took a firm hold on her, but when it did, it had showed within months. The large frame that she had developed after middle age set in was gone, as was her beautifully coiffed hair, and to make matters worse, Tilly had to endure her illness almost alone. Most of her friends were either dead, suffering with dementia or had left to places unknown.

"You have to eat, Tilly!" Olive would often urge whenever she brought over a casserole or chicken soup. "The more you eat, the better you'll feel. If you get too skinny, the cancer takes you faster."

She heard the same dialogue from Beverly, another neighbour who also brought her food. However, the more she ate, the more she had to vomit up and Tilly hated the pain that throwing up caused her throat.

The medications Tilly was administered was slowly diminishing her memory, but the names of Norman Bruhn, Nellie Cameron, Frank Green—who she always cursed whenever his name was mentioned, Phil The Jew Jeffs, Guido Calletti, Fred Moffit, and several others haunted her thoughts. She had done much in her life, some she regretted, others she wished she could do again, but finish the job. Frank Green was one she would have gladly 'run through', but mostly, she was happy with what she had achieved.

7

The telephone ringing late at night was always disconcerting for Tilly. But on the 18th of August 1966 when she heard the shrill ring, a chill ran through her body. She hesitated before answering and placed her left hand over her heart. As she raised the receiver to her ear, John rushed into her bedroom, woken by the loud ring, and the clock on the mantelpiece chimed nine times. Tilly sent her son to bed and told him that she'd be in to check on him when she had finished the call. She waited for him to close his door, and then asked who she was speaking to, explaining that they would need to speak up as she was partially deaf.

A woman's voice on the other end told her that she was a nurse from Melbourne Hospital and that she had the sad task of advising her that James Devine had died an hour ago from pneumonia. Tilly dropped the phone and fell back on her bed.

The last time she had seen Jim was just two years before when she and John had attended the Melbourne Cup. Even though he was seventy-three years old, Jim was still working, and she thought he looked to be in good health. Tilly and John often stayed at his Heidelberg house when they were in Melbourne for the races. Now, the first love of her life was gone, the threads of her past continuing to fray.

Jim was interred at the Fawkner Memorial Park in Melbourne. Tilly and John, who was fond of Jim, were unable to attend the funeral due to the cost and Tilly's bad health.

7

Not many people realised the costs Tilly was forced to pay in legal fees and fines throughout her lifetime. Also, on top of those expenditures, there were the pay offs to police, judges, magistrates, council members, and politicians. Yes, if she had lived a normal life instead of one of crime, she would not have had such expenses. But think outside the square for a minute. With her fines, she brought in a lot of revenue for the state government. She empowered and helped women during times of abject poverty, to care for their children, keep their bellies full and a roof over their head. Her staunch rules on hygiene, birth control, and health checks, educated women in a time when they were considered lower class citizens than men.

Then there's the flipside. Tilly was not the only criminal here. Every politician, policeman, judiciary member and person in authority that accepted a bribe, or bargained for one, was also a criminal, in fact even more so. These men were mostly well-educated and supposed pillars of society holding positions of authority and responsibility…

7

With the new style of male criminal ruling Sydney's underworld during the 1960s, Tilly's brothel was bringing in less and less clientele. Even though she was sick, Tilly still had the fighting spirit that aided her in surviving her violent lifestyle. She stood up to the new age vice kings Abe Saffron, Joe Borg, his girlfriend, Simone Vogel, and Lenny McPherson, as well as several stripling gangsters from The Cross. They all wanted her Palmer Street brothel, knowing that any establishment, no matter how dowdy, that clients had crossed the threshold for more than forty years, was worth its weight in gold. Tilly refused to sell to any of them.

Tilly also knew to live by the adage, 'never say never'. After Joe 'brothel king' Borg was killed by a car bomb, a firebomb was thrown at her Palmer Street brothel, fortunately missing it by several feet. However, for her, the final straw was when her Maroubra home was broken into and vandalised before the intruders stole away with her expensive cut glass collection. She decided that she was too old to play the gangster game. Tilly told her girls that she was retiring the brothel and closed the doors on prostitution after almost six decades.

It was a heartbreaking and metamorphic time for Tilly as she officially hung up her crown as brothel madam and underworld queen. But she did it with aplomb and dignity.

7

Since Eric's death, Tilly played *Are You Lonesome Tonight*, first sung by Charles Hart, and then by Elvis Presley, almost every day as she reminisced the thirteen short years they were married. They were great years, and she felt they more than made up for the many shortcomings of her marriage to Jim. She often wondered why she hadn't left Devine long before she had divorced him. The lies, almost daily beatings, threats, intimidation and forcing her into prostitution almost as soon as she landed in Australia, still angered Tilly. For the first few weeks of living in Australia, she was tempted to scuttle back to Britain, but the money she was making was almost double what she had made in London, thus anchoring her to the Australian shores.

Times were tough for Tilly. She had already used up the two thousand pounds she had received from Eric's war pension, and the widow's pension barely covered her costs. Her expensive car was confiscated by the taxman, along with many other assets which were sold to pay her hefty tax bill. Tilly purchased a cheaper vehicle which most days she was too unwell to drive, so she was forced to rely on taxis whenever her friends were unavailable to drive her, further cutting into her funds. Without the constant flow of money that she was accustomed to, Tilly began to understand how hard it was during the final years of Kate Leigh's life.

However, no matter how bad times were, Tilly still hosted small tea parties which had replaced her lavish shivoos. A pot of tea, biscuits and teacake had replaced the luxuries of champagne, lobster, and duck. During the get-togethers with her old friend, Dulcie Markham, and the few friends still alive from the 'Loo, they would reminisce about the years of their youth, their loved ones, the good times, and then came the regrets of their pasts, the sadness of their losses, and the acknowledgment that their time on earth would also soon come to an end.

Some weekends, her friends would come over for a barbecue, as well as the few neighbours who deigned to associate with her. There was no talk about the brothel and razor gang days during those get-togethers, there were too many children around. Tilly had learned that not everyone was accepting of her previous lifestyle.

When not entertaining, which became less and less due to the perpetual deaths of her friends and her declining health, Tilly remained home watching her serials. Most afternoons she spent helping John with his homework and fussing over him until his bedtime. Dulcie's visits were also infrequent due to her own waning health, but she tried to ring Tilly at least once every few weeks to keep in touch.

One constant in Tilly's life was writing to her favourite niece, Maureen. In the letters, she updated her on her illness, hospital stays and reminisced about the good old days when she had money and her family thought she was important enough to remain in contact with her.

But the main highlight of Tilly's life were the hours that John was home from high school. Of an afternoon, they would sit down and watch the programs on television together snacking on buttered arrowroot biscuits as they talked about his day at high school. On the weekends, sick or not, Tilly attended his sporting events, barracking with her hoarse voice from the sidelines.

Older and becoming more debilitated by the cancer, Tilly realised that the Maroubra house was too much for her. So, she and John took up residence at 193 Palmer Street. She thought about selling the property but had left it vacant.

Tilly found with age came further afflictions. Along with her cancer, bronchitis and gnarled aching fingers and feet due to rheumatism, she was also diagnosed with cirrhosis of the liver. Some days, she wished that she had died in one of the many fights she'd been involved in during her heyday. She felt that way she would have gone out in a blaze of glory, not as a crippled old has-been. The newspapers and magazines didn't make her feel any better. At least once a week would see Tilly shutting the door on a journalist's face or slamming the phone down in a reporter's ear whenever they approached her to do a story about her past and how times had changed for her since her razor gang days.

In 1968, Tilly found it more difficult to manage or pay for the upkeep of such an old house on her limited income and poor health. After much consideration, she applied to the Housing Commission for a two-bedroom flat. No more than seven weeks later, she received a letter to attend the Housing office to inspect a bottom floor flat in Paddington.

Olive drove Tilly to the Housing Commission office, and then onto the address she was given for the flat. Both women were impressed when they saw the newly built block of flats, which Tilly said she was going to accept. "It's a new start for John and me. It's close to shops and the bus stop. John deserves a nice 'ome, not a dump like Palmer Street and no-one 'ere needs to know who I am and what I've done."

Four months later, Tilly put the Palmer Street house on the market, and it was snapped up almost immediately. The buyer, a wealthy developer, paid Tilly cash for the property, which she secreted in her flat.

In March 1969, Tilly was hospitalised due to her rapidly declining health. Olive, who was taking care of sixteen-year-old John whilst Tilly was infirmed, took him to visit her every day after school. Ever the doting mother, Tilly helped her son with his homework and talked about his day at school. While they were working out a mathematics problem, John almost floored his mother when he told her that he wanted to leave school. Usually quick to anger, Tilly thought back to the time that she had left school… times had sure changed since then. "None orf us went through school and you 'ave done your father and I proud. You're smart and you are going to make something orf yourself. If you stay until the end of the year, you 'ave my permission."

Throughout the lonely days and nights in hospital, Tilly often thought about returning home to Camberwell to die. She had even written to her niece, Maureen asking her to visit Australia House to see if they had a little house for her to live in as she was an invalided war widow. Tilly didn't follow up the matter—she couldn't leave her John behind, plus her family over there had all but forgotten her, with some thinking she was already dead.

During a visit, a few days before Easter, John sat on the hospital bed beside his mother excitedly talking about the upcoming Royal Easter Show and how his friends were going. He told her about the rides and games in sideshow alley they had mentioned.

"Mum, we have to go! The Duke and Duchess of Gloucester will be there!" John enthused knowing his mother could never resist a royal visit.

The exuberance of his words, and the glint of excitement in her son's eyes, were all Tilly needed to sign herself out of hospital the following morning. She was past worrying about royalty. Her son's happiness was more important to her.

Before asking the nurse to help her dress, Tilly rang Olive and asked her to pick her up and drive her home. When she arrived at the flat, Tilly made her way to the hidey hole and took out two hundred dollars in smaller notes. She was going to make sure her teenage son would have the time of his life at the show.

John was overjoyed when he arrived home from school and saw his mother sitting on the settee. He dropped his school bag and rushed over and hugged her. "I didn't know you were coming home today!"

"I wanted to surprise you. Tomorrow, you're going to the Easter Show!" Tilly revealed to her elated son.

"Thanks Mum, you're so cool! I'm going to ring John, Keith and Mark and make arrangements to meet them there!"

"They'll be better company for you than this old dinosaur! I'll most probably spend most orf the day sitting in the shade."

Tilly and John were up nice and early to catch the green and yellow double decker bus to the showgrounds. When they arrived, his friends were waiting at the gates. The boys escorted Tilly to a shaded area and made sure she was comfortable. John left to buy his mother a cup of tea and scones from the CWA stall, before he and his mates headed off to hit the rides.

As with all teenage boys, when their stomachs were empty, they returned to Tilly who had been joined by several other elderly folk. They were having a great natter when John excused himself and asked Tilly if she was ready for lunch. She handed him ten dollars to buy whatever he and his friends wanted for lunch and asked for a corned beef and pickles sandwich for herself. When he returned, John handed his mother another cup of tea and her sandwich while his mate, Mark shared out battered savs, hot chips, meat pies and sandwiches amongst them all.

As they ate their food, the boys laughed at the different clothes people were wearing and commented on the show bags that other teenagers were carrying. "Would you like another cup of tea, Mum?" John asked.

"Yes love. See if they can give you a teapot, please."

Tilly watched after her son as he walked to the CWA stall and smiled as he spoke with the lady, nodding his head every now and then as they spoke.

"Here you go, Mum. See that lady over there with the red and white top? She's going to come over to you every now and then with a fresh cup of tea until we come back."

"Your blood's worth bottlin, my darling. Now, you boys scuttle orf and 'ave a good time." Tilly pushed twenty dollars into her son's jeans pocket. "Win me something in sideshow alley."

The boys returned a few hours later loaded up with show bags. John walked toward his mother with a sheepish grin on his face as he handed her a kewpie doll in a blue glittery dress attached to a cane.

"Thank you sweet'eart, she's beautiful! I'll also 'ave some of those sweets in the showbags when we get 'ome!"

"You can eat all the chocolate you want, Mum!"

"Thank you, Mrs. Parsons for giving us a real good time today. We have to go now as Mum is picking us up at the gates at three o'clock." Mark politely stated.

"You're welcome love. I'll see you boys on Saturday at footy training." Tilly said as she waved the boys off.

7

On New Year's 1970, Tilly knew it would be her last year on earth. Most days she found it difficult to get herself out of bed. John had left school and was looking work, but she didn't mind looking after him financially until he found employment. She had Sister's from the church visiting her through the week to make sure she was coping with her illness and her

doctor was also calling on her several times a week. Each visit he told her that she needed to be in hospital, but Tilly stubbornly refused, wanting to spend every precious moment she could at home with her son.

Tilly was proud of John. He had grown up in a home that was frequented by retired gangsters, criminals, prostitutes, and police. He had taken it all in his stride. He was never disrespectful to any of them, nor did he judge her for the life she had led. He knew he was adopted and had met his mother and sister frequently throughout his childhood until they moved to Queensland.

Tilly was always open and honest to John, she told him that she couldn't lie even if she wanted to because there were always stories written about her in the newspapers more times than she'd had roast dinners. She told him she preferred that he knew the truth from her, not lies and gossip from others.

Olive, who had stuck by Tilly through thick and thin over the years, had just turned sixty-five. She wasn't getting around too well with her rheumatoid arthritis. However, during Tilly's final months, she spoon fed her pureed chicken or beef and vegetable broth twice a day. Tilly was unable to swallow whole food anymore and often had trouble swallowing the broth. Her throat cancer had advanced. She knew her days were numbered, as did John and Olive. Tilly refused to go into hospital until it was close to the end. Her son was more important to her than the pain she endured.

On a cold and windy day in May, John left for a job interview. He was concerned that once again he wouldn't be successful. But Tilly wouldn't hear of any negativity, "Listen to me, I feel good today—so take it as an omen…you're going to get this job!"

"I hope so Mum." John said as he kissed her on the cheek before leaving.

When John returned home several hours later, he was armed with a bottle of stout and a bunch of flowers. "I got the job Mum! I start on Monday!"

"I told you that you would! Congratulations my darling!"

The following day, Tilly gave Olive some money to buy John a record player and a portable radio. He was over the moon when he saw the presents and tenderly hugged his mother and kissed her on her cheek. "Thank you, Mum, but you really need to take it easy with your money." He gently admonished her.

One afternoon in early June when Olive arrived to help bathe Tilly, she found her gasping for breath on the floor beside her bed. She rushed to the telephone and rang for an ambulance. While waiting for help to arrive, Olive carefully helped her onto the bed and changed her nightie before packing a bag for hospital. Tilly was trying to say something, but her words wouldn't come out. "It's okay Till, the ambulance is on its way. Stay calm and breathe slowly, sweetheart." Olive said in an attempt to comfort her friend.

The ambulance attendants placed the waif like Tilly onto a stretcher and rushed her to Concord Repatriation Hospital where she was placed on oxygen. Olive arrived at the hospital a half an hour later. She knew Tilly was dying, but she had never seen her looking do deathly ill as she did at that moment.

Olive sat by the bed and placed her hand over Tilly's and told her that she would bring John in to see her after work. Tilly feebly squeezed Olive's hand in thanks, both wanting to see her son, and not wanting him to see her in hospital looking so sick.

Both John and Olive stayed with Tilly at the hospital as long as they could. One day when John was on the way to see his mother, he saw her doctor at the nurse's station and stopped to speak to him. "Dr. Matthews, how is my mother going?"

"I'm afraid John, that your mother will never return home. Her cancer has spread throughout her body. It's only a matter of time now. I'm sorry."

One day whilst visiting a family member at the Concord Hospital, a detective noticed a name board above a bed in a room bearing the name, 'Matilda Parsons'. He took a closer look at the hollow cheeked woman sleeping in the bed and was surprised when he saw the once robust brothel madam and razor gang leader, looking skeletal and weak. When he returned to headquarters, he contacted Police Commissioner Allen and told him what he had seen. Allen summoned his vice squad chief, Detective-Sergeant Vic Green, "Vic, dear old Tilly's extremely ill and she's all on her own. She's in the palliative care ward at the Concord. See if there's anything we can do for her." He ordered, his tone revealing his respect for the aged brothel madam.

Twenty-eight bouquets of flowers and cards were sent to Tilly from several police districts. Tilly may have been arrested and charged two hundred and four times in her lifetime, and at times, fought against the police tooth and nail, but she held the respect of many who knew of her kindness toward the poor, children in hospital, and soldiers during both wars.

John, devastated by the knowledge of the impending loss of his mother, spent as much time with her as possible. He spent his lunch break with her and returned after work, staying with her until visiting hours ended. The Sisters and nurses never chased him out. They didn't mind him staying over time. Tilly was special to many of the nurses and Sisters.

Tilly was no longer able to talk so she wrote some of her thoughts down when she was strong enough. She often wrote messages to John, telling him how proud she was of him and how much she loved him. Other times she asked him to bring a bottle of Sheaf stout. John and Olive would often sneak in a bottle for her. They would do anything to make her last days on earth as happy as possible. Several of the hospital staff knew what was happening, but they turned a blind eye to it.

When John visited, he would talk about work and some of the blokes that worked there, and a girl he was interested in who worked in a dress shop in the arcade. At times, Tilly would drift off to sleep after imbibing a little too much stout, or heavy pain medication. Other times John would read to his mother, even when she was sound asleep. As the days wore on, most times when he came in, Tilly slept the entire time. He stayed with her, holding her hand, and chatting away until Olive arrived, or he had to return to work.

When Olive dropped by on the 20th of November to bring Tilly clean nighties and underwear, she found her most upset. Unable to talk, Tilly feebly wrote on the writing pad that she was at odds again with Freddy.

She had loaned him money to bail out one of their family members and he was refusing to pay her back.

"Don't fret Till. Your health is more important than the money, I'm sure he'll come around."

Tears dropped on the writing pad as Tilly answered Olive, "I don't want to die with my son hating me."

"He'll come 'round sweety." Olive said trying to placate her friend.

"Take me home."

Against the wishes of her doctor, Tilly signed herself out of hospital. She wanted to die at home and on her own terms. Olive wheeled her down to her car and helped her into the back seat where she could lie down. When she arrived home, several of the neighbours helped Olive to take Tilly through to her bedroom. Tilly thanked everyone before asking Olive if she would bring her a glass of stout and a cigarette.

"Tilly, you know you aren't allowed to smoke." Olive tutted.

"I've done plenty I wasn't allowed to do." Tilly rasped.

John was surprised to find his mother at home when he came in from work. He rushed to her bed and hugged her. "Are you feeling better Mum?"

"Yes, love." Tilly rasped. "Please play are you lonesome tonight on your record player, my sweet'art."

"Sure Mum."

As the song played, John held his mothers' hand as tears rolled down her cheeks. She murmured Eric's name several times before falling asleep.

On the 23rd of November when John arrived home from work, he found a note on his mother's bed stand. The writing was barely legible, but he was able to make out the words:

My darling son, everyone has three lives, their public one, their private one, and their secret one. Live your life as you see fit. Don't conform to society standards. We are all not the same. Make your life fit the man you are becoming. Live well, love passionately, laugh, and enjoy being who you are. Life is a gift. Live it to the fullest. Know that I love you with all my heart and I will miss you.

Always,
Your loving mother.

7

They were the last words that John ever 'heard' from his mother. The following afternoon, Tilly suffered a stroke and completely lost the ability to speak. When Olive returned from washing her beer glass, she found her in a terrible state and called an ambulance.

The attendants rushed her to Concord repatriation Hospital. However, this time Tilly couldn't sign herself out—a higher power had that authority. At 10:04 pm on Tuesday the 24th of November 1970, Matilda Mary Parsons looked around the room and smiled before closing her eyes and releasing a long-drawn-out breath. The Queen of the "Loo was dead.

7

The woman who had taken on the establishment and amassed two hundred and four criminal convictions, fought three burly policemen at once, changed the life of many, some for the bad—countless for the good, a woman, who with her bare hands, held society by the throat as she traversed East Sydney by her own moral compass and code of ethics. Matilda Mary Devine Parsons, the woman who survived in a man's world of power, violence, and misogyny, but was still compassionate enough to financially assist the poor, the sick, and the orphaned children of Sydney—had taken her last breath.

Tilly's funeral was not as remarkable as the life she had lived. Few people turned up to pay their respects on the 26th of November. Unfortunately, Tilly had outlived most of her friends, associates, and enemies. If she had died just ten years earlier, the crowd of mourners would have been lined up for miles around the Sacred Heart Church in Darlinghurst.

Tilly was cremated at Botany Crematorium with full Catholic rites under her married name, Matilda Mary Parsons.

There were some scathing and disparaging newspaper articles written about Tilly in the papers after her death, others were more polite. But those editorials were composed by men who had no idea who the real Tilly Devine was. They wrote their pieces from innuendo and decades of old newspaper stories, with misogyny, bias, and ignorance.

But there was one article that was close to who Tilly Devine Parsons was, and that was written in the police journal:

'Matilda Parsons has been in conflict with society all her life. She has fought it with words, with action, and with her bare hands. She has held it by the throat and shaken it. She has spat in its face. Her sense of values, her code of morals and of ethics, are her own and she well tolerated no interference. For the average man, her life had held that singular fascination the criminologist describes as—the fascination of the thunderstorm.'